Death's Sweet Song
Whom Gods Destroy

TWO NOIR CLASSICS BY Clifton Adams

Stark House Press • Eureka California

DEATH'S SWEET SONG / WHOM GODS DESTROY

Published by Stark House Press
1315 H Street
Eureka, CA 95501
griffinskye3@sbcglobal.net
www.starkhousepress.com

DEATH'S SWEET SONG
Copyright © 1955 by Clifton Adams and published
by Gold Medal Books/Fawcett Publications, Inc.

WHOM GODS DESTROY
Copyright © 1953 by Clifton Adams and published
by Gold Medal Books/Fawcett Publications, Inc.

All rights reserved under International and
Pan-American Copyright Conventions.

"The Desert, the Prairie, and the Gutter"
copyright 2014 by Cullen Gallagher

All rights reserved.

ISBN: 1-933586-64-8
ISBN-13: 978-1-933586-64-9

Cover design and layout by Mark Shepard, www.shepgraphics.com
Proofreading by Rick Ollerman

PUBLISHER'S NOTE
This is a work of fiction. Names, characters, places and incidents are either the products of the author's imagination or used fictionally, and any resemblance to actual persons, living or dead, events or locales, is entirely coincidental. Without limiting the rights under copyright reserved above, no part of this publication may be reproduced, stored, or introduced into a retrieval system or transmitted in any form or by any means (electronic, mechanical, photocopying, recording or otherwise) without the prior written permission of both the copyright owner and the above publisher of the book.

First Stark House Press Edition: March 2014

DEATH'S SWEET SONG

What is it about the petite blonde? When Paula Sheldon and her husband Karl pull into Joe Hooper's rundown gas pump motel outside Creston, Hooper can't take his eyes off her. And he sure can't figure why a classy guy like Sheldon would check into his dump of a place. But that night he gets an earful when he overhears the Sheldons discussing a robbery with a local ex-con. Hooper is desperate to get away from Creston, even more desperate to spend time with Sheldon's wife. He takes a chance and convinces the Sheldons that he'd make a better partner. And everything goes smoothly until the old watchman tries to play hero. It's his own damn fault that Hooper has to shoot him. Paula likes a man who knows how to take charge, and she likes what she sees in Hooper. It's enough to make a guy go a little crazy—crazy enough to do anything....

WHOM GODS DESTROY

Roy Foley has hated Lola ever since she laughed at him in high school—the poor kid from across the Oklahoma tracks who was filled with ambition and dared to declare his love. Now he's back in town with some scores to settle. By chance he runs into Sid Gardner, another Burk Street kid, who's running alcohol in their dry state and making pretty good money at it. Roy quickly joins him. But Roy also has eyes for Sid's wife, Vida, with her long white-blonde hair and bewitching manner. Together, Roy figures that he and Vida can take over the booze sales from Barney Seaward, the top dog in Big Prairie, and maybe he can get back at Lola, who is now married to the local D.A., Seaward's kept man. Roy has it all figured out—once he's got Sid out of the way, Barney will be next. But hate is a poor substitute for ambition, and Roy has a long way to go to get ahead of Lola.

CLIFTON ADAMS BIBLIOGRAPHY

Crime:
Whom Gods Destroy (1953)
Death's Sweet Song (1955)

As by Jonathan Gant
Never Say No to a Killer (1956)
The Long Vendetta (1963)

As by Nick Hudson
The Very Wicked (1960)

Westerns:
Desperado (1950)
A Noose for the Desperado (1951)
The Colonel's Lady (1952)
Two-Gun Law (1954)
Gambling Man (1955)
Law of the Trigger (1956)
Outlaw's Son (1957)
Killer in Town (1959)
Stranger in Town (1960)
The Legend of Lonnie Hall (1960)
Day of the Gun (1962)
Reckless Men (1962)
The Moonlight War (1963)
Hogan's Way (1963)
The Dangerous Days of Kiowa Jones (1963)
Doomsday Creek (1964)
The Hottest Fourth of July in the History of Hangtree County (1964)
The Grabhorn Bounty (1965)
Shorty (1966)
A Partnership With Death (1967)
The Most Dangerous Profession (1967)
Dude Sheriff (1969)
Tragg's Choice (1969)
The Last Days of Wolf Garnett (1970)
Biscuit-Shooter (1971)
Rogue Cowboy (1971)
The Badge and Harry Cole (1972; as Lawman's Badge, UK, 1973)
Concannon (1972)
Hard Times and Arnie Smith (1972)
Once an Outlaw (1973)
The Hard Time Bunch (1973)
Hassle and the Medicine Man (1973)

As by Matt Kinkaid
Hardcase (1953)
The Race of Giants (1956)

As by Clay Randall
Six-Gun Boss (1952)
When Oil Ran Red (1953)
Boomer (1957)
The Osceola Kid (1963)
Hardcase for Hire (1963)
Amos Flagg—Lawman (1964)*
Amos Flagg—High Gun (1965)*
Amos Flagg Rides Out (1967)*
Amos Flagg—Bushwacked (1967)*
Amos Flagg Has His Day (1968; reprinted as The Killing of Billy Jowett,1973)*
Amos Flagg—Showdown (1969)*

*Amos Flagg series

Contents

The Desert, The Prairie, and The Gutter:
The Noir Novels of Clifton Adams
by Cullen Gallagher 7

Death's Sweet Song By Clifton Adams 17

Whom Gods Destroy By Clifton Adams 137

The Desert, The Prairie, and The Gutter:
The Noir Novels of Clifton Adams
by Cullen Gallagher

"You were born in the gutter," she said coldly,
"and you'll live in the gutter all your life!"
–Clifton Adams, Whom Gods Destroy

Today, Clifton Adams is primarily remembered as an author of westerns—and for good reason. Twice he won the Western Writers of America's Spur Award for Best Western Novel, first in 1969 for *Tragg's Choice* and then again in 1970 for *The Last Days of Wolf Garnett*. His prolific body of work consists of titles that immediately evoke their genre, including fifty novels with names such as *The Desperado*, *A Noose for the Desperado*, and *Lawman*. Even his short stories and their respective magazines are unmistakably westerns: "Stop-Off in Devil's Creek" and "Girl Gun-Guard for the Devil!" in *Star Western*, "Brand of the Damned" and "Scalptrail Bonanza" in *Fifteen Western Tales*, "There's Hell in His Holsters" in *Dime Western Magazine*, "Blood Buys a Black-Gold Empire" and "Cherokee Strip Range-Pirates!" in *Big-Book Western Magazine*, and "That Pistol-Packin Preacher!" in *New Western Magazine*, to name just a few of the most exciting titles among his body of short fiction, which includes more than 125 stories.

Westerns may have been Adams' specialty, but they're not all that he wrote. In between tales of sheriffs and outlaws, Adams penned five crime novels: *Whom Gods Destroy* and *Death's Sweet Song* (both reprinted here), *Never Say No To a Killer* (as Jonathan Gant), *The Long Vendetta* (also as Gant) and *The Very Wicked* (as Nick Hudson). These works stand out not only as some of his best, most harrowing books, but also as examples of some of the edgiest, innovative, and most gut-wrenchingly honest and terrifying crime fiction of their day.

Adams was born December 1, 1919 in Comanche, Oklahoma. Much of what we know about his personal life comes from *The Roundup*, a publication of the Western Writers of America. Adams fought in European and African campaigns during World War II as part of the Second Armored Division Tank Corps. Later, under the GI Bill, he attended the University of Oklahoma where he majored in creative writing. While there, he met his future wife, Gerry Griffeth, who he married in 1948. In his personal life Adams was a drummer, a guitarist, a jazz aficionado, a book collector, and a cat lover (a cat named El Cazador, "The Hunter," even figures prominently in Adams' *Amos Flagg* series). In an article that he wrote for *The Roundup*, "My Secret Sideline," Adams explained how his interest in culinary arts grew out of the dreadful C-rations he was subjected to in WWII. He outlined what he called The Adams First Rule of Cookery: "No matter what you do to C-ration stew, it can only be an improvement."

The Desperado, Adams' first novel, was published in 1950 by Gold Medal, Fawcett's line of paperback originals. Thus began a life-long relationship that would include *A Noose for the Desperado* (1951), *The Colonel's Lady* (1952), *Two-Gun Law* (1954), *Gambling Man* (1956) (later reprinted as *Outlaw's Son*), *Law of the Trigger* (1956), *The Moonlight War* (1963), and under his Clay Randall pseudonym, *The Osceola Kid* (1963), *Hardcase for Hire* (1963), and all six volumes of his Amos Flagg series: *Amos Flag – Lawman* (1964), *Amos Flag – High Gun* (1965), *Amos Flagg Rides Out* (1967), *Amos Flagg – Bushwhacked* (1967), *Amos Flagg Has His Day* (1968), and *Amos Flagg – Showdown* (1969).

Gold Medal also published Adams' first two noir novels. *Whom Gods Destroy*, published in 1953, is about Roy Foley, a short order cook in a slummy California diner who is called back to Oklahoma when his father passes away. He's so broke he can't even afford to pay for the funeral, but when he hears that the funeral was covered by charity—a charity run by Lola, the girl who laughed in his face back in high school—Roy decides to get revenge by becoming a big man in town, taking over the local bootlegging business, and destroying the reputation of Lola's politically corrupt husband.

Published two years later in 1955, *Death's Sweet Song* is about Joe Hooper, proprietor of a failing motel in the middle of nowhere. When he overhears his guests plotting a robbery, he decides to horn in and take the loot, as well as the girl, for himself.

The first thing that stands out about these two particular novels is their setting: *Whom Gods Destroy* is set in Big Prairie, Oklahoma, and *Death's Sweet Song* in Creston, Oklahoma. Far from the then-archetypical crime settings of Chicago, Los Angeles and New York, Adams' locales foreshadow the country noir trend that is all the rage these days. They also establish a strong bond between Adams' westerns and his noir novels. In these passages, taken early from both novels, notice the intense desolation and violence that Adams locates in the landscape. There's a similar sense of all-pervading loneliness and despair that is often found in more urban noir, however Adams imbues it with a distinctive western perspective.

> Finally the sun comes up, and by this time you've taken off your coat and loosened your tie and you don't care how you look. Your eyes begin to burn from the beat of the desert sun, and a feeling of hopelessness gets hold of you as you watch the wasteland crawl by treadmill-like under the wheels of the bus. Bleak Arizona, standing raw and red; earth-torn New Mexico; the seemingly endless wastes of west Texas. The miles drag out, and out, and now no way you can sit will be comfortable. Your back starts hurting at the shoulders and the ache starts crawling down your spine until it gets to the end, and there it builds a little fire, and the fire gets hotter and hotter. Then some farmer going ten miles up the road sits down beside you, and you swear that, by God, you'll tear his throat open if he as much as asks for a match. (*Whom Gods Destroy*)

> Right next to the railroad are the grain elevators, great towering cement columns standing solid and proud like lonesome skyscrapers in the middle of the prairie. And then there's the big overpass at the railroad. You cross the overpass and drop down on the other side and you're in Creston. You take one look at the town and feel cheated. You'd been led to expect great things and here you are right in the middle of another one-horse prairie town. (*Death's Sweet Song*)

> My own cabin was like a farmer's oven at harvest time. The sleazy marquisette curtains hung limp and still at the open windows. No hint of a breeze. Through the sagging screen door I could see the glistening ribbon of Highway 66, and beyond it the shimmering, sunblasted monotony of Oklahoma prairie. It hurt your eyes, just looking at it. (*Death's Sweet Song*)

The dominant themes of the traditional western novel stem from Manifest Destiny—the heroic spirit of venturing forth into the unknown and emerging triumphant, the ability to reinvent oneself and start anew in the new land, and the individual's capacity to conquer land, animal and person. Clifton Adams, however, puts a perverse noir twist on Manifest Destiny in his novels. Over the course of *The Desperado* and *A Noose for the Desperado*, a young man is wrongly chased into the harsh desert, only to emerge a worse criminal than any could have previously believed—a soldier of fortune, a killer for hire, one with a conscience who fully realizes the depth of his corrupt soul but who continues to kill. This sense of self-knowledge, of recognizing how bad one really is, is the hallmark of Adams' noir novels. Roy Foley and Joe Hooper know exactly what they are doing, every low-down, rotten, corrupt, and horrible deed they commit. As Joe Hooper says to himself in *Death's Sweet Song*, evoking the title of T.S. Eliot's famous poem, "The Hollow Men," "I was a hollow man, without feelings, without conscience, with sensibilities, but I knew that wouldn't last if they left me to myself." Whatever "sensibilities"—qualities that qualified him as human—remained, they were fast fleeting.

Like *The Desperado*, *Whom Gods Destroy* involves a movement westward—Roy Foley's Manifest Destiny, in fact, occurs before the novel even begins, when he flees Oklahoma for California. Instead of prospering, however, he flounders. *Whom Gods Destroy*, then, is an inversion of Manifest Destiny—about the illusion of that destiny, its lies and deceits, the painful road back home, and the deep descent into the lower depths. Foley's attempt to reclaim his own home turf, to quick start his success by stealing someone else's claim to fame, is futile from the start. Even his name suggests as much, being a play on the word "folly." Foley began a failure, and his life goes only downhill from there.

But at least Roy Foley had a chance. Joe Hooper's destiny in *Death's Sweet Song* is so depressed he never even successfully leaves town in the first place. Like Foley, he dreams of leaping from the gutter to greatness by hopping onboard someone else's plans—and like Foley, his ambition is tainted by his own shortcomings, and he is doomed to fail right from the get-go. And like Foley, his name, too, hides his destiny: an average joe fated to jump through hoops, time and again, a western Sisyphus who can never make it to the top of the hill and who will always wind up back in the gutter.

In 1952, the year before *Whom Gods Destroy*, Gold Medal published Jim Thompson's *The Killer Inside Me*, about a psychotic sheriff named Lou Ford who goes on a homicidal rampage in a small Texas town. The influence of that work on Adams is evident—the rural landscape, the first-person narration, the criminal protagonist, and the horrifying murders committed without remorse—however, Adams' work is significantly different from Thompson's. They're all ruthless killers, but whereas Lou Ford is crazy, Roy Foley and Joe Hooper are decidedly sane. Adams' protagonists are all too normal people, their situations and circumstances all too familiar and empathetic, which makes their criminal turn all the more chilling and disturbing.

Ray Foley describes his existence at the start of *Whom Gods Destroy* as if he were already living out a prison sentence: "I thought of the cell that was waiting for me. When I reached it I wanted to be able to drop into dreamless, thoughtless oblivion—and the time was not yet." It's only chapter 1, but he's already invoking a death wish that will only deepen as the novel progresses. "A fry cook's job is a pretty mechanical thing once you get it down, so I just stood there, taking the orders and getting them out, and about the only thing I could think of was, What am I going to do now? About one o'clock, business started to slack off, and in another half hour the place was practically empty. I sat down at the cook table. I guess I ate a sandwich, but I don't remember. One question kept hammering at me—What the hell am I going to do?" Anyone that has ever held a mundane job, where the repetition of labor becomes an exercise in existentialism and boredom borders on suicide, can relate to Joe's frustration.

Where Joe crosses the line from working-class martyr to cold, calculating, and chilling killer is when he starts to channel his ennui into action, when he finds meaning and purpose in past injustice and unrequited emotion:

> You don't sleep that night. You lie there drowning in an ocean of shame, and anger swells your chest and throat until you can't breathe. You beat the mattress with your fists, and you swear that you'll get even with her if it's the last thing you do. You'll be a lawyer, the best damn lawyer in the country, and you'll break her. You'll break her old man. You'll frame him somehow and send him to jail, and see how she likes that! You think of a lot of ways to hurt her, but none of them are good enough. Damn her! Damn her! Goddamn her! And you curse yourself, too, because you know well that you haven't got the guts to face her again. There would be no college; there wouldn't even be a diploma from the high school, because you knew you couldn't face her. And that's the way it is when you're young and your name is Roy Foley and you live on Burk Street. You try, but you can't win. So you run.

First-person, stream of consciousness passages such as this are at least on par with the interior monologues of Thompson. They also evoke the rambling rhythm of Henry Miller, and show off Adams' artistry as a writer and his musical command of language. On a more gut level, there's a brutal honesty to this sort of mundane vendetta whose long gestation amplified it to a monstrous level. The seed of Roy's hatred is something we can all understand, and that is where Adams surpasses Thompson. We never fully comprehend Lou Ford, and we can never place ourselves in his shoes the way we can with Roy Foley.

Death's Sweet Song offers a similarly disturbing empathy; however, Adams' prose here even more acutely captures that sense of ordinary madness unleashed. These passages, pulled from the first two chapters of the novel, progress almost like a poem. The way Joe Hooper tells it, it almost seems just for him to force his way into that robbery, to make that turn from victim of circumstance to circumstantial killer.

It was a pipe dream. And I knew it.

There had been a time when I was going to have such things. There had been a time when I was going to take the world apart and put it together again just the way I wanted it. But it didn't work out like that. Nothing worked out the way I planned it.

[...] Another failure, Hooper; but you ought to be used to it by now. [...] I never got used to it. Every time I went under, something inside me got harder, that anger got hotter. One of these days, I thought, I'm going to do it!

Pretty soon that old feeling of frustration began gnawing at me, that nameless anger that I knew so well began sinking its claws in my guts.

It wasn't any good. The bed was hot, and pretty soon it was clammy with sweat, and I lay there in the darkness smoking cigarettes and wondering when the hell my luck was going to change. When would I be able to pull out of this hole for good?

Times like this were the toughest. It isn't easy to have faith when you're alone. The harder you pray for a break, the more they seem to avoid you, and pretty soon you begin thinking that maybe you've got it figured all wrong, that maybe you're destined to be stuck here the rest of your life, just the way you are now. [...] That's when it gets tough, when you have no money, when you have no special influence, and you know there's no way in the world to go out and make something happen. All you can do is wait and be ready to take advantage of any break that happens to come your way—but they never seem to come. And soon, if you let yourself, you'll get to believe they'll never come.

There's rarely been a purer expression of the dissatisfaction, self-loathing, and fatalism that is at the heart of noir. These passages are an everyman's lament—a mourning for things that didn't turn out the way one wanted, that one didn't live up to his or her expectations, and that the adventure and conquest and prosperity that lies at the heart of Manifest Destiny and the American spirit aren't part of his or her own destiny. This is yet another link between the western and noir worlds of Clifton Adams: protagonists in both genres share this break in tradition, embodying the falsehood of national mythology, the flipside of the American dream.

"Like most writers, [Adams] had at least one obsession and in his case it was the relationship between fathers and sons," observed Ed Gorman, astute critic and himself a damned fine novelist. "On several occasions he had the ability to hurt you with his observations on that theme." Here, Gorman locates one of the central themes of Adams' work, one that is present throughout his career and across genres, and one that "hurts" more than any of the bodily violence that occurs in the stories. From his first novel, *The Desperado* (in which an innocent boy leaves home and is taken under the wing of a notorious fugitive, providing the mentorship he longed for but also sealing his criminal fate) through the Amos Flagg novels (in which a sheriff must renegotiate his relationship to his jailbird father when he is released), fathers and sons have been a recurring preoccupation for Adams. In the two noir novels presented here, there's a youthful sense of rage and rebellion about the relationships.

In *Whom Gods Destroy*, Roy is deeply bitter toward his father—a feeling fueled by his own failings and inability to prove himself better than the broke, drunk, lonely old man his father was. "God, the old man's dead! I turned the words over and over in my mind, trying to give the thought reality, trying to feel something about it. About all I felt was mad—and kind of scared." That sense of fear and anger is multi-faceted—fear that he is all alone and anger that he can't show his father wrong; anger that he finally understands his father, and fear that this is all that Roy is going to be in the end.

In *Death's Sweet Song*, there's a similar repulsion and attraction between father and son, but the difference here is that Joe Hooper's father is still living, still a physical and active part of his everyday existence. "He was the finest man I ever knew—and the only man in the world that I cared a damn about. We never said much. Usually it was just like this, sitting, drinking a beer together, and then he'd leave." But as soon as his father starts intimating that Joe should marry a local girl and settle down, his attitude changes: "I had no wish to hurt my father, the one man in the world that I liked. I guess he figured, like Langford, that someday I would marry a home-town girl and settle down to rot the rest of my life away in Creston. Well, he was mistaken about that; they all were mistaken." The father represents everything Joe Hooper does not want to be—stability, roots, a sedentary and unexciting lifestyle. Later, when Joe is knee-deep in hot water and his criminal plans are beginning to unfold, he makes decisions to save himself knowing that he is taking advantage of his father's protective instincts and endangering his father's life. It's the ultimate act of selfishness—yet there's a naïve sense that, like a child, he believes his father is invincible, that he will be all right in the end. Even in revolt, he still upholds tradition—it's a contradiction that many of us can relate to in our own ways.

"[*Death's Sweet Song*] may be the best crime fiction novel that Gold Medal published in the 50s," critic August West proclaimed on his blog *Vintage Hardboiled Reads*. West goes on to applaud the empathy that Adams is able to locate within the protagonist: "It's a story of how things can spiral out of control once you take that step–and you can't go back. Joe Hooper is a character the reader cares for, even as he goes *bad*. You feel the weight and burden he carries, which slowly drags him deeper and deeper…."

"*Death's Sweet Song* is the best of [Adams' crime novels]," Gorman assessed. "What gives the book its flavor is its desperation. Adams, whatever he was writing, worked in one of two modes. One was irony which he kept broad enough so that mass audiences could grasp it. It played off as humor. The other was a sweaty frantic fatalism that gave several of his westerns a true hardboiled edge. […] I wish he'd written more crime novels."

Bill Crider, the great western and mystery author, wrote that *Whom Gods Destroy* and *Death's Sweet Song* "are of the James M. Cain school, and while they don't quite come up to the best of Cain, they belong on the same shelf. […] The simple plot summaries don't do much to convey the quality of writing in these books. It's the real thing. Uncluttered prose, smooth, and assured, with just the right amount of description to make things real and immediate." Like Gorman, Crider laments the small number of Adams' noir works. "In a way it's too bad that Clifton Adams found his biggest success writing westerns and didn't write more crime novels. He was very good at it."

Gorman and Crider were right—Clifton Adams was damn good at writing crime, and he should have written more. His other three noir novels exhibit the same craftsmanship, innovation, and dark passages that characterized *Whom Gods Destroy* and *Death's Sweet Song*. One year after *Death's Sweet Song*, *Never Say No To a Killer* (1956) was published under the pseudonym "Jonathan Gant" as an Ace Double (the flipside was *Stab in the Dark* by Louis Trimble). It's a homicidal first-person thriller reminiscent of Horace McCoy's jailbreak classic, *Kiss Tomorrow Goodbye* (1948). This one begins with Roy Surratt murdering a prison guard while on work detail and stealing a truck, and in no time at all he's hooking up with the widow of his former cellmate and taking over her deceased husband's extortion racket. It's the most relentlessly vicious of Adams' crime novels, devoid of any moral center or redeeming sympathies, and it gives Thompson and McCoy a run for their money for the vilest main character.

The Very Wicked (1960), published four years later by Berkley under the penname "Nick Hudson," is yet another first-person killer narrative, the difference being that unlike Adams' usual protagonists, this one is certifiably insane. A vice cop on prostitution duty, Bud Creel is sick of living in a world of sex and sin and has decided to wage a one-man crusade to wash the streets clean with blood. Written with unsettling stream of conscious internal monologs and punctuated by sadistic murders rendered with disturbing clarity, *The Very Wicked* is an all-out assault on morality. While it does lack the sympathetic characters and well-crafted plots of his earlier noir novels, *The Very Wicked* more than lives up to its name—it's so nasty it makes sin seem wholesome!

Adams' final noir novel, *The Long Vendetta*, was published by Avalon in 1964, again under the name "Jonathan Gant." Like many of Adams' protagonists, Buck Coyle is guilty of murder—though he is a killer of a different sort. Drawing on his own wartime experience (including his C-ration creations), Adams makes Coyle a WWII tank division veteran who participated in a war crime. Years later, someone has been tracking Coyle and his crew and exacting revenge. While it doesn't possess the emotional depth and introspective darkness of his other works, *The Long Vendetta* is perhaps the most cinematic of Adams' noir novels. It unfolds in an unremitting torrent of action and staccato dialog, fully visualized with the meticulous care of a movie director.

"But all things end, if you wait long enough," Adams wrote in *Death's Sweet Song*. And, in *Whom Gods Destroy*, "So this is the way it ends, I thought dully. One jump ahead of the law, two jumps ahead of the chair." Clifton Adams passed away on October 7, 1971 in San Francisco, CA due to a heart attack. Only fifty-two years old, he left behind a body of work consisting of fifty novels and more than twice that many short stories. Dying so young cut short an extraordinary career still in its prime. It had been seven years since he had published a crime novel, and we can only speculate whether or not he would have returned to the genre. Elmore Leonard and Brian Garfield, two authors who got their start in westerns in the 1950s, made career redefining switches to crime in the 1970s. It's too drastic to think that Adams would have ever fully given up his beloved western, and we can only speculate as to whether he would have made a similar change, or whether he would have continued his regular trajectory and written the occasional noir novels every once in a while, or—well, it's all guesswork at this point. We'll never know the novels that Adams didn't get a change to write, and that we didn't get the chance to read. One thing we do know, however, is that they would have been great.

Of that, I am certain.

—Septemer 2013
Brooklyn, NY

Sources

Adams, Clifton. *Death's Sweet Song*. Gold Medal, 1955.

–. *The Long Vendetta*. Avalon, 1964. (Published under the pseudonym, "Jonathan Gant.")

–."My Secret Sideline," *The Roundup*, Vol. XIX, No. 8, August 1971.

–. *Never Say No To a Killer*. Ace, 1956. (Published under the pseudonym, "Jonathan Gant.")

–. *The Very Wicked*. Berkley, 1960. (Published under the pseudonym, "Nick Hudson.")

–. *Whom Gods Destroy*. Gold Medal, 1953.

Crider, Bill. "The Gold Medal Corner: Clifton Adams." *Mystery*File*, 7 Feb 2010. (http://mysteryfile.com/blog/?p=1817)

Gillson, Gwendolyn. "Adams, Clifton." *Oklahoma Digital Prairie* (Oklahoma Department of Libraries). (http://digitalprairie.ok.gov/cdm/singleitem/collection/okauthors/id/258)

Gorman, Ed, "Clifton Adams," *Ed Gorman's Blog*, 18 July 2008. (http://newimprovedgorman.blogspot.com/2008/07/monday-january-28-2008-deaths-sweet.html)

–. "Forgotten Books: Death's Sweet Song." *Ed Gorman's Blog*, 13 January 2010. (http://newimprovedgorman.blogspot.com/2010/01/forgotten-books-deaths-sweet-song.html)

"Over the Range." *The Roundup*, Vol. XIX, No. 11, November 1971.

West, August. "Death's Sweet Song by Clifton Adams." *Vintage Hardboiled Reads*, 28 January 2008.
(http://vinpulp.blogspot.com/2008/01/deaths-sweet-song-by-clifton-adams.html)

Death's Sweet Song
By Clifton Adams

Chapter One

The blue Buick pulled off the highway about fifty yards past the station. I could see the driver looking back at the cabins, and there was a woman beside him in the front seat. They sat there for two or three minutes while the man made up his mind, and finally the Buick began backing up and stopped in front of the gas pumps.

"Fill her up?" I said.

"All right." He opened the door and got out. "What we're looking for," he said, "is a place to stay for the night. Do you have a vacancy?"

"Sure thing."

There were five cabins behind the station and they were all vacant. Most of them would remain vacant, even during the tourist season. That's the kind of place it was. I wondered about that while I put gas into his car. Here was a tourist with a new car, wearing expensive clothes, so why should he want to put up in a rat trap like mine when there were first-class AAA motels all along the highway?

He must have read my mind.

"Engine trouble," he said. "Nothing serious, but I thought I'd better get a mechanic to look at it."

"Oh. Your best bet is to go back to town and talk to the people at the Buick agency."

He smiled pleasantly. "That's what I was thinking."

He was a pretty good-sized guy, and you could see that he kept in condition. His face was burned to the color of old leather, and I guessed he was the type that spent a lot of time on a golf course, or maybe a tennis court. We talked a little about the weather and how hot it was, and then I hung up the hose and went to work on the windshield. That was when I got my first good look at the woman. And she just about took my breath away.

At first I thought she was asleep. She sat there with her eyes closed, her face completely expressionless. Her hair was blonde and short, and her skin was pale, almost white. She wore tan shorts and a white T shirt. The tan shorts looked almost black against that skin of hers. As I was finishing with the windshield, she opened her eyes. For just an instant we stared at each other through the glass, and then she smiled the smallest smile in the world and curled up slowly like a well-fed cat.

"Will you check the oil?" the man said.

I added a quart of oil. Then we went inside the station and he signed the register: "Mr. & Mrs. Karl Sheldon, St. Louis, Mo."

"You want me to call the Buick agency for you?" I asked.

He smiled again. "Don't bother. I can drive it back to town all right. Anyway, I'd like to freshen up a bit."

I put them in Number 2 cabin, right next to the one I kept for myself. I went around every morning and put the cabins in shape, but it would take more than clean sheets and a few licks with a mop to make them look like anything. They were all just alike, bedroom, bath, kitchenette—lumpy beds, peeling dressers, cracked linoleum on the floors. But I hadn't realized how shabby they really were before I saw the look on that blonde's face.

"Really, Karl! It seems to me—"

"It's just for a little while." And he looked at me, almost apologetically. "Don't bother with the luggage. I'll bring it in after a while."

That was a dismissal, so I went back to the station.

The thermometer on the east side of the wash rack had reached an even hundred. I opened a bottle of Coke and stood in the doorway, watching the endless stream of traffic rushing by on the highway. License tags from everywhere—Nebraska, California, Illinois.... Where do tourists go, anyway, in such a hell of a hurry?

What difference does it make? I thought, with a taste of bitterness. They're not going to stop here!

And who could blame them? No air-conditioning, no fancy lunchroom, no AAA sign hanging out. Why *should* anybody want to stop at a place like this?

That started me thinking about Karl Sheldon and that blonde wife of his. Now, if I could afford a wife like that, you wouldn't catch me putting up in a fire trap like this, not by a long shot. Sheldon seemed like a nice guy, but apparently he wasn't very smart. A woman like that was meant to have nothing but the best.

Several times that afternoon I caught my imagination beginning to get the best of me. That white skin; I'd never seen anything just like it before. I was almost glad when a customer came by and left a flat for me to fix; it gave me something else to think about.

Around five o'clock Ike Abrams, my part-time helper, came on duty, and a few minutes later Sheldon backed his Buick out of the carport and headed toward town.

"I see you've rented one of the cabins," Ike said. "Maybe the tourist business is beginning to hit its stride."

"I hope so. Say, did you notice anything wrong with the way that Buick was running?"

"It sounded fine to me."

Ike may not be the smartest man in the world, but he's as good a shade-tree mechanic as you'll find. When he doesn't hear something wrong with an engine, then there's nothing wrong with it. That started me thinking again.

Now, why would Sheldon bother to hand me that cock-and-bull story about car trouble? And even if it was true, why would he wait until five o'clock to get started for a garage that would already be closed for the day?

Well, a man had his own set of reasons for everything, and it was none of my business, anyway. I was just glad that a cabin was rented.

After a while I checked the cash register with Ike, turned the station over to him, and headed toward my own cabin to get cleaned up for my usual date with Beth Langford. I could hear the shower running in Number 2 cabin, and I stopped for a moment and listened, thinking about that blonde. You'd better hold on to that imagination of yours, I thought.

My own cabin was like a farmer's oven at harvest time. The sleazy marquisette curtains hung limp and still at the open windows. No hint of a breeze. Through the sagging screen door I could see the glistening ribbon of Highway 66, and beyond it the shimmering, sun-blasted monotony of Oklahoma prairie. It hurt your eyes, just looking at it.

I tried to tell myself that the tourist business was just getting started, as Ike had said, and pretty soon I'd be renting the cabins every night and the money would begin rolling in.

It was a pipe dream. And I knew it.

I kicked my shoes off and lay across the scorching bed, and in no time at all I was cursing myself for ever getting into the business in the first place. The heat was getting me down. I was going to be late for my date with Beth, but that didn't seem to matter.

For about fifteen minutes I lay there with the sweat rolling over my ribs. Pretty soon that old feeling of frustration began gnawing at me, that nameless anger that I knew so well began sinking its claws in my guts.

I wondered if Karl Sheldon appreciated the woman he had. I wondered if he appreciated that car of his, the money in his wallet, the way he could afford to live. By God, I thought, I would appreciate them if I had them!

There had been a time when I was going to have such things. There had been a time when I was going to take the world apart and put it together again just the way I wanted it.

But it didn't work out like that. Nothing worked out the way I planned it. Even now I could feel this tourist-court business falling down around my shoulders. Another failure, Hooper; but you ought to be used to it by now.

I never got used to it. Every time I went under, something inside me got harder, that anger got hotter. One of these days, I thought, I'm going to do it!

But not today.

I lay there, groggy and listless in the heat, not caring a damn whether or not I ever got up, whether I ever kept my date with Beth Langford. Finally I did get up and stripped and got under the shower. The cold water jarred me, made me feel a little better. I pulled on some clean slacks and a fresh shirt and got out of that cabin before the heat could get another hold on me. Mrs. Sheldon was sitting on the steps of Number 2.

"Is it always this hot in Oklahoma?" she said.

"In July it is. It usually cools off, though, when the sun goes down."

She shrugged faintly, as though she didn't believe me. A white pique skirt-and-halter outfit had taken over for the shorts and T shirt, but the effect was about the same. Sitting in front of that cabin, she looked crisp and fresh, as out of place as caviar in an Army mess kit.

"This is quite a place you have here," she said dryly. "Do you own it?"

"Me and the bank."

She smiled. It was an expression that came slowly, and you didn't realize that it was there at all until it hit you. Then she stretched those white legs out in front of her and lay back with her elbows on the top step. I must have been staring pretty hard, but she didn't seem to notice.

"Were you ever a fighter?" she asked.

It seemed like a funny question. "I was never a boxer, if that's what you mean."

"You've got the build for it."

I didn't know what to say to that. It made me uncomfortable, the way she looked at me, and I wondered if she was laughing at me. About that time I saw Sheldon's Buick turn off the highway and decided it was time I got away from there.

When I got back to the station I saw that Ike had washed down the driveway and swept the office—things I never remembered to do. "If I'm not back by ten o'clock," I said, "go ahead and lock up." I left my keys with him, then got into my '47 Chevy and headed for town.

When you take 66 into Creston, your first impression is that it's a pretty good-sized place. The first things you see are the oil-well supply houses, big sprawling buildings and sheds, long rows of powerful cementing trucks, pumpers, testing and drilling equipment. Acres of buildings and acres of trucks, millions of dollars' worth of equipment. It's pretty impressive the first time you see it.

Right next to the railroad are the grain elevators, great towering cement columns standing solid and proud like lonesome skyscrapers in the middle of the prairie. And then there's the big overpass at the railroad. You cross the overpass and drop down on the other side and you're in Creston.

You take one look at the town and feel cheated.

You'd been led to expect great things and here you are right in the middle of another one-horse prairie town. I'd lived here all my life, knocking out four years in the Army, and I never failed to be disappointed when I looked at it. It was a fairly clean town, as prairie towns go, once you moved away from the cluster of produce and feed companies that huddled around the grain elevators. Coming down the town side of the overpass, you could see it all. The straight, treeless streets. The frame houses and parched lawns. The new, raw-looking high school, the cement tennis courts, the white afterthought of a steeple on the Baptist church.

It was my home. A place where eight thousand people, more or less, lived, loved, hated, worshiped, spawned. I knew everybody and everybody knew me, and that's the kind of arrangement you can get pretty sick of after a while.

For a minute I thought I'd drive around to the family house and say hello to my dad, but I stopped at a drive-in instead and had a beer. At that moment, with the bank breathing on my neck, I didn't feel up to lying about how good business was and how much money I was making. And I didn't want Dad asking if Beth Langford and I had set the date yet. He didn't know it, and Beth didn't know it, but there wasn't going to be any date. That's one thing I was sure of.

The carhop, the sister of a guy I had known in high school, brought me the beer.

"How's the tourist business, Joe?"

"Fine. Just fine."

What a joke! I thought. They always asked the same question and I always gave the same answer, lying in my teeth. But, at times like this, there was always one comforting thought in the back of my mind—this tourist business was purely a temporary arrangement. A breather, a stopover on the way to something big.

If they thought I was going to stay bogged down in Creston the rest of my life, they were crazy. There was a limit to the number of craps a man could throw, no matter how unlucky he was. Sooner or later his luck had to change, and I could feel it in my bones that my turn was about to come up.

I had a theory about this business of getting ahead in the world. Once, at least once, in every man's life there comes a chance to make a killing, a chance to lift himself out of the dung heap. I'd seen it happen too many times. I'd seen oil-field roughnecks become millionaires, betting their hard-earned cash on good structures that the big companies had missed on. I'd seen two-bit land men become big shots overnight.

There is no mystery about how one man gets to be a big shot while the man right beside him remains a bum all his life. One man saw the once-in-a-lifetime opportunity when it appeared, recognized it for what it was, grabbed it.

There's no mystery about it at all. The only two requirements are plenty of patience and a world of guts. And this is the way it works:

Herb Carter was a small-time land man for a big-time oil company. His job was to go out and lease up land that the company wanted, land that had been proved either by existing producing wells or by geophysical exploration—proved at a cost of maybe a million dollars to the company. It happened that Herb had a friend who was the chief engineer for an exploration company, and this was the once-in-a-lifetime opportunity that Herb didn't miss. From his friend Herb got the exact location of the prize structure and leased the land for himself.

It sounds pretty simple, but it took plenty of guts. Herb Carter had blackballed himself for life, he had practically robbed his company of a million dollars that they had sunk into the exploration of that land. But he took the chance. He let the company scream. He fought off lawyers and began to drill.

Now, there is just one way in God's world to tell you if a structure will produce oil, and that is to sink a hole. They can shoot the land a thousand times and locate faults, salt domes, anticlines, any of which might produce oil, but the only way to tell is to sink a hole. And every time you sink a hole the odds are nine to one that it will be dry. Herb knew this before he started, but he also knew that this was his one chance, his only chance, to hit the top, so he let them scream and he drilled.

It happens that Herb hit it to the tune of five million, and I had heard the story all my life. But the lesson in the story is not that he hit; the lesson is that he had the guts to recognize an opportunity and grab it.

Herb Carter's story was one I never forgot, and its lesson stuck with me. Have patience, have faith, and have the guts when the time comes to act. So when they asked me about the tourist business I could look them in the eye and say: "Fine. Just fine." Because I knew that one day my turn would come.

I tramped the horn and had the carhop bring me another beer, knowing that I was going to be late, knowing that Beth didn't like the smell of beer on my breath anyway, and not caring somehow. I was thinking about that blonde out at the tourist court.

Now, there is a woman, I thought, that a man could get excited about. If I was on my way to pick up a woman like that, you wouldn't find me killing time in a drive-in. You could bet your life on that!

But habit had its way, finally. I settled the tab with the girl and headed the Chevy toward town.

The Langford place was on Third Street, a one-story white frame house right across from the Methodist church, where Beth and I used to go to Sunday school, and where Beth still did. The house had been standing there ever since I could remember, just like my own family place a block away, and it never seemed to change. It got a fresh coat of white paint every other spring, the hedge was always neatly trimmed, the lawn always mowed.

It was a lot like our own place, except that Mr. Langford was not a doctor, like my dad, and had more time to keep the place in shape. It was seven-thirty when I pulled the Chevy into the driveway, almost dark, and Old Man Langford had just finished watering the front lawn.

"You're late tonight, aren't you, Joe?"

Be thirty minutes late for a date and the whole town knew it; that's the way Creston was. "I got held up at the station," I said. "I thought maybe we'd have a sandwich and see a movie. There's plenty of time for that."

"Sure," Langford said doubtfully, then shrugged. "How's the tourist business?"

"Fine. Just fine."

But I wasn't fooling him one little bit. If business was so fine, I'd be driving a better car. Langford was a retired real-estate man and he knew the signs. Then the front door opened and Beth came out.

"I'm sorry I'm late," I said, hardly seeing her.

I'd seen her so many times, had had so many dates with her exactly like this one, that there was nothing fresh or new about it. Long ago I had slipped into the habit of taking Beth for granted. I knew just about everything there was to be known about her; I could guess beforehand just what she would wear, what she would say, how she would react to any given situation. I could look at her, as I was doing now, and never actually see her, because I knew her as well as I knew my right hand, and a man doesn't have to keep looking at his hand to make sure it hasn't changed.

"A sandwich and a movie?" I asked.

She smiled and I knew the exact words she would answer with. "Sure, Joe. A sandwich and movie sounds nice."

There was a drive-in movie on the highway south of town, and that's where we went. But I couldn't tell you what the picture was about. I don't remember her name, but the girl in the picture was blonde and plenty good-looking, and the husky way she had of talking kept reminding me of that girl back at the tourist court, that Mrs. Sheldon.

I kept remembering the funny way she had looked at me, and that remark she had made about my build.

"What is it, Joe?"

"What?"

"I thought you had gone to sleep," Beth said.

I became aware of the giant screen in front of us. "I wasn't asleep," I said. "I was thinking."

"I thought you liked John Wayne. If you want to go, Joe, it's all right with me."

"I like John Wayne fine. Let's watch the picture."

She looked puzzled. Then, almost immediately, she slipped back into that Hollywood dream. I looked at her and had the uneasy feeling that I was sitting beside a total stranger. I looked at her objectively, the way you would look at a photograph of a person you had never seen. By no stretch of the imagination could she be called beautiful, or even pretty, although she was pleasant enough to look at, and certainly she wasn't ugly.

Her face was small, and her hair was rather thick and long, which was the wrong way to wear it. Even I knew that. Her figure was all right, if a little thin. But her arms always freckled in the summer, and they were freckled now. Her eyes, I think, were the best part of her. They were large and startlingly clear.

It's difficult to dislike people with eyes like Beth's, and maybe that's the reason I had fallen into the habit of dating her. But what the hell, I thought. A guy had to do something. If she had let herself believe that it meant something, it wasn't my fault.

She turned her head briefly and looked at me. She smiled and took my hand and squeezed it. The night was hot and her palm was sweaty, and I had to go through an elaborate act of lighting a cigarette to get my hand free. My nerves were beginning to get on edge and I didn't know exactly why.

I settled back in the seat, tried to get comfortable, and stared determinedly at the screen.

It wasn't a minute before I was thinking of that blonde again.

Chapter Two

I went straight back to the station after taking Beth home. The place was dark; Ike Abrams had already called it a day and locked up. I put the Chevy in the carport and then went around and checked all the locks to see that Ike hadn't missed anything. Four of the cabins were still empty, I noticed. Right at the height of the tourist season and only one cabin rented!

The dead, hot air hit me in the face as I went inside my own shack. The lights were still on in the Sheldon cabin, and I could hear the muffled sounds of their talking, without being able to understand what they were saying. Probably, I thought, that blonde is still raising hell about having to stay in such a place.

Well, I couldn't blame her for that.

Think about something else, I thought. Or think about nothing—that's better. Just get your clothes off and hope a breeze comes up and you'll be able to get some sleep before the sun comes up again.

It wasn't any good. The bed was hot, and pretty soon it was clammy with sweat, and I lay there in the darkness smoking cigarettes and wondering when the hell my luck was going to change. When would I be able to pull out of this hole for good.

Times like this were the toughest. It isn't easy to have faith when you're alone. The harder you pray for a break, the more they seem to avoid you, and pretty soon you begin thinking that maybe you've got it figured all wrong, that maybe you're destined to be stuck here the rest of your life, just the way you are now.

That's when it gets tough, when you have no money, when you have no special influence, and you know there's no way in the world to go out and *make* something happen. All you can do is wait and be ready to take advantage of any break that happens to come your way—but they never seem to come. And soon, if you let yourself, you'll get to believe they'll never come.

When I'd got out of the Army I'd gone to work in the Provo Box Factory in Creston—just marking time, I told myself. I'll keep my eyes open and wait for something to come up. Then there had been rumors of a big superhighway project along Route 66 and I had grabbed this tourist court on a GI loan. The superhighway project had flopped, and with it my plans for big right-of-way profits. So I was right back where I'd started, except that I was now saddled with a slipping business.

It was almost midnight and not getting any cooler. Disgusted, I got out of bed and walked around in my shorts. Then I thought: Hell, I might as well go outside if I want to walk. So I put on my pants and a pair of moccasins and went outside.

The lights were still on in Number 2, and they were still talking. That Sheldon! Why didn't he just get in that Buick of his and start driving? That's what I would do if I was in his shoes.

I sat on the steps and started to light another cigarette. But something stopped me. I didn't know what it was at first, but I knew something wasn't right. I listened hard, the unlighted cigarette in my mouth, but the only thing I could hear was the talking over in Number 2. Sheldon and his wife. I listened some more, knowing that something was wrong, but I couldn't put my finger on it.

Then it hit me. It wasn't Sheldon and his wife talking; it was Sheldon and another man!

I couldn't hear what they were saying, but the talk kept going on and on between the men, and only occasionally did Mrs. Sheldon put in a word. The thing seemed funny to me. If Sheldon knew anybody in Creston, he hadn't mentioned it. Then I remembered that car trouble that didn't seem to exist. And the fact that he had chosen one of my shacks instead of a first-class motel. And now he was receiving company at midnight, in a place where he was supposed to be a stranger.

Little things, but put them together and it came to a pretty queer situation.

I had no qualms about eavesdropping; I was trying to hear what they were saying now, but the words were mushy and senseless by the time they had drifted over to where I was. Finally I got up and swung wide around the carport and came up in the shadows by the east window. You're going to have a hell of a time explaining this, I told myself, if Sheldon happens to look out that window and sees you standing here.

I needn't have worried. The shades were drawn, the windows and door were closed. With no ventilation the thermometer inside that cabin must have been reaching for 105, and that only made me more curious. What could be so important that a man would take precautions like that?

I stood there behind the carport for maybe three or four minutes before anything began to make sense, and then I heard Sheldon saying:

"It sounds *too* good. That's the trouble. I don't like jobs that look like pushovers, because there isn't any such thing."

"Just the same," the other man said, "this one is a pushover. I tell you I would have done it myself, all alone, if it hadn't been for that safe."

"Prisons are full of men who thought a job was a pushover. Well, let me see that sketch again."

Then, after a few seconds of silence, "Look. From this first-floor window to the front office, how far is it?"

"I don't know. Forty, fifty feet, I guess."

"I want to know exactly how far it is, right down to the last inch," Sheldon said. "It's going to be dark and we're not going to have a guide to lead us by the hand. I want every piece of furniture listed, in the storeroom as well as in the office, and I want all the electrical wiring checked. That's very important. How about burglar alarms?"

The other man laughed. "Not a chance."

"I know a hundred men who said the same thing," Sheldon said dryly. "They're in cells now."

"Cripes, I can't go in there with a yardstick and measure the place off for you. I'm takin' a big chance as it is."

"All right," Sheldon said flatly, "we'll forget the whole thing. The deal's off. I told you how I work, and that's the way it's got to be."

For several minutes they just haggled, Sheldon saying the deal was off and the other man trying to change his mind. I stood there thinking: Well, I'll be damned! It didn't take a mindreader to figure out what they were planning. They were planning to rob somebody! That realization stunned me for a moment, and I guess a kind of panic took hold of me. This was a hell of a thing. The only thing I could think of was getting to a telephone and calling the Creston County sheriff.

But that would be foolish. What could I tell him? I didn't know who they were planning to rob, or how, or when, or anything else. The only thing to do was wait and see if I could learn something else.

So I waited. They were still haggling about how it ought to be done. After a while I stopped listening to what they were saying and began concentrating on the man Sheldon was arguing with. The voice sounded vaguely familiar. I couldn't pin it down exactly, but there was one thing I would bet on: He was a native of Creston. The thing that puzzled me was how a native of Creston ever got to know a man like Sheldon.

"Now, wait a minute. Maybe a hundred and fifty people work at this factory. They draw between fifty and a hundred and fifty a week, so what does that make a two-week payroll? Close to thirty thousand dollars, the way I figure it. Think of it! Are you saying we should forget thirty grand?"

"I'm saying the job will be done my way or not at all."

"All right, all right! I'll get the information you want. I don't know how I'll do it, but I'll do it. Now is everything all right?"

"Everything is just fine," Sheldon said pleasantly. "Now let's have another look at that sketch. Did you notice what kind of safe it is?"

"All I know is that it's big and looks plenty rugged."

"Get me the make and model and it won't be so rugged. Now tell me about this factory again; I want to hear everything there is to know about it."

I already knew what factory it was, because there was only one factory in

Creston, and that was the one that made boxes. It was owned by a tough old Bohunk named Max Provo, and I had worked there one summer after getting out of the Army. I had sweated off fourteen pounds in the place for a lousy fifty bucks a week. I'd never thought of it before now, but it was a wonder the place hadn't been robbed long ago, considering how it was run.

Old Provo was the kind of penny-pinching gaffer who never put out a dollar if he didn't absolutely have to. Long ago he had figured out that writing checks cost money. A hundred pay checks, costing about ten cents each, meant that he would have to pay out ten dollars every two weeks for nothing. Twenty dollars every month, two hundred and forty every year. Not for a man like Provo. He paid in cash.

And did he have the cash brought out in an armored car? Not Provo; that kind of foolishness cost money. He picked up the cash himself and made the bank furnish armed guards, free of charge. And he picked the cash up the day before payday and made the office force come in an hour early the next morning in order to get the payroll ready by noon. That was Provo's idea of good business, squeezing that extra hour's work out of the office force.

Well, by God! I thought. At that moment I was remembering the long hours and low wages and bad working conditions, and I was almost ready to go back to my cabin and forget that I had heard anything. Let them take the cheap bastard. Let them take him good; it was none of my business, anyway.

I don't know—if I had walked off right then, maybe that's just the way it would have happened.

But I didn't walk off. I heard Sheldon saying: "Now about the watchman; what kind of routine does he follow?"

The other man laughed shortly. "His routine is to sit in the garage and read Western magazines. He's about sixty years old, he's got a gimpy leg, and on top of that he's half deaf. You could probably blow the safe with him right there in the garage, and he'd never even know about it."

I got the unpleasant feeling that Sheldon was not amused. "He'll have to be taken care of," he said flatly, "but that shouldn't be any trouble. Now look. Here's a list of things I want you to do. Today's the seventh, isn't it? Yes, the seventh. Paula and I will leave this place first thing in the morning, and we'll come back on the fourteenth. I'll pick up the things I need and we'll take care of that safe the night of the fourteenth. That's right, isn't it?"

The other man must have nodded.

"All right," Sheldon said, "that's all there is to it. We'll come back to this same place. It's a lousy place, but there's one thing about it—it isn't crowded with tourists who might recognize me. The farmer that runs the place is too stupid to guess anything. He'll think we're just returning from our vacation."

The other man sounded amused. "It's funny, in a way. Joe Hooper used to work at this factory."

"Who's Joe Hooper?"

"The guy that owns this fly trap you're stayin' in."

The meeting was about to break up. Paula Sheldon began complaining about the heat and somebody opened the window, but not until I was well back in the shadows.

Stupid farmer! I thought. Well, by God, we'll see about that! You're going to look pretty silly, Sheldon, when you tackle that safe with a roomful of deputy sheriffs looking on!

I got back to my cabin just in time. I saw the lights go out in Number 2, then the door opened and a man came down the steps. He came right in front of my cabin, whistling softly through his teeth, and suddenly I had him pegged. His name was Bunt Manley. He was a thickset bull of a man, wearing a flapping sport shirt and a wide-brimmed straw sombrero. He walked around the far side of the station, and after a while I heard a car pull off toward Creston.

Well, I thought, the picture is beginning to fall in place. I didn't know Bunt Manley very well, but I knew that he had recently served a year and a day in Leavenworth for some dealings in moonshine whisky, and that was probably where he had met Sheldon.

I lay across the bed again and pieced the thing together as well as I could. It was possible that the robbery had been Sheldon's idea in the first place, but it didn't seem likely to me. Probably Manley had spotted the box factory as a soft touch and had got in touch with Sheldon, who seemed to consider himself an expert on safes.

Looking at it objectively, I had to admit that they were working it very nicely. Almost every man in Creston had worked in the box factory at one time or other, and probably Bunt Manley had too. So he would know the place, and there would be no special reason to suspect that he had a hand in the robbery. Sheldon, of course, was just a man on a vacation. You couldn't arrest a man and his wife for spending the night in a tourist court.

It was a nice setup, with one exception. I knew about it.

Tomorrow, I thought, the sheriff will know about it. Comes the night of the fourteenth and we'll see who's the stupid farmer, Mr. Sheldon!

I couldn't sleep. This new excitement had me alive to my fingertips and I was up pacing the floor all over again. What a hell of a thing this is! I thought. Planning a robbery right here in one of my own cabins—a thirty-thousand-dollar robbery! The thought of so much money stunned me. Thirty thousand dollars, just for one night's work!

Of course, there was going to be a monkey wrench in Sheldon's machinery, and I was going to throw it. But the idea that the thing could be done, if it weren't for me, just about knocked the breath out of me. All that money!

Hooper, I thought, what could you do with that much money? Think of it!

I didn't dare think of it. Sure, I was looking for a break, an angle to grab hold of, but this business of pulling a robbery was too much of a gamble. No, sir, a thing like this just wasn't in my line.

But it was a pile of money, more money than I had ever had at one time, and it was hard getting my mind on anything else. Across the way the lights were still on in Number 2. The door was open now and I could see Sheldon working over some papers at the table. I didn't see the blonde.

Then I did see her. She was outside, sitting on the bottom step of the cabin, and the slant of light from the doorway just fell across the top of that platinum hair. I sat on the edge of the bed for a long while, just watching her, and it was then that I realized that she had hardly been out of my mind from the first moment I'd seen her. All afternoon she had moved back and forth through my consciousness. Even tonight, when I'd been with Beth, she had been in my brain.

Well, I thought, you might as well forget her, Hooper, because in just one more week she's going to be in jail, along with Sheldon and Manley. I wondered what Sheldon was doing there at the table—probably going over those sketches that Manley had made of the factory.

As I watched, the blonde stood up and stretched, and then she called, "How much longer are you going to be Karl?"

"Not long," Sheldon said. "Why don't you go to bed?"

"I can't sleep with the lights on. Besides, it's too hot."

Sheldon said something else and his wife stood there for a moment, smoothing down her hair. Then she turned and started walking out toward the highway—not going anywhere, just walking to kill time while her husband got caught up on his homework. If I had a wife like that, I thought, I wouldn't be fooling with paperwork this time of night; you could bet on that!

But when you're a professional safecracker, I guess you have to work odd hours. I turned around and watched the blonde go past my door, and then I went to the door and watched her walk as far as the station. She didn't do anything. She just stood there and looked at the empty highway, and you could almost tell how bored she was by the way she stood. I lit a cigarette and told myself it was time to get some sleep.

I didn't budge.

As long as she was where I could see her, I couldn't take my eyes off her. After a while she moved around to the other side of the station, making a wide, lazy circle on her way back to the cabin. I went to the icebox to get myself a beer, and when I got back to the door she was standing right there at the bottom step.

She laughed softly, and just the sound of her voice was enough to shake me.

"I saw your cigarette," she said. "The heat keeping you awake too, Mr. Hooper?"

For a moment it was pretty awkward. I couldn't think of anything to say. She had known all along that I had been watching her and it didn't seem to bother her a bit.

Then a cloud slid from under the moon and there was sudden light in front of my cabin. I saw that she was smiling. "Is that beer you're drinking?" she asked.

"There's more in the icebox, if you'd like one."

"I think that would be fine," she said softly, still smiling.

I had a fast pulse as I went for the beer. I kept reminding myself that it was all probably very innocent, that she was just bored and wanted to talk. Still, that was the way things got started.

I didn't have any definite plans; I'd just take her the beer and see where we went from there, if anywhere. When I stepped out of the kitchen I saw that she was no longer outside by the steps.

She was there in my room.

Well, I thought, that's laying it on the line where you can't miss it! She was standing there with an unlighted cigarette in her fingers, and I must have set the beer down somewhere because I didn't have it when I stepped over and held a match for her. For a moment neither of us did anything. We just stood there looking at each other, getting the situation down pat. Then I grabbed for her.

She slipped out of my arms like a greased cat. "Are you always so impulsive, Mr. Hooper?"

"That's the way I am, I guess. And the name's Joe."

"And I'm Paula." She smiled. "Now do I get that beer?"

That was when I began to burn. I felt like the guy who had the wallet pulled away from him just as he was about to pick it up. But I got the beer. I found the can on the kitchen table and gave it to her.

"Now you're mad," she said, still smiling.

I said nothing.

She drank some of the beer and put the can down. "Does it always have to mean the same thing," she asked, "when a girl steps into a man's room?"

"Am I making a beef?"

"No. But you're mad; it shows all over."

I was mad, all right, but not nearly so much as I had been at first. Nothing had really changed. She hadn't turned indignant or tried to slap me, so I knew that nothing had changed but the timing. And I could change my timing. For a Paula Sheldon I could change a lot of things.

"All right," I said, "maybe I'm mad, but I'll get over it. Do you want another beer?"

"No, I'd rather talk."

"All right. What do we talk about?"

Still smiling, she hit me with it. "Let's talk about what you heard at our window tonight."

I couldn't have been more stunned if she had fired a pistol in my face. I stood like a post as she stepped around the bed, looked once through the window to make sure that her husband was still busy with his paperwork, then pulled the shade. She wasn't smiling now. She meant business.

"How much did you hear, Joe?" she said.

I shrugged as if to say I didn't know what she was talking about.

"You heard enough," she said. "I was on the bed when Karl and Manley were talking. You couldn't see me, but I could see you through the gap between the window shade and the facing."

There was nothing I could say to that. She had seen me. What got me was why she hadn't yelled at the time, giving Manley and Sheldon a warning.

She knew what I was thinking.

"You're wondering why I kept quiet about it," she said. "I did it because this job has to go through. There can't be any backing out, because Karl has to have the money. Do you have any idea how many strings have to be pulled to get a man out of prison? It took almost ten thousand dollars to get Karl a parole, and now the string pullers want to be paid, or they'll send him back faster than they got him out. If he's lucky."

I hardly heard what she was saying. She had moved closer, pressing against me, and then those white arms crawled around my neck and she turned her face up to me.

"Do you understand, Joe?"

The only thing I understood was the excitement that took hold of me when she touched me, as the softness of her seemed to melt against me, as I tried to capture that red mouth that kept slipping from one side to the other.

"Joe, do you understand what you must do?"

"I understand."

She was a fire inside me, spreading through me, racing like flame. She was still talking as I forced her back. I tightened my arm around her, bowing her back, bending her knees, and suddenly both of us came crashing down on the bed. She was still talking.

"Joe, nothing must happen to stop this factory job! No one must know about it! No one!"

"I said I understood."

"Promise, Joe, that you'll tell no one!"

"Great God, what do I have to say to convince you? All right, I promise!"

Only then did she stop squirming and fighting, only then did I capture that red mouth of hers. Her arms tightened around my neck in the kind of nervous excitement that is impossible to fake. Her dagger-sharp nails gouged into my shoulders as she pulled me down with her, then she took my hand in hers and guided it, and for a long while there was no sound in the room except that of our breathing.

"Joe...."

I wasn't sure how much time had passed. The bright, clean fire was dead, and the stifling heat of the Oklahoma summer moved into the room.

"Joe...."

I said nothing. The thing to watch about climbing so high is the terrible fall to the ground. I laughed.

"Joe, what is it?"

"Nothing."

I had no wish to touch her or look at her or anything else. After a while she got up and went to the window, again, and I guess Karl Sheldon was still busy with his burglary plans, because Paula seemed in no hurry to leave. She came back and sat on the edge of the bed.

"Joe, you meant it, didn't you? You won't do anything that might affect our plans?"

I looked at her then, amazed that she looked exactly the same as she had before—completely unruffled, as pale as the moon. Even then, at a time like that, with the heat in the room so heavy that it was almost impossible to breathe, all I had to do was look at her and that sure excitement began to take hold again. Instinctively I reached out for her, but she laughed softly and moved away.

She was waiting for an answer, for some assurance that I was going to keep my promise. I wasn't even sure what it was I had promised. I made another grab and she slithered away again, and this time she stood up and moved into the deep shadows on the other side of the room. It was almost as though a powerful field of magnetic attraction had been removed. Now that I could hardly see her, I could think again.

"Well..." she said. Not impatiently, not uncertainly. It was just an invitation to get on with the particular business at hand.

"I gave you my word," I said. "I won't break up your husband's plans."

Like hell I wouldn't break up his plans! What if something got fouled up and something went wrong with the robbery? Where would that put me? I knew where it would put me, if it ever came out that I had known about the robbery beforehand. It would put me in a cell right alongside Sheldon and Manley. Accessory before the fact— I wasn't so stupid that I didn't know what that meant.

I sat up and lit a cigarette to give my hands something to do while I thought it out. She was a hell of a woman, there was no doubt about it....

"I know what you're thinking," she said, almost gently, and I imagined that I could hear that faint half-smile in her voice.

"Do you?"

"You were wondering if the payment was right for the job."

"I was wondering what your husband would do if he knew I had listened in tonight."

"That's easy," she said. "He simply wouldn't go through with the job. That's how he is. If a thing isn't set up perfectly, he doesn't touch it."

"And if he doesn't go through with this one, he goes back to prison?"

She nodded. "Or worse."

I found an ash tray and mashed out the cigarette. "You know," I said, "this thing could be as dangerous for you as it is for your husband. You must love him very much, coming here like this...."

Nothing at all flustered her. She laughed. "As a matter of fact, I don't love him at all." And she had already anticipated the next question. "Then why am I married to him? Maybe I'll tell you someday."

She moved out of the shadows then and came across the room again. This time she didn't slip away when I reached for her. For just a moment the hard fire raged and she gouged her fingers into my shoulders as I kissed her.

"I like you, Joe!" The words came through her teeth, hissing.

Then she was gone. Holding her when she didn't want to be held was like trying to squeeze moonlight in your hands. She was out of my arms and out of the cabin before I could stop her. There was nothing I could do about it.

There was little sleep for me that night. My nerves were strung as tight as cat gut on a violin.

After a while the light went out in the Sheldon cabin and the night was completely quiet. There was not a breath of breeze to move the limp curtains, to relieve the heat. When I looked hard into the shadows I could almost see her standing there. I could reach out and almost touch her. And all I could do was lie there and sweat, giving myself plenty of good advice that I knew I wasn't going to take.

But all things end, if you wait long enough, and finally that night ended. I opened the station as usual around seven o'clock, and about thirty minutes later Karl Sheldon and Paula came around in the Buick.

I lifted my hand when Sheldon waved. "We're going down to Texas to see my wife's people," he called. "On our way back we may be stopping with you again."

"I'll be looking for you."

Paula didn't even look at me. Which was just as well.

As the Buick pulled onto the highway and slipped into the stream of early-morning traffic, panic took hold of me. Christ! I thought. How are you going to explain this to the sheriff, Hooper? What are you going to say when he asks why you stood there and let them drive away?

Then I thought: Now, wait a minute. There's nothing to get panicky about, because, as far as you know, they haven't done a damn thing that they could be arrested for. All they've done is talk. And there was no way in the world I could prove that.

Sure, I thought. That makes sense. The robbery doesn't take place for another seven days, so just phone the sheriff and tell him what you know.

I didn't do it.

The first thing I knew, it was noon, and I still hadn't done anything about calling the sheriff. Something seemed to happen every time I started to call. First it was a farmer wanting coal oil, then a flat to fix, then a lube job, and then the morning was gone. Once I had been putting gas in a car, and the driver got out and said, "What the hell do you think you're doing?" The tank had overflowed and gas had gone over his rear fender and was splashing onto the driveway. "What are you thinking about, anyway?"

I could have told him, but I didn't. I had been thinking about that blonde wife of Sheldon's.

That threw a scare into me. Well, by God! I thought. Are you still remembering that little blonde tramp, Hooper? Is it because of that promise to her that you can't find time to call the sheriff's office?

Oh, she's quite a woman, all right, that Paula Sheldon, but you'd better be sensible about this thing, Hooper, or you're going to have more trouble than you can handle!

Paula, I thought, you're going to look like hell in one of those prison dresses, but there's not a thing I can do about it. I quit the lube job I'd been working on, went into the station, and picked up the phone. After a minute a voice said, "Sheriff's office, King speaking."

"Ray, this is Joe Hooper. Let me speak to the sheriff, will you?"

"The sheriff just left for lunch. Anything I can help you with, Joe?"

"No. Thanks, anyway. It's nothing important." Suddenly I was glad the sheriff wasn't in, because the thing was too involved to tell over the phone. When Ike came on duty, I'd go down to the office and talk to him. That was what I told myself.

"By the way," the deputy said, "how's the tourist business, Joe? They keepin' you pretty busy out there?"

"Yes, pretty busy. Well, see you around, Ray."

I hung up and looked at my hands. They were shaking. I felt like the man who walked away from a head-on collision.

What's the matter with you, Hooper, have you lost your mind completely?

I knew what was the matter with me. I was beginning to get an idea. It came with a rush, and suddenly it stood there full grown, grinning at me. This is the way, it said.

This is how it's going to be!

Chapter Three

About two o'clock that afternoon the sheriff called.
"Joe, this is Otis Miller. Ray King said you called while I was out to lunch. Anything I can do for you?"
"Yes," I said. "I talked to Ray, and maybe I should have told him about it, but I decided to wait until I could see you. I'm afraid I got suckered, Sheriff. I was going through my cash drawer this morning and found a five-dollar bill that looks like it was printed on newsprint."
"Counterfeit?"
"Queer as a thirty-cent piece. I don't know why I didn't notice it before. Too busy to pay attention, I guess."
"Well, that's too bad, Joe, and I don't know of a thing we can do about it. Bring the bill down to the office, though, and it may help catch the man who's passing them. By the way, how's the tourist business out there?"
"Fine, Sheriff. Just fine!"
"Glad to hear it, Joe. Well, you bring that bill around and we'll see what we can do."

I hung up, amazed at how easy a lie could roll once you got it started. I did have a counterfeit five-dollar bill, of course. I'd been carrying it in my billfold almost a year, wondering what I was going to do with it.

Well, now I knew. That bogus bill, the way I figured it, was going to be worth about ten thousand dollars! It had got me off the hook with the sheriff. Because of that bill, and some pretty fast thinking, I'd soon be able to kick this town in the face. I'd soon be on my way to the top!

I felt like a million dollars, just thinking about it.

It seemed fantastic that the idea hadn't come to me right away, as soon as I'd heard Sheldon and Manley scheming the robbery. But it hadn't; it had come at the very last minute, and it had been a damn near thing, too. This was the break I'd been waiting for, that beautiful once-in-a-lifetime break, and I had almost muffed it!

The trouble was I hadn't expected a break to come in the form of a payroll robbery. What I had been expecting was the Herb Carter story all over again, but I knew now that breaks don't come spelled out for you—sometimes you've got to fill out the instructions yourself. Another thing; I hadn't expected my big break to land me on the wrong side of the law. But what the hell! Hadn't Herb Carter broken just about every law in the book? And had anything happened to him? Like hell it had. They're not so anxious to wave that law in your face if they know you've got a bankroll to fight with.

Anyway, I'd finally got it straight in my mind, and I felt fine about it. I walked around grinning. Oh, Sheldon and Manley were going to squeal like pigs under a fence when I broke the news to them that I was cutting myself in for one third of that box-factory payroll. But there was very little they could do about it. They'd either have to accept my terms or give up the job— and I just couldn't see a professional giving up a soft touch like that box factory.

I walked around in a rosy daze the rest of the afternoon. Good-by, filling station, good-by, tourist shacks, good-by, Creston! In another week I'd shake the whole business out of my hair.

But, in the meantime, I had to sit tight. I had to wait for the Sheldons to come back, and I had to act completely normal. That's the important thing, just act as though nothing at all had happened.

So I spent the rest of the day trying to act normal, trying to keep my feet on the ground. I stood in the station doorway, drank Cokes, watched the traffic go by. I thought about that robbery, and the ten thousand dollars, and getting away from Creston. And I also did a good deal of thinking about Paula Sheldon.

But I concentrated on acting normal. Every few minutes somebody from Creston would go by on the highway, and I'd wave, and then I'd think: Christ, what would they do if they knew what I'm thinking right now! They wouldn't believe it. What if I walked up to them and said, "Look here, on the fourteenth of this month I'm going to take part in a robbery. I'm going to help rob old Provo's payroll. What do you think of that?"

I wanted to laugh. They wouldn't believe it! Doc Hooper's boy robbing a payroll? Never!

If they only knew! I thought.

I made a kind of game out of it and amused myself for a while, but after a few hours it began to grow a little thin. Anyway, my thoughts always turned back to Paula Sheldon.

I kept remembering what she had said about her husband. "I don't love him at all," she had said. And she had meant it. And she had meant it when she had pressed that red mouth of hers to mine—there was no faking an excitement like that!

I knew what she was, and it made no difference at all. She was hard, as ruthless as she was beautiful, as brittle as fine china. Well, I could be hard too, and ruthless, and brittle. I had taken it on the chin plenty trying to play according to the rules. Now, for the first time in my life, I felt strong; I felt that I could do something really big, and to hell with the rulebooks.

But it all came back to Paula, eventually. Oh, I had been drunk on heady wine, all right, and only a man with a hangover can know the terrible thirst for more that comes the day after. Paula had known. Knowing that I never intended to keep my promise to her, she had smiled.

She had known better.

It's possible to hate and love at the same time, they say, but I did not hate Paula. Where there had been stale existence, Paula had brought excitement. She had given me something to fight for—herself. Let's face it, Hooper, it's not only the ten thousand dollars that fascinates you—it's that blonde as well, and you know it.

Her husband? I hardly thought of him. What was necessary I would do. But after the robbery Paula would belong to me.

Ike Abrams rattled off the highway in his '46 Ford, drove around to the back of the station, and parked beside the grease rack. I went around to meet him. "Can you take over now, Ike? I've got some things to do. We can check the cash register after a while."

"Sure," he said. "You sick or somethin', Joe? You look a little green around the gills."

"I feel fine."

I went to my cabin and didn't even notice the heat. I lay across the bed for several minutes without moving, without batting an eye, just staring at the ceiling and thinking of all the things I could do with one third of thirty thousand dollars. Ten thousand dollars, right in my pocket! It was more money than I'd ever had, more money than I'd ever seen, even, all at one time.

I must have dozed for a while. It was almost sundown when a knock at the door brought me out of it. I sat up, groggy with sleep and half dazed by the heat, and then I saw my father standing on the steps on the other side of the screen door.

"Son, you in there?"

"Sure, Dad. Come on in, if you can stand the heat."

I was still sitting there scratching my head as he opened the screen and stepped inside. "By God," I said, "I must have been crazy to go to sleep in this heat. I feel like I'd been knocked down with a wooden mallet. Sit down, Dad. I think there's some beer in the icebox."

He looked older than the last time I had seen him, which had been only a day or two before, and very tired. He smiled faintly, dropped into a cane-bottomed chair, and carefully placed his black satchel on the floor.

"Yes. I think a beer might taste good."

I went to the kitchen and washed my face at the sink, then got the beers out of the icebox and brought them in. I dropped on the bed again and for one quiet moment we drank from the sweating cans. I was used to having my father drop in on me like this, every time he had a call out this way. He was the finest man I ever knew—and the only man in the world that I cared a damn about. We never said much. Usually it was just like this, sitting, drinking a beer together, and then he'd leave. I had a feeling, though, that today was going to be different.

"You been out to the Jarvis farm again?" I asked firmly.

He shrugged and smiled that small smile. "The McClellans, this time. The youngest boy stepped on a nail. Luckily, he had been vaccinated for tetanus."

"Why," I asked, "do you keep fooling with these hard-scrabble farmers, Dad? You'll never get your pay, and you know it. You could have a fine practice in town, be making plenty of money, if you'd stay in your office where people could find you."

He glanced at me, then away. "People in the country need doctors too. Besides, it's a little late for me to start making money, isn't it?"

"You could think about your health. It's not too late for that, but it will be pretty soon, if you keep making these farm calls at all hours."

We'd been over it a thousand times and had never found a meeting place. Maybe I would have been a doctor, the way he had wanted, if I could have seen any future in it when I was younger. But getting up at all hours of the night, when you're dead tired, and going out to the very end of God's nowhere to help some farmer's wife have her tenth kid was not my idea of a way to live.

"Joe...." I looked up, almost forgetting that he was still sitting there. He cleared his throat and looked down at his lean, white hands. "Joe, I had a talk with Beth's father yesterday."

"Steve Langford?" I knew what he was thinking.

I didn't want to talk about it. It was the last thing I wanted to discuss right now, with Paula Sheldon whirling in my mind, but I couldn't think of any way to stop it. "What did Langford have to talk about—that front yard of his?" I laughed. "You'd think it was his life's work, the time he puts on it."

"No." He still looked at his hands. "He talked about you, Joe, and about Beth."

"I know," I said, trying hard to keep a hold on my anger. "Langford wants to know if Beth and I have set the date yet. Well, I've got news for Langford. There's not going to be any date. What a hell of a town this is! Go out with a girl a few times and they've got you as good as married!"

I had plenty more to say. I was getting damn tired of people like Steve Langford butting in on my business. But I left them unsaid, the things that were in my mind. I had no wish to hurt my father, the one man in the world that I liked. I guess he figured, like Langford, that someday I would marry a hometown girl and settle down to rot the rest of my life away in Creston. Well, he was mistaken about that; they all were mistaken.

But the look of disappointment in my father's eyes shook me. I suddenly realized how old he was, and tired, and finally I said: "I'll tell you what I'll do. I'll talk it over with Beth."

He smiled, very faintly. "All right, Joe. Whatever you say." Then he reached for his satchel and stood up. We said the usual small things, and after a while he was gone.

I was late, as usual, when I got around to the Langford place that night, and as usual Steve Langford was watering his front lawn as I drove up.

"You're late tonight, Joe."

"Got held up at the station again," I said.

He seemed distant, cool. He had been doing a lot of thinking and had just about decided that he didn't like me.

"Beth's in the house, I think." He went on with his watering.

I sat in the car waiting for Beth to come out. Something made me look at Langford again. He was standing half crouched, rigid as a statue, with the squirting nozzle in his hands, almost as though it were a gun. I got it then. He was waiting for me to get out of the car, walk up to the front porch, and meet his daughter at the door.

Well, I thought, the hell with him! I tramped the horn button and the blaring sound hit the silent dusk like a hammer. Bright crimson rushed to Langford's face as he stood there. I tramped the horn again, just for the hell of it. By God, I thought, if she doesn't want to come out of the house, that's fine with me!

But she came out. I knew she was defying her father in doing it, but she came out.

"Are you ready?" I said.

"Sure, Joe." Not looking at her father, she walked head down to the Chevy and got into the front seat beside me.

That was all we said until we were away from the house. She sat stiff and silent as I worked the Chevy toward the highway. She looked clean and crisp in a white dress, and her tanned arms and small face made her look almost like a young girl. But she certainly was no Paula Sheldon.

Well, I thought, I'm glad the end is in sight. And Beth knew it—it was written in the strained lines of her face. She was thirty years old, which is pretty old for a single girl in a town like Creston, and I could see it written in those lines of desperation at the corners of her mouth, in the steady glassiness of her eyes. There was just one thing I wished for: I wanted it to be calm and civilized. I had no wish to hurt her—all I wanted was to end it as cleanly as possible.

About three miles out of town we turned off the highway onto a graveled road, and before long we could see the dark stand of oak and blackjack that more or less surrounded Lake Creston. It was getting dark now and we began meeting cars heading back toward town, some of them towing small boats on two-wheeled trailers. Local fishermen.

Pretty soon we could see the lake itself, a pretty good-sized body of water for that part of the country, sprawling over maybe three hundred acres and held in check by a big dirt dam. I glanced at Beth, and she looked surprised. It had been a long time since I had brought her out here.

Maybe it was a mistake to come to this particular place, but it was the only place I could think of where we could talk and not be disturbed—where we could get mad and yell at each other, if it came to that, and not be afraid that somebody would hear us. I made a great business of watching the road as the lake rose up before us.

It was always something of a shock to see that much water in a dry country. The lake had been built back in the thirties by the WPA. It furnished Creston with water, and was well stocked for fishing, and a few years back picnic grounds had been constructed below the dam. There was a dock where several fishing boats, and even a few snipe-class sailboats, were tied up. Up toward the head of the dam there was a small blockhouse where you could buy fish bait, fishing licenses, and beer. I stopped and picked up a can of beer before crossing the dam. Now that the sun had set, the night was almost cool near the water.

"You want to take a turn around the lake?" I said.

She said something, I didn't hear what, as I circled the car to get under the wheel. "It's really quite a place," I said. "I wouldn't mind having a cabin out here somewhere, a place where a guy could knock off for a day or so and just take it easy."

I was just killing time, and Beth knew it. I could feel her staring at me, wondering what I was going to say.

There was a narrow, single-lane graveled road that meandered all the way around the lake, and now and then a deep-rutted spur that wandered off to a dead end at some abandoned farm. I put the car in gear and started across the dam, thinking vaguely that the cabin idea wasn't a bad one, at that. Maybe Paula and I would get ourselves one sometime. It would take some money, of course, but Old Man Provo and his box factory were going to furnish that.

After we hit the lake road we had to take it easy. It was dark, and the road crawled crazily in and out of wild-looking blackjack thickets, and you had to watch for cars parked here and there along the road. High-school kids.

About halfway around the lake I pulled my Chevy onto one of those abandoned farm roads and snapped out the lights. I looked at Beth, then lit a cigarette and sat back in the seat. There was tightness around her mouth, a determined look in her eyes.

"Joe."

I looked at her.

"Joe, what's wrong? Something is wrong, isn't there? You've hardly said a word since we left the house."

I didn't know how to say it. Goddamnit, I thought, I should have just called her on the telephone and told her it was all over. She moved over next to me, and I was the stiff one now, and cold.

"Joe...."

"Yes?"

"What is it, Joe? Can't you tell me?"

The situation was ridiculous, and being ridiculous made me mad. "Christ," I said, "do I have to spell it out for you? We're not getting anywhere, that's all, and your old man thinks we ought to knock it off." I looked straight ahead, through the windshield. "I think so, too."

She did nothing for several seconds, sitting very erect, clenching her hands in her lap. Then, finally: "Joe, is it someone else? I know what my father thinks, and it isn't important, but is it someone else?"

"Now, who else would it be?" I said wearily. "If I'd found someone else, it would be all over Creston by now and you know it."

"But... there must be a reason!"

"I told you," I said. "We're not getting anywhere. And I'm tired of not getting anywhere, tired of Creston, tired of those lousy tourist shacks. I'm leaving this country, Beth, and everything in it. It's as simple as that."

"Is it, Joe?"

"Now, what's that supposed to mean? Of course it's as simple as that. I'm sick of it and I'm leaving it."

"And me, Joe?" A very tight voice. "What about me?"

Good Lord, I thought, what do you have to say to a woman like this?

I said, "It's over. If there was ever anything to begin with. That's what I'm trying to tell you. It's over."

She didn't believe me. Womanlike she couldn't believe that after all this time she was being dumped. Behind it all, she probably believed that my motivations were noble and gallant, because she couldn't make herself believe that I was simply sick of her and that was the whole story.

Then she did a hell of a thing. You had to know Beth to understand what a hell of a thing it was. Suddenly she had her arms around my neck and was pressing herself against me, and there was absolutely no mistake about what she had in her mind. This was her one big weapon—the one weapon that all *nice* girls like Beth hold onto to the bitter end, hoping that they'll never have to use it but firmly convinced that it will gain them their ends, a ring and marriage certificate, if the time should ever come.

It left me completely cold. Instantly, Paula was in my brain again, and nothing in the world that Beth could do could stir me. I reached for the switch and snapped it on.

"You might as well go on saving it," I said. "But for somebody else."

Chapter Four

The fourteenth was a long time coming that July. The days dragged as I stood in the station doorway watching the traffic go past, thinking: Maybe the next car will be that Buick, maybe the Sheldons will come early to make sure there are no slip-ups.

Then I'd get to thinking: Maybe they won't come back at all. Maybe something happened and they decided to call the whole thing off.

What would I do then? They *had* to come! I couldn't stand this lousy place much longer. I couldn't stand this flea-bitten service station. I wanted to feel that money in my pocket. I wanted Paula close to me, where I could reach out and touch her.

Meanwhile, I was alone. That business with Beth at the lake—Lord, I hope I never get into a mess like that again. She cried. She didn't say a single word, just lay there with great tears streaming down that pale, pinched face of hers. I had hated her at the time, but now I felt nothing. I hadn't heard a word from Beth since that night. I knew I never would.

Now there was the robbery to be thought about. I wasn't worried about Manley and Sheldon; I was holding all the cards. If they pulled the robbery, there was no way they could keep me out of it. And they would pull it, all right, because Paula would have it no other way.

Still, I was taking no chances.

On the thirteenth I decided to do something that I should have done at the very beginning. I was going over that box factory with a fine-tooth comb. I wasn't going to rely on Bunt Manley.

I thought: This is going to look damn funny, Hooper. You haven't been near that factory since you stopped working there. Is this going to be smart, sticking your nose into things the day before the robbery?

Smart or not, I couldn't take chances on something going wrong. And about that time I remembered Pat Sully—good old Pat Sully, who had loaned me five dollars six months ago and had probably kissed it good-by long since. Well, Pat was going to get a surprise, because I was going to pay him back, and I was going to pay him back because he happened to be a bookkeeper for Max Provo and did his work in the factory's front office, which was exactly the place I wanted to visit.

About three that afternoon I turned the station over to Ike Abrams and took the Chevy into town. The factory was north and west of town, sprawled out on the red slope of a clay hill. There were two main buildings, two-story red-brick affairs, connected by a plank runway at the second-story level.

One building was the factory itself, where the boxes were made, and that one didn't interest me at all. The other was a conglomeration of warehouse-garage-storeroom-office, and this one interested me plenty.

I parked the Chevy in the company parking space at the west side of the factory, got out, and started walking around to where the front office was. There was a good deal of activity at the loading ramp, where two big semis were backed up to be loaded. Sweating roustabouts formed an endless chain with their loaded dollies, warehouse to trailer and back again, working like so many ants around an anthill. I had been one of those ants once. Never again.

The office itself was a busy place and not much to look at. It was just one big room, the working space partitioned off by wooden railings. Truck drivers and warehousemen were coming and going, and some of them were trying to make themselves heard over the noise of typewriters and adding machines. There were maybe a dozen girls on one side of the room, filing things, typing letters, or whatever they do in an office like that; and on the other side of the room the bookkeepers and department managers were going about their business and ignoring everything else.

The temperature must have been a hundred in that room. No air-conditioning, not even an electric fan. Those things cost money, and anything that cost money wasn't for Max Provo.

I had been in that office a hundred times or more, but this time I really looked at it. There was a big double door at the back of the office; one of the doors was open—for better ventilation—and I could look into the warehouse, on the other side of the plyboard partition. Nothing had changed since I had worked here. Everything was the same, but this time I was taking a picture of it in my mind.

Then my gaze landed on the thing I was really looking for, the safe.

It looked like a hell of a safe to me. It looked like the great-great-grandfather of all the safes in the world. I had seen it before, I *must* have seen it before, but I didn't remember it as being that big. It was the biggest, heaviest, ruggedest-looking damn safe I'd ever seen. It was six feet tall; at least six feet tall, and almost as wide, and there was no telling how thick or heavy the thing was. It looked as big as a Sherman tank.

That Sheldon better be good, I thought, because it's going to take more than a can opener to get into that thing.

"Hello, Joe. Not lookin' for a job, are you?"

I looked around and there was a man grinning at me from the other side of the railing, a little sharp-faced, stoop-shouldered man whose name was Paul Killman and who, so the story went, rode in on the first load of brick when they started building the box factory thirty years ago and had been there ever since.

I said, "Hello, Mr. Killman. I just happened to be passing this way and remembed that I wanted to see Pat Sully about something. Do you know where he is?"

"Why, I think he's at his desk. Yes, there he is."

I'd been so busy looking at that safe that I hadn't seen Pat at all. But I saw him now, a big, red-faced guy about my own age, sleepily putting figures into an open ledger.

"All right if I talk to him a minute?" I asked.

"Sure, sure, Joe. You know your way around here."

I pushed open the gate and went around on the business side of the railing. I put a five-dollar bill on Pat's ledger and said, "The age of miracles hasn't passed, after all, and here's something to prove it. Remember that five you loaned me?"

His head snapped up. "Hell, Joe, you didn't have to come all the way out here to give it to me. To tell the truth, I'd forgotten all about it."

Like hell he had. He was quick enough to put it in his pocket.

We talked for maybe five minutes about things that neither of us cared a damn about. Pat kept looking anxiously at Old Man Provo's desk, in the far corner of the room, as though he expected the sky to fall. I was sizing up that room. I was getting a picture of it in my mind that couldn't be erased. That safe was the only thing that bothered me.

I said, "Is the water cooler still in the warehouse? Let's go back and have a cigarette. Old Provo can get along without you for a few minutes."

Pat didn't like it much; old Provo was hell on getting his pound of flesh from the office force. Then he shrugged. Maybe he was getting tired of the job anyway. "All right, but just for a minute."

I wanted to get a good look at that warehouse, because that was the way we had to come in. We couldn't come in the front way; that was well lighted and facing the highway. It had to be the back way, through the warehouse. I deliberately counted the steps from Pat's desk, which was about in the center of the room, to the warehouse partition.

I swung close enough to the safe to get the brand name; it was a Kimble. A Kimble Monarch, the lettering said, Model K-467. It was an elephant of a safe. Why hadn't I noticed it before? No wonder the place had never been robbed, with a safe like that. If you're smart, I thought, you'll drop this thing right where it is. Let Manley and Sheldon beat their brains out trying to get inside that iron blockhouse. It's crazy to think that a man could ever open a monster like that.

Then I was crazy, because I was not dropping it now. Sheldon was the expert on safes; let *him* worry about it.

The water cooler was a big galvanized can with two spigots at the bottom, sitting on a couple of sawhorses just on the other side of the office partition, in the warehouse itself. Entering that warehouse was like stepping into the bleak, empty spaces of a desert. It looked as big as those hangars they used to house dirigibles in. The ceiling was two stories high, and up there somewhere, in the gloom, cranes rolled back and forth, the noise echoing and bouncing from one wall to the other. All over the floor there were skeleton crates filled with flattened cardboard cartons of every size and shape imaginable, and the roustabouts were continually bringing them in or taking them out.

At the back of the building there was a giant steel sliding door, and I immediately counted that out. A door like that might turn out to be tougher to open than the safe. That left the windows, and they didn't look much better. To start with, they were small, and they had iron bars on them.

I stood there at the water cooler talking to Pat, but I don't know what about. I was studying those windows at the back of the warehouse. Then one of the workers, a big swarthy guy in overalls, saw me and yelled.

He had a grin a yard wide. His name was Matt Souel and he had been just another roustabout when I had worked at the factory, but now he was the warehouse foreman.

"What the hell you doin' out here with us workin' folks, Joe?"

Pat Sully was nervous and happy enough to make a quick excuse and get back on the job before Provo discovered that he was missing. I went back and talked to Matt Souel for a while, glad that he had called to me. It gave me a chance to have a closer look at those rear windows.

We'd wake the whole town trying to get past those iron bars. But the thing that really decided me had nothing to do with the bars. The thing that decided me was about twenty feet of makeshift electrical wiring and an oblong box fixed to the rear wall, above the windows.

There were limits, it seemed, to how far even a man like Max Provo would go to save money. He was tight, all right, but he hadn't been too tight to invest in a burglar alarm.

The windows were out.

Everything was out unless I could find a way of disconnecting that burglar alarm, and I didn't know a damn thing about burglar alarms. I didn't know where the switch was, or how it was set, or anything else. And even if I did know, I couldn't very well start fooling with that wiring when there were fifteen or twenty roustabouts looking on.

Matt Souel was still talking, and I stood there grinning like an idiot while my spirits sank like a truck falling down an elevator shaft.

Hell, I thought, we're beat even before we start. If the back of this building is wired, then so is the front. Touch one of those doors or windows after closing time and the whole town is going to know about it. You'll have Otis Miller and the rest of the police force on your back before you know what hit you.

Then I remembered something. I remembered the garage, on the other side of the warehouse, and I remembered the two master switch boxes that controlled the electrical output to both buildings. They were in the garage. And the garage wasn't locked at night, because that was where the night watchman stayed most of the time.

I was beginning to feel better. I felt fine. Burglar alarms were electrically operated; all we had to do was open the circuit to this warehouse building, and you could knock the walls down and the burglar alarms wouldn't do a thing.

I felt great. I felt like a man whose parachute had finally opened a hundred feet above the ground. Not even those barred windows worried me now. Not even that steel monster of a safe could worry me.

The next day, about four in the afternoon, the blue Buick pulled under the station shed and Karl Sheldon said pleasantly, "Here we are again. I hope you've got a vacancy for us."

I felt as big as a house. I grinned right in his face and said, "Yes, sir, I've been saving one for you."

Paula was back in shorts again, white duck shorts and white T shirt and thong sandals. Just looking at her was all I needed to get me excited again. She didn't say a word. She just sat there smiling that slow smile, knowing that she was being stared at and liking it.

She knew what I was thinking, all right. She knew what was in my mind.

Sheldon said, "We're in luck, honey. He's saved a place for us."

You sonofabitch, I thought. Do you think I'm so stupid that I don't know sarcasm when I hear it? I was tempted to hit him with it right there. I wanted to grab him by the throat and say, "Listen to me, you pompous bastard, I'm cutting myself in for one third of your take tonight. What do you think of that?"

But I played it straight. I signed them in, then took them to the cabin.

Sheldon came around to the back of the car and began unlocking the trunk. I didn't offer to help. Somewhere in that car there was enough nitroglycerin to blow us to hell, and I wanted no part of it. I unlocked the cabin and opened some windows. When I turned around, Paula was standing right behind me. I grabbed her.

I hadn't meant to. I had it all planned not to do a thing until I got everything settled with Sheldon. But I simply couldn't keep my hands off her. That bright hot arc jumped between us and suddenly she was straining against me.

"You haven't changed," she said huskily.

"It's been a long time."

"Only a week."

"Do you know how long a week can be?"

"Yes, I know."

That ripe mouth didn't slip away this time as I kissed her. I felt her nails digging into my shoulders again, into my arms. "You're strong, aren't you, Joe? Hard and strong."

"Yes."

"I believe it. I've thought about you, Joe. Your arms like leather rope. I like men with arms like that."

"You've got some points too that I've thought about."

Her arms went around my neck and pulled tight. The words came through her teeth. "There's no future in this, Joe. You know that, don't you?"

"We'll talk about that later."

"There won't be any later. Tomorrow I'll be gone. Besides, there's Karl."

"You said you didn't love him."

"That has nothing to do with it."

I had the feeling that she didn't like what was happening, but she was unable to stop it, just as I was unable to stop it. A handful of iron gets caught in an electrical field and jumps to the magnet. The iron has nothing to say about it.

Outside, an impatient horn blared out, and I knew it was somebody at the station wanting gas or oil. Then Sheldon called, "Hooper, you've got a customer."

I had forgotten about Sheldon, the station, and everything else. Sheldon hit the steps, but before he got the door open Paula was out of my arms. She threw herself on the bed and lay there like a marble statue, as white and unmoving as a marble statue, that red mouth of hers partly open.

She lay there on her back, her arms and legs forming a white letter X on the bed, her eyes closed. For just a moment I remembered some paintings that I had seen once. They were nudes, painted by some Italian with a name I couldn't pronounce. The nude women all looked alike and they were all painted orange; their bodies, their faces, everything was orange but the hair, and they were the nakedest women I ever saw.

Sheldon was in the room now, standing there by the door. I looked at him but couldn't tell what he was thinking.

"I think you've got a customer,' he said again.

"Yes. I heard."

I'd have to wait until Ike relieved me at the station before I could hit him with the robbery business. Anyway, I needed to calm down a little. I got out of there.

I went back to the station, took care of the customer, and tried to keep my feet on the ground until Ike came. I didn't hear any noise from the Number 2 cabin, so I figured Sheldon hadn't noticed anything out of the way. I didn't give a damn whether he had or not.

Maybe fifteen minutes had passed when Sheldon backed the Buick out of the carport and headed toward town. That meant he was going to make his contact with Manley and get their plans jelled.

Sheldon had been gone almost an hour when the telephone rang.

"Hooper?"

"Yes." I didn't recognize the voice at first.

"This is Karl Sheldon. Would you give my wife a message for me?"

"Sure, Mr. Sheldon."

"Just tell her that some important business has come up and our plans have been changed. Please ask her to get everything packed and I'll be back as soon as possible."

"You're checking out, Mr. Sheldon?"

"That's right. Sorry if we've inconvenienced you, Hooper, but of course we'll pay the usual rental fee."

"I see."

I didn't see worth a damn. But something had gone wrong. Something had exploded right in my face and I didn't know what it was. All I could think of was that I had to talk to Paula and talk fast before her husband got back. Maybe, between the two of us, we could straighten the thing out.

Then Ike Abrams drove up in that jalopy of his, and I was never so glad to see anybody in my life. I turned the station over to Ike, then went to my own cabin, as I always did. When I saw that Ike was busy in front of the station, I went over to the Sheldons' cabin.

Paula was still on the bed, but she came off it the minute I stepped through the door.

"Something's wrong," I said. "Your husband just called and said for you to get packed."

"What?"

"That's all he said. He's checking out as soon as he gets back and he wants you to get packed. Do you know what it means?"

Something happened to that beautiful face of hers; it wasn't so beautiful now. "Yes," she said, almost hissed. "I know what it means. It means he's backed out on the factory job."

"Why would he do a thing like that?"

"Because everything has to be perfect. If everything isn't absolutely perfect, he won't touch it."

"I still don't get it," I said.

I had never seen anger just like hers. It was almost as though she could turn it off and on by throwing a switch. Now she switched it off, sat on the edge of the bed, and put her hand to her forehead. "I really can't blame him so much. He spent five years in a cell for making a mistake once, and he doesn't want to make any more. Probably Bunt Manley couldn't get the information he wanted, so he called it off."

"Just like that he'd turn thumbs down on thirty thousand dollars?"

"It's more than thirty thousand dollars—it's his life."

I remembered what Paula had said about how much it had cost to get her husband a parole. "It's the string-pullers you're worried about, isn't it? What happens to your husband if they don't get paid?"

"They always get paid, one way or another."

"How much time does he have?"

She looked up. "It ran out a week ago. Karl thinks he can outrun them, but I know better."

It would suit me fine to let the string-pullers take care of Sheldon in their own way, but I needed him myself. That safe had to have an expert's attention, and Sheldon was the only expert I knew.

"This is important to you, isn't it?" I said.

I am convinced that she could read my mind. "No, Joe. Not you!"

"What's the matter with me? Am I made of old china? Do I go to pieces when I'm dropped? You say you're not in love with your husband—that's good enough for me. Maybe you'll tell me someday why you're so concerned about him, but that isn't important now. If I get your husband off the hook by convincing him that this job can be brought off, with my help, would you drop him?"

"For you, Joe?"

"For me."

For one long moment she said nothing. Then, without looking at me, she said, "You wouldn't like it, Joe. I would want things that you couldn't give me."

"Don't believe it. All I need is a little time."

"You wouldn't like my world," she said. "You wouldn't like me, either, after you got to know me."

"The way I feel about you has nothing to do with liking you. I just have to have you. As for this world of yours, all I ask is that it be different from the one I've known all my life.'

I moved in front of her, lifted her chin, and made her look at me. "You've been in my brain ever since I first saw you. After that night in my cabin I started cutting myself away from Creston and everything connected with it."

She smiled faintly. "You're a convincing man, Joe."

"It's a deal?"

She nodded. "It's a deal, as you say. Now tell me how you're going to convince Karl."

That was when we heard the Buick outside. It pulled into the carport beside the cabin and I said, "I won't have to tell you. You can see for yourself."

Sheldon was surprised to find me there with his wife, but not too much surprised. He said, "Well, Hooper..." then stepped over to the table and put down a brief case and some papers. Maybe he was used to walking into situations like this. He eased into a chair at the table and Paula lay across the bed, her eyes alive, her body tense.

Sheldon said, "Did you want to see me about something, Hooper?"

"Yes."

"Well, out with it."

The way he said it did something to me. A spring snapped. The words came out like pistol shots. "All right, Sheldon, here it is. It has to do with you and me and an ex-convict named Bunt Manley. It has to do with a box factory and a thirty-thousand-dollar payroll. Does any of that ring a bell?"

He was surprised this time and showed it.

"I'm afraid I don't know what you're talking about."

I was impatient now and wanted to get it over with. "Look," I said, coming toward him. "I know what you and Manley are planning to do. It would scare hell out of you to know how close I came to telling the police. But I didn't. I got to thinking."

I let it hang, watching Sheldon's face. One second it was red with rage, and then it was gray. Paula sat up on the bed, her mouth half open, looking as though she were going to laugh.

She didn't laugh. After a moment she lay back on her elbows and stared at me, not making a move, not even blinking.

Sheldon's anger was pretty thin when he said, "I think you're crazy, Hooper. I still don't know what you're talking about."

"Goddamnit! I haven't thought this thing out just for the sake of argument. Get that through your head, will you? I came here to talk business."

He'd had a pretty bad shock, but he was quick to regain his poise. He began putting things together, slowly at first, and then it came with a rush, like a summer storm, and he had the whole picture.

He looked at me and a suggestion of a sneer began to form at the corners of his mouth.

"You punks," he said hoarsely. "You all think you can ride luck, nothing but luck, to the very top, but you never think of the long fall down. Eavesdropping must be very interesting, Hooper. You must hear some interesting things in these cabins, even some profitable things, maybe, although I doubt that you have the brains or imagination to bring them off."

I almost hit him. He was big and in good condition, but I could have taken him. But I didn't. I snapped a steel trap on my temper and held it.

I said, "I think we should talk business."

"With a punk like you, Hooper?" He looked as though he might laugh, but didn't. Instead, he dropped back into his chair and sat there looking at me, shaking his head.

I said, "There's thirty thousand dollars in that factory, Sheldon. That's ten thousand a man, not bad for about an hour's work."

I could see that he wasn't going for it. He wasn't the kind to let himself be pushed into a thing he didn't like. My ground was falling out from under me.

Then I noticed the papers that Sheldon had put on the table, and I could see what they were. There was a detailed diagram of the factory layout, streets and highway, and there were other sketches that I took to be diagrams of the office interior and warehouse. I took a step forward and scooped up a fistful of the papers. When I straightened up I was looking into the muzzle of a .38.

It was a Police Special. Most of the bluing had been worn off around the muzzle and the front sight had been filed off even with the barrel. In Sheldon's brown hand it looked businesslike and deadly.

"Those papers," he said, holding out his free hand.

"You've already talked to Manley, haven't you?" I said. "You didn't like the way he laid it out, so you called off the job."

I studied that pistol for one long second, then handed him the papers.

"You punks," he said again. "I don't know anyone named Manley. I don't know anything about a box factory. I'm just a tourist who made the mistake of spending the night in this rat trap of yours—and after these papers are burned, you can't prove I'm anything else. Besides, I don't think you'll holler cop, Hooper. You'd have a bit of explaining to do yourself."

He smiled.

The robbery *couldn't* be called off! My whole future was built on this one thing, this one night. Without its support, all my tomorrows would come crashing down. "Look" I hardly recognized the voice as my own. Sheldon still had that pistol in his hand, but I ignored it now. "Look," I said again, and stepped right in front of him, right in front of the muzzle of that gun, "look at these sketches." I grabbed them from his hand, scattered them out on the table. Then, with one sweep, I brushed them all to the floor. "I told you I was here to talk business," I said. "Get me some paper and a pencil, and I'll prove it."

For one long moment he did nothing. I could see a thousand things going on behind his eyes, like lemons and plums and bells whirling past the windows of a slot machine. Paula still lay back on her elbows, staring with a kind of dumb fascination.

Then, at last, things stopped happening behind Sheldon's eyes. I heard the soft sound of breath whistling between his teeth. There was a little click as he switched the safety on that .38, then he slipped the pistol into his waistband and said, "Get it for him, Paula. Pencil and paper."

Paula got up lazily, almost bored now that the moment of tenseness was over. She got several sheets of note paper and a fountain pen out of one of the suitcases and brought them over to the table. Sheldon didn't say a thing. He just waited. I picked up the pen and went to work.

I had the inside of that office and warehouse and garage down perfectly. I had stepped them off, I even had the approximate dimensions. I put it all on paper and shoved it over for Sheldon to look at.

Two full minutes must have passed before he said, "Are you sure about all this?"

"I was in the place yesterday. I made it my business to find out."

"And also to make a suspect of yourself." The sneer was beginning to show again.

"There's a guy in the place I know," I said. "I owed him five dollars and just dropped in to pay him."

The sneer disappeared. "What about the safe?"

"The biggest goddamn safe I ever saw. A Kimble Monarch, Model K-four-six-seven."

He began to relax. He even smiled, very faintly. "Given time, I could open it with a nail file. However, that won't be necessary. What about burglar alarms?"

"The place is wired, all right, front and back. But the master switch box is in the garage, where the watchman stays. It shouldn't be much of a job to find the right switch and cut off the power to the building."

I could see that he was interested, and I began to breathe normally again. "When we cut off the power," I said, "it will darken the building, of course, but I don't think it will be noticed because the front of the factory is lighted with floodlights."

"How do we get in—*if* I should lose my mind and decide to try it your way?"

"Through the front door. It's the only way."

"With all those floodlights?" An eyebrow lifted, that was all.

"I told you it's the only way. The back door is a big power-operated steel affair and out of the question. It would take all night to saw through the bars on the rear windows. What we'll have to do is take the keys from the watchman, watch our chance, and go right in the front door."

He wasn't even listening. He was back to studying that sketch I had drawn. Paula was standing behind him, looking over his shoulder.

"It looks all right," she said. "Everything you want is there."

Sheldon said nothing. He was thinking.

"It's a lot better than your pal Manley could do," Paula went on.

Sheldon ignored the gentle prod about Manley. "It could be a soft touch," he said thoughtfully, "if something hasn't been overlooked. That could be a big if. I should have scouted the place myself. It was a mistake to leave it up to Manley."

"Manley!" Paula spat the name. "You were a fool to listen to an ox like Manley in the first place. He's small-time. He'll never be anything else."

"But he spotted the factory," Sheldon said, as though he felt somehow obligated to defend Manley.

Paula said one word, a word that is not often heard, even among men. There was nothing sleepy or passive about her now. There was an almost electrical energy about her. She walked across the room, snapped a cigarette out of a pack, and lit it.

"Leave Manley out of it," she said. "Forget him. He's contributed nothing so he gets nothing."

Until now I had been satisfied to remain quiet and let Paula get my argument across. But this business about leaving Manley out of it was no good.

She took one nervous drag on the cigarette and then ground it out on the floor, ignoring an ash tray less than twelve inches away.

"I know what you're going to say, Hooper," she said to me, as though she had never seen me before. "That is your name, isn't it? You're going to say that we can't leave him out. But we will. Manley's a fool, all right, but he's not fool enough to yell cop in a situation like this. When he reads about the burglary in the morning paper, he may not like it, but there'll be nothing he can do about it."

I shook my head, and Sheldon started to speak, but she stopped both of us. "Think of that five thousand dollars, that extra five thousand that will be yours, Hooper, if we leave Manley out of this. Anyway, what are you afraid of? Manley doesn't know that you've cut yourself in. There's no way he could hurt you."

Sheldon managed to break in this time. "I'm afraid there's one small detail you've overlooked," he said. "I haven't decided to take this job."

"I have decided," Paula said. "We have to have that money, Karl. It's not too late to set yourself right with those people, but we've got to have the money!"

She could be beautiful and decorative when she wanted, but she could also be other things. We stood there looking at each other over Sheldon's head. She's a hell of a woman, I thought, realizing vaguely that my argument about Manley was slipping away from me. One hell of a woman!

Chapter Five

I went back to my cabin feeling nine feet tall. Fifteen thousand dollars! What a man could do with that much money! I looked at my watch and saw that it was already six o'clock. I'd been in the Sheldon cabin almost two hours and the thing was settled.

Everything was all right, it was fine. Paula had everything, brains as well as looks. What a hell of a team we would make!

And then I saw Ike Abrams peering through the screen door. "Where the hell have you been, Joe? Your dad was around a while ago and we couldn't find you anywhere."

"Where have I been? Nowhere."

Wait a minute, I thought. That won't do. "Oh," I said, "I was over in Number Two. The shower was leaking again and they wanted me to fix it."

Just in case he had seen me go over there.

He kept standing there, one foot on the step and his face almost against the screen. "What is it?" I said. "Is something wrong?"

"No, I guess not. It's just your father. He looked worried."

"He's always worried about something. Probably he's pulling another of his hard-scrabble farmers through another siege of malaria."

"I think he's worried about you, Joe." He had something on his chest and he wasn't going to rest till he got it out. He said, "I know this is none of my business, Joe, but if you and Beth have had a fallin' out about something, well, it's never too late to make up, they say."

"Great God!" I exploded. "Ike, will you get back to the station and stop sticking your long nose into my business?"

He looked as though I had pulled a knife on him. Backing away from the steps, he mumbled, "All right, Joe... I'm sorry."

I hadn't realized I was so on edge. I almost called Ike back to apologize to him, but I didn't. What difference did it make? I was cutting away from Creston anyway.

I prowled the cabin for maybe thirty minutes, but the place wasn't big enough to hold me. I wanted to see Paula. I wanted to make plans for the future—a future with just me and her and no Karl Sheldon. But I couldn't talk to her now, and I couldn't very well just sit in the cabin until time for the robbery.

I looked through the window and Paula was sitting on the steps of Number 2 again, but this time her husband was standing in the doorway behind her. What the hell, I thought. I pulled on a clean shirt and went out.

"Hooper?" Sheldon said.

"Yes?"

"What do you usually do this time of day?"

"Do? Nothing in particular, I guess."

He opened the screen door and stepped outside. "It's important," he said soberly, "to keep to your regular routine, if you have one. Are you sure there isn't some kind of pattern? Don't you have a girl friend in town that you see pretty often?"

I looked straight at Paula and she smiled faintly. "No, I don't have a girl friend."

"Then why don't you drive into town and see a movie, if you're not going to stay at the station? The less we see of each other, the less chance there is for suspicion. Just be sure you're back by midnight."

Maybe he was right. I had to do something to kill time, and sitting alone in my cabin was no way to do it. Of course, there was always the chance that I might get a few minutes alone with Paula if I stuck around, but odds were long. Everything would go to hell if he caught us together.

"All right," I said. "Midnight.' I headed toward the station to get the Chevy.

It was the longest movie I ever sat through. It was the first time I had missed Beth, or even thought much about her, since I had made up my mind to break away. I was so used to having her sitting there beside me that it was almost like being lost. It was strange at first—but I had a cure for that.

All I had to do was think of Paula.

I didn't see a thing that happened on the screen; I just sat there and thought of what Paula and I would do after the robbery. Then I began thinking about the robbery itself, and that was when the first stirrings of uncertainty made themselves felt in my bowels. What if I had overlooked something at the factory! What if that switch had nothing to do with the burglar alarm at all? After all, I didn't know a damn thing about burglar alarms. Maybe the wiring on it was independent of the original circuits. What a hell of a thing that would be!

I never hated a thing in my life as much as I hated that movie. Every instinct told me to get out of there. Get out in the cool clean air and get this thing straightened out before it strangled.

That's just what I did, and it worked. The minute I got outside, the uncertainty was gone and I felt fine. I killed some time at a beer drive-in, then took a ride out north of town, and the first thing I knew there was the box factory looming up in the darkness. I don't know what had pulled me in that direction, but there I was.

Looking at it made my guts draw in a little. At night the place looked much more formidable than it did in the daytime, those two solid brick buildings squatting on a clay hillside. They looked almost prisonlike, with those floodlights pouring down the front of the main building, and I thought: I hope to hell that's not an omen.

I kept driving until I came to a section line and turned around. On the way back to town I tried not to look at it, but the thing was too big, too formidable to ignore. How were we ever going to get inside the place with all those floodlights pointed right at the front door? I had seen the factory a hundred times at night, but I had never noticed that there were so many of those floodlights or that they were so bright.

Then I thought of all that money. Thirty thousand dollars, maybe more. I thought of what Paula and I could do with money like that, and it would be just a beginning. The factory didn't look so tough after that. I drove straight through town and headed for the station. It was getting close to midnight.

Chapter Six

Karl Sheldon said: "Have you got a gun?"

"We don't need guns to take care of the watchman."

"I hope you're right. But in case you're not, take this." It was a nicely blued Colt's .38, and it looked as though it had never been fired. "I'll take it," I said. "But I'm telling you now, I'm not going to use it."

He looked at me. "Let's hope not." It was almost a prayer, the way he said it.

The time was twelve minutes past midnight and the three of us were back in Number 2 cabin. Paula still had on those white shorts and halter and was lounging on the bed.

"Well," Sheldon said, "I guess there's no use waiting."

"I guess not."

He took up a satchel, similar to the one my father carried his medical supplies in, and the two of us went out the door. Paula said nothing. She lay there on one elbow, her eyes quick and alive, but she didn't make a sound.

"We'll take the Buick," Sheldon said. "You drive."

I got under the wheel and Sheldon sat on the other side, holding the satchel very carefully in his lap. "There's one thing," I said, before pressing the starter. "This old night watchman, he's kind of a friend of mine. He might recognize me, so you'll have to take care of him. Tie him up or something, but don't hurt him."

"My friend," Sheldon said dryly, "I understand that they have not yet installed a lethal gas chamber in your state penitentiary, and the electric chair is a very nasty way to die. You may be assured that I want no part of murder."

"I'm glad we understand each other." I started the car.

The traffic on Highway 66 was very thin, and there was almost none at all in Creston, but I played it safe anyway. I didn't want to be seen driving that Buick, so I took the side streets through town until we hit the north highway. Sheldon seemed lost in thought and neither of us said anything until we saw those floodlights in front of the box factory.

Then he said, "Keep in the shadows as much as possible and drive around to the back, where we can't be seen from the highway."

"Do you think I'm crazy enough to park under those floodlights?"

He looked at me coldly. I was just about ready to turn onto the factory road when a car topped the hill ahead of us, headed toward Creston. I had to drive on to the next section line, turn around, and try again. This time there were no cars. I tried not to look at those floodlights as I shoved the Buick into second and skidded onto the graveled factory road.

"Take it easy, you fool!" Sheldon snapped. "There's enough nitro in this satchel to blow us both to hell!"

I didn't look at him. I kept out of the light as much as possible, but I couldn't get off the road and leave tire tracks everywhere. When we neared the factory office building I cut sharply to the right and pulled around to the back. The car lights had been snapped off.

"Who's out there?" a voice called as I cut the motor.

"I thought this old man was deaf," Sheldon said.

"He's not so deaf that he can't hear eight cylinders charging down on him."

"What's his name?"

"Otto," I said. "Otto Finney."

And about that time the voice called again, "Who's that out there?"

"All right," Sheldon said, "you just sit here and watch the satchel. I'll be back in a minute."

I sat there feeling sweat popping out on my forehead. Sheldon seemed very cool as he got out of the car. He walked forward and called, "It's me, Otto."

"Who?"

"It's me," Sheldon called again.

I could see Otto now. When he opened the garage door a thin slice of light fell across the parking area in back of the building. The old man was standing in the light, holding a big hog-leg revolver in front of him. Sheldon kept walking toward him. "Can't you see a damn thing, Otto?" he said jokingly. "Don't you know who I am?"

"Oh," the old watchman said uncertainly. "Well..." Then he let his revolver sag at his side. He still couldn't see a thing, standing in the light the way he was. Sheldon walked right up to him, and hit him.

That's all there was to it. I heard Sheldon's fist crack against the watchman's jaw, and then the old man's revolver clattered to the cement driveway, and he fell as though he had been shot. It was all very neat and clean and I felt weak with relief.

Sheldon dragged the old man inside the garage. I drove the Buick up against the building, in the shadows, then I got the satchel and Sheldon stuck his head through the doorway. "All right, Hooper. We can't take all night."

The garage was a big affair, almost as big as the warehouse itself, and the air was heavy with the smell of gasoline and oil. Four big trucks were parked in there and they seemed almost lost in the vastness of the place. A whisper could ricochet from one wall to another, building itself up until it sounded like a scream. "Over here, Hooper!" Sheldon called, and the loudness of his voice startled me.

The old watchman was as limp as a rag and pale as death, but there was only a trace of blood where Sheldon had hit him.

"Is he all right?" I asked.

"Sure he's all right. Now where is that master switch to the office building?"

I couldn't take my eyes off the old man. Sheldon already had him bound and gagged, but it looked like an unnecessary precaution to me. Otto Finney was dead! I would swear it! He lay there as still as any corpse I had ever seen, and his face had that yellowish cast that the dead or dying always have. As I stared at him I could feel the cold feet of panic walking right up my spine.

"He's dead!" I heard the words, but I didn't recognize the voice as mine.

"I told you he's all right," Sheldon said impatiently. "Now where is that switch?"

I wheeled on Sheldon with a kind of rage that I had never felt before. "You sonofabitch! He's dead! Do you think I don't know a dead man when I see one?" I went down on my knees and put my hand over the old man's heart.

I felt like a fool. The beat was there, as strong and steady as the tides.

"Are you satisfied?" Sheldon said dryly.

"All right, I'm sorry. The switch boxes are over on the west wall, over there by the workbenches. You want me to take care of it?"

Sheldon was all business. "You go back to the garage door and keep your eyes open. I probably know more about electrical wiring than you do. Besides, you don't want the old man waking up and recognizing you, do you?"

I hadn't even thought of that. I got out of there.

The minutes crawled by. Every minute seemed like an hour as I stood there in the darkness behind the garage with a thousand insane fears tearing through my brain. What if Sheldon fouled it up? What if he pulled the wrong switch, cut the wrong wire? What if the sky fell? What difference did it make? I was in it to my neck and there was no pulling out.

Then the lights went out. The garage was black. The whole building was black. But the lights were still on in the factory building across the way, and the floodlights were still on. I heard my breath whistling through my teeth in relief.

Sheldon had done the job right. Sheldon was a good man. At that moment I almost loved him. I heard him walking carefully across the cement floor of the garage, and then he was at the door.

"All right," he said, "I got the keys off the watchman. Let's go."

We went around to the far corner of the building, then under the catwalk, and walking into those floodlights was like walking into machine-gun fire. We cast shadows twenty feet long. We stood out like tarantulas in the snow.

"Jesus!" Sheldon said. We stood there blinking, our backs against the office building. I felt that if we walked under those lights they would be able to see us all the way to Tulsa. But there was absolutely no other way to do it. We had to go right up to that front door and open it.

"Well," Sheldon said finally, "at least we can be thankful that traffic is light on the highway."

"Give me the keys," I said.

Sheldon was still staring at that highway. "I'll take care of the door," he said at last. "You move back in the shadows and let me know the instant you spot a car. The first damn instant, understand?"

I was getting tired of being treated like an irresponsible idiot, but I kept telling myself that it wouldn't last much longer. I moved back against the wall, then went back to the catwalk and crossed over to the factory building, where I could stand in the shadows and still see the highway. Sheldon glanced at me and I nodded. He slipped around the corner and headed for the door.

He cast a shadow as big as an elephant against that brick wall. He went up the two cement steps to the door and I could hear the keys jingle as he went to work. I was so busy watching Sheldon that I didn't see the headlights on the highway until it was almost too late. Maybe it wouldn't have made any difference, maybe the people in the car wouldn't have noticed. But at that moment it seemed absolutely impossible that they could fail to notice Sheldon's enormous black shadow under the glare of those lights, and if they ever noticed, it was sure going to look fishy. People just don't fool around factories at that time of morning.

"Sheldon!" I called hoarsely.

He didn't hear me. He was so busy with that lock, concentrating so hard on which key to try, that he didn't hear a thing.

"Sheldon!" I practically yelled it this time, and this time he heard and reacted instantly. He hit the ground as though a bomb had gone off. He dropped off those steps, maybe three feet down, and hit face down in a flower bed. The car roared past the factory and hummed off into the night.

After a minute I gave him the go-ahead and he picked himself up and went back to work. It didn't take long. Not more than a lifetime. But he got the door open and motioned me to come on.

I crossed back over to the office building and sidled along the edge of that brick wall as though I were walking a tightrope. By the time I got inside, Sheldon was ready to go to work. It wasn't dark in there, with those floodlights pouring through the front windows, and Sheldon had already spotted the safe.

"Well," he said, sounding pleased, "this shouldn't be difficult."

It still looked like a hell of a safe to me, but Sheldon was supposed to know. He was the expert.

"How long will it take?" I asked.

He shrugged, walking back and forth in front of the safe, looking it over from all angles. "That all depends. I'd say about fifteen minutes if I could use an electric drill, but I can't. As it is, it shouldn't take longer than thirty minutes."

That was going to be long enough for me. Already the echoing silence in the place was making me edgy. Sheldon was down on one knee, his black satchel open. He pulled on a pair of tight black suede gloves and tossed a pair of white cotton work gloves to me. "Put these on and wipe both doorknobs. Wipe the doorframe, too, while you're at it, and any other place that you think you might have touched."

By the time I had done that, Sheldon had his tools laid out—a hand-operated brace, diamond-tipped drilling bits, a teaspoon, a small bottle of yellowish liquid resting on a cushion of foam rubber.

"All right," I said, "what do I do now?"

"When I blow the door," he said, "we need to have something over the safe. Something like a very heavy quilt or blanket would do, but we'll have to make out with what we can find."

"How about a canvas tarp?" I said. "They usually keep them in the warehouse."

"Fine!" He locked in a drilling bit. "I couldn't have ordered anything better."

The warehouse was dark and ringing with silence. I could hear my own breathing, I could hear the wind sliding softly over the high tin roof. The echoes of my footsteps sounded like an army of marching men in the darkness.

I had no light, but I knew my way around back there, and I finally found the pile of heavy tarps that I was looking for. They were big pieces of canvas, maybe twenty feet square and very heavy. They used the tarps to protect new shipments of material from the weather when there wasn't enough storage room in the warehouse. The thing was too cumbersome to carry, so I dragged it across the cement floor and through the partition to Sheldon.

"How's it coming?" I said.

He just grunted. He had shed his coat and loosened his tie, and in the floodlight glow I could see the drops of sweat beaded on his forehead as he struggled with the brace and bit.

"Anything else you want me to do?" I asked.

"Just keep out of my way," he said shortly. "Go over to one of those windows and keep an eye on the highway. Don't bother me until I'm finished."

It looked like Sheldon's show from here on in. I went over to one of the far windows and stood staring out at the night. This was the part I didn't like. As long as I was too busy to think, it wasn't bad, but just standing and waiting began to get on my nerves. I began thinking about that Buick sitting outside. It was in the shadows, of course, hard against the building, but it would be a lot better if we could just open that big back door and drive it into the warehouse.

Then I began worrying about Otto Finney. What if the old man was really hurt? Hurt bad? What a hell of a mess that would be!

I looked at my watch and it was almost one-thirty. We had been there in the office almost forty minutes. What was taking Sheldon so long? Then I heard him throwing the tarp over the safe.

"You going to blow it?" I asked.

"That's what we came here for, isn't it?"

"You need any help?"

"All I need is for you to keep out of my way. Get over there by the partition and stay on your belly until this door's off."

I thought: One of these days I'm going to shove that nasty voice down your throat, Sheldon. But not now. I was going to be a good boy and do exactly as he said, because this was Sheldon's party.

"You ready?" he called.

"Yes."

"All right." He set the fuse, then took about five quick steps and lay down behind the safe. The building seemed to bulge with the explosion.

It wasn't such a loud noise—most of it was muffled by the tarp—but it was loud enough for me. It was enough to make the windows rattle. It was enough to make my teeth rattle, too.

But it did the job. The safe door flew open as though a bomb had gone off inside, and a little whitish smoke drifted up in the darkness. Sheldon and I began picking ourselves up.

I couldn't be as casual about it as Sheldon was. I rushed to one window and then another, not knowing exactly what I expected to see, but something. It seemed impossible that nobody had heard that explosion. But evidently nobody had. Everything outside was nice and quiet, the highway empty. I began to breathe again.

When I got to the safe, Sheldon was grinning. "Well, here it is."

"It sure as hell is!" I had never seen so much money. The explosion must have broken the inside compartment, because money was scattered all over everywhere, nice new, clean, crisp, green bills, tens and twenties and fives and ones. It was beautiful.

I said, "What are we going to carry it in?"

"Carry it in the box it was in," Sheldon said. So we began crawling around on the floor, grabbing bills and stuffing them in the tin box. All that money! More money than I had ever dreamed of—and half of it was mine!

"Well," Sheldon said when we'd got it all together, "how does it feel to be rich?"

"It feels fine! But it will feel even better when we get away from this factory."

That was one time Sheldon gave me no argument. He got his satchel and I picked up the box of money, all that beautiful money, and we headed for the door.

We waited until the highway was clear and then made a run for it. Going under those floodlights was nothing now. I had thirty thousand dollars under one arm and was on top of the world. By the time we reached the garage I was four stories tall and growing by the minute.

"By God," Sheldon said, "I'll have to hand it to Manley. He said this would be a pushover, and it was. I'd never have believed there could be such a pushover if I hadn't seen it with my own eyes."

"Good old Manley!" I felt like laughing. "He's going to have a fit when he reads the morning paper."

"The hell with Manley," Sheldon said. "The sooner we get out of here, the better."

We had already started for the car when I heard it. I didn't know what it was, but it hit me like a hammer. Sheldon looked around at me.

"What's the matter?"

"I don't know. I thought I heard something."

"Heard something? Where?"

"I don't know. I think it was in the garage."

Both of us stood there as rigid as a pair of department-store dummies. I listened until my ears ached, every nerve drawn to the snapping point. Then it came again, a scuffing, shoving sound that started an unscratchable itch on my scalp.

I glanced at Sheldon. "Did you hear it then?"

He shook his head.

Maybe it was nothing. Maybe it was just an overactive imagination, or maybe it was just the strain. After all, a man doesn't commit a thirty-thousand-dollar robbery every day. But I had to be sure. It was much too late to begin taking chances.

I said, "Wait a minute. I want to have a look in there." I opened the door and stepped into the pitch-darkness of the garage. There was no sound, absolutely no sound at all. Hooper, I thought, you'd better get hold of yourself before you go off the deep end. Then, just as I turned to go, the light hit me right in the face.

It was brighter than any light I had ever looked into. Brighter than those floodlights. Brighter than the sun. It hit me right in the eyes, that ball of brightness, and I couldn't see a thing. I lunged to one side just as the revolver crashed and resounded with unbelievable violence around the walls of that high garage. I felt the hot breath of the bullet. I heard the instantaneous *spat!*

as the slug smashed itself against the brick wall.

I turned to run. I fell over something—God knows what—there in the darkness and went sprawling just as that revolver exploded again. Then I knew, somehow, instinctively, that running was not the answer.

That light had been on my face. The owner of that pistol was not only trying to shoot me, *he knew who I was!*

There was no time for rationalization. That deadly .38 of Sheldon's was in my hand. I fired once, twice, three times at the sweeping ball of light that was trying to pick me out of the darkness. I heard the incredible reverberations shatter the silence of the night, and I knew, somehow, that there was no use shooting any more.

It had happened with unbelievable speed. One second? Two seconds? No more than that. By the time Sheldon came crashing into the garage, it was all over. Realization of what had happened was just beginning to hit me, and it left me cold and weak.

"Hooper!"

"It's all right," I heard myself saying. "It's all over." That flashlight still stabbed the darkness. I could hear it rocking back and forth on the cement floor. Its beam swept shorter and shorter arcs across the floor, and finally it stopped, pointing directly at me.

Sheldon said, "For God's sake, Hooper, what happened?"

"I just killed the watchman," I said.

Chapter Seven

Sheldon took about four quick steps in front of me and picked up the flashlight. He turned the beam on the watchman's face.

He was dead, all right. There was no use feeling for a pulse this time. Those pale old eyes stared directly into the beam of light, unblinking. A broken little man, completely dead. He had fallen on a small heap of waste rags, the kind you find in every garage, and for a moment he looked as though he were another pile of rags and not a man at all. Sheldon moved the flashlight beam up and down, slowly and carefully, and it was easy enough to see what had happened. The watchman's feet were still tied, but he had somehow managed to loosen his hands. He had pushed himself over to the garage wall, to a workbench where the pistol must have been, and the flashlight. Probably he was just beginning to untie his feet when I heard him.

Sheldon suddenly shot that beam of light at me. "Well, Hooper," he said tightly, "you've fixed things this time. You've fixed them good."

"I fixed them!" I stepped forward and knocked that beam out of my face. "You were supposed to have him tied and gagged! A fine fix we'd have been in if I hadn't stopped him before he threw that switch."

"Did you have to kill him?"

"What was I supposed to do? He had that flashlight right in my face!"

"But you didn't have to kill him. It could have been some other way."

Sheldon's voice was almost a whine now. I could look right through that tough front of his and see his guts deserting him. This was something I hadn't figured on. If anybody went to pieces in this operation I had expected it to be me. But I should have known. I'd seen the signs—I'd seen how Paula could shut him up. From personal experience I knew that he would not touch a job unless he figured it to be an absolute pushover. The signs were there, all right, but I hadn't seen them until it was too late.

Now Sheldon wiped his face on his coat sleeve. "This isn't just robbery now, it's murder! I didn't agree to anything like this."

"You didn't agree! Listen!" I grabbed the front of his shirt and twisted hard. "Listen to me! Do you think I wanted it? I liked this old man. I liked him a lot, and about the last thing in the world I'd want to do is kill him. But I had to do it. Do you hear me? He had the flashlight in my face!"

"Christ!" I could feel him shaking. "I didn't plan on anything like this!"

"You didn't plan! You gave me the gun, didn't you?"

It was amazing, really. I had never killed in my life and I had never imagined that it could be so easy. I was sorry that it had been Otto; it would worry me for a long time, but still it wasn't as bad as I had heard. It had been Otto or me. Otto had shot at me and I had shot back, and there was no way in the world to change it now. I had to accept it. Besides, there were other things to think about. It was staggering how many things there were.

"Hooper, we've got to get out of here!"

"Wait a minute. I think I've got something."

The one word that kept hitting me was "murder." To me it didn't have the usual meaning. It was like thinking of cancer or TB. You get yourself branded with it and it kills you, only with murder you die in the electric chair instead of in a bed.

I said, "Sheldon, you wait right here." Then I went down on one knee and lifted the dead watchman to my shoulder. Sheldon looked as though he had been clubbed. He stared dazedly as I hurried out of the garage with the dead man across my back. What I had in mind wasn't going to fool anybody for long, but it would cross the sheriff up for a while, at least, and maybe that would be long enough.

It seemed, by now, that I had run that gantlet of floodlights a hundred times, but that didn't make it any easier this time. It was pure gambling; I just had to hope that no one saw me. Old Otto Finney had been a frail little man, and I was glad of that as I raced along the front of the building with him across my shoulders. I didn't even look at the highway. I went right up to the door, pressed Otto's palm to the latch and in two or three places along the door frame. Then I dragged him inside and did the same thing there. Finally I went over to the blown safe and made sure that Otto's fingerprints would be found on the door as well as other places.

That was that. I was breathing as though I had been swimming underwater, but I hoisted the dead man to my shoulders again and headed for the door. Just as I stepped outside I heard the sound of a motor, and then the headlights of a car cut a thin gash in the darkness of the highway. I hit the ground. The dead watchman hit and rolled a few feet ahead of me. As the car hummed past and out of sight, I lay there for several seconds, breathing hard. And Otto was looking at me. Those pale, sightless eyes were wide open and staring right at me.

I said, "I'm sorry, Otto!" And I knew I had to get hold of myself or I was cooked. What was done was done. I wasn't going to crack up about it. That was the one thing in the world I couldn't afford to do. I shouldered the corpse and made another run for darkness.

Sheldon was right where I had left him, there by the garage door. I hadn't been afraid of his running out on me because I still had the key to the Buick. "Get the car door open," I panted. "The back seat."

By this time Sheldon had guessed what I was up to. "It won't work, Hooper," he said tightly.

"I know it won't work for long. But maybe it will buy us time, let the trail cool a little. Now get the door open."

He did it, and I dumped the dead watchman on the floor. Then the two of us went back to the garage and cleaned the place up. We picked up all the bloodstained rags, the gun, the flashlight. "Now," I said, "let's go!" I brought Otto with us.

It was a long, long ride back to the tourist court; I hope I never take another ride as long as that one. Every car we met I expected to be the sheriff's car. I expected something violent to happen every second but nothing did. Nothing happened at all. What we were going to do with the dead watchman, I didn't know. I was beyond thinking. It took all my concentration just to keep the car in a straight line.

Then at last we reached the cabins, and I pulled the Buick behind the station and into the carport next to Number 2. There were no lights in the cabin, but Paula had the door open the minute we pulled off the highway, and she was right there the second we hit the carport. She jerked the door open on my side.

"What took you so long? Did anything go wrong?"

I could smell the perfume she wore. Or maybe it wasn't perfume, maybe it was just her.

"Something happened, didn't it?" she said. "Tell me!"

Sheldon hadn't said a thing. But now he turned toward his wife, and his face looked a hundred years old. "The trouble," he said, "is back there."

Paula opened the back door and made one small sound when she saw the dead man. Then she looked at me. "Who did it?"

"I did."

She frowned. "I might have known it couldn't have been Karl."

"I guess we need to talk this thing over," I said, and got out of the car.

Sheldon sat where he was. "Paula," he said, "we've got to get out of here. Get your things together right now."

"The three of us?" she asked coldly, glancing at the back seat.

"Oh." He looked pretty foolish and he knew it, and that did more than anything else to snap him out of it. "Well, maybe Hooper's right, maybe we should talk it over, coolly, calmly."

There was a moon out that night. I didn't notice it until I got inside the darkened cabin and saw the whitish moonlight pouring through the open door. "Turn the light on," Paula said.

"It will be safer if we don't," I said.

"We can't count the money in the dark."

First things first. I felt a crazy impulse to laugh. The hell with the dead man outside, we had money to count. She turned the light on.

It really didn't make much difference. The cabins, as usual, were empty, and I was too tired to care, anyway. I was having trouble keeping my thoughts organized.

Then I thought: Christ, I've forgotten all about the money! I kicked the door open, went out to the car, and got it. I didn't look behind the front seat; I didn't want to see those pale, wide eyes again. Just don't think about it, I thought. He asked for it, didn't he?

Paula's eyes were alive with excitement as she dug her hands into the green bills. "Thirty thousand dollars!"

Sheldon said, "We don't know how much there is. We haven't counted it."

"I can tell! Just by feeling of it!"

"For God's sake," I said, "stop playing with the stuff and let's count it!"

Then Paula turned on me with a tight little smile. "First," she said, "tell me about the watchman."

The look in her eyes shook me. "Forget it," I said.

All this talk was rubbing right through to my nerves. "The old man shot at me and I had to kill him. That's all there was to it."

"I knew it!" She almost sneered, looking now at Sheldon. "I knew it couldn't have been you, Karl!"

I didn't know what she was talking about, but Sheldon must have. He stood rigid for just a moment, his eyes stormy, and then, without a sound of warning, he back-handed her. The back of his fist slammed into her mouth, knocking her across the room and onto the bed. "Now keep quiet, goddamn you!" he said hoarsely.

I felt the muscles become tense in my shoulders. Stay out of it, I warned myself. This is between just the two of them. You can't afford to butt in now—not until we make the split, anyway.

His knuckles had broken Paula's lower lip and a thin little stream of blood dripped down her chin. She didn't come fighting back, as I had thought she would. She felt of her lip. Then she opened a suitcase, took out some paper tissue, and held it to her mouth. She didn't say a word, but there was plenty in her eyes. Sheldon dumped the money on the table and began counting it out. I helped him.

It came to $31,042. We cut it right down the middle without a word: $15,521 each.

"Not bad," Sheldon said.

"If we live long enough to spend it!"

"Oh, yes," Sheldon said softly, as though he had been trying to forget it too. "The body."

I glanced at Paula and she was still sitting exactly the way she had been for fifteen minutes, there on the edge of the bed, holding the bloody tissue to her mouth. Now she stood up and I could see that all the fight hadn't been knocked out of her.

"Why did you bring the body with you, anyway?"

"Because," I said, "I went to a good deal of trouble putting the watchman's fingerprints all over the safe before we left the factory."

"Oh." She was getting it now, but I stopped her before she had a chance to carry it too far.

"Don't get the idea," I said, "that the sheriff's going to be fooled. He's not going to think for one damn minute that Otto Finney robbed that factory. Still, the evidence is going to be there and he's going to have to look into it. And if we can get rid of the body, the sheriff is going to have to look for it, and that's going to take time."

"Time for us to get far away from Oklahoma," Sheldon said softly. "Well, the rest is up to you, Hooper. What do we do with the body?"

That question had been drumming at me ever since I pulled the trigger. So far, I had been pretty successful in keeping it impersonal. I tried to think of it as a problem to be solved, and nothing else. "The lake," I said. "It's the only thing I can think of. Drop the body in the lake."

Sheldon frowned. "Tell me about this lake."

"Creston's water supply, a man-made affair about four miles out of town. There's a deep hole at the north end that would give them plenty of trouble if they tried to drag. Anyway, there are a lot of garfish in that water, and I doubt if a body would be recognized after a day or two, even if they got it up."

Keep it impersonal, I reminded myself. But the thought of those scavenger fish wasn't pleasant.

Sheldon turned it over in his mind. "All right, that's the way it will have to be. We haven't got time to think of something better."

I shook my head. "There's something else about this lake that you'd better know about. It's kind of like a local lovers' lane. When couples don't have anywhere else to go, they head for the lake."

"At this time of night?"

"At any time of night. That's what I'm trying to tell you. There's just a chance we might be seen."

"Then the lake's out," Sheldon said shortly.

"The lake's all we have," I reminded him. "Paula could go with me; the two of us could handle it. If we happen to be seen, nobody's likely to give it a second thought." Time was running out and I had to talk to Paula. This was the only way I could think of doing it.

Sheldon didn't like it, but this was no time to smooth out the rough places. What Paula thought about it she didn't say. The three of us stood there, looking at each other, and then I said, "I'll be back in a minute." I gathered up my half of the money and went out.

I put the money under the mattress in my cabin, and then I went to the station and rummaged around in the darkness until I found what I wanted—a cast-off flywheel and a set of rusty mud chains. I was working smoothly now. Just keep cool, I thought, and everything is going to work out all right. Then I went back to the Buick to put the flywheel and chains in the back seat.

About a minute later Sheldon came out. "What's the matter?"

"Nothing. We've got to move the body to my car, though. I can't afford to be seen in this Buick."

"Hooper, are you sure this lake business is all right?"

"Can you think of anything better?"

He wasn't worried about the lake, he was worried about Paula. But he merely shrugged. Between the two of us we got the old watchman's body into the back seat of my Chevy and covered it with a piece of canvas from the station. Then we loaded the flywheel and chains and everything was set—as set as it would ever be. I looked at my watch and it was almost three o'clock.

The thing went like clockwork. There was just enough moon to make driving without lights possible on that twisting lake road. The place was deserted, not a car, not a soul anywhere, and the lake itself was motionless. Not a ripple was on the water. When I reached the spot I was looking for, I drove on for maybe a mile to make sure that the way was completely clear, and then I turned around and came back.

It was just as I had remembered it, shelves of brownish rock jutting out of a red clay bank, and below it the lake. I knew how deep it was there, for as a kid I had seen the bulldozers gouging it out. There was no need of a boat, no need of taking the body out to the middle of the lake before dumping it. Just drop it over that shelf of rock and let the lake settle over it and keep it forever and ever, amen. He was an old man, I thought. He wouldn't have lived much longer anyway.

"Is this the place?" Paula said.

"Yes."

I got out of the car and lugged the chains and flywheel over to the edge of the rock. Then I went to the car and carried the body—the amazingly light, frail old body—over to the rock and put it down. I then slipped the chains through the flywheel and fastened the other end of chain to the body with several pieces of strong wire.

"Can I help?" Paula said.

"No." I eased the dead watchman over the ledge, then gave the flywheel a shove, and there was a silvery splash as the body and weight plunged down and down, and I stood there watching as they sank out of sight.

"Good!" Paula said huskily. She looked as soft and pale as the moonlight.

I knew we should get away from there as fast as possible, but there were still some things to get settled. I wasn't fool enough to think the killing hadn't changed things. I couldn't possibly just pack up and leave with Paula; that would look too fishy now, right after the robbery. But she was in my blood and something had to be worked out.

I walked over to her and she stood there looking at me with that tight little smile at the corners of her swollen mouth. Then she reached out and touched my shoulder, and she said, "You've got guts, Joe Hooper."

Staying there was idiocy, but I couldn't seem to move. "I like a man with guts," she said huskily. "I like a man to be strong."

"What about your husband?"

She made a small sound. "Karl spent a long stretch in Leavenworth, and do you know why? Because he was afraid to pull the trigger. He let the cops take him because he was afraid to shoot."

"That isn't what I meant. What do we do now, you and me?"

Like a lusty young animal, she wrapped those white arms around me. She was fire in my arms. The taste of blood was in my mouth when I kissed her.

"What do you want to do, Joe? About us."

"I want to hold you just like this and never let you go. But that's impossible now. Within a few hours cops are going to be swarming all over this part of the country, and they're going to be asking a hell of a lot of questions."

"Then you want me to go tonight with Karl?"

"It looks like the only thing for the present. How can I get in touch with you as soon as things cool off here?"

She thought for a moment. "I have a sister in Missouri. Mrs. Stella Bundy, Box Three-forty, Route Three, St. John, Missouri. She'll know how to find me. Can you remember the address?"

Chapter Eight

It was almost five o'clock when we got back to the cabins and Sheldon was fit to be tied. He grabbed his wife and jerked her out of the car as though she were a bag of groceries. "Goddamn you!" he snarled. "Where have you been?"

He looked as though he were going to tear her head off and she just smiled. "Don't get excited, Karl. You know where we've been."

He knew where she had been, all right. Or he was guessing pretty close to it. A family ruckus was the last thing in the world I wanted right now, and I didn't like the ugliness in his voice. I stepped out of the car and said, "Did you ever try to get rid of a body, Sheldon? You don't just dump it in a gully. You have to do it exactly right or it's too damn bad. I didn't know it was going to take this long, but it did, and there's nothing we can do about it."

Glaring at me, he took one deep breath, then he flung his wife against the side of the car and went into the cabin. "Well!" Paula said softly. "You'd almost think he was a man, wouldn't you, when he's mad?"

I said nothing. The sky along the eastern edge of the prairie was beginning to pale, and I could feel all the strength going out of me. I felt a hundred years old. I didn't let myself think about the things that would start happening within the next few hours. That robbery was going to turn Creston upside down and shake it, and I just hoped that I would be able to ride it out.

Then Sheldon came out with the luggage. He threw it into the car without a word and Paula glanced at me and shrugged. "Maybe we'll meet again, Mr. Hooper," she said dryly.

She smiled again and slipped onto the front seat beside her husband. Karl Sheldon looked at me once. He didn't say a word, he just sat there and looked at me with all the hate that was in him. Then, with one savage movement, he jammed the Buick into gear and they were on their way.

I stood there for maybe five minutes. I watched as the Buick slammed violently onto the highway, spewing gravel and dust into the still morning air, and I listened with relief as the car dropped behind a small rise and the roar became a drone, and the drone became a hum, and the hum became nothing. Silence.

Strangely, I felt nothing. I stood there and the pale sky became suddenly bloody as the violent sun lifted into a widening sky. Finally I turned and walked to my own cabin.

There was no use going to sleep. I had to open the station within an hour, because I always opened the station at six-thirty in the morning, and this morning had to be exactly like all the others. I made a pot of coffee, black as evil, strong as temptation, and I sat at the tiny kitchen table and watched that savage sun begin its violent work. Even my bones ached with weariness. I looked at my watch and it was nearly six, so I turned on the light and went to the bathroom to shave.

My face looked back at me from the bathroom mirror, and nothing could have shocked me more. It seemed incredible that I could have survived such a night without changing, but there was no change at all. The face was mine. The eyes seemed faintly tired, but no more so than they often did in the morning. I don't know just what I expected to see in that mirror, but the sight of my own unchanged face almost made me sick.

This is fine! I thought bitterly as I lathered to shave. Just a little more of this and you're cooked, Hooper. Get a hold on yourself, and you'd better be damn sure you keep it.

I felt a little better after the shave. Then I stripped and showered and got into my work clothes—and only then did I remember the money. I grabbed the mattress and threw it to the floor.

The money was still there.

I took it in my hands. The bills were crisp to my touch. The smell of ink and silk-fibered paper was like the smell of roast beef to a starving man.

For a while I had trouble thinking of a place to put the money. The woman who cleaned the cabins might run across it if I left it here, so I took it to the station with me when I opened up. The first thing I did was wrap the money in clean waste; then I moved several cases of oil and loosened a plank in the flooring. That's where the money went, under the floor, and the cases of oil went back on top of it. That would have to do until I thought of something better.

I felt all right now. It was almost seven o'clock by the time I'd finished unlocking the gas pumps and connected the hose for water and air. The tourists were already beginning to hit the highway, getting an early start on the heat. I went back into the station and turned on the radio.

"...between midnight and four in the morning, according to the authorities," the announcer was saying. "No details are available as yet, but it is believed that the entire Provo Box Company payroll was taken in the robbery. Otis Miller, Creston County sheriff, has issued no statement concerning the disappearance of Otto Finney, the factory's watchman. The robbery was discovered less than an hour ago, when Paul Millman, shop foreman, delivered a company truck to the garage..."

They knew nothing. They weren't even sure how much money had been taken.

By noon they knew a little more, but not much.

"It is not known whether more than one person took part in the robbery, but it has been determined that entry to the company's office was made possible by use of a key—probably the key that watchman Otto Finney kept on his person. Also, it was learned that the factory's burglar-alarm system was rendered ineffectual by a circuit break at the master switch box in the garage. This has led to speculation that the burglar or burglars must have been familiar with the factory layout, and it has been suggested, off the record, that an employee of the Provo Box Company may soon be named as a suspect. However, Sheriff Otis Miller claims he suspects no one at the present time, although the watchman was still missing as we went on the air. Ray King, Miller's deputy, said this morning that several fingerprints were found on and near the blown safe and that these will be checked...."

I could smile. The sheriff knew as well as I did that Otto Finney had nothing to do with the robbery, but pressure for investigation was being brought down on him and he would have to look into it. While the real trail grew colder. And colder. By the time they permitted Otis to stop chasing his tail, there would be no trail at all.

It was exactly the way I had figured it. But there was small satisfaction in it for me. I was too sick with fatigue to feel satisfaction or anything else. All I wanted right now was for Ike Abrams to relieve me and give me a chance to get some sleep. And that was the day Ike had to be late. It was almost one o'clock when that Ford of his rattled off the highway.

"Where the hell have you been?" I said. "It's almost one and I haven't even had lunch yet."

He was a lanky, easygoing guy, but that day there was excitement in his sleepy eyes. "By God, hell's bustin' loose in town, Joe! I guess I forgot what time it was. You heard about the robbery, didn't you?"

"The box factory? It was on the radio."

"Well, it's the damnedest thing you ever saw, the way it's got the town boilin'."

I was too tired to care, but I couldn't walk off without showing a normal amount of interest. "I figured most people hated Max Provo's guts," I said. "Why should they get worked up because he lost some money?"

"It ain't Provo that bothers them, it's old Otto Finney. Half of them say he ought to be caught and lynched. They claim old Otto's the only one could have done it, him having the keys and knowing about the burglar alarm and all. And the other half claim the old man's probably dead somewhere, wherever the burglars buried him after they killed him."

"And what do you think, Ike?"

Ike shrugged. "Old Otto never cared about money. He never showed it, anyway. But it's goin' to look bad if those fingerprints on the safe turn out to be his."

"Has the sheriff got any clues besides the fingerprints?"

Ike grinned faintly. "Otis ain't talking. Half the City Council is pullin' him one way, half the other."

Just the way I had planned it. I was pleased. "I wouldn't want to be in the sheriff's shoes," I said.

And Ike said, "I wouldn't want to be in the *burglar's* shoes. The harder they make it on Otis, the more determined he'll be to catch them. And he'll do it, too. In spite of the City Council or anybody else."

I rubbed my face, only half hearing what Ike said. "Well," I said, "it's the sheriff's baby, not mine."

I went to my cabin, too tired even to wash my face and hands. I dropped on the bed and began to sweat in that blistering heat. Almost immediately unconsciousness began closing in like a steaming blanket.

And it was night again.

And there we were, Sheldon and I, racing under the blinding brilliance of floodlights. It was an endless, vacant avenue lighted by a thousand suns, and we were racing up that dazzling stretch where there was no sound, no shadow. That was the thing I noticed, there was no shadow. Just Sheldon and I racing through that shocking brilliance. There was a heavy load on my shoulders. I felt myself falling and I called out to Sheldon but he did not hear. He continued to run, and the load on my shoulders bore me down.

Now it seemed that all the lights, every dazzling little sun turned upon me as I fell. The load was suddenly lifted from my shoulders as I struck the ground, and I lay there for a long while, breathless, as the gathering suns watched and waited. And that was when I saw the eyes, two old eyes, very old and very dead, and they were staring right at me.

I awoke staring into the brilliance of the sun, the real sun. Its furnace-like heat reached through the cabin window and struck my face.

I rolled over and lay drunkenly on the soggy bed. The dream was still with me and the terror of it was in the room. Automatically, I shoved myself up from the bed. I stumbled to the bathroom and washed my face. I sloshed cold water on the back of my neck until I was fully awake. I stood there for a long while, rigidly, waiting for the lingering terror of the dream to slip away. I soaked a towel and wrapped it around my neck, and then I went to the bedroom and then into the kitchen, touching things as I passed in an effort to prove to myself that I was awake and that the dream was gone.

I opened a can of beer and went to the bedroom. A strange thing happened then—or perhaps it wouldn't seem so strange to people who knew about such things. I began to hate Otto Finney.

It came slowly at first, and then with a rush, and within a matter of minutes I hated the old watchman more than I had ever hated a man in my life. I was *glad* he was dead. I was *glad* I had killed him. In my mind I had a completely new picture of what had happened, and now Otto was the villain, not I.

I don't know.... Maybe it's what a psychiatrist would call "defense mechanism." Maybe they would say that turning my hate on Otto was an attempt to "justify my crime." I don't know....

I only know that hate came when I needed it most. It saved my sanity.

Killing a man was not so difficult—I had learned that. But to go on liking him is not compatible with sanity—I had learned that, too. Killing and hatred are brothers. They go together, they are inseparable. If one is missing, it must be created from what is at hand.

And so it was.

But it came slowly at first. I thought: It should never have happened. If he hadn't shone that flashlight in my face, it never would have happened. If he hadn't shot at me, it never would have happened.

And the inevitable tangent to this circle of thought was: He had no right to shoot at me! I wasn't trying to take his money! But he had shot at me. He had tried to kill me. Goddamn him, the whole thing could have been so easy and simple. A pushover, Sheldon had called it. But that watchman had to be a hero, he had to try to ruin everything just at the last minute.

And so hate was created. At the time, of course, I did not look at it objectively and I did not question it. The terror of the dream was too close for objectivity. I welcomed my new hate and held it close. I thought, I'm *glad* I killed him!

If it is true that hate is a defense mechanism, it is an effective one. It stands head and shoulders above fear. And it has strength, that's the important thing. I could feel myself growing stronger, and it was good to know that I would be able to sleep again and not dream.

The hell with Otto Finney!

Chapter Nine

The sheriff's office was in the courthouse basement. I walked down the corridor of dirty marble and was almost sick at the steaming smell of unemptied spittoons and filthy toilets and stale cigar smoke, and I wondered why it was that the sheriff's office was always in the basement, and why it was that small-town courthouses were always so filthy. Near the end of the corridor there was a sign that said: 'Otis Miller, Sheriff."

Ray King was sitting at a desk just inside the front office. "Well, Joe, what brings you down to the courthouse?"

"Hello, Ray. I'd like to see Otis, if he's around."

"Sheriff's tied up right now, in the back office. He ought to be free in a minute. Take a chair."

I sat down in a straight-backed hard-oak chair, hoping that coming to the sheriff wasn't a mistake. Mistake or not, I felt that it would be a good idea if I could find out what Otis thought about the robbery. It had been three days now and the papers had printed the same thing over and over again, and the sheriff had said nothing, nothing at all, and there was no way of telling what he was thinking or doing. And I had to know. Before I could think of contacting Paula, I had to know.

Ray sat there grinning for a few seconds, then he pulled some papers in front of him and picked up a pen. 'Excuse me a minute, Joe. Otis will be on my back if I don't get this report finished."

"Sure. Sure."

There was nothing else to do, so I sat back and tried to ignore the heat and watched Ray working on the white form. He didn't look much like a deputy sheriff, but the business was in his blood and it was more or less taken for granted that he would get Otis Miller's job when Otis decided it was time to step down. Ray's dad had been a U.S. marshal when Creston was just a stage stop in Oklahoma Territory, and there was a stone monument out west of town marking the place where he had been killed in a gun fight with two Territory badmen.

So it was natural enough that Ray should take up the law-enforcing business, although he looked pretty light for that kind of work. He was a lanky, easygoing sort of guy, not much older than myself. He looked more like a lawyer or a businessman than a deputy sheriff. Most of the time, when it wasn't too hot, he wore a dark, double-breasted suit. No cowboy boots and white hat for Ray King, and he never wore his gun where it would show, but he knew the business of a sheriff as well as Otis Miller did.

Maybe ten minutes passed, and finally an inner door opened and out came Pat Sully, the guy I'd paid that five dollars to that day at the box factory. That jarred me for a moment. Surely Pat hadn't suspected me! The big red-faced bastard was too dumb to put two and two together.

Still, it was something to think about. It turned me cold for just a moment, until I heard Sully say, "I hope I've been some help, Sheriff."

Otis Miller followed him out. "Well, we can't tell about that, Pat, until we put all the pieces together. I've called in everybody on old Provo's office force on the long chance that they might know something." Then they shook hands and Pat turned to leave.

He saw me then. "Why, hello, Joe. What are you doing in this part of town?"

"Got a little business with the sheriff, nothing important. How are things out at the box factory?"

Sully shook his head. "It's a mess. You never saw such a mess in your life. Old Provo's fit to be tied about this robbery." He grinned faintly. "Well, I guess I'd better get back to it."

I breathed easier. Nothing to worry about, I told myself. The sheriff's talking to the entire office force. A matter of routine.

The sheriff looked at me and I could see the tight little lines around the corners of his mouth. They were putting the pressure on him, all right.

"You waitin' to see me, Joe?"

"If you're not too busy, Sheriff. It's about that bogus bill I took in."

"Oh." He rubbed his face and I could see that he was annoyed. "Well, all right," he said after a second. "Come on in the office."

The sheriff was a short, squat barrel of a man. He wore cowboy boots and the pants and vest of a blue serge suit. He had a big pearl-handled .45 that he wore cowboy style on his right hip, even in the office. Looking at Otis Miller for the first time, you'd think that here was just another small-town politician who had seen too many Buck Jones movies, full of wind and nothing else. You couldn't be more wrong. Otis Miller was as tough as steer hide, and his reputation as a lawman was spotless.

He planted himself behind his desk, as solid as an oak stump. "Well," he said, "let's see it."

I gave him the bill and he held it up to the light. "You've got stuck, all right."

"It looks like it," I said. "I guess there's not much to be done about it now," wondering how I was going to get around to the robbery.

Otis was still squinting at the bill. "When did you say you got this?"

"Four or five days ago. I found it in my cash drawer."

He grunted. Then he got up and went to a small office safe in the corner of the room. He took another bill from the safe and held them up to the window. "I'm no expert," he said finally, "but I'd swear these two bills came off the same press." He handed them to me. "Look at the scrollwork in the upper left-hand corners."

I held the two bills up to the light, and sure enough, they were exactly the same. The same engraving flaws were in both bills. "Where did this one come from?" I said, holding out the bill he had given me.

He shrugged. "Don't remember exactly. Several of them were passed here in Creston about a year ago. Directly after that the counterfeiters were caught in Tulsa."

Otis was looking at me. It was just a look, I told myself, and didn't mean a thing, but I felt that chill again.

"They were caught?" It was all I could think to say.

"A year ago. They're in Leavenworth now."

"How about the plates?"

"They were taken, too. They were so bad that the counterfeiters had stopped using them." The sheriff dropped the bill and let it flutter to his desk. "Very few of these bills were passed," he said thoughtfully, "according to the federal men who were on the case. Look at them. That kind of work wouldn't fool an idiot—no offense, Joe."

Goddamnit! I thought. Why did I ever think of this bogus bill, anyway? "Well...." I didn't like the way he was looking at me. "Where do you figure this bill came from?"

He shrugged.

"Somebody must have held onto it for a year and then passed it off on me."

"It's possible," Otis said.

But not probable. Bogus money as bad as this stuff just didn't stay in circulation. I couldn't tell what he was thinking, if he was thinking anything. He just looked at me and fingered that bogus bill.

"Then," I said, "I guess there's nothing much we can do about it, if the counterfeiters are already in prison."

He smiled faintly. "Maybe the experience will be worth five dollars to you, Joe. From now on you'll look at your bills before ringing them up."

I had an almost irresistible impulse to wipe the sweat from my forehead. It was nothing. I was just imagining things. The sheriff said, "Was there anything else on your mind, Joe?"

"No. No, that's all," and got up. "I guess this robbery thing has got you pretty busy," I added.

"Yes. In fact, there are some people I want to talk to right now. So if you don't mind...."

That was a dismissal. He stood up and hitched his holster. "Well, take it easy, Joe," and he walked out of the office.

I hadn't learned a thing. That didn't occur to me until I had reached the sidewalk in front of the courthouse. I had been on the defensive every minute; I hadn't had a chance to ask questions.

I was tempted to go back and talk to Ray King and see if I could get anything out of him, but that would be too risky. If Otis *did* get to wondering about that bogus bill, everything I did would begin to mean something to him. He was a bulldog when he got hold of a thing. Let well enough alone, I told myself. Give Otis no reason to believe that I tried to fool him with that piece of counterfeit and everything will be all right.

I looked at my watch and it was three o'clock. Three days, almost four, since the robbery, since I had seen Paula. It seemed like a lifetime.

Across the street from the courthouse there was a bar, and that's where I headed. I stood there with my foot on the rail for maybe fifteen minutes, nursing a schooner of beer and wondering what I was going to do next. I was free; Ike was taking care of the station for the afternoon. Free to visit with my dad, free to do anything I wanted, and I wanted to do nothing. I didn't even want the beer. Then a paper boy came in with the afternoon paper, the only paper Creston had, and I took one. It was in the headlines.

FINGERPRINTS ON PROVO SAFE
IDENTIFIED AS MISSING WATCHMAN'S

> Otis Miller, Creston County sheriff, said this morning that the fingerprints found on the blown door of the Provo Box Company safe had definitely been identified as those of Otto Finney, missing company watchman. Finney has been missing since the night of the robbery....

I read it and felt myself smile. The paper, without coming right out and saying it, made it sound like an open-and-shut case against Otto. Now I knew why the sheriff had been annoyed at my bothering him with that bogus bill. He knew perfectly well that the old watchman was innocent, but that wouldn't keep the political wolves off his back. There was only one thing for him to do, and that was to find Otto. By the time he did that, if he ever did, the details of the case would be so fogged that the trail would never be picked up again.

Suddenly I felt good. I felt fine. I had another schooner of beer and this time I enjoyed it. It was strange, the way that story in the paper affected me. It was difficult to believe that it had anything to do with me, anything at all. A factory had been robbed. An old watchman was missing. That was all. I could even think back to the night when Paula Sheldon and I had dumped the body over the rock ledge into the lake and feel nothing but a kind of cold savagery. The old bastard had tried to kill me! He got what was coming to him!

I had another beer, and this time the bartender leaned over the bar to look at the paper. "Well, I'll be damned," he said. "That makes it look bad for old Finney, don't it? But you want to know what I think? I think the old man's dead."

I looked at him. "Why?"

"Just a hunch, maybe." He shrugged. "That's the way I've got it figured, though. I've been thinking about this thing, and I just don't believe the old man could have done it. I don't give a damn about the fingerprints. I think the robbers killed him and dumped his body in the lake."

I must have jumped.

"What's the matter?" he said. "You look kind of funny."

"Nothing's the matter. But what made you think of the lake?"

"Well, it just seems like the logical place to me. I ask myself how would be the best way to get rid of a body in a hurry, and I think right away of the lake. I don't know why; it's just the obvious place, I guess."

It was obvious, if this stupid bartender had thought of it. Dangerously obvious.

"It's my guess," he went on, "that the sheriff would be dragging the lake right now if he could get the officials together on it. There are too many damn fools in town, though, that think the old man actually took part in the burglary and is hidin' out somewhere. But they'll come around in time. Then you'll see I'm right."

I wanted to get out of there. I was beginning to realize that the lake hadn't been such a fine idea after all, and if it weren't for the wrangle in the City Council I'd be in a hell of a mess. I said, "Well, I guess the sheriff knows what he's doing."

"Sure, if they'd just let him do it. You know, I've got another theory about this thing. I'll bet somebody right here in Creston took that money and killed Finney. Otis Miller will get them, though. I'll bet on it."

I downed the beer and got out of there. I'd heard enough. I got back to the station around sundown and Ike Abrams said, "Anything new in town?"

"Not much. I talked to the sheriff about the counterfeit bill. We'll have to chalk it up to experience."

"I heard on the radio that the fingerprints on the safe belonged to Otto Finney. That's hard to believe, isn't it?"

"You can't ever tell about people, I guess. Anything new out here?"

"Everything's about the same." Then he grinned. "By golly, there is something. You remember the guy with the blonde wife, the ones in the blue Buick?"

An anvil dropped in my stomach.

"Well," Ike said, "they're back."

Chapter Ten

I couldn't believe it. It was impossible! They couldn't be stupid enough to come back here at a time like this!

But they had. That blue Buick was parked in the carport beside Number 2, like the returning of a nightmare. "I don't know what we've got," Ike said, "but they must like it. This is the third time they've stopped here, isn't it?"

"I don't remember."

"Sure, two times before. I remember the last time was the night the box factory was robbed."

I was about to blow up. Why had they come back? "Maybe you're right," I said, and my voice was surprisingly calm. I felt like yelling.

"You goin' to town tonight?" Ike asked.

"No. There's no need of your staying on; I'll close the station myself."

"I don't mind staying."

"Ike, take the night off. I want to go over the books, anyway." He stood there grinning, and I could have slugged him. "What's the matter with you? What are you grinning at?"

"Why, nothing, I guess. Is anything wrong?"

"No, nothing's wrong. Go on, Ike, take the night off."

"Whatever you say, Joe."

I was tingling all over. I wanted to get that Sheldon by the throat and beat some sense into his stupid skull. And Ike wouldn't leave. He kept puttering around for maybe five minutes while I tried to keep from yelling.

"Well, if you're sure you won't need me tonight..." he said finally.

"I won't need you, Ike. That's the truth."

I was as tight as a drum. Just about another minute of Ike and I would have exploded. But he left. I was never so glad to get rid of anybody in my life.

Now that he was gone, I didn't know what to do. I had to see Sheldon. I had to find out if he had completely lost his mind. He must have lost his mind, coming back here at a time like this! At least Paula should have known better.

I was afraid to leave the station untended, but it looked like the only way. As soon as Ike was out of sight, I headed for Number 2. There was a coldness inside me; I was ready to take somebody's throat in my hands and start squeezing.

Paula was at the door when I got there, and the sight of her jarred me. She looked as though she hadn't slept for a week. That blonde hair wasn't as blonde as it had been before, and it looked as though it hadn't been combed since the night of the robbery. I jerked the door open and said, "What the hell do you mean, coming back here?"

She took two steps back, like a sleepwalker, and glanced at the bed. Sheldon was stretched out on the covers, his face flushed, his lips tight. One shirt sleeve had been ripped off at the shoulder and his left arm was bound with what looked to be dirty rags.

"Hooper?" he almost whispered.

"Goddamn you, why did you—"

"I've got to have a doctor," he said, talking through clenched teeth.

I wheeled on Paula, who still hadn't made a sound. "What's wrong with him?"

She smiled then, without humor. "He's been shot."

The full implications still didn't hit me. "How did it happen?"

"We'll go into that later."

"We'll go into it now!"

She shrugged. "All right. We were in Texas. We saw this drugstore, a little hick drugstore in a little one-horse town in Texas. I was buying some aspirin and I saw the druggist go to the safe, and I saw the money there. It looked easy." She sighed wearily. "There must have been a week's take there in a safe that I could have opened myself."

"And then what happened?"

"For God's sake," Sheldon said hoarsely, "don't stand there talking. I've got to have a doctor!"

"And then what happened?" I said again.

Again Paula smiled that smile that wasn't a smile at all. "We took the drugstore that night. Or we almost did. The town marshal, a hick town marshal, just happened to see us as we were leaving. The whole town was asleep, but not that hick marshal. He was a hero. He had been wearing that six-shooter for God knows how long, just waiting for a chance to use it. And he used it on Karl."

"But why come here, all the way from Texas?"

"Karl's got blood poisoning, I think."

"But why did you come here?" I insisted.

She sank to a chair beside the kitchen table. "Because," she said, "Karl has to have a doctor. And because doctors don't treat gunshot wounds without reporting them. And," she added, "because I remembered that your father was a doctor and I thought maybe he would overlook the report if it was for a friend of yours."

That stunned me. It had been obvious all the time, but she had to spell it out for me before I got it.

"You're crazy!"

She shrugged, very lightly.

"You must be insane," I almost yelled. "Or maybe you just don't know what an honest man is like. Well, that's what my father is. Nothing in the world could make him take a case like this and not report it!"

"Not even to save his son from the electric chair?"

She had me.

She knew she had me, and she could start turning the screw any time she felt like it. And she felt like it right now. She stood up suddenly, and she didn't look so tired now. She pushed her hair back and looked straight at me with those cool blue eyes. "I'm not going to argue about this. Karl has to have a doctor."

"Then get one of your own!"

"You know that's impossible. Your father is the doctor we want, the one we're going to have."

And then a car honked outside and the sound made me jump.

"What's that?" Her eyes brightened just a little.

"Somebody at the station. A customer. I've got to get back."

"Have you got a telephone at the station?"

"No."

The corners of her mouth turned up again. "Sure you have. Well, call your father and tell him to get out here, understand?"

The car honked again and we stood there staring at each other, and even then, at a time like that, I kept thinking what a hell of a woman she was. She had looks, she had brains, and she could set a man on fire. I hated her guts at that moment, and it was all I could do to keep my hands off her.

"For God's sake!" Sheldon groaned.

"You'd better go, Joe," she said, and fatigue crept back into her face. I turned on my heel. "And don't forget to call your father," she added as I went out the door.

I was shaking with rage when I got back to the station. The guy was just beginning to honk the horn again as I rounded the corner. "All right!" I yelled. *"All right!"*

They were tourists, a fat old geezer of about sixty and a little pinch-faced woman. I looked in the car window and said, "Fill her up?"

"No, we just want a cabin," the man said.

Of all the times to get business! "I'm sorry," I said, "we're full up."

"You've got a 'Vacancy' sign out," the little old woman said peevishly.

"I just forgot to take it in, ma'am. Sorry."

"Don't look like you're full," the man complained. "There ain't but one car back there. I looked as we drove up."

I could feel my nerves unraveling. "Mister," I said tightly, "I've got no vacancy. Why don't you try one of the other motels? There are plenty of them down the road."

"The good places are all filled," the old woman whined.

The man said, "Look here, son, I'm not as young as I used to be. Driving tires me, and I've been driving all day. You sure you haven't got some kind of place?"

"For Christ's sake!" I exploded. "How many times do I have to tell you? We've got no vacancy!"

"Well!" The little old woman pulled herself up, outraged. The fat man got red in the face. I turned my back on them and went back to the station as they drove off.

I was still shaking. I took the "Vacancy" sign down and put the "No Vacancy" up, the first time it had been up since I started running the place.

At that moment Paula stepped through the station doorway. She had washed her face and combed her hair and put on fresh lipstick and she looked like ten million dollars.

"Have you called your father?" she said.

"I'm not dragging my father into this, Paula. That's something you'd better get straight."

Surprisingly, she smiled. "All right. If that's the way you want it." She stood up, lazily, like a young savage. Then she stepped to the wall phone and picked up the thin directory.

"What are you doing?"

"I'm going to call a doctor, any doctor."

"You can't! Any doctor you call will have to report that gunshot wound!"

"It can't be helped," she said, as though it didn't make any difference to her one way or the other. "Karl will die if that arm doesn't get attention."

"Then let him die!" I took Paula's arms and held her tight. "What do you care what happens to him? You don't love him. You despise him. I can see it in your eyes every time you look at him."

I must have been hurting her, but she only shrugged. "Maybe, Joe," she said softly, "but he's been good to me."

"What's that supposed to mean?"

This time her smile was edged with bitterness. "Joe," she said huskily, "could you guess what I was before Karl married me? Could you guess what I did for a living?"

I turned her loose. I could guess.

"That's the reason I won't let him die," she said. "Love has nothing to do with it. Karl has everything to gain and nothing to lose by calling a doctor. If the wound is reported, if the story gets to the police—well, it was you that killed the watchman, Joe." She found a number, then lifted the receiver, and I could hear the operator answer.

I slammed the hook down with my hand.

"Well, Joe?" she asked softly.

She had me and she knew it. I picked up the phone and gave the number. "Hello, Dad?"

Chapter Eleven

It was closing time but I was still at the station, waiting, wondering what I was going to say when my father came out of that cabin, wondering how I was going to explain it to him. Then I heard his footsteps—those slow, weary footsteps—as he came around to the front of the station. He looked a hundred years old as he came in and set down his bag.

"How's the patient, Dad?" It sounded insane, but he didn't seem to notice.

"Blood poisoning," he said heavily. "Another day without attention would have killed him. He still stands a chance of losing that arm." He reached for the phone and I jumped.

"Who're you calling, Dad?"

"The sheriff's office. That man has a gunshot wound and I have to report it."

"But it was an accident, Dad. Didn't they tell you?" I was hoping that he wouldn't notice how I was sweating. "You don't have to report it, do you, if it was an accident?"

"All gunshot wounds have to be reported and investigated, Joe. You know that." He reached for the phone again and I stopped his hand with mine.

"Dad, as a favor to me, don't report this one. These people are friends of mine and I know it will be all right. Just don't bother them.'

Those old eyes looked puzzled, and I couldn't tell whether he suspected anything or not. "Joe," he said slowly, "you know I have to make a report. I'd be breaking the law if I didn't."

"Then you'll have to break the law, Dad." And that was when he began to notice things. He noticed the sweat, the veins standing out on my forehead, and I guess he saw some things in my eyes that scared him. He felt for a chair and sat down very slowly.

"What is it you're trying to tell me, Joe?"

I couldn't tell him. I couldn't bring myself to hurt him any more than was absolutely necessary, but he knew something was wrong, and he knew it was bad. And he was waiting.

"Joe," he said finally, "you're in trouble, aren't you?"

"Yes."

"Is it bad?"

I couldn't look at him. I nodded.

He just sat there, looking at his hands. Those white, thin hands. After a moment he said quietly, "Why did you do it, Joe? Was it because of that woman?"

I didn't understand at first. Then it began to come, and an unexpected hope began growing inside me. He thought I had shot Sheldon! I took hold of that hope and held it tight, I held it with all the strength that was in me.

And then I was talking. "Dad, I don't know how it happened. I'd tell you if I could, but I don't know." I saw the opening and the words came pouring out. "You saw what kind of woman she is. When she came playing around, I lost my head, I guess. I know that's not much of an excuse, but that's the way it was. And then her husband found out what was going on, and there was a scuffle. I don't know.... There was a gun in it somewhere, and it went off, and when it was over there was a bullet in his arm."

He just sat there.

"Dad," I said, "don't you see why you can't turn in that report? The whole story would come out and the whole town would know about it."

He folded and unfolded those white hands, saying nothing.

"Dad, the rest of my life depends on what you do about this report. Should one mistake be that expensive? Just one mistake!"

"I was thinking about Beth," he said heavily. "I didn't want to meddle any more in your affairs, Joe, but that woman, that man's wife, is she the one? Is she the reason you and Beth stopped seeing each other?"

I said nothing and let him think what he wanted to think. His hands trembled as he fumbled for his handkerchief and wiped aimlessly at his forehead.

I couldn't tell how I was doing. I couldn't tell what he was thinking or how much of the story he believed. "Dad," I said tightly, "you hold the lives of three people in your hands. What happens to us now is up to you."

He was hurt, but not nearly as hurt as he would have been if I had told him the truth. He looked at me once, then picked up his bag and slowly got to his feet. "I'm tired, Joe, very tired. I think I'll go home now."

"The report, Dad. What are you going to do about it?"

He smiled then, and it was the saddest expression I'd ever seen. "It's a terrible thing," he said, "holding other people's lives in your hands. It makes an old man out of you. Maybe you were right, Joe, in not wanting to be a doctor."

"The report?"

"I've never broken the law, that I know of." And he smiled that sad smile again. "Maybe I'm overdue." He walked out of the station, a little older, a little more bent, a little more tired. Relief washed over me like an icy sea. "I'll come back tomorrow," he said wearily, "and treat the man's arm."

"Tomorrow night, Dad, after I've closed the station. It has to be at night."

"All right. Tomorrow night." He got into his car, a battered old Dodge, and I stood there in the station doorway as he drove onto the highway and headed toward town. I felt as though the weight of the universe had been lifted from my shoulders. I took great gulps of air into my lungs and felt young again, and strong.

I never closed the station faster than I did that night. I took in the hose and oil displays, I locked the pumps and the door, and when I headed for Number 2 it was all I could do to keep from running.

Paula had the door open for me. "What happened?"

"It's all right," I said. I walked over to the bed where Sheldon lay quietly, his eyes closed. "How about him?"

"He's asleep. What did you tell your father?"

"I told you everything was all right. He thinks I shot your husband."

She blinked. That was all. Then she laughed. "Your father didn't like me very much. He didn't approve of me. He thinks I led you astray, doesn't he?"

"Something like that."

"And he knows about the robbery?"

"Not a thing. He doesn't even suspect anything."

"Well," she said, smiling, "you've got brains. I'm glad you didn t disappoint me by not using them."

There never was another woman like Paula Sheldon. She didn't have to talk. What she had to say she could say with her eyes and her body. I lit a cigarette for her and one for me, and we stood there for one long moment saying nothing. Suddenly I reached for her, but she stepped aside as gracefully as a cat.

"No!"

"What's the matter with you?"

"I think you'd better go to your cabin," she said. "You look like you could use some sleep." Carelessly she dropped her cigarette to the floor and stepped on it, then she went over to the bed and placed the back of her hand to Sheldon's forehead. I followed and put one arm around her.

"That's enough," she said flatly.

I wheeled her around, pinning her arms to her side, and when I put my mouth to hers it was like setting fire to a keg of powder. Her arms went around my neck. She melted and flowed against me and I could feel the nervous ripple of her body, the softness of her, the heat of her.

Then it was over. She slipped away.

"You'd better go."

"Like hell!" I reached for her again and she whipped her hand across my face with a crack like a pistol shot in the silence of the room.

"Get out of here!" she hissed.

I almost hit her. I could feel the muscles in my shoulders and arms grow taut as I took a quick step toward her. She didn't move. She just stood there smiling that insolent smile, and I grabbed her by the front of her dress and slammed her against the wall. She went reeling back, then fell over a chair and went down to her hands and knees. Even then, in the midst of rage, I thought what a hell of a woman she was. I had to force myself to turn and walk out. If she had said one word, I would have come running. But she made no sound.

I took a shower and felt a little better. I opened all the doors and windows of my cabin to let in what little breeze there was. I lay across the bed in my shorts and tried to think about my life before Paula came into it, but the picture wouldn't come. It was hard to believe that I had ever been such a person.

Relax, I told myself. Relax and get some sleep.

Easier said than done. Paula had played hell with me. I could feel myself winding up tighter and tighter, and pretty soon I'd be ready to get up and start kicking holes in the wall.

That was when I heard it. A quick, soft shuffling outside. Then my door opened and Paula was standing there in the doorway, framed in moonlight, as pale as the moon herself. I sat up in bed as she came toward me.

She didn't say a word. She slipped onto the bed and her fingers were like a hundred snakes crawling over my body. "Goddamn you," I said, "I ought to beat your brains out!"

She laughed softly. That hot mouth found me in the darkness and I pulled her down with me.

"Joe?"

"Yes?"

"What were you thinking about before I came?"

"Nothing."

She laughed again.

Chapter Twelve

It was about two the next afternoon when Ike Abrams came back with the news. His drowsy eyes were bright with the excitement. "By God," he said, "Creston's about to bust loose at the seams! They just found old Otto Finney's body in the lake!"

"They what!"

"The old watchman at the box factory. They just found his body."

I couldn't believe it. Otto Finney was at the bottom of the lake, where I had dumped him. He *had* to be!

"A funny thing," Ike said, "the way it happened. You know that upper part of the lake has always been bothered with garfish and big cats. Well, the city opened that part of the lake to commercial fishermen, hoping they'd clean out the scavengers before they ruined it for game fish. Well, this morning these fishermen brought up something that damn near tore their nets to pieces, and it turned out to be a body. It was pretty much of a mess, I guess. All they had to go by for identification was his clothes."

"Is it a positive identification?"

"According to the sheriff, it is. And you know what kept old Otto underwater all this time? They had him wired to a flywheel."

I couldn't think of a thing to say. I was stunned.

"They say Otis Miller is fit to kill about it. I sure wouldn't want to be in the killer's shoes, with the sheriff in that frame of mind."

"Does he have anything to go on, any clues?"

Ike shrugged. "You know the sheriff. He doesn't say a thing until he's ready to slip the noose around somebody's neck." Then he noticed the blue Buick in the carport next to Number 2. "I see our star boarders are still with us." He grinned.

That Buick! I should have got rid of it somehow, but it was too late now. I said, "Mr. Sheldon picked up some fever in Texas and doesn't feel like driving. They'll probably be staying over for a day or two."

It didn't sound too good, but Ike took it in stride and was already beginning to sweep the driveway. Then he stopped. "Now that you mention it," he said, "Sheldon didn't look so hot when they came in yesterday. His wife was driving, if I remember right."

I didn't want to talk about the Sheldons; I wanted to hear more about the body. "You say the sheriff hasn't got any clues to go on?"

"Who knows what Otis Miller has in his mind? All I know is they've got a body and a flywheel. If he could trace the flywheel, it might mean something, but that don't seem very likely. Lot of flywheels around. I think we've got one ourselves in the back of the station."

A coldness was gathering in the pit of my stomach, and I didn't like it. "We had that hauled away the last time the junkman was around," I said quickly.

"Oh?" Ike paused in his sweeping. "I don't remember. The flywheel came out of your dad's old Dodge, though—I remember that much. You don't see them very often these days."

I'd heard enough. I turned the station over to Ike and went to my cabin. Then, when the way was clear, I made it over to Number 2. Sheldon was awake but he looked like hell.

"How do you feel?" I asked.

"Lousy." It was barely a whisper.

I went into the kitchen, where Paula was warming some canned soup on the apartment-sized range. She looked at me blankly and it was almost impossible to believe that she was the same woman who had been in my cabin the night before.

"We're in trouble," I said. "They found the body."

She took the pan off the stove. "We had guessed that much, hadn't we?"

"But I hadn't guessed they'd find it this soon. Some commercial fishermen found it this morning, caught that flywheel in their nets."

She didn't seem worried. "It served its purpose. The trail is cold now, just the way you said it would be. They'd never think of looking for the killer in Creston."

"It's the flywheel!" I said. "That goddamn flywheel that we tied the body to. There's just a chance they might trace it back to me. It came out of my dad's old car and I just learned that there aren't many exactly like it."

She thought about it. "That seems pretty farfetched."

"My robbing a payroll and committing murder is pretty farfetched, too, but I did it."

"Has anybody said anything to you, anything at all?"

"No."

She poured the soup into a bowl. "Then stop worrying about it."

I was just beginning to worry. But I let her take the soup in to Sheldon and watched him sip from the spoon a few times before he fell back to sleep. I took Paula's arm when she came back to the kitchen.

"This is too damn risky," I said, "sitting here right under Otis Miller's nose. You two have got to get out of here, out of Oklahoma."

She smiled wryly. "You weren't so eager to get rid of me last night." She jerked away from me and rinsed the bowl at the kitchen sink. "Besides," she said, "Karl can't be moved."

"He'll *have* to be moved. My helper at the station is beginning to wonder what the hell is going on back here."

"Let him wonder. He's just a stupid farmer."

"Your husband thought I was a stupid farmer, too, but I cut in for half of that payroll. Get this through your head: We're not as stupid out here as you people seem to think. And we've got a sheriff that's tough, as tough as they come."

She smiled teasingly, and those white arms of hers went around my neck. "You don't really want me to go, do you, Joe?" She knew the effect she had on a man when she plastered herself against him like that. I grabbed her, holding her tight enough to crush her, but she only smiled.

"Not now, Joe."

"You started it, I didn't!" I forced her head back, and when our mouths came together the contact shocked both of us. Everything went to hell when I touched her. I didn't give a damn about anything or anybody.

I don't know how long we stood there wound up in each other, and I don't know how long Ike had been hollering before I finally heard him.

"Joe! Joe, you in there?"

I almost ignored him. I was tempted to tell him to get away and leave me alone, because that's the kind of effect Paula Sheldon had on me.

"Joe, the sheriff wants to talk to you."

That jerked me out of it. It was like having ice water poured on you. Paula hissed, "The sheriff?" and she couldn't have got away from me faster. "What does he want?"

"I don't know."

"Get out there and see. We can't have him coming in here."

I felt sick. I couldn't imagine what Otis Miller wanted with me, but every bad thing in the world flashed through my mind as I stepped to the door, where Ike was waiting.

"Who did you say wanted me?"

"The sheriff. He and Ray King are over by your cabin."

Ike was beginning to think things. There were questions behind those sleepy eyes of his that I didn't like at all. Just before I opened the door I thought of something. "Just a minute, Ike." I went back to the kitchen, where Paula was standing like a statue.

"Joe, get out of here!"

I headed straight for the kitchen stove, lifted the grating from one of the cold burners, and smeared my hands good with the collection of burned grease at the bottom. Then I got out.

Ike had already gone back to the station when I came out of Number 2, and the sheriff and Ray King were standing beside their car, which was parked in front of my own cabin.

"Hello, Sheriff. Hello, Ray. Always something breaking down in a place like this—I just had a kitchen stove to fix for those people." I made sure that they saw the grease on my hands. The sheriff was sweating, and so was Ray, but I had never felt colder than I was at that moment.

"Just wanted to ask a few questions, Joe," Otis said, "if you can spare us the time."

"Sure, but let's go inside where I can wash up a little." I needed the time to get set for whatever was coming. We went inside and I went into the bathroom and washed my hands. When I came out I felt that I was as ready as I would ever be.

"All right, fellows, what can I do for you?"

Otis sat on the edge of the bed, Ray took a chair, and I stood there in the doorway. "Well," the sheriff said slowly, "it isn't much, but I can't afford to overlook a thing. You've heard that they found Otto's body in the lake."

Not trusting my voice, I nodded.

"He was a fine old man," Ray King said softly, and I nodded again, watching the sheriff. Otis was staring down at his hands, and I couldn't tell what was going on in his mind. Ray King went on: "The picture's pretty clear now, Joe. Old Otto was killed during the robbery and his fingerprints were planted all over the place to throw us off the trail. The whole town's worked up about it. So is the sheriff, and so am I. We want that killer, Joe, we want him bad!"

"I know how you feel," I said. "I liked Otto, too. I guess everybody did." My voice sounded all right. It was calm enough.

The sheriff raised his head. "The point Ray's trying to make, Joe, is that we can't overlook a thing, no matter how small, if there is a chance in a million it might help us. That's the reason we're here."

"I understand, Otis."

"Well, here it is. The day before the robbery you were out to the box factory, weren't you?"

So that was it. "That's right," I said. "I stopped by to pay Pat Sully some money I owed him."

"So Pat told me. Joe, were you going somewhere else and just happened to drop by, or did you make a special trip just to see Pat?"

"Why, I guess I made the trip special. I was downtown and just happened to think of it—that's the way I do things sometimes." I didn't like the way this was going. I couldn't tell where it was leading or what they were thinking. They just sat there dead-faced, their eyes expressionless.

"Now tell me this, Joe. Did you notice anything out of the way while you were out there that day?"

I could hear my heart pounding. "What do you mean, Sheriff?"

"I mean you used to work at the box factory and were pretty familiar with the place. You knew all the people, the buildings. It occurred to me that a person who hadn't been out there for a while might notice something that people who work there every day might pass by. I just want to know if you noticed anything out of the way, no matter how small—something that might help us."

I made a show of thinking it over. "I'm sorry, Sheriff, I can't think of a thing."

"Tell me just what you did while you were out there."

"Did? Well, not much. I just went in and gave Pat the money I owed him and left. I wasn't there more than two or three minutes."

"I see." Otis took off his Stetson and wiped the sweatband with his handkerchief. "Well, it was just a chance. I've talked to everybody at the factory, and they're not much help. There's one more thing, Joe, if you don't mind."

"Sure."

"It's out there in the car. I want you to take a look at something."

What was he getting at now? Was it a trick? Was he beginning to suspect something or was it just routine? I felt as though my nerve ends had worked to the top of my skin. If anybody had touched me I'd have yelled.

But I managed to keep a straight face as we filed out of the cabin. Ike Abrams was standing at the corner of the station, watching us, and Otis called to him. "Come on back here, Ike, if you're not busy." And then he opened the car door and there it was, on the floor.

The flywheel that I had tied to the body.

"Have you ever seen this before, Joe?"

At that moment I was completely defeated, crushed. My tongue was thick and my throat tight, and I knew I couldn't utter a word if my life depended on it. To gain time, I pushed my head and shoulders into the back of the car and pretended to take a close look at the flywheel. My God, I thought, he knows everything! He must! Why else would he bring that thing straight to me?

It was a bad moment. But it passed. I made my hands stop trembling. By sheer force of will I made myself stand up and say calmly, "Is this the flywheel that was tied to the body?"

"That's right. Did you ever see it before?"

"I don't think so. Of course, I can't be sure. Ike works on cars sometimes, back of the station, and leaves extra parts around."

"What do you do with those extra parts?"

"Have them hauled away with the tin cans and other trash that piles up in a place like this. Maybe once a month I call a truck and have the stuff taken out to the dumping grounds."

"I see." Then he said, "Ike, how about you? You ever see a flywheel like this before?"

"Sure," Ike said, and my insides seemed to shrivel.

"Have you ever seen *this* one before?"

"Can't be sure about that. But it looks like one that used to be back in the station."

"What makes you say that?"

"Well...." Ike pushed closer and had a good look. "Well, the ring gear is still on it, for one thing. See how chewed up it is? It looks like the assembly I took out of Dr. Hooper's old Dodge not too long ago. He had a bad habit of pushing the starter while the engine was running—absent-minded, I guess—and that's the reason the ring gear is chewed up the way it is. Had a hell of a time with the pinion gear jamming."

"Is that the reason you replaced the flywheel?"

"Hell, no. Just a new ring gear would have fixed that part of it. That old car of his had a bad clutch that scored a flywheel. Had to replace the whole assembly."

"When was that?"

"Maybe a month ago. A little longer."

Otis turned to me. "Have you had the trash hauled since then?"

That was the big question. That was the jackpot question, and it could kill me if I didn't come up with the right answer.

That clutch, that flywheel, they had been taken out together, and it was reasonable to assume that they had been hauled away together. If they had been hauled away. If both of them were still in the station, everything would be fine. But I knew they weren't. If both of them were gone, that would be fine, too. But that clutch was still there.

You'd better think fast, Hooper.

And I couldn't think at all. I stood there with my forehead screwed up, trying to look as if I was thinking, but there was just a roaring emptiness in my brain. There was only one thing to do. I had to bluff it. I had to lower my head and bull my way through, and hope that Otis Miller would take it.

I heard myself saying, "Sure, all that stuff was hauled away almost a month ago. It's about time I called the truck again."

"Ike would remember the hauling, wouldn't he?"

That was the end. I might as well get set for it. I looked at Ike and knew that he would be no help at all. "Sure," I said, surprised to hear that my voice was still normal. "I guess Ike would remember."

Ike was scratching his head, looking a bit sheepish. "Sheriff," he said slowly, "I can't be sure when the last hauling was done, but I think I know what you're getting at. You're trying to trace that flywheel, is that right?"

"It's the only clue we have. That's right, Ike."

"The flywheel I mentioned we had in the station, do you figure it's the same one you have in your car?"

The sheriff said nothing. He just waited.

"Well," Ike went on, "like I said, I don't remember exactly about the hauling. But I do remember that clutch assembly, because I took it home with me."

The sheriff's eyes widened. He looked as though he had reached for his gun and discovered it wasn't there. "What do you mean, Ike—you took it home with you?"

"Well...." Ike was sweating now. He knew that he had just kicked one of Otis Miller's ideas full of holes. I felt like the man who got a reprieve after they had already strapped him to the chair. I could hear relief whistling through my teeth. Suddenly I could smile. I could breathe again. Riding this kind of luck, nothing could stop me. Nothing! It was all I could do to keep from laughing.

The sheriff was waiting.

"Well," Ike said again, "I figured Joe wouldn't mind. I had an idea I could use some of the parts sometime."

"Have you still got that clutch assembly?"

"Sure. At home." Then Ike got smart, as he sometimes did. He stopped talking.

The sheriff looked at Ike, then at me, then he took off his hat and wiped his face. Then, surprisingly, he grinned. "Well, I guess that's all. Sorry to have bothered you, Joe."

"Not at all, Sheriff." He could never in the world pin anything on me now, no matter what he was thinking behind that grin.

Then Otis turned to Ray King. "We'd better be going. I want to check with all garages and salvage yards on this thing."

Ike and I stood there as they got into the car and drove out to the highway. My feeling of elation began to melt as the car disappeared. It had been a close thing—too close for comfort. If Otis had caught me in that lie about the flywheel, it would have been all over.

Chapter Thirteen

I used the stove repair excuse on Ike again and went back to the Sheldon cabin. Paula had the question ready before I got the door open.

"What did the sheriff want?"

"I don't know what he wanted. He was very polite, but that doesn't mean a thing with Otis Miller."

"What kind of questions did he ask?"

"It isn't the questions that matters. Most of them didn't make sense. But he had that damn flywheel with him. That's the important thing."

Sheldon was awake again. He had been following the talk with his eyes closed, but now he opened them. His voice was husky, not much more than a whisper.

"He didn't trace the flywheel to you, did he?"

"Not for sure, but he may have ideas. There's no way of telling about a man like Otis." I went over to the bed and said, "How do you feel?"

"Like hell."

"You'd better take a turn for the better, because you've got to get out of here."

Paula stepped between us.

"Look," I said tightly, "I know what I'm talking about. This sheriff's no dummy. Sooner or later he'll begin tying all the loose ends together, and that will be the end of us."

"We'll leave," Paula said calmly, "when the doctor says it's all right. Not before."

I could feel anger swelling in my throat. Tread lightly, I told myself. Take it easy and think straight. I turned and walked out.

Paula followed me out of the cabin and caught me at the bottom step. "This is the way it has to be, Joe. I don't like it any better than you do, but I can't leave him to die." She looked at me. Then she took my hand and I could feel the current going up my arm. "It's going to work out all right, Joe."

"You don't know the sheriff."

"It's going to work out. I can feel it. Karl will be ready to travel before long. When things cool off, you can contact me through my sister, just the way we planned."

I wanted her, but I also wanted to stay alive. I said, "That husband of yours is going to get us nothing but trouble. Leave him to me and I'll get rid of our troubles before they kill us."

Her eyes snapped angrily. "No! Can't I make you understand? I owe Karl something, I owe him plenty, and this is the only way I can pay him back. Seeing him through this is the only way I'd ever feel right about leaving him."

"This is a hell of a time to develop scruples about paying your debts!"

"Nevertheless, that's the way it is. I'm no good, Joe, but neither am I completely rotten."

"All right!" I was mad, but not so mad that I didn't realize that I had to get away from there. "Nurse him back to health, if you can. Take your time. Everything's going to be just dandy." I went back to the station and worked on the grease rack until I had calmed down.

It was a long day. They don't come any longer than that one.

I couldn't keep my mind on business for wondering about the sheriff and whether or not he actually suspected anything. I knew one thing—I had to get hold of my father and have him patch Sheldon up well enough to travel. Every minute they remained in Creston piled more odds on Otis Miller's side of this thing.

I called my dad twice that afternoon but he wasn't home. There was nothing to do but wait.

I was on edge again when Ike came in, wearing that stupid grin of his.

"Well," I said, "maybe you'll tell me what's so goddamn funny."

Ike didn't bat an eye. "You know," he said, "you're beginnin' to act just like Frank Sewell when he broke up with his wife. Damn if he wasn't the hardest man to live with you ever saw."

"If I'm so hard to live with," I said, "maybe you'd like to gather up your work clothes and quit."

"Nope," Ike said quietly. "I figure you'll get over it after a while."

I never figured that Ike fancied himself as any cupid, but I could see that he was trying to swing the conversation around to me and Beth Langford. That was about the next to the last thing in the world I wanted to talk about.

I had to get away. I went around to the wash rack and cleaned the place up a little, and pretty soon I began to cool off. After a while I went back to Ike and apologized for blowing up. I had to stay on the good side of him. I wanted him to go on thinking that everything was exactly the way it always had been.

Around six o'clock I told Ike that I'd close the station myself and sent him home.

It was well after dark when my dad came back to have another look at the patient. He was a very old man that night as he got out of his car and said heavily, "You all right, Joe?"

"Sure, Dad, I'm fine. I want to talk to you when you finish back there."

He took off his hat and ran his fingers through his thinning hair. All the things my son could have been! I could see him thinking it. I could see it in those ancient, melancholy eyes. Then he nodded. "All right, Joe." And he walked heavily back to Number 2.

That was when the black Ford rolled up in front of the station. I went out automatically and reached for the gas hose. The car door opened and a man said, "Never mind, Hooper."

I froze.

He was a big man with a big, humorless grin. He wore a straw sombrero and a loud sport shirt. His name was Bunt Manley.

Chapter Fourteen

He didn't get out of the car. He sat there for a moment, grinning. Then he started the car and drove around to the side of the station and parked. When he came back I was still standing there, frozen, feeling the bottom falling out of everything.

"Wasn't that your dad headed back toward the cabins, Hooper?"

There were no words in me at that moment.

"Sure it was your dad," Manley said. "Could it be there's somebody back there needs a doctor? You know, that's a right interesting idea. I think I'll just go back and give the doc a hand."

"Stay where you are," I said. "My father doesn't like to be bothered when he's caring for a patient."

"I'll bet," he said dryly. "Especially if the patient happens to be a man named Karl Sheldon."

That was it. I didn't know how he knew, but he did. He knew everything. He stood there looking at me, half grinning, then he fished out a cigarette and lighted it. "You know," he said roughly, "you're really quite a boy, Hooper. Tell you the truth, I didn't think you had the guts for a thing like this."

I had to bluff it, there was no other way. "I don't know what you're talking about, Bunt."

He laughed suddenly. "You know damn well what I'm talking about." Then, surprisingly, he turned on his heel and went to his car. But he was back almost immediately, with a newspaper in his hand. "Here," he said. "I want to read you a little piece of news that turned up in yesterday's paper. Datelined Crowell, Texas. 'Last night Frank Hennessy, city marshal of Crowell, Texas, prevented the burglary of a city drugstore....' So on and so on, but here's the interesting part. 'Hennessy was able to provide descriptions of the would-be burglars. The man was of tall, athletic build. He had dark, thick hair, and was well dressed. In all probability the man is carrying one of the Marshal's bullets in his body. The man's woman companion was slight of build with short blonde hair.'"

Looking at me, Manley folded the paper. "You heard enough, Hooper?"

"I still don't know what you're talking about."

He wasn't grinning now. "I'm talking about that blue Buick back there in one of your carports, Hooper. I saw it this afternoon and began putting two and two together." He snapped his cigarette straight at my feet. "Funny thing about it, though. I never tied you in with them until just now, when I saw your old man headed back to that shack. Sheldon's been here two days, hasn't he? And your old man has been taking care of him. Now, does it stand to reason that Doc Hooper would treat a bullet wound and not report it—unless he had a mighty good reason?" He reached out quickly and grabbed the front of my shirt. "I know the reason, Hooper. He's doing it to keep his son out of the electric chair!"

Something snapped when I felt those thick fingers grab me. A rage caught fire inside me and I wasn't afraid any more, I was just mad. I knocked his hand away and then grabbed his arm and slammed him against the station wall. "Listen," I said hoarsely. "Listen to me, you sonofabitch. If you try to drag my father into this thing I'll kill you!"

He was startled. He hadn't expected this kind of reaction. "Look here!"

"You look, Manley! And don't you forget! So help me God, I'll kill you if my father is brought into this!" I let him go and he almost fell.

I had learned one thing these past few days. You had to be tough if you didn't want people stepping on you. You had to let them know who was boss, even if you had to beat it into their thick skulls.

"All right," I said, still shaking with rage. "You think you know something. You think you've got me nailed, don't you?"

"Wait a minute, Hooper! For Christ's sake!"

And only then did I realize that I was about to hit him. My fist was a hard club, ready to smash into that thick face of his. I think I would have killed him at that moment, right on the spot, if I hadn't suddenly snapped out of it. And Manley knew it. Maybe, at that moment, Bunt Manley was remembering that old watchman that they had fished out of the lake.

When I relaxed he began to breathe again, but not very well. "For Christ's sake, Hooper, I haven't got anything against you! It's them!"

"Who's them?"

"You know who I mean. Karl Sheldon and that wife of his. I've got something coming from them, but not from you, Hooper."

"What have you got coming from Sheldon and his wife?"

"Well, it was my idea, wasn't it? That box factory?" He was thinking a little faster now. "After all, I was the one that got in touch with Sheldon and told him about it. He was supposed to cut me in on it. I want my share of the money, that's all."

"You're not getting a penny, Manley. And you're not going to mention my father. Is that clear?"

"Sure, Hooper, I told you it wasn't you I was after. And what could I gain by bringing your old man in on a thing like this?"

"I just wanted to be sure you had it straight."

I was thinking. Maybe—just maybe—Bunt Manley had a point here. It was a lousy piece of luck that he had to know at all, but he did, and there was nothing I could do to change that. If he could somehow talk Sheldon out of part of his take, maybe it would be a good idea. Maybe that would satisfy him and he would be quiet.

But I knew, even then, that it was wishful thinking. Manley would never be satisfied. There was too much greed in those quick little eyes. And besides, Paula would never turn loose a penny of that money. I had seen enough of her to know that.

The answer was clear, and I think Manley was beginning to get it now. I went around to his car and took his keys, just in case he decided this wasn't such a good place to butt in, after all.

"What are you doing?" he asked quickly.

"Nothing. I think we ought to talk this over with Sheldon and his wife, that's all. After my father gets out of there."

I had a tire tool in my hand, a nice, solid piece of iron, and Manley knew I would use it if he made a move. He didn't make the move. After a while I heard those dragging steps again and my dad came around the side of the station. I took hold of Manley's arm and squeezed it hard. "Just remember," I said. "Dad, is that you?"

"Yes, Joe."

I went around to the side of the station where he was standing, as though he didn't want to look at me in the light. "Is he all right, Dad?"

"Yes, he's better, Joe."

"Is he able to travel, Dad? They want to go as soon as possible."

"Yes," he said, "he'll be able to travel tomorrow." I had almost forgotten how stooped and small he was. He said quietly, without looking at me, "Is that all, Joe?"

"Yes, Dad, I guess that's all. And thanks for everything."

He made no answer. He stood there for a moment, his head bowed, and then he turned and walked slowly to his car.

I stood there, feeling lousy about the way I had hurt him. Then I thought: Just be glad he doesn't know the real truth. That's the one thing in this mess you can be glad of.

I turned to Manley, the tire tool still in my hand. He must have been a mindreader, that Manley. He stared at me for maybe five seconds and knew all the answers. He could look into his future and see nothing but the endless darkness of death.

"Joe, for Christ's sake!"

"Just shut up," I said, "until I get this station locked up." And that was when he started to run. He knew now that he had made a mistake—a lot of mistakes. In the first place, he should have brought a gun with him if he figured on taking a slice of that thirty thousand dollars. But the small detail of a gun had slipped his mind, and now there was no way out except to run for it.

He moved fast. It's hard to believe that a man his size could move as fast as he did—but it wasn't fast enough for the tire tool. I drew back and let it fly, and it caught him right in the middle of the back, about three inches below the shoulders. He dropped as though he had been shot.

I thought he was dead at first. I turned him over with my foot and his eyes had that glazed look that I had seen before. But his pulse was still there, and he was still breathing. I rolled him over to the wash rack and locked up the station.

I had no feeling at all for Manley. The lousy chisler had tried to horn in on money that I had risked my life for, and he deserved to be dead. But I was glad he wasn't, just yet. This time somebody else was going to pull the trigger. This time somebody else was going to have the pressure put on him, not me.

I was thinking fast now. There was one thing I knew—Paula Sheldon was the one woman in the world for me. That I was sure of. But how could I be sure that I was the man for her? What if she turned against me sometime in the future? She was the one person who could get me electrocuted, because she knew that it was my gun that had killed Otto Finney.

Think this out carefully, Hooper. You need Paula Sheldon the way an alcoholic needs his booze. But what if she decided to leave you? There's nothing you can do about it, because she's holding a knife at your throat.

What I needed was a knife like hers, and I thought I knew just how to get it.

There was very little traffic on the highway, and for once in my life I was glad that there were no customers. After I got the station locked up, I went around to the wash rack and saw that Manley was just beginning to come out of it. I pulled him up by one arm and half dragged him back to the Sheldons' cabin.

Paula's pale face got even paler when I came in with Manley. Even Sheldon showed signs of life.

"Hooper, what the hell...."

I dumped Manley right in the middle of the floor and looked at both of them. "So you had to come back to Creston," I said tightly. "I told you this thing was going to blow up right in our faces if you didn't get out of here."

Paula was standing very erect, as cold and pale as marble. "How much does Manley know?"

I had the feeling that she was scared, actually scared for the first time. It was good to know that I wasn't the only person in this thing with some feelings. "He knows everything," I said. "Every damn thing there is to be known."

"How?" Sheldon asked.

"Because of that stupid drugstore job of yours in Texas. It was in the paper and Manley saw it. Then, out of curiosity, probably, he drove out this way and saw that Buick of yours. Not even Manley is so stupid that he couldn't fill in the rest for himself."

"What does he want?" Sheldon said weakly. "A share of the money?"

"That's what he said. But I've got an idea he won't be satisfied for anything less than the whole take."

Sheldon looked even sicker than before. He'd had enough. There was nothing in the world he would like better than to undo everything that had happened and forget that he had ever heard of Creston, Oklahoma. At that moment I think Sheldon would gladly have given up every penny.

But not Paula. She had recovered from the first shock of seeing me drag Manley into the place, and now that gleaming, steel-trap brain of hers was working as coolly as ever. She turned her gaze on Manley, who was trying to lift himself to his hands and knees without much success. Shaking his head dumbly, he moved as though the right side of his body were paralyzed, and maybe it was.

Still looking at Manley, Paula spoke to me. "You shouldn't have brought him here. You should have killed him."

"I've had my share of killing."

Her head snapped up. "You've gone yellow?"

"If you want to call it that. It's just that I don't intend to carry more than my load in this thing. You brought this on when you came back here. You can get out of it the best way you can."

Surprisingly, she smiled. "I think I called you a stupid farmer once. I apologize."

There was absolutely no way of knowing what she would do or how she would react. She showed admiration only when I lashed out the hardest.

"What are we going to do?" Sheldon asked hoarsely from the bed.

"That's up to you. Or your wife." I looked at both of them and knew that it was going to have to be Paula. Not until then did I realize that I was still carrying that tire tool in my hand—but Paula had noticed. She took it from me.

Manley never knew what hit him. Still dazed, he was trying to bring himself to his knees when Paula swung. It was the first time I had ever heard the mushy sound of a skull caving in. It's a sound I won't soon forget. Manley fell on his face, kicked once, and then was completely still. There was very little blood.

Everything in the room seemed to freeze for just a moment. I hadn't been ready for anything as cold-blooded as this, and neither had Sheldon. He lifted himself up in bed for just an instant, staring wide-eyed at Manley, who was dead. There was no doubt about that; he was dead. Then Sheldon made a thin little sound, almost a kittenish sound, and dropped back on the pillow.

Only Paula took it completely in stride. She looked at the tire tool, then wiped it neatly on Manley's shirt and put it to one side. She said, "He came in a car, didn't he?"

I nodded.

"Get it. Bring it back here." Her breathing came slightly faster than usual, it was the only way her excitement betrayed her. She stood very straight and brushed her hair away from her forehead. "Mr. Manley," she said, "is going to have a very bad accident."

An "accident" was the only way. My father had seen Bunt Manley with me just a few minutes before; that fact immediately canceled out any attempt to get rid of the body. Sure as hell the sheriff would be back asking more questions, and that was the last thing in the world I could allow to happen. I said, "All right. I'll get his car."

Chapter Fifteen

I knew just where it had to happen, and how. I looked at my watch and it was almost eleven o'clock—just about time enough if we worked fast. I carried Manley's body out to his car and dumped him into the front seat. Paula stayed behind long enough to clean up what little blood there was on the floor, and then she came out and said, "I'll follow you in the Buick."

"All right. We don't have far to go.' My heart was beating like a hammer against my rib cage.

"This part is up to you," she said. "Do you know exactly what you're going to do?"

"Exactly. Now get in that Buick and follow me. Turn your headlights off when you see mine go out."

She touched my arm. "You're all right, Joe," she said huskily. "You're a lot of man."

"Thanks," I said flatly.

"I wanted you to know, Joe."

"You told me. Now get in the Buick."

She got into the Buick and I got into Manley's car. The body was sprawled all over the floor boards and I had to shove it over in order to get my foot on the brake pedal. I turned on the switch and started the motor.

When I got to the highway I slowed down until the Buick's headlights showed in my rear-view mirror. I looked at my watch again and it was ten minutes after eleven—still enough time. I hit thirty-five on the speedometer and held it there. Take it slow and easy. This is the one time in your life when you can't afford to pick up a highway patrolman, Hooper.

About two miles outside of Creston, just on the other side of the oil-field supply houses, I turned off the highway and eased down to a crawl until I was sure that Paula was still behind me. We followed the graveled road for maybe a mile, until I could see a stand of tall cottonwoods in the headlights. That was the thing I was looking for. Just beyond the cottonwoods I saw the outstretched arms of a railroad-crossing sign and I snapped off my lights. The Buick's lights went out behind me and both of us slowed down to a crawl again. Just before reaching the crossing I stopped the car.

Eleven-twenty, my watch said. It was time. I got out of the car and the country road was completely deserted. Paula, in the Buick, was about fifty yards back, pulled off on the gravel shoulder. I knew that she must have figured it out by now, because she made no move to get out of the car.

I walked up the slight grade to the crossing and listened until my ears hurt, but there were only the million little sounds that come with the night. I got down on my knees and put an ear to the rail, but I couldn't be sure whether I heard anything or not. My watch said eleven-twenty-five.

The Rock Island Rocket, unless they had changed schedule, hit Creston at eleven-fifteen on the dot, stopping just long enough to take on express. From this crossing to Creston, as well as I could judge, was about eight miles. It shouldn't take a train like the Rocket more than ten minutes to cover eight miles.

Then I heard it. The rasping sound of its horn cut the night like a knife. I hurried back to the car and got it started. I slammed it forward until it exactly straddled the tracks, and then I saw the light. The dazzling brilliance of that single enormous headlight sprang up like a thousand suns on the other side of the cottonwoods. I thought, I've got to get out of here, and fast! I kicked the door open. All I could think of was getting out of there. Then I caught my arm on something, my wrist. I didn't know what was holding me and I was too excited to find out. That locomotive was crashing around that stand of cottonwoods, the noise filling the night, and then I gave my arm a hard tug and it was free. I ran.

I never ran faster.

Paula had the Buick running by the time I got there. She had the door open and I dived in.

"Is everything all right?"

"Yes."

"Joe, are you sure?"

"Goddamnit, I said yes!"

Then she slammed the car in gear, and we had traveled maybe fifty feet when all hell broke loose behind us. Fire lit up the sky like worlds colliding, and the locomotive slammed into Manley's car. The engineer didn't have a chance to stop, he didn't see the car until he was on top of it. I heard the nerve-shattering screech of steel on steel, and the racket of coupled coaches slamming together, and then the locomotive crashed headlong into the car, scattering it all over the countryside. I looked back once and that was enough.

Paula and I rode in tense silence until we hit the highway. Then she said, "Joe..." and I stared straight ahead. "Joe, are you sorry?"

"About Manley? It's a little late to be sorry, isn't it?"

She smiled. At a time like that she could smile. After a moment she said quietly, "You're quite a man, Joe, you really are. You're hard and you're tough. You're a lot tougher than you think."

I said nothing. I was still hearing that locomotive slamming into Manley's car.

She leaned against me for just a moment. "I mean it, Joe. I've been thinking. I know a place in Arkansas," she said, steering the car through the night, "near Hot Springs. A friend of Karl's lives there. For a price he would take care of Karl for a week or two, however long it takes his arm to get well. Then it will be the two of us, Joe. Just you and me."

I looked at her. "You just now thought of this place?"

"Not exactly," she said softly, almost crooned. "I'll tell you the truth, Joe. Until tonight I wasn't absolutely sure about you."

"Are you sure now?"

"Yes."

And then we were back at the station. Paula drove off the highway and put the car into the port. When she switched off the ignition I reached out for her, brought her hard against me, and pressed her back against the seat, my mouth on hers.

"Yes," she said again, "I'm sure."

She twisted expertly and was out of my arms, but her eyes were glistening with the brightness of excitement. I followed her into the cabin, almost ran over her, for she was standing frozen in the doorway.

"Joe!"

I saw what had stopped her. It was her husband, Karl Sheldon, lying face down on the floor.

I went down on one knee beside him and turned him over. His face was flushed, and the heat of his fever burned my hand as I felt of his forehead. I looked around and saw two suitcases partly packed, and I guessed that, in his eagerness to get away from here, he had tried to pack himself while Paula and I were out disposing of Manley's body. In the middle of the job he must have passed out.

My only emotion was one of anger. Goddamn him, I thought, why didn't he stay in bed? I had a crazy urge to close my fingers around his throat and choke out the little life that was left in him, but instead I lifted him and put him on the bed. Paula felt of his forehead and looked at me.

"Joe, we'll have to get your father."

I tried to hold onto my anger. "Look," I said. "It will just take more time, and time is a thing that could kill us. Not more than an hour ago my father was here. He looked at your husband and said he was able to travel."

"That was an hour ago. He wasn't this sick then. Look at him—does he look in any shape to travel? Do you want him to die?"

"Why not?"

The pressure was being applied and the only thing I could think of was kill. It got to be a fever, a worse fever than the kind Sheldon had. Great God, I thought, what has happened to me in just a few short days? After a moment I took Paula's arm and held it for a moment. "I guess I didn't mean that," I said.

She was in complete control of herself. "You know how I feel about Karl," she said evenly. "I'll leave him, but not now, not like this."

"I said I didn't mean it!" Then I turned for the door and walked out.

There was a night light burning in the station and it felt as bright as those factory floodlights as I lifted the receiver and gave the number. I could hear the ringing. It must have gone on for a full minute before my father answered.

"Dad, can you come out to the station? Right away?"

He didn't say a thing. I could hear his heavy breathing. I could almost feel his weariness. "Dad," I said, "it's important."

"All right, Joe." He hung up.

I sat down at the plank desk and tried to tell myself that it was going to be all right. After all, my father didn't know I had anything to do with the robbery and killing. For all he knew, I had just got myself into some kind of fool scrape over a woman. People got into that kind of trouble every day. And Sheriff Miller—if he had anything to throw, he would have hit me with it long before now. Miller meant business. He would have jumped on me good if he'd had any idea I was mixed up in a killing.

He hadn't jumped, so everything was all right. But it didn't feel all right. There was this thing with Manley and my nerves were still raw from that, but I couldn't see how they could possibly tie me up to a train wreck That part had been foolproof, much better than the lake.

But it didn't feel right. As I sat there I could feel the cold emptiness growing in my guts.

I remembered then how easy it had seemed at first. A pushover robbery, fifteen thousand dollars in my pocket. Easy. What a joke that had been, but I wasn't laughing. Somewhere along the line my future had gone up in a bright, hot flame. It started the day I first looked at Paula Sheldon, and it was sealed the night I eavesdropped at Sheldon's window.

I needed sleep. I got up, went to the far wall of the station, and began moving cases of oil. When I had all the money together I locked the station again and went to my car and stuffed the money under the rear seat. I was just beginning to realize that I was actually preparing to leave Creston, preparing to wipe out in one night the plans that had been half a lifetime in the making. As far back as I could remember I had known just what I wanted—position, respectability, family; the same things, more or less, that every man wants out of life.

And what do you have now, Joe Hooper?

Fifteen thousand dollars. That's a lot of money in any man's language. And Paula Sheldon, if I wanted her on her terms. And I did.

The door to Number 2 opened and Paula said, "Joe, is that you?"

"Yes."

She came outside and over to where I was standing. "He seems to be sleeping. Did you call your father?"

"He's on his way." She leaned against me and it was like a charge of electricity against my bare arm. I grabbed her, pulled her hard against me, and she squirmed like a snake.

"Joe, not now!"

"What's wrong with now?"

She laughed softly, moving her head to one side as I tried to kiss her. "What were you thinking, Joe, when I called to you just now?"

"Nothing."

She smiled. I felt her hands on my arms, crawling up and down my arms and across my shoulders. Then, deliberately, she gouged her sharp fingernails into the muscles of my shoulders. "You're hard, Joe. I like men who are hard!"

That mouth of hers found mine and everything seemed worth while again. Who gave a damn about the past or the future, as long as there was a present? I held her tight, so tight that I knew I was hurting her, but she made no sound of complaint. My arms and legs felt weak when I finally released her.

"We're getting out of here," I said. "Tonight."

"If your father says it's all right."

"All right or not. It's got to be tonight; I've got to get away from Creston."

She was silent for a moment, then turned her face up to mine. "You really mean it, don't you, Joe? Don't you have any roots here? Don't you feel just a little sorry to leave this place?"

"No."

"What about your father?"

"He'll be better off without me."

"Karl asked you once if you had a girl here in Creston. Do you, Joe?"

"Not any more."

"No girl, no roots."

"Nothing."

"Just me?"

"Just you."

She laughed. The sound of that laughter cut like a whip, and at that moment I could have killed her, and I almost did. I knocked her back against the car and grabbed for her throat. But she was too fast for me. She slipped out of my arms and moved quickly along the side of the car, and there was a flash of uneasiness in her eyes. Not fear, just uneasiness that came from the knowledge that she had done something very dangerous. By the time I got my hands on her again that first unreasoning burst of anger had disappeared, but Paula didn't know it.

"Joe, what's wrong?"

"Nothing's wrong," I said roughly. Then, very gently, I put my hands on her throat and slowly let my fingers begin to squeeze. "Just you, Paula. That's the way you want it, isn't it?"

That was when the first fear showed in her eyes. In my mind were all the things I was giving up for her, and she had laughed at them. I don't know what would have happened if the car hadn't pulled off the highway just then, if the headlights hadn't cut a bright swath across the row of cabins and snapped me out of it. I turned her loose and said, "That must be my father. You'd better go back to Karl."

She slipped away quickly, as silently as the night itself, and I stood there by the car as rigid as steel. Slowly I made myself relax. I told myself that what had happened had been for the best. She knew who was boss now. That was Sheldon's trouble; he had never let her know who was boss.

It didn't occur to me that my father, in his old Dodge, hadn't had time to reach the station. I watched the headlights coming toward me from the highway, and when the car stopped a little way from my cabin I stepped out and said:

"Dad, is that you?"

"No, Joe." A thick, squat figure stepped out of the car and said, "It's the sheriff, Joe. Otis Miller."

Chapter Sixteen

The muscles in my legs turned to milksop. The sheriff waited for Ray King to get out of the car and then the two of them came toward me. If my legs could have worked I would have started running in stark panic—but they wouldn't work and that was the only thing that saved me.

Otis Miller said, "Hope we didn't wake you, Joe, comin' out here like this in the middle of the night."

"Not at all, Sheriff." I was amazed that my voice could sound so calm. "Too hot to sleep in that cabin of mine—but we could go in and have a beer. What have you got on your mind?"

"Just some questions, Joe," Ray King said.

At this time of night! But I merely nodded at the door to my cabin and the two of them went in ahead of me. I followed and turned on the light. Otis sat heavily in the room's only armchair and Ray took the edge of the bed. They were very businesslike. Their faces told me nothing.

"How about that beer?" I said. "There's some in the icebox."

Both of them shook their heads. "Later, maybe," Otis said, wiping his face with a handkerchief. "Joe, didn't I see somebody with you as we drove off the highway just a minute ago?"

I was sure they could hear my heart pounding. I had to stand there looking them right in the eye, not knowing what they were thinking, or how much they knew. "Oh, yes," I said, and again my voice sounded all right. "That was the lady from the next cabin. Her husband came down with the fever. She knew my father was a doctor and wanted me to call him."

"Did you do it?"

"Sure, just before you drove up. He'll be here soon."

I was going to have to explain my father some way when he got here, and I might as well do it now. If Otis and Ray already knew about the Sheldons, there was nothing I could do about it, anyway. I needed a minute to get myself set for whatever was coming, so I said, "Ray, you sure you won't have a beer with me?"

"No, thanks, Joe. Maybe later."

I went into the kitchen and got a can out of the icebox and opened it. Why had they come here at this time of night? Why in heaven's name had they come? I forced myself to calm down. By sheer will power I stuffed my fear down to the bottom of my guts and held it there. Then I went back to them.

"About those questions. Is it anything special, Sheriff?"

"Can't say yet about that. Joe, have you been here all night?"

"No, not all night. I closed the station and went into town to see a movie."

"By yourself. No one was with you?"

"No, I was by myself." I tried to grin. "Maybe you've heard; me and Beth Langford kind of called things off."

He hadn't heard and he wasn't interested.

I said, "What's this all about, anyway? Is it so important that it can't wait till morning?"

"It's important enough," Otis said. "Joe, how well did you know Bunt Manley?"

Here it comes, I thought. But my voice was a thing apart; it answered calmly. "Bunt Manley? Why, I don't know him very well. He put in some federal time for bootlegging a while back, didn't he?"

"When was the last time you saw Manley?"

I started to say I couldn't remember, but I recalled just in time that my dad had seen me with Manley just a couple of hours ago. It would take too short a memory to forget a thing like that.

I said, "Come to think of it, I saw Bunt Manley tonight. Not more than two hours ago."

"Here at the station?"

"Sure." I felt a little better. I was convinced that I could make up lies as fast as Otis could ask the questions. "Sure," I said again. "He drove up to the station just as I was closing up. He wanted some gas."

"I see. Does Bunt Manley usually trade with you?"

"No, not as a rule. Nearly everybody in town, though, drops in on me at one time or another."

"What did Manley do after he got his gas?"

"Paid me and drove off, that's all. Say, couldn't you give me an idea what this is about?"

"In a minute. When was the last time you saw Manley before tonight?"

I made a show of thinking. "I can't remember, Sheriff. I might have seen him in town, but not to speak to."

"I see. Joe, could you give me the time?"

"Sure." Then I looked at my wrist and my watch wasn't there. "I must have left my watch lying around somewhere," I said, and started toward the dresser. But Otis stopped me.

He held up a watch and said, "Is this yours, Joe?"

That was when the roof fell in. That watch! I didn't know just what part it was going to play in my future, but I knew it wasn't going to be good. I could see it in the sheriff's eyes, in the tight lines at the corners of Ray King's mouth. There was absolutely no use denying it was my watch. On the back was the legend "Joseph Hooper, Jr. May 16, 1938," engraved in the gold. My dad had given me the watch when I was graduated from high school, and if that engraving wasn't enough to settle it, the local jeweler had the records.

It was my watch, all right. But where had it come from? How had the sheriff got hold of it? I remembered having it on my wrist only a short time before, because I had been counting the seconds while waiting for that train.

Otis Miller said again, "Is this yours, Joe?"

"Yes, it's mine." That was all I could say.

"Could you guess where we found this watch, Joe?" he asked, his voice silky-smooth, his face bland.

It was like playing barehanded with a swamp moccasin, but I had to play with him until I found out where he was headed. "No, I have no idea where I lost it."

The sheriff stood up, a rare smile touching the corners of his thick mouth. "You sonofabitch!" he said softly. "You know, all right."

Ray King came out of his chair. "Hold it, Otis. Take it easy."

"Stay out of this, Ray. I swore I'd get the bastard that killed Otto Finney, and by God, I'm going to do it." He stepped in front of me and shoved the watch in my face. "It's yours, isn't it? You admit it?"

"I told you it was mine." My heart sank. I could feel the ground falling out from under me.

"All right, now I'll tell you where we found your watch. Just about an hour ago we picked it up near the railroad tracks where Bunt Manley was murdered. See this leather strap? The stitching is rotten. That's how you lost the watch. You killed Manley, probably while he was here at the station, then you put him in his own car and put the car on the tracks to make it look like an accident. But while you were fooling with that car you caught your watch strap on something and the stitching pulled loose and you lost it. That's the way it happened, isn't it?"

That was *exactly* the way it happened. But the first shock had worn off and now I was more angry than afraid. I said, "Otis, that's the craziest story I ever heard of. Are you actually accusing me of killing somebody?"

"I'm not accusing you, I'm telling you!"

I turned to the deputy. "Ray, for God's sake, what's got into him? Has he gone out of his mind completely?"

Ray only looked at me. This was Otis Miller's play and he wasn't going to try to take it from him. I wheeled back to the sheriff.

"Tell me one thing," I said, "just one thing, before you make any more of these crazy accusations. Why in the world would I want to kill Bunt Manley when I hardly even knew the man?"

"Maybe you didn't want to kill him," the sheriff spat. "But maybe you *had* to kill him. Maybe he came around wanting a bigger share of the money and you decided you had to kill him."

"What money are you talking about? This gets crazier all the time!"

"You know what money, Hooper. The same money you and Bunt Manley took from old Provo's box factory. If I have to spell it out for you, by God, I'll do it. I've been keeping my eye on Manley ever since he got out of the pen. He's never been any good and I knew sooner or later he'd get himself in bad trouble. So Manley was the one I thought of first when you broke into the factory and killed the old watchman. But Manley couldn't have done the job alone. Somebody had to be in it with him, so when I started looking for a partner I found you."

The sheriff's voice was still, soft, and sure.

I was practically yelling. "What the hell do you mean? I thought you were a responsible man, Otis, but here you are building a case on nothing but thin air and making these insane accusations! Well, I've had enough of it! I demand that you offer some proof or shut up and get out of here!"

He grinned. "That suits me fine. We'll start with that bogus bill that you brought around to my office right after the robbery. I knew at the time you were lying through your teeth about just getting it, because that kind of paper hasn't been seen in more than a year. That was a mistake, Hooper, because I started to wonder why you'd go to that much trouble to pump me about the robbery."

I snorted. "I didn't pump you. I might have mentioned it casually. Hell, the whole town was talking about it. If I mentioned it, do you call that proof that I had a hand in it or killed Manley?"

"And Otto Finney, too," he said softly. "Don't forget Otto. No, it doesn't prove anything in particular, but it all adds up to a jury."

We stood there glaring at each other and nobody had to tell me that he had me by the throat and I was fighting for my life. From here on out it would be brass knucks, and I knew it. I tried to get set for it.

"All right," he said, and his voice was hard now, hitting like a hammer. "Here's something maybe you didn't know. We knew Manley got some ideas during his stay in Leavenworth. We figured he'd try something like this before long. But Manley was smart, we didn't learn a thing from him, so we figured our best bet was to find the man who was in it with him. That turned out to be easier than I had hoped, when we found Otto's body in the lake with that flywheel tied to him. That was your big mistake, Hooper, that flywheel."

It wasn't "Joe" now, it was "Hooper," and he said it as though he had a mouthful of quinine.

"That flywheel is the thing that cooked you, Hooper. We have Ike Abrams' word that he took it out of your father's car and left it in the back of your station. No mistake about it, it's the same flywheel. The jury will take Ike's word for that. You and Bunt Manley robbed the box factory and killed the watchman; then you smeared Otto's fingerprints all over the safe to throw me off the track. Finally you brought the body out here, weighted it with that flywheel, then took it out to the lake and dumped it. It's as simple as that and I can prove every damn word of it.

"Have you heard enough? Well, I'm not through yet. There's plenty more. There's something else that started me thinking about you, Hooper. That visit of yours to the box factory. You hadn't been near that factory for years, not since you used to work there, but on the day before the robbery you made the trip just to pay a five-dollar debt. I ask you, does a story like that hold water? Like hell it does! You went out there to get the exact layout in your mind because the robbery was all set for the next night, when you knew the entire payroll would be in the safe. You prowled around the front office, where the safe was, then you went back to the warehouse and talked to some of the workmen."

I was almost ready to explode. "All this talk doesn't prove a damn thing and you know it!"

Otis grinned tightly. "It proves plenty, and I can see your guts crawling. Do you know how long the factory burglar alarm had been installed, Hooper? Just two days! That means that whoever took the money and killed the watchman gave that place a thorough going-over not more than two days before the job. And you're the man, Hooper. I can put my hands on at least twenty people who will testify to it. How does it look to you now, Hooper? The jury will throw the book at you. When the story gets out, you'll be lucky if they don't lynch you on the courthouse lawn."

My voice deserted me. I couldn't make a sound.

"I'm not making any promises, Hooper, but if you'll sign a statement I'll at least see that you get a fair trial."

My brain was numb. I just stood there too sick to move.

Then a light stabbed the darkness outside the cabin, and I heard the sound of my father's old Dodge pulling up in front of my door.

Ray King said, "It's your father, I think, Joe."

"Look," I said. "Don't say anything to him about this. Not now, anyway. He has a patient next door. That's the only reason he's out here."

Otis Miller said nothing. The two of them looked at each other and finally Ray nodded. I went to the door and said, "Dad, is that you?"

"Yes, Joe. It's pretty late for you to be up, isn't it?"

"Some friends of mine dropped in. Anyway, I wanted to stay up till you got here. I don't know how important it is, but his wife seems to think he's getting worse."

I could see him standing there, a stooped, bone-tired old man. After a moment he turned and walked heavily toward Number 2.

"How about it, Hooper?" Otis said. "You ready to sign that statement?"

The brief escape from the sheriff's hammering had given me a chance to get things straight in my mind. At first I felt empty and helpless. I knew they had me. There was absolutely no doubt about it, and I might as well do what they said. So this is the way it ends, Hooper.

After a moment I turned to the sheriff and looked dully into those eyes of his.

That was the thing that saved me.

I had expected to see the iron-hard glint of victory in those eyes. But it wasn't there. There was anticipation, anxiety, expectation, but not that glint of complete victory. At last I recognized what I saw there. Otis Miller's eyes were the eyes of a gambler who had just run an outrageous bluff and was waiting for his opponent to call.

The implication struck me like an icy shower. It jarred me awake, it released the numbness in my brain. Otis Miller didn't have a damn thing on me! Maybe he had tried to run the most fantastic bluff in history, but he still didn't have a leg to stand on and he knew it.

Oh, he knew I was guilty, all right. He was mixed up about Manley, but he had me pegged every inch of the way. But he couldn't prove a bit of it. All that loud talk of his had been so much hogwash in the hope that he could panic me into a confession.

I felt like a teen-ager on his first drunk. I wanted to laugh right in Otis Miller's face and then kick him and Ray King out of my cabin. What I did was look at Otis and grin.

"Now," I said, "are you through, Otis?" The glee of the top dog was bubbling inside me. "Are you finally through shooting off that fat mouth of yours? Because if you are, I've got a few things to say that might interest you."

He reacted just the way I had known he would, as though I had whipped him across the face with a pistol butt.

I had to laugh then; I couldn't hold it back. "Who the hell do you think you are, Otis? None of your talk means a thing. That flywheel story, for instance. There's no way in the world you can prove the flywheel was in my station on the night of the robbery. It was hauled away to the dumping grounds almost a month before, where anybody could have picked it up. As for the bogus bill, I always thought it was a sheriff's duty to take care of things like that. You can suspect anything you please, Otis, but you'd better be damn sure you have proof to back you up before you accuse people of robbery and murder."

He opened his mouth but I didn't give him a chance to say a word.

"That visit to the factory," I said. "No jury is going to convict a man for going out of his way to pay an honest debt. That burglar alarm doesn't prove a thing, either, because any top law officer will tell you that any burglar worth his salt takes care of burglar alarms as a matter of course. That just about blows your conviction sky-high, doesn't it, Otis?"

I wasn't through yet. When you got Otis down, it was a good idea to kick him, just to be safe.

"What else is there?" I said. "Oh, yes, the watch. Well, listen carefully, Otis, because this is what happened to my watch. I missed it tonight just before Bunt Manley drove up for gas. I figured at the time the strap had broken and I'd dropped it somewhere, and I intended to look for it when I wasn't busy. While Manley was here I saw him pick something up, but I didn't think anything about it at the time. Manley wouldn't be above picking up a watch, of course, but I didn't think about that until it was too late. So that's what happened to my watch. Also, while Manley was here I noticed that he had been drinking and mentioned that he shouldn't be driving in his condition, but he wouldn't listen to me. Half drunk, he stalled his car on the railroad tracks and got himself killed by a train. Later, you found my watch near the scene of the accident, which isn't surprising. I'll bet you found a lot of other things, too, didn't you, Otis, scattered clear to hell and gone, probably?"

I had shown the cape to the bull but he hadn't charged. He got red in the face, his throat swelled, veins stood out on his forehead, but he didn't charge because he knew that he couldn't win. Ray King stood stiffly, looking grim, but Otis was almost crazy with rage and frustration. Maybe a full minute went by before he made a sound, before he trusted himself to open his mouth.

Suddenly he wheeled and went to the door, then he turned and came back. "You think you're smart, don't you, Hooper? Well, listen to me."

"You listen to *me!*" I said. "If you think you've got something, you're welcome to use it. Take me down to the courthouse, lock me up, bring me to trial. You try that, Otis, and you'll be the laughingstock of the country. The jury wouldn't be out thirty seconds before they came in with a verdict of not guilty."

That was the reason I was so sure that nothing was going to happen. Otis wasn't going to bring me in until he had the evidence he needed, and he didn't have it. The law of double jeopardy worked in Creston as well as it did in other places, and once they found me not guilty it would be over, no matter what Otis might turn up later.

Ray King touched his boss's arm. "Well, Otis?"

I could see the angry blood pumping in the sheriff's throat, but he took a tight rein on his voice. "You're guilty, Hooper," he said softly. "You're guilty as hell and I won't let up on you until I see you cooked. You can bank on it!"

Then he tramped out, stiffly, like a mechanical man operating on overwound springs. Even the back of his neck looked angry as he went out.

I stood at the door as the two men got in the car, circled the cabin, and headed toward the highway. Well, I had won that round, but he was a bulldog, that Otis Miller. He had his teeth in my throat and he wasn't going to turn loose until I was dead. There was only one answer—I had to get out of Creston, far away from Creston, before he scraped together a real case against me. I heard the door slam at the Sheldon cabin, and when I looked out the window I saw my dad heading for his car. I went to the door and started to speak, but he didn't even look in my direction. He leaned against the car for a moment. Then he looked up at the white clouds sliding under the pale belly of the moon and I thought I heard him say something, but I couldn't catch what it was. Finally he got into his car and drove away.

I kicked the door open and headed for Number 2.

I ran into Paula at the door of the Sheldon cabin; she was just coming out. "Joe," she said quickly, "I'm afraid we're in trouble."

"You can say that again. Do you know who I've been fighting with for the past half hour? The sheriff!"

"At this time of night!"

"The time of day or night doesn't mean a thing to Otis Miller. Didn't you hear the car?"

"I heard it, but I thought it was your father. I thought he had stopped to talk to you before looking at Karl."

"It was the sheriff, all right, and he threw the book at me. He hit me with everything he could get his hands on. Luckily, it wasn't enough to panic me into a confession, the way he had hoped."

Her eyes widened. "Do you mean he actually suspects you of that robbery?"

"He doesn't suspect, he *knows*. There's absolutely no doubt about it in his mind. But he doesn't have the evidence to convince a jury, and that's the only thing that saved me. Paula, we've got to get out of here, and we've got to do it in a hurry!" I went inside, dropped on a chair, and looked at Sheldon, who seemed to be asleep. "What did Dad say about him?" I asked.

"He has a high fever, but he should be all right tomorrow. We'll leave tomorrow night."

I was too tired to argue. Anyway, I needed some rest. All of us did, before starting the trip to Arkansas. Then I remembered something. "You said something about trouble," I said, looking up at her. "What is it?"

"Your father. He knows everything."

I felt the nervous tingling of my scalp. "The factory, the killing? How could he know?"

"He saw those sketches you made for Karl. I had meant to burn them, but so much has happened.... Anyway, he saw them, and the minute he looked at them he knew everything."

A cold void opened in my bowels. This was the beginning of a sickness that I knew would never be cured. Paula sat on the arm of the chair, then put her hands on my shoulders and gently massaged the back of my neck.

"He can just guess," I said. "He doesn't really know."

"He knows," she said, "because I told him. I thought if I laid it on the line for him, it would scare him so that he wouldn't dare go to the police. Now I don't know."

"What do you mean?"

"Your father has a conscience," she said. "A strong one. It will eat at him until he'll finally have to do something about it."

I got out of the chair so suddenly that I almost knocked her off the arm. I went to the door and looked out at the darkness, remembering how he had looked standing there beside his car, his face turned up to the black sky. Paula came over and stood beside me.

"What are we going to do, Joe?"

"What *can* we do?"

Her voice was suddenly brittle, and it was one of those rare times when I felt that she actually understood what it was to be afraid. "Don't you understand?" she said. "He knows everything! Sooner or later—maybe not tomorrow or the next day, but pretty soon—he won't be able to hold it inside him. He'll start talking and he'll tell everything he knows."

"By that time we'll be far away from Creston."

"That won't help us. For murder, they'll come after you, no matter where you are."

"All right," I said tightly, "you think of something. It was your idea to tell him everything."

She said nothing. She just stood there beside me looking out at the night. But somehow I knew what she was thinking. I knew her well enough to guess the solution that would come instinctively to her mind. I took one of her arms and jerked her around to face me.

"You can forget it!" I said. "You can damn well forget it right now!"

There was a flicker of pain in her eyes. "Joe, I don't know what you're talking about."

"You know, all right!" I let her go and she almost fell.

There was nothing—absolutely nothing—that she wouldn't do. She would have killed my father in a minute, because he had become dangerous to her. Several long seconds passed as we stood there staring at each other, as we sized each other up like two savages. Then she closed her eyes, swayed, and leaned against me. Those arms of hers went around my neck and her face tilted up to mine.

"I'm sorry, Joe. You can see right through me, can't you? You can read me like a book."

I said nothing.

"I'm over it now," she said huskily. "Things will work out fine. You'll see."

Chapter Seventeen

The first thing I did the next morning was write a letter.

> Dad:
> I guess you knew this would happen sooner or later. The station and tourist-court business just didn't work out. Everything seems to have gone to pieces this past year—first the business, then breaking up with Beth. There's no reason why I should stay on in Creston, so I'm pulling out. The bank can take over the station, if they want it. They would have done it anyway in another month or so....

I wrote the letter for the jury's benefit, in case I ever had to face a jury. At least they couldn't say I was running away without a legitimate reason. When I finished the letter I went to the station and opened up as usual.

It was a long day, that day. I kept telling myself that in a few hours Creston and all its memories would be behind me, and Paula and I would start building something for ourselves. I never thought about our future, just the beginning of it.

The end I didn't want to know.

I wasn't afraid of my father's telling what he knew. After all, I was his son, and a man doesn't go out of his way to send his son to the electric chair. I actually hated Paula every time I thought of her telling him everything. The hate became so powerful at times that my hands ached to get around that pale, soft throat of hers—but I knew what would happen if I tried it. She would look at me and I would be kissing her.

The best thing to do was forget it. My father was hurt and there was no way to ease the pain. And there was no changing the way I felt about Paula, either. Forget it.

I tried. I cleaned all around the grease rack and straightened things in back of the station, and somehow the morning became afternoon and after a long while Ike came, as he always did.

"How's it goin', Joe?"

"All right, I guess. You take over for a while. I think I'll go back to the shack and wash up a little."

"Sure."

Ike thought I was acting strange, and I guess I was. But every hour now seemed like a year, and I kept looking at my wrist for the watch that wasn't there. Every time I did it I thought of Otis Miller and wondered if he and Ray King had dug up anything else or if they would be back to take up the questioning again.

They didn't come back. Maybe they had somebody watching me, but I doubted it. So I went to my cabin, took a cold shower, and gave myself a few minutes to settle down, and then I began packing. I threw all my clothes into suitcases, rounded up a few other things I would need, like toilet articles and razor blades, and not until that minute did I remember the gun. That revolver that Sheldon had given me. The one that had killed Otto Finney.

I didn't want to keep it on me, but I sure couldn't leave it here in my cabin. Finally I shoved it into my waistband, under my shirt. It felt cold and deadly, like a coiled snake.

It was almost sundown when I left my cabin. Ike was doing something in front of the station but he didn't seem to be looking my way, so I went over to the Sheldons'. Paula and her husband were having what sounded like a serious talk when I came in, but they broke it off and Paula stood up.

"Are you ready, Joe?"

"I was ready days ago." I looked at Sheldon. "How do you feel?"

"Better than I did yesterday. Have you heard any more from the sheriff?"

"No, but that doesn't mean he's stopped working on me." I turned to Paula. "You've got everything ready to go, haven't you? I want to pull out as soon as it's time to close the station. With a little luck we ought to be well into Arkansas by sunup tomorrow."

"Everything's ready," she said. "But I want your father to have another look at Karl before we leave."

I stared at her. "Are you crazy? We've pushed my father just about as far as he'll go. It simply won't do to have him come again."

"Would you like it better if Karl's arm became infected again, and we had to go to another doctor somewhere? A doctor we didn't know?" She turned suddenly, went to the window, and stood looking flatly at the sleazy curtains. "It doesn't seem very smart to me," she said.

"The answer is no," I said.

"All right. But it seems like a little thing to fight about. If your father just brought out some sulfa, we'd have nothing to worry about. We wouldn't have to depend on doctors."

"No."

But I was weakening, and she could tell it. She turned from the window and said, "I know what's worrying you. You just don't want to see him, do you? Well, you won't have to. I can drive into town and pick up the drugs and dressings we'll need; all you have to do is let him know I'm coming."

It seemed a little thing. It didn't seem possible that it could cause my father any more pain. After a moment I said, "It's no good. You don't even know where the house is."

"I can find it. I've been in bigger towns than Creston. All you have to do is give me the directions."

What a hell of a fuss about nothing! I thought. It was beginning to grate on my nerves. "All right!" I said finally. "If it will make you happy, you can drive in and get the medicine you need. I guess it's all right."

"Of course it's all right," she said. "The sheriff doesn't suspect me and Karl. If I should be seen, it wouldn't mean anything."

"I know all that, and I said it was all right!"

I was getting jumpy, much too jumpy. I just wanted to get away from here—far away. That was the only thing I could think of. I walked to the door and said, "I think I'll go to the station."

Sheldon said, "You'd better send your helper home and close the station yourself when the time comes."

I nodded and went out.

Darkness had settled over that bald Oklahoma prairie, but it was still early and there was plenty of traffic on the highway. As I came around to the front of the station I saw that Ike had washed down the cement driveway by the gas pumps, and now he was spraying water around the station to settle the dust.

I didn't know just what to do about Ike. We were friends and he had been a lot of help to me with the station, and I didn't feel like picking up and leaving him without a word. He turned and grinned when he heard me come up.

"Hot as hell tonight."

"Yeah." I went inside and checked the cash register. I took out enough to cover Ike's salary for two weeks and it just about cleaned it out. "Ike," I called, "can you come here a minute?"

"Sure." He hung up the water hose and came inside. I handed him the money.

"What's this, Joe?"

"Two week's pay, Ike. It looks like you're out of a job." He looked as though he had been slapped. "You mean I'm fired, Joe?"

"I mean the business is on the rocks. You know as well as I do that we've barely made expenses these past few months, if that."

He stood there for a moment, looking stupid. He scratched his head. "You mean you're throwin' it up, Joe? You're quittin'?"

"There's nothing left to do. If you can't make this kind of business pay during the tourist season, then you might as well give up."

He looked uncomfortable as he took the money, folded it slowly, and put it in his pocket. "By golly, Joe, I'm sorry to hear it. I kind of liked working out here. You've been a good boss."

"Thanks, Ike."

"If there's anything I can do...."

"Just one thing, Ike." I counted out forty dollars, most of it from my pocket. "This is what I owe the gas company on the last delivery. Will you contact them tomorrow and pay them off?"

His forehead wrinkled at that one. "Ike," I said, "I'm just sick of this place. When I close up tonight I don't want to have to look at it or think about it again. Maybe I'll just pack up and go fishing or something. Anyway, I'd appreciate it if you'd take care of the gasoline people."

"Well, sure, Joe, if that's the way you want it. I guess I know how you feel. The business has been pretty much of a disappointment, at that, I guess."

"Ike," I said, "that's the understatement of the year." I had expected something of a fuss, or at least a pep talk, for Ike was a great one for seeing a thing through to the end. But he was surprisingly calm, as though he had seen it coming from a long way off—and maybe he had. "Well, Joe...."

"I guess that's it, Ike."

We said a few more things, none of them making much sense, and finally I got Ike in his Ford and headed him for town.

The last small thread was cut. I was free. Automatically, I began locking up, bringing in the display cases of oil, disconnecting the water hose, locking the pumps. I looked out at the highway and thought: I'm free! Free to go anywhere I damn please!

Far up the highway I could see the lights atop the towering grain elevators. Creston, Oklahoma. If I never saw it again, it would be fine with me.

Just as I finished locking up I heard Paula starting the Buick. She drove around to the front of the station. I went around to the driver's side of the car and thought: Christ, she can be beautiful when she wants to! I'll never forget how she looked at that moment as she reached through the window and traced her fingers lightly over my chest.

"It won't be long now, Joe. Within another hour this town will be behind us."

"I'm ready."

"We'll start just as soon as I get back. Just as soon as I pick up the medicine and dressings from your father. You didn't forget to call him, did you?"

"I didn't have a chance. Ike left just a few minutes ago. But I'll do it now, if you're still sure it's necessary."

"I explained it to you, Joe. It's insurance we've got to have. If Karl's arm should get bad again, we won't find another doctor as co-operative as your father."

I still didn't like it, but when Paula got hold of something she wouldn't turn it loose without a fight. And right now I didn't feel like a fight. "All right," I said finally, "I guess you'll have it your way."

I had to unlock the station again to get to the phone. I got the number and listened to the ringing at the other end, and at last a thousand-year-old voice, a voice without life, said, "Hello."

"Dad, this is Joe. I've got a little favor to ask of you."

He didn't say a thing. For a moment I thought he had hung up on me, but then I heard the hum of the open line and knew that he was still there.

"Dad, this is the last thing I'm going to ask of you. Believe me, it is. You know this man you've been treating; well, he and his wife are pulling out tonight. They're pulling out for good and you'll never hear of them again. But the woman wants you to give her some medicine, just in case her husband's arm starts acting up again. I'm sending her over to pick it up. Is that all right?"

There was only the hum of the wire.

"Dad, are you still there?"

"Yes."

"You'll let her have the medicine, won't you? Sulfa, or whatever you think best."

"Do I have a choice, Joe?"

I felt like hell. For a moment I just stood there with the receiver in my hand, unable to think of anything else to say, and finally I hung up.

I went outside, where Paula was waiting. "It's all right," I said. "But make it fast. Don't drag it out any longer than is absolutely necessary. I'm afraid he's had just about all he can take."

I told her how to get to the house, which wasn't much of a job. The town wasn't big enough to get lost in, and anyway, the streets were clearly marked. She smiled faintly and squeezed my hand, then she put the Buick in gear and left me standing there. God, I thought, I'll be glad when it's over!

After I got the station locked again, I went around to Number 2 to see how Sheldon was doing. He was doing fine. He had his clothes on and was doing some packing as I came in.

"You're looking pretty good," I said.

He looked at me, then looked away, fast. "I'll feel better when we're away from here."

"Well, it shouldn't be long now. It won't take Paula long to pick up the medicine."

He wouldn't look at me. He kept fiddling with a shirt that he was trying to get folded, keeping me behind him. He looked nervous and pale, but I put that down to his sickness.

I said, "You want me to help you with that?"

"No!" He turned on me then, and there was something in those eyes of his that put ice in my veins.

"What's the matter with you?" I said.

"Nothing! Just get out of here and leave me alone! Do you have to stand there watching me, watching every move I make?"

"Look," I said, "you're pretty jumpy, aren't you? Hadn't you better just sit down and take it easy?"

I thought for a minute that he was going to spring at me. Then he seemed to go to mush inside. He leaned against the bed, then he sat down and put his face in his hands. I guess that was when the first germ of fear became implanted in my brain. I looked at Sheldon and knew that something was wrong, something was wrong as hell. Here he had just pulled through a serious sickness and within an hour would be on his way to freedom, and he looked like a man getting ready to walk his last mile. I stepped over to him, pushed his head back, and made him look at me.

"What's eating you, Sheldon?"

"Nothing."

"Oh, yes, there is! Something's got its fangs in your guts and I want to know what it is."

"I tell you it's nothing!"

I think I already knew. In the dark cellar of my mind I knew what it was. Panic's cold feet raced up my spine as I grabbed the front of Sheldon's shirt. I heard myself saying it, before the thought was really clear in my mind.

"Out with it, Sheldon! Does it have anything to do with my father?"

He whined, and I slammed him across the face with the back of my fist.

"Goddamn you, you'd better tell it and tell it fast, or you're going to curse the day you were born! Has it got anything to do with my father?"

But he was too sick and too scared and too weak to make a sound. I hit him again, knowing it was hopeless, knowing that it was a waste of time, but I hit him. His mouth came open and his teeth were red with blood.

"It's Paula, isn't it?" I almost yelled at him. "What's she going to do? What's she got in that hard little brain of hers?"

But I already knew. It was in Sheldon's eyes, gleaming there in the twin small seas of pain. Paula was going to kill my father. He knew too much about her, so she was going to kill him.

I should have guessed. I should have known when I first saw that look in her eyes the night before. That was when she had made up her mind.

I felt sick. All day she had been planning it. She had made up that story about having to go after medicine, knowing that I wouldn't have the guts to face my father myself, now that he knew all about us. She was going to murder him. Right this minute she was on her way.

It seemed like a lifetime as I stood there, my fist doubled, ready to hit Sheldon again. I thought: She must have known that I'd find out. She couldn't keep a thing like this a secret. How she meant to explain it to me, I couldn't guess—but she would think of something. I knew her well enough for that. With the help of that ripe mouth and soft body she would think of something, and make it sound logical enough, when the time came.

But the time would not come. I was almost sorry as I thought it. The end had already arrived.

I let Sheldon go and he fell to the floor, still whimpering. I could have killed him without a qualm, as easily as stepping on a spider, but there was no time for it. I was out of the cabin and racing through the night toward my car.

I drove like a crazy man, deaf and dumb, blind to everything but the grayish highway and the dazzling lights that rushed at me from the darkness and then fell swiftly behind. I assaulted the night with speed, split it open and made it scream. Past the floodlighted oil-field supply houses, the wind rushing. Past the big motels and the crumby shacks. Past the towering grain elevators; pale, unbelievable giants in the darkness, topped with blinking red lights. Over the railroad overpass and down the breath-taking slope on the other side to Creston.

How I got there, I didn't know. But I was there. I had not passed the Buick—that was one thing I was sure of—and that meant that Paula had reached Creston before me. I drove as though each second were a matter of life or death. And it was. I skirted the heart of town to avoid traffic. Maybe, just maybe....

The tires screamed as I took a corner too fast, too sharp. There was a spine-shattering jar as the front wheel hit the curb. The explosion blew a ragged hole in the night, in my hopes. The right front tire went out and the Chevy careened sideways, jumped the curb, crashed into a squat cement marker, and came to a shuddering halt.

The starter wouldn't work. I jabbed it and there was nothing but silence. Up and down the street doors came open, people came out to see what the noise was about. The car wouldn't start. Maybe it was a battery cable broken loose, maybe it was something else. Whatever it was, I didn't have time to look into it. I got out of the car and began running.

People were pouring into the street. I ignored their shouted questions. I ran.

Through alleys, up streets, across yards, over hedges I ran. From one end of town to the other, almost, I ran, with fire in my lungs and ice in my belly. I almost forgot why I was running. The muscles in my thighs quivered, my knees wanted to buckle. Just a minute, I thought. Rest just a minute. Give yourself a chance to breathe. And then I would remember and keep going.

The Buick was the first thing I saw. I passed the church and the Langford house, and then I wiped the sweat from my eyes and there was the blue Buick parked at the curb in front of my father's house. How long it had been there, I didn't know. But not too long. Paula would have taken it easy on a strange street in a strange town. She couldn't have driven so very fast. Whether or not it had been fast enough, only time would tell.

I almost fell on my face when I reached the car. I couldn't get enough air into my lungs, no matter how hard I tried. Then I saw that the car was empty, and that gave me a new strength. I staggered like a drunk man, a straw man, an empty shell of a man. I shoved the front gate open and stumbled up the walk to the front porch. The porch light was on. The front door was open, because of the heat, and there was a light in the front room. There was also a light on the south side of the house, in my father's bedroom. I noticed all this as I stumbled toward the porch. And then I saw Paula.

She was standing almost in the center of the front room, calm and erect, with no flicker of emotion on her beautiful face. In her hand was Sheldon's .38 revolver and it was pointed at the door of my father's bedroom.

An ocean of hopelessness washed over me. I was too late. I wanted to let go and sink to the bottom depths and never look up again.

And then I heard my father calling, his voice muffled, "Just a minute. I'll be with you in just a minute." Thank God! My heart took up its beating again, and now I could see the situation as it was. My father had been napping, probably—about the only kind of sleep he got. Obviously, Paula had got here just ahead of me. She had stepped into the front room and called out, and now....

And now the nightmare was reality. My father would open the bedroom door. Perhaps he would get one startled look at Paula and the gun, and then he would be dead. Panic and exhaustion held me frozen. I tried to call out to Paula, and no sound came from my throat.

The door to my father's bedroom opened. He stood framed in the doorway, wearing a faded blue bathrobe and ragged carpet slippers. His thin hair was tousled, his eyes swollen with sleep, and I don't think he even saw Paula's gun before the sudden blast cracked the night.

I stood there, my throat swollen with a yell that would not come out. My father did not fall. Startled, he jerked to one side. With wide, unbelieving eyes, he stared at Paula as she took one step toward him, then another....

Slowly, languidly, gracefully—almost beautifully—she died.

She seemed almost to melt to the floor. There was hardly a sound as Paula went down to her knees, and then she fell over on her shoulder and lay staring blankly at the front wall of the room. The thing I noticed was how cold and beautiful she looked. Her mouth seemed brazenly red.

Not until later did I realize that I had taken my own .38 from my waistband, and that the barrel was hot, and that a whisper of burned powder had become mingled with the clean smell of the summer night. Perhaps several seconds went by before I realized fully that Paula was dead and that I had killed her.

There seemed nothing to do after that. Nothing I wanted to do.

I sat on the front porch and held my face in my hands, and after a while the sheriff came.

Chapter Eighteen

The wall clock in the sheriff's office said seven o'clock. We had been there almost eight hours, Otis, Ray King, and a county stenographer taking down everything I said. The sheriff didn't know it, but he was doing me a favor by keeping me there. I didn't want to be left alone. Every time I closed my eyes I saw Paula. I could imagine what it would be like if I tried to sleep. A great numbness had taken hold of me now, and that was the way I wanted to keep it. I was a hollow man, without feelings, without conscience, with sensibilities, but I knew that wouldn't last if they left me to myself.

Otis Miller, his thick face beginning to sag with weariness, sat staring at me with red-rimmed eyes. Unbelieving eyes. He had known me all my life, I guess. Doc Hooper's boy. Tackle on the high-school football team, soldiered with a tank outfit in Africa and France. A little erratic, maybe, but would settle down eventually and marry Steve Langford's girl. That was the way he'd had me pegged, more than likely, before the robbery. He was trying to figure out what would make a boy like that turn to robbing and killing.

He wasn't having much luck. Fatigue had dulled the edge of his imagination. He had all the facts before him—I had given them to him, almost gladly—but they were just the bare facts and didn't tell the whole story. I was guilty, all right. There was no doubt in the sheriff's mind about that. It was the *why* of the thing that stumped him.

"All right, Hooper," he said heavily, "let's hear it again."

He wasn't giving up yet, and I was glad of that. I wanted to keep talking, I wanted to have people around me. That was the important thing. I just didn't want to be taken to a cell and left to myself.

"All right, Otis. What do you want to know?" My voice sounded lifeless. I felt lifeless and hollow. It was a strange, cold feeling.

"First," the sheriff said, "let's get the main facts straight again. Is it true that on the night of the fourteenth you and this Karl Sheldon robbed Max Provo's box factory?"

"It's true."

Like a wooden dummy talking.

"And on that same night you killed old Otto Finney and disposed of the body in the lake?"

"True."

A wooden dummy. You put your hand inside the hollow dummy, and you press on something, and its mouth comes open and it seems to talk. That was the way it seemed to me. The words just came out and I had nothing to do with them at all.

"Who helped you dispose of the body?"

Something went wrong with the dummy. The mouth came open but the words wouldn't come out. I couldn't make myself say Paula's name.

"The woman?" the sheriff said. "The Sheldon woman?"

I nodded.

"Then what happened?"

"That's about all. We split the money and they went away."

"Where did they go?"

"Somewhere in Texas, I think."

"All right. We have all the details about Bunt Manley and the Sheldon woman. You killed them, too; is that right?"

I nodded.

"The stenographer has it all down. Do you have anything to add to your original statement concerning the deaths of Manley and the Sheldon woman?"

"I guess not."

He turned to the stenographer. "For the record, you'd better put in that this confession was not obtained through duress or force. Is that right, Hooper?"

"Yes, that's right."

"Do you have anything else to add to the statement before it's typed up?"

At some point during the night Otis had dropped his toughness. He was almost gentle now. "Do you want to talk to a lawyer before signing the statement?"

Sheldon was still alive and would talk his head off, and I knew it. I said, "A lawyer couldn't help me."

Otis gave the signal and the stenographer gathered up his notes and left the room. The sheriff and his deputy sat there staring at me.

It was all over. Otis said, "Well, Hooper, we might as well go over to the jail."

For the first time in eight hours a real emotion went to work on me. Fear. Fear of being put in a cell and left to myself.

Ray King said, "Is there something else you want to say?"

Suddenly I felt an insane urge to laugh. "We almost got away with it," I heard myself saying. "We came so close!"

"You're wrong, Hooper," the sheriff said. "You couldn't be more wrong if you tried." Suddenly he pushed himself back from his desk, still not satisfied with the bare facts. He still wanted an answer, but he wasn't sure of the question. He said, "You never had a chance, Hooper. We're not completely stupid down here. We had you nailed to that box-factory job and, in spite of what you think, we could have made a good case in court. But we also knew you didn't pull the robbery alone. I figured Bunt Manley helped you, but I was wrong in that. Anyway, we didn't want to pull you in until we found out who was in it with you. With all the circumstantial evidence we had on you, do you think we'd just forget about you?"

He snorted. "We had you watched day and night, Hooper. Ike Abrams or one of my deputies reported every move you made. You thought you were going to leave this town scot-free, didn't you? Well, let me tell you, you couldn't have got away in a Patton tank. We were just waiting for you or the Sheldons to make a mistake, and when you did make one it was a lulu!"

I stared at him. "You had Ike spying on me all the time?"

"You're a murderer, Hooper. Ike was doing a job for the sheriff's office. And it didn't take him long to tie you up with Sheldon's wife. After that it was just a matter of waiting. There's one thing I'm curious about, though. Why did you kill her?"

I closed my eyes and there she was.

I could almost feel sorry for Sheldon; he wouldn't die easy in the chair. Maybe I wouldn't, either, but the prospect was not frightening now. I had died the instant my finger had pulled the trigger on that .38. With a woman like Paula it seemed ridiculous to think such thoughts—but I had loved her. I must have loved her to have done the things I had done.

Ray King said, "Maybe I'll never understand it, Joe, but I'd like to try. You threw over a fine girl like Beth Langford, then turned to robbing and murdering because of a woman like Paula Sheldon. Why?"

I thought of the cell that was waiting for me. When I reached it I wanted to be able to drop into dreamless, thoughtless oblivion—and the time was not yet.

I looked at them and they were waiting for the answer. They wanted a simple, clear-cut answer, and there wasn't any.

It was a long story. Almost a month ago, I thought; that was when I saw her for the first time. That was when the Buick stopped on the highway in front of the station. Less than a month ago it had been. It seemed like a thousand lifetimes.

Otis and Ray were waiting and I didn't know where to begin. And then I thought dully: Begin at the beginning, and maybe there will be an answer there for you, as well as for them. And I said:

"This is the way it was...." And I started at the beginning.

THE END

Whom Gods Destroy
By Clifton Adams

Chapter One

I was in Bakersfield, California when the news came. It was the busiest part of the lunch hour and I was slicing tomatoes to go with two orders of cutlets when the Western Union kid came back to the kitchen and said, "You Roy Foley?"

I said I was and he handed me the telegram and a pad to sign.

Somebody was dead. I knew that much because, in my family, that's the only thing a telegram can mean. For a moment I held the envelope in my hand, looking at it, knowing what was in it, and feeling absolutely nothing. Not even curiosity. The orders were piling up and it seemed more important to get those orders out than to see what was in the telegram.

So I went ahead and fixed up the two orders of cutlets and dished up the vegetables and put the two platters in the service window. Then there was a little breathing spell so I took out the envelope and opened it. It said: "George passed away today. Funeral Friday." It was signed "May Lou Smothers."

So help me, it took a full minute or more before it finally came to me that "George" was my old man.

About that time Charley Burnstead, the counter man, put his head in the service window and said, "Burn two on one!"

I put the two hamburgers on the grill and split the buns and put them on to toast. And that was the way I got the news.

They kept me hopping all through lunch hour. But a fry cook's job is a pretty mechanical thing once you get it down, so I just stood there, taking the orders and getting them out, and about the only thing I could think of was, What am I going to do now? About one o'clock, business started to slack off, and in another half hour the place was practically empty. I sat down at the cook table. I guess I ate a sandwich, but I don't remember. One question kept hammering at me—What the hell am I going to do?

I really didn't get down to thinking about the old man until the relief cook came on at four o'clock. Then I took my apron off and went around the block to where my rooming house was. That day I think I saw the rooming house for the first time—really saw it as it actually was. A two-story clapboard house, the porch sagging, the roof patched crazy-quilt fashion with split-open tin cans, the dirty white paint peeling and the rotten wood showing through like open sores. I thought, You've come a long way, Foley!

I went up the ancient stairs and down the dark hall and unlocked the door to my room. I stood in the doorway for a moment, just looking at it—the scabby iron bedstead, the sagging mattress, the almost-black bureau with the mahogany veneer peeling back at the edges, the litter, the dirt, windows smeared. A great place you've got here, Foley! Just like home, you might say. Exactly like home. Geez, it was, and that's the thing that made me sick.

It began to work slowly then, the association of stray thoughts. The rooming house, Big Prairie, home, the old man—and finally the telegram. I lay on the bed and I thought, God, the old man's dead! I turned the words over and over in my mind, trying to give the thought reality, trying to feel something about it. About all I felt was mad—and kind of scared.

This May Lou Smothers who sent the telegram, I couldn't remember her at all. Whoever she was, she kept a damn tight jaw when it came to paying for telegrams.

I got off the bed and started walking up and down the room, smoking one cigarette after another as fast as I could burn them. There was one thing you couldn't get around; dead people had to be buried, and burying cost money. This was the thing that scared me And he'd left it to me!

I wasn't sure just what it was that made up my mind, but I knew I had to go back. I hated it and it scared me to think about it, but when I looked into the mirror and saw my face looking back at me it was like opening the book on the future and reading the last page. A man can run just so far before he goes over the edge.

All right, I thought, stop running. Go back and start again. And fear stood there beside me, empty and gutless, and it laughed. You haven't got the guts, Foley! What would you say to her? What would you do if she laughed? The thought left me weak. But there is something stronger than fear. It grows inside you, poisonous and festering, and it tells you its name is Pride, but it's a liar. Its name is Hate.

That night I went around to the sandwich joint and told them I'd got some news from home and had to go back to Oklahoma. The next morning I went around to the used-car lot to see what I could get for my prewar Chevy, and then I went back to my room and counted up what I had. It came to a little over four hundred dollars.

Four hundred lousy dollars to show for fourteen years' work.

I spent eighteen dollars and ninety-five cents on a second-hand suitcase, and I brushed it until it looked pretty good. There was one good suit in the closet, a single-breasted drape I'd bought the day I hit the three-horse parlay at Tan Foran, and a pair of black Florsheims. I packed them carefully, along with plenty of white shirts, and threw in underwear and socks. I went downstairs and used the rooming-house phone to call the bus station, and the girl said I could catch a Greyhound for Big Prairie, Oklahoma, at five o'clock that afternoon.

I had plenty of time to think during the next couple of days. Maybe you never rode a cross-country bus halfway across the United States, and if you haven't this is what it's like. The first couple of hours aren't so bad. If a baby starts crying, you shrug it off and look at the scenery. You get off at the rest stops and have a Coke and a sandwich and you feel pretty good. Then night comes and you rent a pillow. You doze for two or three hours and then you wake up with a baby yelling in your ear, and you've got a crick in your back. Then you begin to notice that you feel dirty. You rub your fingers together and there's grit. You touch your face and it's the same thing. Your beard starts coming out and scratching your neck, and you see that you've got cigarette ashes all over you.

Finally the sun comes up, and by this time you've taken off your coat and loosened your tie and you don't care how you look. Your eyes begin to burn from the beat of the desert sun, and a feeling of hopelessness gets hold of you as you watch the wasteland crawl by treadmill-like under the wheels of the bus. Bleak Arizona, standing raw and red; earth-torn New Mexico; the seemingly endless wastes of west Texas. The miles drag out, and out, and now no way you can sit will be comfortable. Your back starts hurting at the shoulders and the ache starts crawling down your spine until it gets to the end, and there it builds a little fire, and the fire gets hotter and hotter. Then some farmer going ten miles up the road sits down beside you, and you swear that, by God, you'll tear his throat open if he as much as asks for a match.

About that time you had better be getting close to your destination.

It was midmorning when the bus finally got to Big Prairie and I had almost forgotten what I'd come for. I stood on the sidewalk waiting for the driver to get the bags out of the luggage compartment. What I was going to do next, I didn't know. It was hard to believe that I had ever seen the town before. The bus station and a lot of other places had gone up since I had lived there as a kid. I got my bag finally and asked a porter if there was a place where I could clean up, and he said there was a pay shower in the men's room.

I used the shower. I lathered and let hot water run over me, and then I lathered again and just soaked. After I shaved and changed into a clean outfit from the skin out I began to feel a little better. My blue suit was wrinkled but it looked pretty good. A hot bath, clean clothes, a well-cut suit—they can do wonders for a man. I looked pretty good. I tried to think of the old man, only a few blocks away, lying dead. I accepted it, but it still didn't change the way I felt.

The cab driver sized me up as somebody, and he jumped out of the front seat and grabbed my bag and said, "Yes sir! Where to, sir?"

"Seven-twelve Burk Street."

He turned his head and gave me a quick look, and I could see what he was thinking, the punk. Geez, Burk Street! He slammed the cab into gear.

Every town has a Burk Street, or one just like it. It's usually on the east side because most towns grow to the west, and it's right down there with the mills and warehouses and railroads, where the center of town used to be but isn't any more. Big Prairie started out as a little crossroads place. Then they discovered oil across the river, to the south, and Big Prairie became what they call a boom town. Oil-field workers moved in with their families, and there wasn't any place for them to stay so they started building these little knock-up houses of clapboard and cement blocks down by the river, and that was the way Burk Street got started. When the boom was over the oil-field workers moved out, and the houses started falling down until people like us moved in and began patching them up. That was twenty years ago, and people still lived down there. The houses were still falling down and they were still trying to patch them up.

But the rest of town had changed since I had left. It was a long way from being a city, still it was a good-sized place, sprawling out across the prairie like these Oklahoma towns do. Down by the river I could see the smokestacks of a factory.

I leaned forward and said, "Isn't that Cedar Street down there?"

"Yeah." He had me spotted. He wasn't wasting any "sirs" on me now.

"Turn left on it," I heard myself saying.

I don't know just why I did it. On the bus I'd told myself a thousand times that Cedar Street was in the past, and so was *she*. I told myself to forget it, take care of the funeral and then get out of Oklahoma. It didn't do any good. When the time came, I had to see it again, although I knew it wouldn't be the same.

"Stop here," I said.

The driver pulled up to the curb.

It was still there, but it didn't seem the same. The paint was peeling and one shutter was gone and another was hanging by one hinge. The house didn't look as big and proud as it had looked to me as a kid, but there was still something about it that made my guts draw in. There was a cardboard sign staked in the weedy front yard that said "Room and Board." She didn't live there any more.

I said, "Do you know where the Johnsons live now?"

He turned around, not knowing just what I was getting at. "You mean old Judge Johnson? He's dead."

"He had a daughter. Her name was Lola."

"Mister—" He was beginning to get tired of this. "Mister, a lot of people have daughters named something or other. I don't keep up with all of them."

He started to fish for a cigarette, then thought of something. "Come to think of it, the old judge did have a girl, but I forget what her name was. She's married to the county attorney."

That would be Lola. Just thinking of the name made me shrink up inside, and for one wild moment I thought I was going to be sick.

We hit Burk Street and it looked even worse than I'd remembered. What I remembered as houses were now unpainted, patched-up shacks stuck away here and there between junk yards and garages and used-car lots. The ones with front porches were piled high with secondhand hub caps and radiators and maybe a fender or two. The driver pulled up at 712.

God, I thought, is this really the place? Is this the house I lived in for eighteen years?

I took my bag and walked up to the picket fence. Most of the pickets were missing, and the ones that were still there were unpainted or broken. The gate sagged open on one hinge. The house was older, tireder, sagged a little more, but it was the same house all right. I stepped up to the front porch and a board cracked, almost gave away under me. I pushed the torn screen door open and walked into the front room. There was a stale, dusty smell about the place in spite of the open doors and windows. I walked to the kitchen, the bedroom, the little lean-to affair that had once been my room. There was nothing familiar about it. I was a stranger walking around in an empty house.

All I could think of was, What am I going to do? They've probably got him in a funeral parlor somewhere. But would a funeral parlor take him if there wasn't somebody there to pay the expenses? I wondered if three hundred and fifty dollars would be enough to take care of everything. If it wasn't, would they let me pay it out so much a month, like buying a car? I knew one thing, though. The county wasn't going to bury him.

I decided I'd better go somewhere and start calling the funeral parlors and find out where the old man was. Then it would be time to figure out a way to swing it. Just as I got to the front door, a battered '41 Buick rattled to a stop by the front gate and a little bald-headed guy and a fat woman got out.

I walked out on the porch and the woman made some kind of noise in her throat before she said, "Roy?"

And that minute it came to me who May Lou Smothers was, the woman who'd sent the telegram. She was the old man's sister, but I had forgotten that. I hadn't even known if she was still alive. They started coming toward me then, both of them looking kind of funny, and about the time May Lou reached the gate she started bawling.

"Roy!" she sobbed. "Roy!"

She grabbed for me, but I side-stepped and opened the door again. May Lou's husband—his name was Albert, I remembered—looked about as uncomfortable as I felt. We shook hands and his wife stood there with tears running down her fat face.

"I just got into town," I said. "My plane got grounded in Albuquerque and that made me a little late, but I got here as fast as I could after I got your telegram."

Albert Smothers nodded heavily. "You can't tell about airplanes, I guess, but we forgot that you might be flyin'. It's a sad thing, though—a sad thing that you couldn't get here in time. Your Pa's put away, boy. They put him away real nice."

That left me stunned for a minute. The telegram said Friday, and today was—I counted the days in my mind, and, by God it *was* Friday!

"But how?" I said. "I mean there were things to be taken care of. How could they go on and have the funeral if there wasn't anybody here?"

I knew one thing: Albert and May Lou hadn't taken care of the funeral expenses. And about that time a thought hit me and I must have lost my head for a minute. I reached out and grabbed the front of Albert's shirt.

"The county didn't do it, did they?" My voice rasped like a saw on a bone, even in my own ears. "I've never taken charity, and, by God, I'm not going to start now!"

Albert shook his head quickly. I think I was twisting his collar too tightly to let him talk.

"Then how did he get buried? I know he didn't have any money of his own."

May Lou stopped bawling and got a hold on herself. "Roy, we didn't even know you was comin'," she managed. "We didn't even know if you had the money to come." Then she brightened a little. "You look like you're doin' right well, though."

I had held myself in about as long as I could stand it. "Goddamnit, can't I get a simple question answered? Who buried the old man?"

"Why, the Women's Christian Aid Society."

I felt myself growing cold all over.

"A lady came around yesterday," she blubbered on. "A real nice lady. She said she understood how it was and all, and said the Women's Aid Society was to help people like that, good God-fearin' people, when we was in trouble." Then she began to whine. "Roy, we didn't know you was doing so good. You never wrote to your Pa. You never let us know. But we knew you wouldn't want the county to put him away—and Albert and me, we didn't have the money."

"So the 'nice lady' came around," I said bitterly, "and you let her Women's Christian Aid Society do it! Just like the old man was a pauper."

"Well, he didn't have any money...."

"I'll pay them back!" I was almost yelling by this time. "I'll give them back every damn cent. Get out! God, you make me sick, both of you! Just get out and leave me alone!"

They got out. I paced up and down the floor like a wild man until I heard the old Buick pull away, then I went out of the house and across the street to the salvage shop.

There was a pay phone and I had a hell of a time finding a coin. My hands shook so much that it must have taken two or three minutes to get the change and find the number in the directory.

"Hello?"

"Is this the headquarters for the Women's Christian Aid Society?"

"Yes, it is, sir. May I help you?"

"You took care of the funeral expenses for a G. A. Foley today. I want to know what those expenses came to."

"Oh, yes. Mrs. Keating took care of that personally."

"Who?"

"Mrs. Lola Keating, our president."

I sucked my stomach in as though I had been gut-shot.

"Mr. Keating wouldn't be the county attorney, would he?"

"Why, yes, he is. Just a moment, sir, and I'll get the information...."

I hung up. If anybody had spoken to me at that moment I would have killed him.

Chapter Two

This is the way it begins. This is how it is when you're young and your name is Roy Foley and you live on Burk Street.

To begin with, you don't remember much about your old lady because she died when you were six. Your old man is a cobbler when he's not drunk. He works in shoe repair shops putting half soles and rubber heels on shoes for people like us who can't afford to buy another pair. Sometimes he comes home at night, sometimes he doesn't.

At first you don't realize that anything is wrong. You roll hoops and fish for mud-cats and play on-and-over with the rest of the kids on Burk Street, and you figure that's the way things are. It's not a big town, still you don't see much of it except Burk Street until you start going to school. There's a law or something that says all kids have to go to school, and that's when it begins to come to you that everybody isn't the same.

The kids on Cedar Street, for instance. They go barefoot two or three days out of the summer just for the hell of it. Not like you, from June to September. You begin to understand that some kids don't have to worry about wearing out shoe leather, because their parents are lawyers or doctors or something and they've got plenty of money and live in big white-painted houses on Cedar Street. But it's not a big town, and you all go to the same school.

It doesn't take you long to find out that most of the Cedar Street gang are pretty snotty. So you get into fights with them and usually beat hell out of them because you're pretty good at that kind of thing. You've got a vague idea that the thing can be settled as simply as that. If you just beat hell out of a few of them they'll come to believe you're as good as they are.

It doesn't work that way. It takes you quite a while to see that you're not getting anywhere, but finally you see that fighting isn't the answer. So you start studying, long hard hours.

The teachers say you've got a good brain, better than any brain in the room, maybe. You don't know just why it's so important to make these snotty Cedar Streeters see that you're somebody, but it is. You lie awake at nights and it gnaws at you and you ask yourself, Why is it so important? I'm smarter than any of them, I can whip any of them. But I'm not one of them.

In your second year of high school you think you've found the answer. You go out for football. You're big and tough and fast and you've got a head on your shoulders. You're a natural quarterback. You get your picture in the paper and write-ups and State University sends scouts down to watch you do your stuff. But what really gets you is the yelling from the sidelines. You hear them yelling your name and it goes to your head like high wine. And after you make a touchdown they all pound you on the back and holler at you and tell you you're the best damn quarterback old Big Prairie High ever had, and you feel so proud that you're ready to bust. You're finally getting somewhere.

And there's a girl, too. But we'll have to go back again to understand that.

You have to go clear back to the beginning to understand about Lola, because it was Lola who put the hunger in you to pull yourself out of Burk Street and be somebody.

Lola was a symbol at first, and hardly a person at all. She was nine years old and she wore a white dress and black patent-leather slippers, and she was the most beautiful thing you'd ever seen because she represented something that you were just beginning to understand. She represented class. She lived in a big white house on Cedar Street and her old man drove a new Dodge sedan. She didn't even know you were alive.

There is one day that you remember in particular. It was in September, and you remember standing around in front of the school building that afternoon after school was out, with the rest of the bunch. Then Lola came out, talking to some girl that you didn't know but who must have lived on Cedar Street, too, and they passed right by the group of boys, their heads in the air, not even seeing them.

"Snotty little dames," one of the kids said under his breath.

Somebody snickered. "I wouldn't kick that Lola Johnson out of bed, though."

Nine years old. You learned fast on Burk Street. The boys began shoving each other and pushing and snickering wisely to cover up their embarrassment, and for the first time you could remember you were ashamed of them, ashamed of being one of them.

"What's the matter, Roy?"

"He's stuck on Lola Johnson."

"Like hell I am."

"Goddamn, let's go down to the slough and see if the mud-cats are bitin'."

"I've got somethin' else to do."

You walk off, careful not to take the street Lola and the other girl had taken, but as soon as the other kids are out of sight you cut quickly across vacant lots and come out on Cedar Street.

You can think of no logical reason why you did it. But your chest was pounding and aching, and not just from the run, as you fell in quietly behind Lola and the other girl, almost a full block back. She looked so clean—even after a full day at school she was clean and white and starched. *I love you, Lola!* The thought explodes in your mind as you watch her from a distance. You don't know what love is, of course; you only know that she represented something that you craved.

The girl dropped off at one of the houses on Cedar and Lola walked on alone. She reached her house finally and went inside and for a long while you stood across the street, just looking at the house, with a strange kind of ache inside you.

In some strange way, in the remote, dark places of your mind and heart, you came to a decision that afternoon. Somehow, you had to reach that other world of Cedar Street. You had to be someone that Lola Johnson could look up to.

It took a long time. When you had the football in your hands and when you heard the crowd yelling from the sidelines, knowing that Lola was yelling too, then you thought you had made it.

In your senior year you were sure you had. You were "somebody" now. People pointed you out—*That's Roy Foley—all-state quarterback*. Not even Lola could ignore a thing like that. When you spoke to her in the halls, between classes, she spoke back. Sometimes she smiled, and when she did your insides would go to mush.

"Lola, ah— That is, well, I'm going your way this afternoon. If I could carry your books...."

"Oh, I'm sorry, Roy, but I'm not going straight home this afternoon. I promised Patsy that I'd go over to her house."

Well, you never walked home with her. But, on the other hand, she didn't look down her nose at you either. She knew who Roy Foley was, and that was something.

You told yourself it was something—but you began to wonder. Had you really made progress, or had you been kidding yourself? It was Lola herself who put your mind at ease—for a little while, at least.

"Lola— Well, I was thinking, if we beat Classen Friday, ah— Well, they'll be having a dance in the gym, I guess...."

You'd stopped her in the hallway, between classes, on some flimsy excuse, and the words came blurting out. You were alone with her for just that moment. The warning buzzer was sounding outside the superintendent's office, the signal that classes were ready to begin. For a moment she looked blank, and you were afraid that she was going to rush on to class without bothering to answer. Then she paused, glancing almost furtively, you thought, up and down the empty hall.

Suddenly to your amazement, she became a different person. She smiled. She almost blinded you with the dazzling warmth of it.

"Oh," she said. "Roy, I *do* wish I could go to the dance with you!" You could feel yourself glowing inside. And you felt eight feet tall. "But I've already promised Bob Carney I'd go with him. I *will* see you, though, won't I, Roy?" And then, miracle of miracles, she took your hand in hers and squeezed it!

There was one thing you were sure of, as you stood there, struck dumb in your rose-colored trance. She liked you. It was in her eyes, in her quick response as she squeezed your hand. The only thing you could think of was, She likes me! Maybe she even loves me!

And maybe it was true. Probably she did love you, or at least was infatuated with you, but of course things are never as simple as that. How were you to know or understand the complexities of women? It never occurred to you that when Lola smiled or showed a warmness toward you, it was always when there was no one to see her.

The entire team was at the dance, of course, and people kept pounding your back and telling you what a great guy you were. You weren't a very good dancer, but the girls didn't seem to care that night because you were a hero. You were the greatest guy around.

"I never was so excited in my life, Roy, the way you made that touchdown in the last quarter!"

You've forgotten the girl's name. You probably didn't even see her because you were watching all the time for Lola. You saw her come in and she was so beautiful that it made you ache inside just to look at her. You let her have one dance with her date, and then you cut in.

"Hello, Lola."

She smiled and you could see that she was glad you'd tagged in. She's proud to be dancing with you. Lola is more than a symbol now, she's everything you want or will ever want. She's cleanness and sweetness and softness, everything that Burk Street isn't. When you put your arms around her, you want to mash her to you. But you don't do that. You dance, a little more clumsily than usual, and you feel sweat breaking out on your forehead.

This is a hell of a thing. On the football field you're not afraid of anything and you know just what to do, but you're dancing with a girl and she's smiling at you and you're scared to death.

"Is anything wrong, Roy?"

"Wrong? Oh, no, not a thing. Everything's fine. I guess I don't dance so good—so well, though."

"We could sit this one out," she says, "if you don't feel like dancing."

Now you've done it. Just keep talking and talking and finally you'll ruin everything.

"It was a wonderful game." And she looks up at you and her eyes are soft and she's still smiling that gentle smile.

"I guess we could get Cokes," you say. "We could go outside on the steps and drink them. It's pretty hot in here."

So you do that. You get Cokes and go outside.

"It's a nice night," you say, and then you think, God, that's a new opener for you! It's a nice night!

"The moon's just coming up on the other side of the river—see it?"

You say you see the moon. You say a lot of other things just as bright, and all the time you're wanting to put your arms around her and kiss her.

"It was a wonderful game," Lola says again. "I shouted until I was hoarse in the last quarter."

You begin to feel a little better. "If I'd known, maybe I'd have done better."

"You did wonderfully, Roy. You won the game."

There's nothing to be afraid of, you tell yourself. She's talking to you just as she would to anybody else. The thing is, you don't want her to talk to you the way she would talk to anybody else. You want it to be special. You want her to feel the way you feel. And you think, Maybe she does. She likes me. I can tell when somebody likes me.

An idea hits you then, and you say, "Are you going to college, Lola, when you finish high school?"

"Why, I suppose so, Roy. Why?"

"I think I'll go, too. I can get a scholarship if I want it. I want to study law or something."

"I think that would be nice."

"Maybe we could see each other there, if you go to State University. I'll be going out for football, probably."

"Why, that would be nice."

You're not sure just how it happened, but you have one arm around her now. And all the feeling inside you starts rushing up in your throat and you can't talk any more. You drop your Coke and put both arms around her, and you pull her against you so hard that you know you're hurting her, but you can't help yourself. You mash your mouth onto hers and time seems to stop. The world stops and waits. And for the first time in your life you feel good and clean and at peace.

When you release her, her eyes are wide and startled. Then suddenly she smiles and says, "My!"

You start talking then, and you can't stop. "Lola, I love you. I've loved you ever since I can remember, almost. I want to marry you—not right now, of course, but not too long off, either. I'm going to amount to something, Lola, you wait and see. They can't keep me on Burk Street if I don't want to stay there. I'll be a lawyer or something. Maybe a doctor, and you'll be proud of me, Lola."

At first she just has that startled look, and that little half smile. Then abruptly, right in your face, she laughs.

She throws her head back and howls, and tears of merriment form at her eyes and run down her cheeks. She gasps for breath and holds her sides as if she's in pain, and then she starts all over again, howling and laughing.

You turn cold. Your insides sag like rock. "Lola!"

She gets her breath finally. "Oh, Roy!" she gasps. "You're the funniest thing!" And then she starts laughing again.

You start backing up, a step at a time, at first. Then you turn and try to slip away.

"Hey, Roy!" someone calls, and you know it's one of the team but you're too sick with shame to turn around. You walk faster, staying in the shadows, and the only thing you want is to get away from there. As far away as you can get. And then you hear the others coming out of the gym to see what all the excitement is about, and you hear Lola laughing, starting all over again.

"Lola, what on earth!"

Then, standing in the darkness, praying frantically to a God that you know won't hear you, you hear Lola gasp out, between spasms of laughter: "Oh, this is just too funny! Roy Foley—*Roy Foley* just said to me...."

You don't hear any more. You turn blindly and run.

You don't sleep that night. You lie there drowning in an ocean of shame, and anger swells your chest and throat until you can't breathe. You beat the mattress with your fists, and you swear that you'll get even with her if it's the last thing you do. You'll be a lawyer, the best damn lawyer in the country, and you'll break her. You'll break her old man. You'll frame him somehow and send him to jail, and see how she likes that!

You think of a lot of ways to hurt her, but none of them are good enough. Damn her! Damn her! Goddamn her! And you curse yourself, too, because you know well that you haven't got the guts to face her again. There would be no college; there wouldn't even be a diploma from the high school, because you knew you couldn't face her.

And that's the way it is when you're young and your name is Roy Foley and you live on Burk Street. You try, but you can't win. So you run.

Chapter Three

You would think that fourteen years would be long enough to forget. I thought I *had* forgotten, but there it was, the same thing all over again. The shame was just as sickening as it had been fourteen years ago, and the hate and anger were just as sharp.

I went across the street and into the house again, and I guess I went absolutely crazy for a few minutes. I picked up a chair and slammed it against the wall, and I kept slamming it until there was nothing but splinters left. Then I pounded the walls with my fists and cursed. Foley, you're a phony, no-good sonofabitch! Oh, you were going to do great things! You were going to show her that she couldn't get away with treating you like that. A lousy fry cook in a crumby eight-stool hash house. Great God, you make me sick!

The rage finally burned itself out of its own violence and left me weak and gasping. I lay across the bed and tried not to think about it. Well, what do you do now, Foley? I knew I couldn't stay in Big Prairie. Sooner or later I would run into her, and what would I do then? Now that I had cooled off I knew that I didn't have enough money to take care of the funeral expenses. What would I say to her? Here's three-fifty, Lola. Thanks for burying my old man for me. I'll pay you the rest when I get a job.

I knew what I was going to do. I was going to run, just the way I had done before.

I went back to the salvage shop and called a taxi, then went outside to smoke a cigarette and wait for it. I felt like I was just coming out from under a long, hard drunk. My hands shook. The muscles in my legs had gone to milksop.

The taxi came finally, and I went back to the bus station and found out that it would be another hour before I could catch anything going west. So I checked the suitcase and started walking the streets to kill time just looking around.

The red Ford passed me, making about forty-five miles an hour right through the middle of town. I'd just stepped off the curb and he missed me by about six inches, and I thought, The sonofabitch, I hope he gets himself killed! Then, while I was still looking, the Ford screeched under tramped brakes, then made a U turn right in the middle of the street and came back toward me. It was a new convertible, but the top was up because the day was sharp.

I jumped back on the curb and started to yell, but then I saw the girl sitting next to the driver. Her hair was long and so blonde that it was almost white. Her mouth was as red as an open wound. She wasn't beautiful—she was a long way from that—but there was something witchlike about her, and once you looked at her it was hard to take your eyes away.

"Roy," the driver called. "By God, it's Roy Foley!"

I saw the driver for the first time. He was a heavy-set guy with eyes that were pale and vaguely weak-looking, and mousy hair that was beginning to get thin on top. He had the flushed, slightly puffy face of a heavy drinker. The first thing I thought was, How did a pig like that get a girl like that? The red convertible explained part of it, I guessed. Then it hit me who he was and it almost floored me.

I gouged in my mind for his name, and then I had it. It was Sid Gardner. He was from Burk Street, just like I was, and he was one of the dumbest guys I had ever known. But he had that new car and that girl.

By the time I got it all figured out I was over pumping his hand, and he looked tickled to death to see me.

He turned to the girl and said, "Vida, this here's Roy Foley. He was the sweetest damn running back you ever saw."

"Not without you making the holes for me," I said. I had him pegged now. He had been a guard or a tackle, as well as I could remember. The girl looked at me and smiled as though it was a debt that had to be paid.

"By God," Sid said, and then he remembered something and got serious. "Say, I heard about your old man. That's too bad."

There was nothing much I could say to that, so I nodded.

"Look," Sid said, "why don't you climb in? I've got to take Vida home, then I've got some running around to do, but that won't keep us from talking."

"Well—"

I was thinking about the bus that would be pulling out in less than an hour, but I was calmer now and not so anxious as I had been back on Burk Street. Anyway, I still hadn't got over the shock of seeing an ordinary Burk Street punk looking so rich. There were two things I knew, he hadn't done it by working and he hadn't done it with brains. Then, how?

I made up my mind right then to find out, if I could. There would be other buses.

The girl, Vida, looked vaguely annoyed as she moved over to the middle of the front seat and I got in. Sid put the car in gear.

The longer we rode the more I remembered about him and the better I understood him. Sid Gardner was one of those men who never grow up and never forget. He was still Burk Street, even with his red convertible and expensive-looking girl, and he would never forget that, either. But it would never bother him.

He drove north from town, where the new residential district had grown away from the river. I expected him to let Vida off at some apartment house, because it looked like that kind of setup to me. It shook me when he pulled up in the driveway beside a rambling new brick house. And it dawned on me then that Vida was his wife. A dumb guy like that with a new car, a big house, and a wife like Vida. God!

But maybe he wasn't so dumb at that, because he could see what was going on in my mind after we let Vida out and started back toward town.

"Not bad for a Burk Street boy, huh?" he said, grinning.

"That's just what I was thinking."

"You don't look bad yourself, Roy. You look like you've been doing all right."

I thanked God then that I had one good suit. "I can't complain," I said, and hoped Sid would let it go at that for now.

Then he pulled the convertible into a side street and began to check a list of names that he'd taken out of his breast pocket.

"What's this?" I said.

He looked kind of puzzled. Then he laughed. "Hell, I keep forgetting you've been away. But, with your old man and all, I guess election day doesn't mean anything to you. This," he explained, nodding at his list of names, "is a list of every good church-going voter in this precinct, and it's my job to see that they get to the polls and vote."

"Vote for what?"

"For prohibition," he grinned. "Boy, you've got a little bit of catching up to do! Look, how do you think I can afford these things I've got? By working in a salvage shop on Burk Street? Hell, no! I can afford them because I'm a bootlegger."

That jarred me for a minute. I'd had the notion that bootlegging had gone out with the Volstead act about twenty years ago. But then I remembered that Oklahoma was one of the two states still hanging on to prohibition, and something about that struck me as being funny. There was no other place in the world, probably, where Sid Gardner could have made a living, but here he was, raking it in.

I laughed and said, "Well, I'll be damned."

"You see now why I've got to work to get these voters to the polls?"

"Sure, you've got to keep the state dry or you go out of business. But why pick on the church-going voters?"

He looked at me as though I were feeble-minded. "Why, they're the ones that vote dry."

I lay back in Sid's glossy new car and howled, feeling better than I had felt for a long time.

"Why, hell, I even took Vida down to vote," he said. "This is hard work. It's impossible to buy a pint of whisky in Big Prairie County today—until the polls close, that is. All us bootleggers are working to get the vote out."

That hit me just right and I started laughing again.

I forgot all about that bus I was supposed to catch. Sid had planted the seed, and now the idea was growing, growing faster than weeds in a rose garden. I knew then that I wasn't going to leave Big Prairie, after all. If Sid could get all this, I could get more. A lot more. And there was one other thing I knew. I would see Lola again. And when I did, I would be ready for her.

After I made up my mind, Sid couldn't have shaken me even if he had wanted to. But he didn't want to. He wanted to talk about all the old days on Burk Street and the fights we'd had and the football team, and I listened to every word as if it were the Gospel. And in between, we'd pick up the voters and take them to the polls—nobody but church members, the solid citizens of the community.

Toward the end of the day, I hit Sid with it. I told him I wanted a job working for him.

At first he didn't think I was serious. "Hell," he said, "you wouldn't have any kind of job I could give you. The only boys I have working for me are the runners, and you can't make any money at that."

"How much?"

He shrugged. "Maybe seventy-five a week."

I wondered what Sid would think if he knew I'd been working fourteen hours a day in hash houses for a hell of a lot less.

"Seventy-five's all right."

When he began to get that careful look I knew I was going too fast. But I'd already laid it on the table, and there didn't seem to be any way of backing up. "Of course," I said, and tried to look hurt, "if you don't want me, it's all right. There won't be any hard feelings about it. I was doing all right out on the Coast. I've got plenty of contacts out there and I can raise all the money I need any time I want it. I was going back out there, anyway. So if you don't want me, there're no hard feelings. I'm just curious to see how this bootlegging works, that's all."

"You figure to go into business for yourself?"

I shrugged. "Maybe. If I decided to do it, I'd go somewhere else. Maybe Oklahoma City or Tulsa. I wouldn't try to horn in on your own business."

He thought about it for a long minute, and then he grinned. "Hell, why not?" He did have one idle thought, though, and he said, "It'll take money, if you decide to open up."

"I told you money didn't worry me."

That decided it for him. He punched me on the shoulder and said, "You're hired, then, if that's the way you want it. I was going to have to put on another runner anyway. When do you want to go to work?"

"The sooner, the better."

"You'll have to have a car."

"I'll get one tomorrow."

We had been cruising around, not heading anyplace in particular. "I've got to get back to the house," he said, 'and pick up Vida. Where can I let you off?"

"Downtown at one of the hotels will do until I find something better."

When he let me out I pumped his hand. "Sid, I want you to know that I appreciate this."

"Hell, don't give it a thought." He was about ready to pull away when an idea hit him. "I just thought of something," he said. "Some of the boys are getting together tonight to play some poker and listen to the election returns. It wouldn't hurt you to mix with them a little."

"That sounds fine. Who are the boys?"

He grinned. "I'll tell you later. Pick you up at eight in the lobby of the Travelers."

The Travelers Hotel was a four-story building on the corner of First and Main, right in the middle of what passed as Big Prairie's downtown section. They gave me a room on the top floor, which was as good as you could expect in a town of that size, and the bellhop hustled around opening windows and turning on lights while I stood at the corner window and looked down at the town.

"Would there be anything else, sir?" the hop said.

"What else have you got?"

"Whisky," he said and grinned. "Women. About everything."

It was quite a town at that. Just for the hell of it, I said, "Bring up some ice and soda and a bottle of Johnny Walker."

He was back in about five minutes with the Scotch and mixer. I asked him how much it came to.

"Twenty dollars, sir."

I paid him off and when he left I made myself a drink and stood at the window again, thinking, Geez, twenty dollars for a bottle of whisky! Somebody sure as hell is making money.

Then I felt myself grinning. I'd finally found a place to grab hold and start climbing, and I didn't care who I knocked down getting to the top. I remembered the old man, and it was almost impossible to believe that he had been buried just that afternoon. But the old man had finally done something to help me, even if he'd had to die to do it. He'd brought me back to Big Prairie.

Then, out of nowhere it came, that feeling of darkness and queasiness, and I thought, You're forgetting Lola. The future that had only a moment ago been so secure, began to crumble senselessly, just because I had thought her name.

Forget it, I told myself. It was a kid thing, and all kids get hurt at one time or another, but they get over it. Besides, she probably doesn't even remember you. Not Lola, she had more important things to do than carry grudges against Burk Street nobodies. She had ambition, she had a husband who would probably be governor of the state some day. Roy Foley?—she wouldn't even remember the name.

I tried to tell myself that it was coincidence that Lola happened to be the president of the charity that buried the old man. But it was no coincidence. And no accident. You can't put your knife in a man, even accidentally, and then walk away without hating somebody. I remembered something then, and at first I had no idea why a thing like that should bob suddenly to the front of my brain.

There had been a dog—an ancient, slat-ribbed, crippled hound—that used to lie in the sun beside the sidewalk in front of our house. The dog never bothered anybody. I had passed him a thousand times without thinking about him. And then one day, for no reason at all, I kicked him. I could remember laughing at the way he yelped and jumped up. He couldn't run, because of his crippled leg, so he hobbled around, bewildered and hurt, in a tight, wobbly little circle, and several people gathered around and there was a lot of laughing for a little while. Then suddenly it didn't seem funny any more, and we all stopped laughing and stood there feeling vaguely uncomfortable, and not knowing exactly why. I could feel them looking at me, and then they all walked away. I looked at the dog and felt sorry for him at first, and I began to get mad at myself for doing such a damn fool thing. But what the hell, he was just a dog, wasn't he? What right did people have to look at me that way just because I'd kicked a goddamn dog? So I kicked him again. Harder this time. You mangy mutt, that'll teach you to keep out of my way! I kicked him every time I saw him after that, and pretty soon he went away. I heard later that he turned mean and somebody finally had to shoot him. I was glad. I'd hated the mutt.

I made another drink, a strong one this time, and poured it down.

The whisky helped. It put fire where there had been nothing. After a while the sureness and feeling of strength came back. Think about Sid, I told myself. Nobody kicks Sid around—not even a dumb guy like that—so what are you sweating about? Money is the thing that counts. With enough money, you can handle people like clay; even Lola. And there's money, plenty of it, in bootlegging.

To hell with Lola. Forget about her.

I drank to that.

When the hop got back with my suitcase I got out some clean things and soaked for about thirty minutes in the bathtub. After I finished shaving I gave my suit a brushing and got into it. By the time I was dressed and down in the lobby it was eight o'clock. Sid was just coming in.

"You ready, boy?"

His face was redder than usual and I could see that he had been belting his own merchandise. "I'm ready. Where do we go?"

"Vida's got the car outside." His grin seemed a little forced. "She's kind of mad, I think. Don't mind Vida if she's kind of mad. Hell, a man's got a right to celebrate on election day, hasn't he?"

"Sure he has. Let's go."

We went out to Fourth Street where Vida had that red convertible parked. She didn't even give us a glance when Sid opened the car door and piled in. She stared straight ahead with her jaw set like a bear trap. "Damn!" she said, as Sid tilted over and almost dumped in her lap. She snapped her head around and said to me, "What's your name again?"

"Roy Foley."

"Roy, you'd better let Sid sit next to the door, just in case."

That was fine with me. I elbowed Sid out, then I slid in next to Vida and Sid got in next to the door.

"Hell, I'm not drunk," Sid said. "I'm not drunk by a damn shot."

Vida slammed the car into gear. "You'd better roll the window down for him," she said. "Let him get some air."

So I rolled the window down and Sid hung his head out for a minute. When he pulled his head inside again he looked as sober as anybody. "I guess I needed some air at that. I feel fine now, though."

Without looking at him, Vida said, "Sure. You look fine." They threw it back and forth for a while, as if I weren't there. While they were at it, I studied Vida.

She was one of those women who are almost ugly, but with something about them that knocks men flat. She had practically no color in her face except for her mouth, which was painted blood red. Her eyes slanted just a little, or maybe it was the way she made them up. Her hair, almost white, hung as straight as a board and came to her shoulders. She looked as cold as frosted glass—still it was hard to look at anything else.

She was wearing a thing that was probably called a cocktail dress, but with a fur stole over her shoulders I couldn't tell much about it. After a while she caught me looking at her, so I started paying attention to what was going on in front of the windshield.

"Look," I said, when the traffic got heavier, "where are we going, anyway?"

"Across the river," Vida said, "to Barney Seaward's place."

"Am I supposed to know Barney Seaward?"

Sid fumbled for a cigarette and seemed to be glad to change the subject. "Barney Seaward is the wholesaler for Big Prairie County," he said. "He ships the booze in from Texas and spends money in the right places for protection and keeps things running smooth."

"He sounds like quite a man."

"He's the biggest man in Big Prairie County, and don't forget it. Me, I'm just one of the retailers. There are two of us in Big Prairie, and four or five more scattered around the county."

"You mean this Seaward supplies all the bootleggers in Big Prairie County?"

"All the big ones. There's a few wildcatters, but they don't do enough business to bother us." He got his cigarette going and thought for a minute. "I guess I'd better fill you in," he said, "if you're thinking of going into the business. To begin with, we'd better not say anything about you going to work for me. Not tonight, anyway. I'll just introduce you as a guy who used to live on Burk Street. If I vouch for you, it'll be all right."

"Whatever you say. Who's going to be there besides Seaward?"

"Well, there'll be Joe Kingkade, the other retailer. He works the west side and the business district and part of the river area. And there'll be Clyde Somers, the county sheriff, and McErulur, the chief of police."

"This begins to sound more like a peace officer's convention than a get-together for bootleggers," I said.

Sid looked at me. "How do you think these people get elected to office? Who do you think pays their campaign expenses and sees that they get good write-ups in the paper? They wouldn't be anybody without the whisky dollars backing them, and they know it." He grinned faintly. "This being election night, Paul Keating will probably be there, too. He's the county attorney."

I guess I should have expected that. As long as Seaward was buying up all the county offices, he might as well buy the county attorney while he was at it. But the thing knocked the wind out of me for a minute.

"The women folks will be there, too, probably," Sid went on. "On election night, it's kind of like a party."

For a few brief seconds panic seized me and left me weak. Then something else hit me and I almost laughed.

"Well, I'll be damned!"

"What's the matter with you?"

"I was thinking of something."

For a moment a picture had come clear in my mind, and that was what I was laughing at. I saw Lola catering to a crowd of bootleggers and crooked politicians, and hating every minute of it. But catering to them anyway, because she was the county attorney's wife and she was ambitious. I would bet that right at this minute she had her eye on the state capitol and the governor's mansion.

"Do you want me to run this down for you or not?" Sid said, and he was a little peevish because he couldn't see anything to laugh at.

"Sure. I didn't mean to interrupt you."

"Well," he said grudgingly, "this is the way we do things. And wherever you go, it'll be the same way. To be a whisky dealer, you've got to buy a county, and you do that by starting with the county seat. The first thing you do is organize, like me and Seaward and Kingkade. And then you buy the county newspaper and see that it prints what you want it to print. Next you take in the county offices—the sheriff, the county attorney, the chief of police of the county seat. It's cheaper to put your own men in office than to try to buy the ones already in, and that's easy enough, if you own the newspaper. The county attorney is the key man because it's up to him to get clearance from the state officials. After you do all that, buy your trucks and start bringing the stuff in.

"And then you have more trouble. You can't buy protection for your transportation across the state line because that's up to the Federal officers and the highway patrol, so you've got to figure on losing a truck now and then. And the sheriff's got to make a raid once in a while to make it look good. On top of that, wildcatters try to hijack your trucks for you, and there's nothing you can do about it except fight them. We're not bothered too much with hijackers, though. Seaward's boys carry sawed-off twelve-gauge shotguns, and they know how to use them."

Sid had been looking at the tip of his cigarette and talking to the windshield. Now he turned and looked at me. "I'm telling you all this to give you an idea of what it's like. Bootlegging in Oklahoma is big business. It takes big money to start it and big money to keep it going. There are big risks to take and there's a chance you might even get killed. Do you still think you want in?"

Sid would never know how much I wanted in. I said, "I haven't changed my mind about that. But I'm beginning to see why the price of whisky is so high."

"You're damn right it's high," he said self-righteously. "We've got expenses." Then he settled back in the seat, looking satisfied with himself. "Well, that's that, then. You can work with me for a while until you catch on. I know a county up in the Panhandle where you can get started on your own."

To hell with the Panhandle counties, I thought. Drinkers up there could drive across the state line and get their own booze at legal prices. I wanted a place like Oklahoma County, or Tulsa County, right in the middle of the state, but I knew there wasn't a chance of moving into places like them. I figured Big Prairie would be just about right, to start with.

"By the way," Sid said. "How much money can you raise, when the time comes?"

I was tempted to look him in the eye and say, "I couldn't raise a goddamn penny," just to see how he would look. What I said was, "Ten thousand. Maybe fifteen." And I was afraid that was being too extravagant.

"That won't be enough," Sid said. "A load of merchandise can come to twenty thousand."

God! I hadn't realized that there was that much money. But I held onto that sinking feeling and tried to make myself sound convincing. "I can raise it." Here I was going to work the next day, and I couldn't even buy a car that I would have to have. Still, I had that feeling that I could work it out somehow. I had hold of something good at last, and it was going to take a damn hard blow to knock me loose from it.

We left Big Prairie behind and headed south toward the river. About a mile on the other side of the river Vida turned off on a section line road, then after another mile or so we saw the house. It was a big brick place with a brick wall around it and a lot of trees. We turned off the road onto a graveled driveway. A pair of iron gates stood open, so Vida pulled up to where five or six cars were parked.

An old lady wearing a white apron and a lace cap met us at the door and let us in. She took our hats and coats and told us that the women were in the front room and the men were in the clubroom listening to the radio. Vida went off down the hall without even a nod to us.

"The hell with her," Sid said. "Let's go get a drink and see if the returns have started coming in."

We went down the hallway and turned into a brick-walled room where five men sat around the fireplace in big leather chairs listening to the syrupy voice of an election reporter coming from a combination radio-record player-bar. One of the men got up and came at Sid with an outstretched hand.

"Sid, have you heard? Clyde's run away with the sheriff's race. It wasn't even a contest."

"We spent enough money on it," Sid said. "What did you expect?" Then he took my arm and said, "Barney, I want you to meet Roy Foley, the sweetest damn quarterback Big Prairie ever saw. I didn't think you'd mind if I brought him along."

"Not at all," Barney Seaward said. "Any friend of Sid's is all right any time." We shook hands and he was smiling all the time, but when the formalities were over I knew that I had been sized up by an expert. Seaward was a trim, well-dressed guy somewhere in his late forties, and at first glance he seemed a quiet, well-mannered man who had somehow drifted into the wrong business and didn't quite know what to do about it. But on second glance you knew that he was as hard as gunsteel. He had regular, straight features, dark hair beginning to go gray around the temples. His complexion was dark but, in the artificial light of the room, I couldn't tell if it was a natural swarthiness or if it came from a sun lamp.

His eyes were very sharp. He looked at Sid and I had the feeling that he could tell to the ounce how much liquor Sid had put away since noon, and I also had the feeling that he didn't like it. But he was smiling all the time, and talking, a fine picture of a perfect host. A nice guy, but I wouldn't want to put a knife in his hand and turn my back to him.

"How's the vote going on the prohibition amendment?" Sid asked.

"How do you think it's going? A preacher came on awhile ago and wanted everybody to thank God because the drys are winning."

Barney and Sid had a good laugh over that, then a squat little guy in an expensive blue suit and cowboy boots came over and said, "It looks good, Sid."

"It looks that way, Clyde. Barney tells me they're declaring it no-contest in the sheriff's race. By the way, I want you to meet Roy Foley, the damnedest football player you ever saw when he was in high school."

"Glad to know you, Foley."

I made myself a quick drink at the bar and we ran into Thad McErulur, the chief of police, and Joe Kingkade, the other retailer, and then we went through the handshaking again and talked some more about the election. I tried to keep my mind on who I was meeting and what was being said, because it was going to be important to me later on. But I could feel myself winding up tighter and tighter, like a dollar watch just before the spring snaps.

"Something wrong, Roy?" I heard Sid saying.

"No. I just remembered I haven't eaten today. I guess I'd better go easy on the liquor."

"Nothing to worry about," McErulur said. "Barney's whisky won't hurt you. He serves nothing but the best." McErulur was a big, red-faced ox of a man, looking much too prosperous to be the chief of police of a hick town like Big Prairie. But that figured. Kingkade was a quiet little man in a bow tie and a sloppy blue serge suit. He nursed a coke while the others poured down Seaward's free liquor and I pegged him right away as the most dangerous man in the house, next to Seaward himself.

The room was beginning to get smoky, but even so I noticed how drunk Sid was getting. I watched him pour three fingers into a highball glass, down it straight, and before it had time to hit his stomach he was pouring again. He weaved a little.

He saw me watching him as he hoisted another shot. "You think I'm drinkin' too much." His tongue was thick.

"It doesn't make any difference to me. Seaward might not like it, though."

"The hell with Seaward," and I could see the drunken belligerence begin to look out from behind his eyes. "You met everybody?"

"I think so," I said, wondering why Seaward would have a lush like Sid in his organization.

"How about Paul Keating?"

I almost dropped the glass I was holding, because I had begun to hope that the Keatings wouldn't show up after all. Sid grabbed my arm and hung onto it. "You got to meet Paul Keating," he said ponderously, pulling me away from the bar. "Hell, Keating's going to be governor some day."

Keating had just come in from the hallway and was shaking hands with the sheriff when Sid pointed him out, but I think I would have known him anyway because he was just the kind of man Lola would marry. His suit was cut from beautiful Oxford gray flannel, but it was so conservative that it looked more like a period costume than a suit. It was single breasted and all three buttons were buttoned. His shirt collar was stiff, of course, and his tie was of the best navy silk with a small red stripe running through it. He wore an Acheson-type mustache, and I would bet my last penny that as soon as he got out of Big Prairie he would buy himself a walking stick. I hated his guts on sight.

"Roy," Sid said thickly, "I want you to meet Paul Keating, our county attorney. Paul, this is Roy Foley, the best damn quarterback you ever saw."

I thought savagely, if Sid mentions football one more time I'll hit him! Paul Keating nodded politely, but I could see distaste in those cool, supercilious eyes of his as we shook hands. I could see him thinking, Great God, another Burk Street hoodlum! But for all he knew I was a personal friend of Seaward's, and if I was, he was going to be nice to me if it killed him.

"It's a great pleasure, Mr. Foley." We shook hands limply, and then we stood there, looking at each other and trying to think of something to say, but the words wouldn't come.

The sheriff saw Keating, came toward him, and Sid and I got away.

I should have kept my mouth shut, but there was so much boiling inside me that I had to let a little of it come out. "You boys sure bought yourselves something," I said, "when you got that county attorney."

"Paul?" Sid grinned vaguely. "Hell, he's all right. Comes from a good family, got a good record. He's done a lot of good for Big Prairie County."

"Like what?"

"He cleaned up prostitution, for one thing. Used to have some cribs down by the river, but things like that go bad with the churches. Anyway, bootlegging is the big business. We clean up prostitution and gambling and people figure that's doing damn good."

"Do you mean there are no tramps or gambling joints in Big Prairie?"

"Sure there are tramps. And you can get a bet down without any trouble, if you want to, but it's all under control. It's a nice quiet business."

"Barney Seaward's business?"

Sid was drunk, but he wasn't that drunk. He gave me a long, careful look and said, "Roy, the next time you think of a question like that, just forget it."

I should have been ready for it, but I wasn't. When Barney Seaward came back into the clubroom, the wives behind him, I could hear the breath whistling between my teeth as if I had been kicked in the stomach. I couldn't move as I stood there, feeling the blood draining out of my face, waiting for her to recognize me. There were others around us, but I didn't even see them. I could hear Seaward making the introductions and I could hear myself mumbling something, I don't know what. There were just Lola and me, and we could have been alone in the middle of a desert.

She was standing so close to me that I could have touched her, and I saw the vague shock in her eyes. She moved her head slightly, as if shaking off some unpleasant mental image, and for a moment I noticed her dark hair framed the pale oval of her face, and how her mouth half smiled, uncertainly, the expression as rigid as a smile on a statue. And for that moment it was hard to believe that she was real. She was just a woman after all. Open her flesh and she'll bleed, I thought. Hurt her and she'll cry out. And only then, after I was convinced that she was flesh and blood and not a myth, did the hate begin to come. For both of us.

I heard Barney Seaward saying something and I bowed slightly, sick inside. "How do you do, Mrs. Keating."

She smiled then, and I wondered if the others saw the savageness behind it. I wondered if the others had ever kicked a dog and then grown to hate it with such a viciousness that it made you weak to think about it. That's a crazy thing to think of now, I thought. But Lola would have understood.

Chapter Four

"Are you all right now?"

"Sure. I'm all right."

"Here, wipe your face with this." Sid handed me a towel and I wiped my face. Then I went over to the basin and splashed water on my face. I rinsed my mouth and I felt a little better.

"You sure you're all right?"

"For God's sake, yes, I'm fine. Look, Sid, will you leave me alone for a minute? Go get me another drink. That's what I need now."

I was giving Sid a hard time. Here he had brought an old pal uninvited to a party and the first thing his pal did was throw his guts all over the host's bathroom. But I wasn't worrying about Sid. I could close my eyes and still see Lola. I could hear her laughing at me. I leaned on the basin and tried to pull myself together.

After a while Sid went out, and then he came back with a highball glass half full of straight bourbon. I gagged it down, and pretty soon I could feel it start burning some of the sickness away.

"Thanks, Sid. That's what I needed."

Vida was waiting for us in the hallway when we came out of the bathroom. "Well," she said coldly, "have you had enough, or won't you be satisfied until the bar is cleaned out?"

"It wasn't Sid," I said. "It was me."

Sid said, "Look, honey, why don't you take him out on the back porch for a minute? He's all right, he just needs some fresh air."

The corners of that red mouth turned down. "He's your big friend, why can't you take him out?" And then she said, "Oh, hell. You couldn't stay away from that bar long enough, could you?" Without looking at me, she jerked her head and started toward the back of the house.

Friendship was all right, I thought, but this was going pretty far. If Vida was my wife, inviting her out on the back porch with another man would be the last thing I'd do. But if it was all right with Sid, it was all right with me.

We went down the straight hall and into a kitchen and then onto a screened-in back porch. I went out and leaned against a wooden pillar, breathing deeply. The air was clean and cool.

"Can you find your way back?" Vida asked.

"Sure."

"Then I'll go back. I'll have to be ready to catch Sid when he starts falling."

I could see that dress, now that she had taken off the stole. It was probably expensive, but somehow Vida made it look like a streetwalker's uniform. The black material accented the pale nakedness of her arms and shoulders. It pulled tight across her small breasts, then flowed like water over her flat belly and long thighs. I said, "Sid must be crazy," and the sound of the words shocked me because I hadn't meant to say a thing.

She was starting for the door when I said it, but she paused and looked around. "Why?"

"You don't have to be told that, do you?"

It was all a mistake and I knew it was a mistake and still I couldn't seem to stop it. Maybe it was because of Lola and because I was still seeing that savage half smile of hers. And I kept thinking helplessly, Goddamn her! But there was nothing I could do, no way to hurt her, and I knew that I had to lash out at somebody, hurt somebody back. Vida was there, so I guess that's the reason I said it.

She was quiet for a minute. Then she walked slowly over to where I was and looked hard at me. She said coldly, "Look, Roy, or whatever your name is. You're a friend of Sid's and that's all right with me. There's one thing you'd better get straight, though; it doesn't go any further than that.'

I don't know how I knew she was lying. But I knew. She looked like a woman who would cut your heart out if you as much as touched her. She looked hard and tough. But the moment I put my hands on her, she went to nothing.

I pulled her to me and it was like leading a sleepwalker. And then she plastered herself against me, and those white arms went around my neck, her fingernails digging like daggers into my shoulders as that blood-red mouth found mine.

"Roy."

She flowed against me, and that hungry red mouth was hot and alive. God! I thought. That crazy bastard, Sid! I could have had her right there on the back porch, but then she got my lip in those sharp front teeth and began to sink them in and I could feel the blood spurting. My blood! Instinctively, I jerked my knee up and kicked her with everything I had.

That broke her loose. Her mouth flew open and she half doubled, her eyes sick with pain. I got my handkerchief out and wiped the lipstick and blood off my mouth. She had barely broken the skin inside my lip, but the taste of blood was still there.

She was still pretty sick. I put my arm around her and held her up. "Are you all right?"

She nodded. Maybe a minute went by while she dragged in deep gulps of air. I thought she was going to cry, but she fought it back.

"Look, Vida, I didn't mean—" I started. But she cut in.

"Let's don't talk about it. We'll forget about it and it won't happen again." She straightened up and arranged her hair. "We'll forget about it," she said again. Then she went back inside.

My lip had already started puffing, but maybe it wouldn't be noticed. For several minutes I stood there in the cool night air and tried to get myself to settle down. What had just happened with Vida was in the past and I could forget that. The prospect of going back in there and seeing Lola was the thing I had to face.

What I wanted to do was start running and not stop until Big Prairie was behind me for good. What I did was light a cigarette and go back in the house.

"I was afraid you'd got yourself lost, Mr. Foley," Barney Seaward said when I came in.

"Just an upset stomach. I'm fine now."

Then McErulur came over and said, "How's about a little poker, Barney? Foley, you'll join us won't you? Nothing big, just table stakes."

Table stakes could get pretty damn big, but I figured I could hold my own by playing close to the vest. So I said, "That sounds all right with me."

Vida wasn't around, but Lola came into the room again and I could feel myself squeezing the highball glass hard enough to break it. Instinctively, I tried to get away when I saw her looking at me, smiling at me with that damned fixed smile of hers, but my feet could have been in cement for all the good they did me. I saw her stop for a minute to say something to McErulur's wife, then she turned, smiling, and came toward me with an unlighted cigarette in her hand.

"I seem to have misplaced my lighter, Mr. Foley," she said. "I wonder if I could bother you for a light?"

"Of course, Mrs. Keating," I heard myself saying. I found the matches somehow, struck one and held it for her. Even through the haze of hate I thought, She's just as beautiful as she ever was!

"I've been trying to place you, Mr. Foley," she lied pleasantly. "I think I have—it was Big Prairie High, wasn't it? Football, I believe."

I thought savagely, You remember, all right. I said, "Yes. Football."

"Oh, I remember now," she smiled. "You were going to be a doctor, I believe. No, a lawyer." She frowned slightly. "But Barney didn't mention that when he introduced us."

"I didn't get to be a doctor. Or a lawyer, either," I said. Damn you, I didn't get to be anything but a fry cook.

"A businessman, then?" she asked brightly. "As I remember, you were terribly bright in school."

I felt sick and didn't even try to answer it. Sure, a businessman! I make so much money I let your charity bury my old man just because a little detail like that skipped my mind.

But, God, she was beautiful, more beautiful than I remembered. Hair as black as a witch's heart pulled back severely from the pale oval of her face. Her eyes were dark, with no questions in them. Her mouth thin and smiling as she waited for me to say something when she knew there was nothing I could say. And then I remembered that night, and the high-school kid running blindly away from the laughter, too sick with shame to cry. How Lola must have hated herself that night—but just for a little while. Only until she had found a way to justify the thing and turn the hate around and start it going in the opposite direction. But for a little while she must have hated herself almost as much as I hated her now.

I stood there like a statue for what may have been a few seconds or an hour. Time had stopped for me. Lola brought the cigarette to her mouth and dragged on it, smiling, and behind those eyes of hers I could see her thinking, A doctor! You're a Burk Street hoodlum and that's all you'll ever be. And I saw her glance quickly at her husband on the other side of the room with an almost savage pride, a pride born of possession and ambition. I had a feeling that when she looked at Paul Keating she was looking right through him and seeing the governor's mansion.

"You goin' to play?" I heard Sid saying huskily. I had forgotten that Sid was in the room. I had forgotten that there was anybody in the room except me and Lola.

"Of course," she said evenly. "Please don't let me keep you from the game."

When she was gone it seemed to me that everyone in the room must have heard the pounding in my chest. I looked at Sid and he was still holding onto the edge of the bar, glass in hand. Finally I took a deep breath and poured myself another drink. "I thought I'd sit in for a while," I said.

Sid nodded heavily. "You find out what a man's like when you play poker with him. Maybe you won't be so hot for bootleggin' when you find out what kind of men they are...."

He was even drunker than I had thought. He wiped his face, and when I looked into his eyes I could see his mind drifting from one thing to another. "Vida's sore as hell," he said. "Went out to the car. Won't even talk to me." Then he reached out and took my arm. "See Kingkade over there, that little dried-up guy? Looks like a prune, don't he? The little punk would move in on me tomorrow if he thought he could get away with it."

"You mean take over your territory?"

"Sure. He can't do it, though. I'm a friend of Barney's. I did Barney a big favor once. Old Barney won't let me down." He laughed abruptly. "The sonofabitch'll be sorry if he tries it."

"What kind of a favor did you do for Barney?"

But that was going too fast. I could see that Sid wasn't apt to ever get drunk enough to answer a question like that. "Roy," he said ponderously, "you better play poker." But when I started to move away he grabbed my arm again, and his face was deadly serious. "You were talkin' to Paul Keating's wife."

"There's no law against it, is there?" I managed to say it tonelessly.

"I'm not so dumb, Roy. And I'm not so drunk that I can't figure out a few things. Stay away from Lola Keating."

"I wouldn't touch her with rubber gloves!"

Sid grinned faintly. "That's what I mean. Everybody in town knew why you left Big Prairie fourteen years ago. She's Paul Keating's wife, and Paul Keating is the county attorney. That's the way it's got to be—if you want to stay in Big Prairie."

We stood there looking at each other, and I could feel myself about to blow up. Lola hadn't been satisfied with what she'd done, she'd had to brag about it. Sid handed me a glass, and I poured it down without tasting it.

"Just forget, Roy."

"Sure."

Seaward, McErulur, and Kingkade were cutting for the deal when I pulled a chair up to the table and sat down. "Half a dollar ante, Mr. Foley," Seaward said. "Is that all right with you?"

That could run into big money, and the three hundred dollars in my pocket was all I had in the world. But there was no easy way to back out now. McErulur cut a king and began to deal.

It was the kind of night that you have once in a lifetime, if you're lucky. I was still boiling, and every chance I got I'd sneak a glance at Lola and curse her under my breath. Half the time I didn't even know what I had in my hand, but it didn't make any difference. The cards kept falling one on top of the other and I couldn't lose.

"Are you sure you're not a beginner at this game, Mr. Foley?" Joe Kingkade asked gently. "I don't believe I ever saw anything like this except in what they call beginner's luck."

When I could count my chips I found a little over five hundred dollars in front of me. It jarred me. "Luck like this can't last all night," I said, and tried a laugh that didn't come off very well.

Sid wandered off somewhere. Then McErulur fell out and Paul Keating sat in. They jumped the ante to a dollar and the pots got bigger, and that was when my luck started going downhill. I had almost a thousand dollars in front of me at one time, but then I started playing the cards close, or jumping in on wild hunches, and pretty soon it had dribbled down to about seven hundred. Every card got to be harder to play and I started trying to outguess them. But you don't outguess men like Seaward and Kingkade.

I thought, How the hell am I going to get out of this? I can't just get up and say I've had enough. Kingkade would squeal like a stuck pig. As the game got hotter the women stopped their talking, and pretty soon there wasn't any sound at all except the few words mumbled by the players. I could feel Lola watching me, and that didn't help my game. Roy Foley! I could almost hear her thinking it. Burk Street Foley. Roy, you're the funniest thing! Then I could hear her laughing.

It wasn't my imagination this time. She was really laughing. The sound was hard, bouncing like bullets around the brick walls of the room. One of the women said, "Lola, what on earth—?" And she said, "I—I just thought of something. It struck me as amusing."

"Are you going to call, Foley?" Seaward said.

I looked at my cards and all I could see was Lola's face. I turned them over and said, "I fold."

Then I heard the front door slam and the click of high heels coming down the hall and into the living room. It was Vida.

"Roy," she said, "I don't want to break up the game, but I've got to have your help."

"What is it, Vida?" Seaward asked.

"Sid's down," she said, spitting out "Sid" like a curse word. 'He's wallowing like a pig in the front yard, and he says he won't talk to anybody but Mr. Foley."

"I hate to quit when I'm this much ahead," I said, shoving the chair back. "But maybe we can finish the game some other time."

Seaward did make an attempt to be pleasant, but his eyes looked worried and I could see that it had nothing to do with the game. "Sure, we'll get together again, Foley. You go on and take care of Sid." Keating was being dignified about it. Kingkade was calling me thirty kinds of bastard under his breath, but he kept a straight face. I shoved my chips to the center of the table and collected my money from the game's bank.

"Well, it's been a pleasure, gentlemen," and I shook hands around the table and with McErulur. I nodded to the women and almost made it to the door before Lola said:

"Oh, Mr. Foley, I do want you to know that I'm awfully sorry about your father. If there is anything else my Christian Aid Society can do to help you, please let us know."

I don't know how I got out of the house. At that moment I could have killed her. My hands ached for that lovely white throat of hers, ached to choke her slowly, slowly, slowly....

Somehow I got to the front porch, shaking, feeling that if I didn't start hitting somebody I'd go crazy. I stepped up to the porch railing and smashed it viciously with my fists and the pain shot up my arm like a bright needle. It was good.

"Roy, are you crazy?"

I smashed the railing again and heard a sickening crack in my hand. Then pain washed over me and blotted out everything.

"I'm all right now. Where's Sid?"

We found him on his hands and knees in a rose bed to one side of the steps. He was trying to get up and couldn't make it. I got a shoulder under him and swung him across my back in a fireman's carry, then dumped him in the car. I sat on the outside and Vida got under the wheel, holding Sid up between us. As she slammed into gear, she said, "He makes me sick! He makes me so damned sick I could die!"

"Does he get this way often?"

She made an ugly sound in her throat. "Seven nights a week is all. You'd think he'd take a holiday sometime, but not Sid. Not one of Big Prairie's most prominent bootleggers. He has to get drunk and shoot off his mouth and tell everybody what a big shot he is."

I knew by this time that I had broken something in my hand. The sharp pain eased a little and a pounding ache took its place. It worked its way up my arm and across my shoulders, and the hammering set up at the base of my skull. It hurt like hell, but I welcomed it. It gave me something besides Lola to think about.

Sid's chin dropped on his chest, he sagged over toward me, and pretty soon he began to snore. Vida had worked up a full head of steam and had to let the pressure off some way, so I let her talk.

"If he drinks like this all the time," I put in finally, "how does he take care of his business?"

She stared at the windshield hard enough to break it.

"Oh, he doesn't get this drunk often. Tonight was something special. Oh, Sid's smart, he'll tell you so himself. He takes care of his business and does his drinking at nights. Every goddamn night. Can you imagine what it's like having a lush for a husband?"

I could imagine. And I was beginning to understand Vida a little better. When a girl's husband goes out on a bust once in a while, that's one thing, but when he does it seven times a week it's something else again. Especially at nights. A girl like Vida could get very restless at night if a thing like that went on too long.

The car moved across the river, then through the heart of Big Prairie. Finally Vida braked the Ford and turned into the driveway of their house.

"I'll help you get him to bed," I said.

"How does your hand feel? We can always leave him in the car."

My hand was throbbing and, without looking at it, I knew it was beginning to turn an ugly blue. "Never mind the hand. Just get the door open and I'll bring him in."

Using my left hand, I managed to wrestle Sid upright in the seat. Then I eased under him and got him across my shoulders. I couldn't stand touching anything with my right, and it was a ticklish job getting him up with just the left, but finally I managed it. I got him to the front door and went inside where Vida had switched the lights on.

"Show me where the bedroom is and open the doors for me."

She shrugged and held a hall door open. I took Sid down the hall, into the bedroom and dumped him. He fell on the bed like a sack of oats.

I pulled his shoes and coat off, and loosened his tie. He never stopped snoring.

"I can get you a drink," Vida said.

"I think I need one."

So we went back to the front room and I waited there while Vida got the drinks in the kitchen.

"Bourbon?" she called.

"That's fine."

The room looked like something right out of Better Homes and Gardens. The furniture was what they call "modern," and every piece of it was a monotonous blond. The floor was carpeted from wall to wall in pale green shag, and the walls were draped in Japanese prints. Everything was neat and clean and completely without imagination. Vida came in with two full highball glasses on a silver tray.

"Let me look at that hand."

"It's all right," I said, but she took it anyway and I winced.

"Sure," she said dryly, "it's fine. If you're lucky, maybe there's a bone or two that isn't broken."

"I'll have a doctor look at it in the morning."

She looked into her glass, rattling the ice. "Sid said you were going to work for him," she said after a pause. "He said you were thinking of going into business for yourself in another county."

"That's the idea."

She had something on her mind but I didn't guess what it was until she said, "You don't have to work for anybody to learn how to be a bootlegger. It's the same in every county and Sid can tell you all there is to know in five minutes."

I thought I was beginning to get it then. "You don't want me to stay in Big Prairie," I said. "Is that it? If it's about that business on Seaward's back porch, we'll forget it. It didn't even happen."

"It's partly that," she said bluntly. "You probably won't believe me, but I've been a good wife to Sid. I'm not the kind of woman you think I am—but sometimes it isn't easy." She took a quick drink. "But I was really thinking of Lola Keating."

I turned the glass up and drank until the ice hit my teeth. "Go on."

"Sid told me about you and Lola," she said quietly. "I didn't think much about it then. That was a long time ago. But when I saw you tonight, you scared me. A woman shouldn't be able to do things like that to a man—not after so many years."

She continued to look into her glass again, not at me. "Leave Big Prairie, Roy. You can't hurt her, she's hurt-proof. Her husband's the county attorney and before many years he'll be the governor, because the liquor dealers like him. He does what they say."

"What makes you think I want to hurt Lola Keating?"

She smiled then, but very faintly. "When you broke your hand tonight on Seaward's porch railing, you weren't hitting the railing, you were hitting Lola. It will always be like that—the harder you hit, the more you'll hurt yourself."

"You're quite a philosopher. But why are you so interested in getting me out of Big Prairie?"

She looked at me, and those eyes were cool. "Because I signed a marriage contract with Sid and I mean to stick to it. For better or for worse, as they say. I'm afraid of you, Roy."

Then, as she stood there looking at me, I could see a shudder start at her shoulders and go all the way down. Her mouth parted as if to say something, but no sound came out, and that shudder went over her again. And a strange thing happened. As I stood there looking at her she stopped being Vida and became Lola. It was Lola and she was laughing without making a sound. Laughing. I stepped over to the wall and snapped the light out.

I could see the nakedness of her pale arms and shoulders and that was about all. I heard myself saying, "You lousy, rotten bitch!" But it was Lola I was talking to. I went up to her and she didn't move. "Goddamn you!" I took the front of her dress in both hands and ripped it wide open.

If there was any pain in my broken hand, it never reached my brain. "Crawl, Lola, goddamn you! Let me hear you beg!" The dress fell somewhere and she stood there, shaking, her body seeming to glow in the darkness. Oh, you're beautiful, all right, I thought. You never thought this would happen, did you, Lola? A thing like this couldn't happen to a proud, snotty little bitch like you. But it is!

"Roy! Don't!"

It was the first sound she made. But it was too late then.

The house was full of small sounds. As from a great distance we heard Sid's snoring. Somewhere an electric clock whirred. There in the front room Vida and I lay in the darkness, on the couch.

It took me several long minutes to pull myself away from that first rush of madness. I was convinced now that I was crazy—or at least partly crazy.

I had seen Lola, I'd had my hands on her, but it was Vida beside me now. She had her arms around me, pressing my face to her breasts, and she was crooning something softly. It had a soothing, pleasant sound in the darkness. "Lie still," she crooned. "Lie still...."'

But it scared me—whatever had happened in my brain. I had to figure it out, and I couldn't do it by myself. "I went crazy," I said. "As crazy as a whole carload of loons. I saw her, right here in this room. She started laughing and I—God, Vida, I'm sorry."

"I'm not. It had to happen sometime, and I guess I've been hoping it would happen. I'm not made like some women. I can't keep holding on and on forever. And a lush is no husband, Roy. It happened and I'm glad—even if you thought I was someone else."

"It wasn't that. But I saw her. She started laughing and I went nuts."

Vida ran her fingers through my hair and kind of twisted it, and then I lifted my face and she kissed me with that red mouth, slow and warm. "I'm glad it was you, Vida. I'm glad it was you instead of her." She began shuddering again.

Chapter Five

I woke up in the hotel the next morning without knowing exactly how I got there. My hand was swollen and discolored and I lay there feeling the pain spreading all through me. I looked at my watch and it was ten o'clock, so I figured I ought to find a doctor's office open at that hour. It was a job getting dressed and I didn't even try to shave. There was no way I could hold the hand without hurting it. I thought of Vida then and the whole thing was clear enough in my mind, but still it didn't seem real. No more of that, I thought. Sid is too important to you for you to take chances like that with his wife.

There was a doctor half a block from the hotel. He looked at the hand, prodded it in different places with his finger, frowning. "It's a fracture, all right."

He shot something into me with a needle and I felt my arm growing numb. That was about all I remembered, except for the red haze of pain and the shock of splintered bone ends snapping into place. It took maybe twenty minutes, getting the cast on and everything, and then he said, "That's all there is to it."

I ate something, later got a shave, found a used-car lot and bought a '46 Ford for five hundred dollars. It was noon by the time I phoned to see if Sid was at home.

Vida answered, and I said, "This is Roy. Is Sid around?"

Nothing happened for a minute, and it occurred to me that maybe she thought I was angling to take up where we'd stopped the night before. The hell with that, I thought. It was too risky.

"It's the job," I said. "I've got the car and everything's ready to go. I want to know where I can find Sid so I can get started."

"Oh," she said, in a voice that didn't mean anything one way or the other. "I think he's at the office," she went on, cool and impersonal. "That's the telephone office. The address is 116 West Main; it's over a department store." She hung up.

I stood there for a minute, the receiver in my hand. It seemed kind of crazy to have it broken off like that after what had happened just a few hours before. But I reminded myself that that was the way I wanted it, and apparently Vida wanted it the same way, so that made everything fine. Just fine.

I found the telephone office without any trouble. It was on the second floor of a two-story building, over a department store as Vida had said. It wasn't much of an office, really—a ten-by-twelve affair with bare walls and unswept floor. There was a long table against one wall where two men sat with six telephones, answering them as they rang. On the other side of the room there was an old-fashioned, roll-top desk and a tilt-back chair, and that was where Sid was sitting, looking weakly at a ledger. He looked up when I came in. He'd made a good comeback from the night before but he still looked pretty hung over.

"I thought maybe you'd changed your mind and left town," he said. Then he noticed my hand. "What the hell did you do to yourself?"

"I took a swing at Seaward's porch railing. I was pretty far gone."

He didn't know just what to make of that, so he let it alone. "Vida tells me you helped get me to bed last night. Thanks."

He didn't suspect a thing as far as I could see, so I grinned.

"What do you think of our setup here?" he said, nodding toward the other side of the room.

"It looks pretty wide open to me, for an illegal business like bootlegging. Don't you keep yourself guarded?"

Sid snorted. "Hell, who would bother us here? We pay for protection, and besides the building belongs to Seaward. The thing to remember is that bootlegging is a nice, quiet, everyday business, the way it's run now. We've made it respectable—almost respectable, anyway—here in Oklahoma, and that's the reason we don't have any more trouble than we do. People are going to drink, it doesn't make any difference about the laws."

"I guess so," I said.

"Sure they are. Well, you saw last night how we begin by buying up men like Keating and McErulur and all the rest of them, so there's no sense in going for rough stuff when you've got a setup like that. But the telephone end is what you're interested in now. I've got six phones and I'll get a couple more as soon as I can find good numbers; numbers easy for the customers to remember. I got one good one yesterday; had to pay fifty dollars for it. Five two's."

He opened a desk drawer and took out what seemed to be a box of five hundred business cards and handed it to me. One of the cards I picked out said: "Call Curly for Fast Delivery. The Best Brands at the Best Prices. 2-2222."

"Had the cards made up as soon as I got the number," Sid said. "Take these and pass them around. You have to advertise in bootlegging just like in any other business. Drop them in mail boxes. Shove them under doors in apartment houses. Leave them beside the customer's telephone when you make a delivery."

"Who's Curly?" I asked.

"Nobody. Every runner has a different number and a different name and works his own territory, as close as he can stay to it. A good runner can work up a damn good following; the boozers won't buy from anybody else but their regular man if they can help it."

Sid put his hand to his face and rubbed it. "God, I've got a head." Then he opened another drawer and took out a fifth of bonded stuff and broke the seal. "You want one?" he said.

"It's a little early for me."

He swigged from the neck, sat looking at it for a long moment, and finally put it back in the drawer.

"Anyway," he said, "here's the way you work it. We don't keep anything here, it's down at a warehouse in the south part of town. You go down there and pick up what you need, maybe a lug of bourbon and a split of gin and bonded stuff—they're about the only things you'll get calls for around here. After you do that you call the office here and they'll give you the addresses to go to. After you make a delivery you use the customer's phone and call the office back to see if they have any more deliveries to make in the neighborhood you're in. You keep it up that way until you run out of liquor, so then you go back to the warehouse and check out some more."

"Why don't I start out with several lugs to begin with?"

"Hijackers," Sid said. "Don't get caught with a big roll or a big load. Bootleggers are fair game for every south-side punk in town, and we can't go crying to the police about it if we get knocked off. Not even in Big Prairie."

"How does this other retailer, Kingkade, fit into it?"

"He has his own customers and I have mine. We cut it up like Big Prairie was two towns. What kind of car did you get?"

"A '46 Ford."

He nodded. "That's all right. A runner doesn't want anything fancy, it attracts too much attention. Well, we'll go down to the warehouse and I'll show you how it goes."

Sid had his warehouse in a little run-down grocery store near the south edge of town. The store, of course, was just a front, and the back end of the place was stacked high with cardboard cases of every kind of liquor you could think of. We parked the Ford in the alley behind the place and went in the back door. There was a kid about nineteen sitting on a case of Belmont, reading a comic book. A twelve-gauge shotgun leaned against the wall within easy reach.

"Hello, Sid," the kid said.

"Burt," Sid said, "this is Roy Foley. He's starting today as a runner." I shook hands with the kid, and Sid went on, "Either Burt or his brother will check the stuff out to you. They keep the records and run the grocery store for me; one of them will be here all the time." Sid stood there, his face sagging. After a minute he went over to a case of Yellowstone, tore the top back, and took out a pint. He took a long drink, then another, then he capped the pint and put it in his pocket.

"Is there anything else to know before I go to work?" I asked.

"I guess not." He looked at a phone on the wall. "You can call the office and see if they've got anything for you."

I went over and began dialing 2-2222, and Sid said, "Not that number, for God's sake. A customer may be trying to get it and you'll have the line tied up. Try 8-8627, that's the office phone all the runners use when they call in." So I dialed it and a voice said, "Yeah?" Sid took the phone out of my hand.

"Morgan? This is Sid. I'm starting a new runner going under the name of Curly. He'll handle north of Twenty-third Street, on the west side. Have you got anything out there?" He waited a minute and said, "218 Willow Drive. You'd better write that down, Roy."

Sid hung up, still looking pretty wrung out. "Well, there it is. You're in business, Roy. You've got your first customer."

"What do they want?"

"Two pints of Old Quaker. That'll be nine dollars." He took out his bottle, looked at it, and then hit it. "Burt, you get him straight on the prices, will you? I'm going back to the office and try to lose this head."

After Sid was gone the kid straightened me out on the prices; then he checked me out and loaded me up, putting the stuff under the front seat of the Ford. He stood in the back door grinning as I turned the car around with one hand to pull out of the alley.

Well, this is the first step, Foley, I thought. You've got the wedge in. All you have to do now is find a hammer and split the thing wide open. And by God, I'd do it! I could feel it.

It took me about a week to find out that I could make money on the side in bootlegging, as in most other things. When I got a call to a party I could sell them red-stamp stuff for green-stamp prices and, if they were drunk enough, they would never know the difference. And some of the customers would have the runners bring other things out with the whisky—cigarettes, sandwiches, whatever they wanted—and that would always mean a tip.

But being a runner for a bootlegger was like scrambling for pennies just outside a gold mine. There was no telling how much Seaward was making out of his operations, but it was plenty. I didn't intend to scramble for pennies any longer than I had to, but I couldn't rush into the thing. I had to wait and take my time, and then one day I'd find an angle and work it for all it was worth. In the meantime, there was Lola. There was no way of getting away from her, so I tried to forget her and concentrate on my job. I kept telling myself to take it one thing at a time. After I discovered a way to move in on Seaward's bootlegging business, then there would be plenty of time for other things.

Then there was Vida. I thought it was all over with Vida after that one night, but I learned pretty soon that Vida wasn't a girl you could think about or not think about, the way you would switch a light off and on. I kept reminding myself that she was Sid's wife, and right now, Sid was a man I couldn't do without. Keep out of her way—that was about all I could do.

I moved into a rooming house on Fourth Street and began to work on the million small details that had to be taken care of before I could make a push against a guy like Seaward. I learned that Seaward and Kingkade were pretty sore about the way I'd taken seven hundred dollars off them in the poker game, especially when they found out that I had hired on with Sid as a common runner. But it didn't bother me. As long as I attended to business and kept my mind off Lola and Vida, I was all right.

I'd had my hand out of the cast for about two days when I made a routine call to the downtown office and they gave me an order out on West Twenty-first. The place was a tourist court and I had made deliveries there before, so I figured it was just another traveling salesman letting off steam. But when I got there I saw that red convertible of Sid's parked in the garage next to the cabin.

Well, I figured, maybe Sid's gone to solitary drinking. The order was for Scotch so I got a bottle of Ballentines from under the front seat and went up to the door. I didn't get an answer at first, but I could hear water running inside and I guessed that somebody was taking a shower. Then the water was shut off and I knocked again.

"Come in."

I would have recognized that voice anywhere. It was Vida. When she opened the door and stood there smiling at me, I knew what was going to happen.

"Come in, Roy."

"Are you crazy?" I said. "That red convertible can be spotted clear to the highway!"

"There are a lot of red convertibles. But I'll come in a cab the next time, if it bothers you."

She wore a long white terry-cloth robe that covered her completely from her throat to the floor. Her hair hung even straighter than I remembered it, and the ends were damp where she had missed getting it inside her shower cap.

"While I waited for you to get here," she said, "I took a cold shower. I've taken a lot of cold showers, Roy. They're overrated."

She came toward me, floating almost, inside the loose folds of the robe. I reached out for her and only then did I realize how much I wanted her. How much I had missed her. I put my mouth on hers and we stood there for a long time. Finally she said, "Roy?"

"Yes?" I touched her hair. It was amazingly soft. "You're not mixed up this time, are you?"

"No. I'm not mixed up at all."

A strange thing happened then. I began pulling at the robe and it loosened. I put my hand inside and caressed the cool curve of her back, still damp from the shower, and I felt a kind of gentleness that I had never felt before. I pressed her close, but not hard. When I kissed her again, the fire was still there but the savageness was gone.

"Roy, is anything wrong?"

"No."

Her eyes were puzzled when I released her and the folds of her robe fell back into place. I couldn't explain it to her because I wasn't sure what was happening myself.

There was a wall phone near the head of the bed, so I used it to call the office and tell them I had car trouble and they would have to give my orders to another runner. Then I went into the two-by-four kitchenette and made two drinks with plain water. I came back in with the drinks and Vida was sitting on the edge of the bed, watching me with those silent eyes.

"Did you ever think what would happen," I said, "if Sid found out a thing like this was going on? Sid can be a tough boy. He could kill you if he got mad enough."

She shrugged faintly.

"It doesn't matter to you?" I asked.

"Not much."

I sat down beside her and looked at my drink. Two or three minutes went by before I said, "It looks like we'd better get ourselves straight, Vida. A thing like this isn't very smart for either of us. You've got Sid, and I've got plans."

"I think I already know what they are. You mean to move in on Sid, don't you?" I almost dropped my drink at that, but she went on before I could say anything. "And that means you'll have to move against Seaward, too. That will be dangerous, Roy."

I tried to sound surprised. "Now that's a hell of an idea! What makes you think I'd try to shove around a man like Seaward?"

She looked at me and then at her drink. "I don't know exactly. I think it's Lola Keating. Are you still in love with her, Roy?" But she didn't wait for an answer. "I think you are," she said flatly. "You think you hate her—still, you're willing to fight men like Seaward for her special benefit. What are you trying to prove?"

"I'm not trying to prove anything. I hate her guts."

"Love and hate are very close sometimes," she said. "What do you feel with me, Roy?"

She put her drink down and lay back on the bed. The robe fell open.

"Come here," she said softly.

Those white arms came up and went around my neck and pulled me down.

"Don't talk. We can talk later. Don't talk," she kept crooning. And I didn't.

There was no way of knowing how much time had passed. I lay in the soft circle of her arms, thinking nothing, drinking in a great feeling of peace. It was strange, the way I felt about her. For that moment it was almost as if we were the only two people in the world.

"Did you like it?" she asked.

"What do you think?"

She laughed soundlessly. "What do you think of me, Roy? Do you think I'm bad?"

"No—but you scare me."

She lifted her face from my shoulder and looked at me. "I think I can see what is going on in your mind," she said finally. "You think I do this all the time, don't you? Because my husband is a lush, and he's no good in bed, then it makes sense for his wife to take her loving where she finds it. You wouldn't believe me if I told you there had been nobody else before you, would you?"

"I believe you."

"Then what is it?"

"I'm afraid I'm falling in love with you."

I hadn't meant to say it—but there it was. A minute passed, or an hour, and there in the quiet of the room I could feel my insides winding up tighter and tighter. I think I prayed then, the first time I'd ever tried it. God, don't let her laugh! I pleaded.

She didn't laugh. She said, "Hold me close, Roy. Hold me as close as you can."

The worst was over. The terrible sickness that had been closing in on me began to retreat.

She said softly, "When did you decide, Roy?"

"Just a little while ago. When I first came in, I guess."

"What was it like?"

"I—I don't know. When I kissed you, I wanted you but I was afraid of hurting you. I've never been very particular about hurting people before. And you were cool and clean and alive. I don't know how to say it, but I knew you were what I wanted."

"Did I remind you of—someone else?"

"No. It wasn't that."

But that wasn't the truth; I realized it the moment I said it. Somewhere in the cellar of my mind I could see Lola—cool, clean, alive, as she had been that night so long ago. I began to wind up again and I think Vida felt it. But if she did, she said nothing about it. After a while the feeling went away and Vida was saying, "I think I'll take that drink now."

But before I could get dressed she said, "I've got a confession to make, Roy. Until now I wasn't sure why I came here and tricked you into meeting me. But I know now. I'm afraid I'm falling in love with you, too."

It was an awkward thing for both of us. I looked at her, then finished tying my shoes and went into the kitchenette to get the drinks. When I came back, Vida was sitting crosslegged in the center of the bed, the white robe draped over her shoulders like a cape. Her figure was almost perfect, wasplike at the waist, flaring at the hips, and tapering into long, smooth legs.

"Do you want to talk?" she said.

"Not unless you do something to that robe."

She laughed softly and pulled the robe about her like a tent. Most women would have started right in with "What are we going to do now?" But all Vida said was, "Do you want to tell me about your plans, Roy?"

I knew she didn't mean about us And I wasn't sure how much I ought to tell her about the other business. At last I said, "Do you know much about how Seaward runs things?"

"No," she said evenly. "But I imagine I could find out from Sid."

"Could you find out when he's bringing a shipment into the state? I'll need to know just what kind of truck he's using, who's driving, who's riding guard. I'll also have to know what route he takes and approximately the time he hits the state line."

She didn't even blink. "I can find out from Sid, but I'll have to do it a little at a time and it may take several days. Men have been killed hijacking whisky trucks. Don't underrate Seaward. He can be hard." Then she smiled. "You told Sid you could raise the money when you needed it. You can't, can you?"

It was good to have someone that I didn't have to lie to. "I couldn't raise a penny," I said. "But all I need is one load of liquor, and Barney Seaward is going to furnish that." I leaned forward and took Vida's shoulders. "Before I'm through, Vida, I'm going to own this county. I'm going to own it harder, and squeeze more out of it than Barney Seaward ever dreamed was possible. I'm going all the way to the top, Vida, and I'm going to step on a lot of people getting there, but that can't be helped. Will you go with me?"

She almost whispered. "I guess there's no place for me to go now, except with you. But what about Lola?"

"What about her?"

"Every time her name is mentioned you freeze up," she said. "You get cold and hard and I can see the hate flame up behind your eyes. Do you have to hurt her, Roy? Is that the reason you have to take this risk?"

I couldn't lie to her. I said, "Yes—I guess that's the reason."

Chapter Six

Vida didn't like the idea of hijacking one of Seaward's trucks, and I didn't like it much either, after I started thinking about it. But that was the way it had to be. I couldn't very well break into bootlegging without anything to sell, and I sure couldn't raise the money to buy the stuff.

The actual job of stealing the whisky was going to be tough, but even at that it would be easier, I figured, than the job of keeping it after I had it. It would almost certainly mean that I'd have to sit on it for a while before doing anything with it, and probably I'd have to move out of Big Prairie County. It wasn't going to look right for a common runner to suddenly turn retailer, and especially it wasn't going to look right to Barney Seaward who supplied the retailers and furnished the protection in the county.

But moving out of Big Prairie was the thing I hated most. In the first place, the county sat right in the middle of the state and that meant that not many people would be driving over to Kansas or Texas or Arkansas for their liquor. Big Prairie was the ideal spot for bootleggers because the drinkers had to depend on them. And there was Vida, too. Maybe if I said the word she would leave Sid and go with me, but it seemed a shame to break up that direct connection to the county's political machine. Big Prairie was a tailor-made spot for a bootlegger and it made me sore to think of leaving it.

But I think Lola was the real reason I hated to leave.

I would go along for days keeping her locked in the back of my mind, then suddenly, unexpectedly all that dammed-up hate would break loose again. When that happened I'd go a little crazy, because I knew there wasn't a thing I could do about it. There was no way I could hit back at her. No way I could hurt her. God, I kept thinking, if I only had the money Seaward had! If I only had the power he had! Oh, I could make them crawl, all right. I could put the screws on that husband of hers and that would bring her to her knees. Paul Keating was Lola's weakness, and the startling thing about it was that I hadn't realized it before. Lola was ambition. She lived it. She breathed it. God, I thought—and the idea was as bright as a new sword—if I only had Seaward's power!

There was no easy way of doing it and no good way of doing it. I'd have to take all I could and play it as well as I could, and the rest would depend on how much I could do in how little time. Assuming, of course, that I didn't get killed in the hijacking. Or if Seaward didn't get suspicious and track me down and send me to the bottom of some river. There were a thousand "ifs" and all of them were deadly, but as long as there was a chance in the gamble, I had to take it.

So that is the way it would have gone, probably, if it hadn't been for the phone call.

It was a routine call to the telephone office and they gave me an address out of my territory, way out in Western Heights, where the big homes were.

"What the hell!" I said. "That's not my territory."

"It's nobody's territory," the phone man said wearily, "but you have to make the delivery just the same. A lug of Scotch, two fifths of gin, and a lug of green-stamp bourbon."

"I haven't got it with me. I'll have to go back to the warehouse."

"Then go to the warehouse, but get it out there."

"Who lives there, anyway?"

The phone man laughed. "Big Prairie's promising young county attorney. By the way, there's no charge on this. It's on Sid."

I got to the car somehow, sitting there for a long while until the wildness began to die. The lousy snob, I thought, she did it on purpose! But that didn't make sense either. If anybody like Lola Keating had asked for a special runner, the phone man would have said something about it. It was just a lousy break and there was nothing I could do about it.

By the time I got to the warehouse I had cooled off some and begun to think straight again. Probably Keating was throwing a party, and if that was the case Lola would be so busy with that end I wouldn't even see her. The kid checked me out with the stuff and, on the long chance that there might be another runner around, I asked him if somebody else could make the delivery. There wasn't anybody else. So that settled it.

I almost had myself believing that everything was going to be all right as I wound around the crooked, elm-lined streets looking for the address. When I finally found the place it was pretty much like all the others, a low, ranch-type brick house set back from the street behind a well-cared-for lawn. I looked at the house and thought, So that's where she lives. And then I realized that I was gripping the steering wheel tightly enough to snap it in two.

I drove between two brick pillars and up a graveled road that curved around the back of the house, and I thought sourly, The back door's the place for you, Foley. I parked near the back steps and got the stuff out from under the front seat. The back door opened then and a young, dull-eyed girl stood holding the door open for me as I came up the steps with my arms full.

I put the stuff on the kitchen table and looked around. "You alone here?"

She nodded suspiciously, as though she expected me to start making passes at her. The hell with her. I was breathing freely now, feeling a queer sort of excitement take hold of me. *Her* house, I thought. This is where *she* lives. I wandered through the big white kitchen and came into a richly carpeted dining room where a lot of stuff was laid out, all kind of nuts in little copper bowls and trays of tiny sandwiches. It was going to be a party, all right.

"Look," the girl said worriedly, "you can't go in there. Missus Keating won't like it."

"What she doesn't know won't hurt her." The house fascinated me, now that I knew Lola wasn't there. I went into the front room and stood there staring savagely at the richness of it, while the girl followed behind me, complaining and whining.

"Shut up and get out of here!"

She got out. She scurried like a rabbit in loose leaves. It was the wrong thing to do and I knew it. She would tell Lola and Lola would tell Keating and finally the word would get back to Seaward and Sid and I'd be out of a job. I'd be out of everything. But right then I didn't give a damn. I don't know how much time passed before the front door opened and Lola came in. She stood there, faintly startled, a key in her hand.

She said coldly, "What are you doing here?"

I said nothing.

"Cora," she called, "come here this instant!" The girl came in from the kitchen. She had been crying. "What is this man doing here, Cora?" Lola demanded.

The girl made a strangled sound, too scared to talk.

I said tightly, "I brought the liquor you ordered from Sid."

"To the front room?"

The rage broke then. The dam washed out. "No," I said, "I brought it in the back door. That's right, isn't it? You wouldn't want the neighbors to see a Burk Street bootlegger coming in the front way, would you, Lola?"

Her mouth turned down in a sneer and she wasn't beautiful at all. "I can see it's no use trying to be civil to you. Get out of my house."

"I'll get out," I said, "but not until I'm damn good and ready." It was funny, but I wasn't afraid of her then. In the back of my mind I knew that I was tearing everything down, destroying everything completely. But I was drunk with the knowledge that I could stand in front of her and look at her and not feel torn apart.

"You were born in the gutter," she said coldly, "and you'll live in the gutter all your life!" She laughed harshly. "You were going to college! You were going to amount to something! That's funny, it's really very funny!" She laughed again, but the laughter seemed forced, as though she wasn't quite sure of herself.

"I guess it was pretty funny at that," I said. "You thought it was funny when I first said it."

Her face seemed to drop and the laughter stopped. "You're sick," she said.

"Your brain is sick and twisted. No one but an insane person could keep a hate alive that long."

"You ought to know, Lola. I understand you. I've been afraid of you for a long time, but I'm not afraid any more. You know why, Lola? Because I'm going to break you before I'm through. I'm going to make you crawl, Lola."

She tried to laugh again but the sound died abruptly. "You are insane!" she said, and she sounded vaguely frightened. "By tomorrow you won't even have a job! I'll see to that. You won't even be allowed in Big Prairie!" She put her hands in front of her face, and I wasn't sure what was going on inside her until she said hoarsely, bitterly, "Oh, God, how I hate you!"

And then I could laugh, because I knew that I had been right about her. I threw my head back and let my laughter roll and the sound of it filled the room.

She sank into a chair, still holding her hands in front of her face. Her shoulders began shaking as I turned and walked out.

It didn't take long for Lola to make her threat good. When I got back to my rooming house the hall phone was ringing and when I answered it, it was Sid.

"Where the hell have you been?" He was mad.

"Out making deliveries. I just checked in at the warehouse."

"I want to see you, and damn quick."

I knew that was the end of it. I hung up. When the phone started ringing again I let it ring. I went upstairs and numbly started putting clothes into a suitcase.

I should have been panicky, but somehow I wasn't. I sat down and thought about it for a few minutes, and I still wasn't sorry for what had happened. But had it been worth it, really? How was the thing going to settle after the elation had worn off? Jesus, I thought, here I was within reach of money and power and I threw it all away on one crazy impulse!

It began to come then, the big emptiness as the elation slipped away. If it would have done any good, I think I would have gone back out there and begged her to call it off. She could do it. But she wouldn't, and I knew she wouldn't. She would laugh and I would probably kill her, and that would really be the end of everything. God, I thought bitterly, if I only had Seaward's power!

And I guess that's when I began to get the idea. If I only had the power Seaward had! That thought stuck in my brain and I couldn't get rid of it. All right, what *was* the power he had? Money, for one thing, and plenty of it. But, it wasn't the money that made him big, it was his political power and the knowledge that he could make or break any politician in Big Prairie County. He could make or break Paul Keating.

Then the thought hit me, the whole plan, full grown. It stunned me for a moment. It's too simple, I thought, there must be a catch in it somewhere. I turned it over in my mind, looking at all sides of it for the flaw, but I couldn't see it. I came to my feet. "Well, I'll be damned!"

The way I saw it, Paul Keating was the key to the whole thing. The key to Lola's weakness—her ambition. All I had to do was find a club to hold over Paul Keating's head. Or if I couldn't find a club, manufacture one. I couldn't see any reason why it wouldn't work, at least for a little while. Keating seemed spineless enough, which was probably the reason Seaward had put him in the county attorney's office in the first place.

If I tried it and it didn't work—I didn't like to think of what would happen. I was in enough trouble already. Out of a job and in bad with Barney and Sid. And Vida hadn't had a chance to get the information I had to have to try the hijacking.

It was settled, actually, even before I went over all the arguments against it. I had to try it. It was either that or lose everything.

Not more than fifteen minutes had passed between the time Sid said he wanted to see me and I made up my mind to take the gamble. If I didn't show up pretty soon Sid would be looking for me, and probably some of Seaward's truck drivers as well, so I had to get out of there. I looked at my watch and it was three-thirty.

The first thing I did was visit a camera shop. Then I went to the Travelers Hotel and rented a room on the fourth floor. The bellhop hustled around the way hops do when they show a guest to a room, pulling blinds, raising windows, snapping lights off and on.

"Will there be anything else, sir?"

"Yes," I said. "I want a girl."

He blinked, then grinned. Nothing much could jar him.

"Yes, sir. Things're kind of hot on girls, but I think I can get you something."

"Not just something," I said. "She has to be young, reasonably good-looking, and put together like a brick out-house."

"I know just the one."

He was already heading for the door when I caught him and gave him five dollars. "This is to help make a bad memory worse," I said.

"Yes, *sir!*" He was on his way.

I stood in the middle of the room for a few minutes, trying to decide what I should do next. Then I went over to the closet and began prying one of the panels off the door. After I got that done, I put the panel back in place and pressed in two small moulding nails to hold it there. Then I sat on the bed and unwrapped the camera I had bought.

I had the whole works, two dozen flash bulbs, a flash attachment, and one of those cameras that takes a picture and develops it and gives you the positive print all in sixty seconds. I'd never snapped a picture in my life, and now that I was finally going to snap one, it had to be perfect. I needed practice and I needed it in a hurry.

The instructions seemed simple enough. I put the flash attachment on, then put in one of the bulbs, and fiddled with the lens until I guessed it was about right. The panel in the closet door came out again. I got inside the closet, aimed the camera through the hole in the door and pressed the shutter lever.

The whole room lit up for an instant as though lightning had struck it. When I pulled the film out, sixty seconds later all I had was a black piece of glossy printing paper. Without a thing on it.

I read the instructions more carefully this time, and went back into the closet to try again. It still wasn't good, but when I took the film out I could make out the ghostly image of the bed. Too much exposure, I decided, so I made more corrections and shot again. I used up a dozen flash bulbs, with a chair placed in the middle as a target, and every picture got a little better.

Then the knock came.

She didn't wait for an invitation. She tried the knob of the door and saw that it wasn't locked so she came in. If she was surprised at seeing me standing in the closet looking through the hole I had made, she didn't show it. She sat on the bed, staring vacantly around the room, until I came out. Then she smiled. The smile was vacant, too.

"The boy said you wanted some fun, honey."

She was perfect for what I wanted, a broad-rumped, heavy-breasted, Jersey-cowlike girl.

"Stand up," I said. "Let's see what you look like on your feet."

She got up, stretching lazily. "This all right, honey?"

"That's fine. Right there by the chair." I went back into the closet and took aim at her. She was a long way from being ugly—her hair was rich brown and long, but uncared-for. She was about twenty, and it took only a brief glance to know that her young, overripe body was her stock and trade. Her dress was a sleazy off-the-rack print pulling almost to the bursting point across her bulging hips and breasts.

"All right," I said. When I pushed the shutter lever, setting off the flash bulb, she jumped. "What is this?"

"Just a minute and I'll show you.' I came out and she looked on curiously as I began pulling the film out of the camera.

I handed it to her and she said, 'Well!" in a tone that didn't mean anything. "It makes me look a little fat, don't you think? But it isn't bad."

"It could be sharper," I said. I changed the shutter speed the least bit, snapped off the ceiling lights and turned on a floor lamp. "Let's try it again, this time without clothes."

"Look, honey," she said patiently. "I've seen plenty of strange ones, so if you want to take pictures it's all right with me. Clothes or no clothes. But I have to have my money in advance."

I gave her a ten and a five and she smiled in a vague sort of way, then put the two bills in a leatherette bag. "Honey, I can be real nice. Are you sure you want it this way?"

"I'm crazy about it this way. I just like to take pictures all the time."

She shrugged the smallest shrug in the world, and began stripping.

She was perfect. That overripe body, those swollen breasts—she looked like the great grandmother of all the whores in Babylon. For a moment she stood alone, pale, deadly white, in the midst of the flash bulbs' silent explosion. I came out of the closet, snapped the ceiling lights on, and after a minute we looked at the picture. It was perfect.

I said, "All right, you can put your clothes on and we'll talk business."

I went over to the window and looked down on Big Prairie until she was dressed.

When I turned around she was sitting there, fully dressed, waiting for me say something. I got out my wallet, took out five twenties, and laid the crisp green bills on the bed. She looked at them hungrily, not moving.

"Do you want to make a hundred?"

"What kind of a question is that, honey?"

"All right," I said, "we're going to make one more picture and the hundred's yours. But you're going to have a partner in the next one. This is the way it's going to be. First, you've got to have a robe of some kind, something good and long that you can wrap yourself in and look dressed, even when you've got nothing on under it. The next thing you do is make a telephone call to the county courthouse and tell them you want to talk to the county attorney. His name's Paul Keating. When you get Keating on the phone you tell him you've got some information that his grand jury will be interested in. Tell him it's about Barney Seaward. Tell him it's so bad you're afraid to talk about it over the phone, and when he asks where he can talk to you, you give him this room number in the Travelers Hotel."

She looked up then, beginning to get it. "So when this Paul Keating comes around, I get him in the room, shuck my robe, and you snap a picture of us."

"That's it."

She got up slowly, reaching for the bills, but I grabbed them first.

"After," I said. "Now get going. Get that robe somewhere and make the telephone call—and don't put it through the hotel switchboard."

She picked up her bag and walked toward the door, switching her rump at me. She opened the door, then paused. "Honey, will you take care of the bellhop? After all, this isn't like a regular trick."

"All right," I said impatiently. "Now get out of here." She left.

The whole thing seemed pretty damn crude. Still, I couldn't see any reason why it wouldn't work. I felt sure that Paul Keating would jump fast if he thought Seaward was in trouble. After all, Barney was the man Keating was depending on to put him in the governor's mansion.

The whole thing depended on Keating himself—how much guts he had and how much of a bluff he would swallow. If it didn't work—I couldn't allow myself to think about that. And if it *did* work....

I liked to think about that.

In about thirty minutes the girl came back.

"Tell me about it," I said. "What did Keating say?"

"I've got a name," she said. "It's Rose—that's the reason I got this robe with the roses on it." She held the robe in front of her and admired herself in the dresser mirror. "Well, he was interested all right," she said, looking over her shoulder at me. "He wanted me to come to his office, but I told him what you said, that the information was too bad and I was afraid Seaward was having me followed. He didn't like it much, coming to the hotel, but he finally gave in."

"When?"

"Four-thirty," she said.

I looked at my watch and it was a little after four. "All right. Let's see how the robe fits."

She could have gone into the bathroom to change, but I guess it never occurred to Rose. She stripped right in the middle of the room.

Then she posed for me, turning clumsily, imitating the fashion models she'd probably seen in newsreels.

"That'll do, I guess. Can you shuck the thing fast when the time comes?"

"In less than a second, I'l bet. All I have to do is pull the tie and shrug my shoulders. You want to see me do it?"

"Never mind, I'll take your word for it."

We had almost a half hour to kill and it was a long half hour. But Keating was right on time. At four-thirty sharp there was a light rap at the door and I grabbed my camera, making elaborate gestures for Rose to get her robe on right. Keating was knocking the second time when I closed the closet door on myself. I didn't see him come in, but I heard the door open and Rose saying, "Mr. Keating—?"

She was a pretty good actress, at that. She did it just right, not too eager but kind of nervous. Keating said something and I began easing the loose panel up, making a crack to look through.

Keating didn't look very comfortable and he didn't like the setup at all. He looked around sharply as Rose slipped behind him and snapped the latch on the door. He took out an immaculate handkerchief and daubed at his forehead. "Well— Very well, Miss Carson. Now what is this information you mentioned over the phone?"

By now she had maneuvered him into the center of the room, the way we had planned it. "Do you promise," she asked anxiously, "not to tell where you got the information?"

"Of course, Miss Carson. It will be confidential, I assure you." Keating was beginning to get interested now. She had him in profile to the closet, which was just right. I saw her working with her belt then, and that was my cue to go to work. Keating started to say something, but no sound came out. His mouth merely came open and stayed open. She brought it off as calmly as she would light a cigarette. One smooth motion broke the bow in the belt and the robe came open. She shrugged her shoulders; the robe fell away completely.

I almost laughed at the look on Keating's face. He was completely frozen, shocked beyond speech, beyond movement. He stood there like a stone statue as Rose wriggled against him and slipped her arms around his neck, and by that time I had the panel down and the camera aimed. She flattened her bare belly against him and hung onto his neck, leaning back from the waist up. For just an instant they stood that way. The camera clicked and the silent crash of light lit up the room.

Keating reacted to that. He whirled, knocking the girl against the bed. When I stepped out of the closet I thought he was going to faint. His face went white as he began to realize what had happened. Then he sprang at me, growling deep in his throat and grabbing frantically at the camera.

As a lawyer, Paul Keating may have been pretty good, but as a fighter he was less than nothing. With the camera in my left hand, I stepped to one side and hit him full in the face with my right fist. I could feel the ache all the way to my shoulder. I shifted the camera and slammed my left in his belly, low. He went to his knees.

I made sure that Keating was in no hurry to get up; then I gave Rose the five twenties and waited for her to get dressed. It could have been a minute or an hour—but after a while she finally eased out.

Keating kneeled on all fours, gasping, sick from that low punch. I realized then that I still had the camera in my hand. The realization almost sent me into panic. Maybe I had left the exposed film in too long and it was ruined! But the picture was all right. I pulled it out of the camera and tore it off.

"How do you like it, Keating?" I held it in front of him and jerked it back before he could grab it.

His mouth worked. "It— It was a trick," he said painfully. He shook his head, blood from his split mouth dripping to the carpet. "It was a trick—she was in on it all the time." He looked up then, at me. "This is extortion, Foley. Do you know what they do to extortionists in this state?"

"It isn't extortion unless I try to get something out of you. Now get up."

He got up slowly, wiping his mouth on his handkerchief. "It was a trick," he said again. "I can prove it in any court in Oklahoma. If I have to, I can get experts to swear that it's a composite picture you had made up for the purpose of blackmail." His legal brain was beginning to work now, and he was gaining confidence. "Give the picture to me," he said, holding out his hand. "If you refuse, I'll see you behind bars."

I laughed. "The last thing you would do," I said, "is bring this up in court. Sure, you could prove that it was a trick. You could even send me to prison, maybe—but you're not going to. Do you know why? It would be the end of your political career, that's why. No matter how many experts you brought in and how completely you proved it. Look," I said, holding the picture in front of him again, "do you know what I'll do if you ever mention this? I'll get a hundred thousand copies of this picture printed and I'll send a copy to every voter in Big Prairie County. Do you think your good church members would believe what an expert told them or what they saw with their own eyes? Look at the picture, Keating. Does it look faked?"

His brief moment of fight was over. He looked as if someone were turning a knife in him.

"Why—?" he said hoarsely. It was almost a sob. "What have I done to you? What do you want from me?"

"First, I want you to call Sid and tell him not to pay any attention to anything your wife might have told him earlier today. Tell him she was upset or something and it was all a mistake and there's no reason to take me off the payroll."

He stared blankly. "What is this? I don't even know what you're talking about."

"You'll find out later. Just do as I say."

Now he looked more puzzled than hurt. He just stood there for a moment, studying me; then he picked up the room phone and gave the hotel operator the number of Sid's office.

"Sid? This is Paul Keating. I believe my wife talked to you today about one of your runners—" Sid said something—I could guess what it was. "It was nothing," Keating said. "Lola was upset, that's all; it's been a hectic day, we're planning for a few people tonight." He listened for a minute. "Yes, I'm sure, Sid. Will you get in touch with Barney and tell him everything's all right? No, it's perfectly all right. There's no use saying anything to Foley about it."

"That was very good," I said when he hung up.

"Is that all?" he asked coldly.

"Just keep on being smart," I said. "If you ever get an idea about turning

Sid and Seaward against me, just remember this picture and what it would do to your political career."

He got out.

I could breathe now. Then I looked at the picture and laughed. I fell across the bed and howled. I would give plenty to see Lola's face when she first laid eyes on it.

Chapter Seven

What I should have done was find a photographer that I could trust and have the copies made up right away. But I figured Keating was too stunned and scared to do anything about it right now.

The more I thought about the setup the better I liked it. By holding that picture over Keating, I thought, there was even a chance that I could put pressure on Seaward. Barney had spent a lot of money getting Keating where he was in the political setup, and he wasn't likely to let all that fall out from under him if he could help it. I had a bargaining point now, and before it was all over I was going to bargain myself right into a Big Prairie retailing position. But the thing that excited me most was the knowledge that I could smash Lola anytime I felt like it. I could make her crawl; I could make her beg!

It was almost dark when I got back to the rooming house. The hall phone was ringing again and when I answered it was Vida.

"Roy!" The word came out as a gasp. "Roy, I've been trying to get you all day. Roy, listen to me. Something's wrong, horribly wrong!"

"How do you know?"

"Sid was mad. He just left here, Roy, and he was half drunk and crazy mad. He said he was going to get you. He said Barney was after you too."

I grinned. "Maybe they *were* after me," I said, "but not any more. There was a little trouble but it's all straightened out now."

I could almost feel her gripping the phone. "Roy, are you sure?"

"Of course, I'm sure. I saw that it was all straightened out. Can I see you tonight?"

We didn't even mention Sid any more. By ten o'clock he would be too drunk to notice or care if Vida was even in the house. "All right, Roy."

I hung up, went to my room, and sat on the edge of the bed, thinking. Maybe it wouldn't be necessary to try the hijacking after all—but I didn't believe it. Even if I could bluff Seaward into installing me as a retailer, I didn't have the money to make the start. Twenty thousand dollars, Sid had said.

I sat there for a long while, letting the thing filter through my mind. Finally I decided that there was only one thing to do, and that was to hijack the liquor, get rid of it, and then get out of Big Prairie fast and take Vida with me. The hell with holding a club over Keating's head and praying that he and Seaward would play along with me.

All right, I thought, the idea running fast now, finish it up good and get out. The only reason you wanted to stay in the first place was because of Lola, and now you can bring her to her knees and get the money too, all in one giant sweep! I'd do it just the way I had threatened Keating I would. I'd have a hundred thousand copies of that picture made. I'd flood the county with them. There was no reason why I couldn't. The only bad thing about it was that I wouldn't be able to stay and watch Lola as her world started falling down around her shoulders. But I would know how she felt—and I could laugh.

The thought was fully grown. I stood there holding it, fondling it, proud of it. And then it exploded in my face.

"Sid just left here," Vida had said on the phone!

Just left here.

That bomb had lain there for fifteen or twenty minutes and I hadn't even noticed it until it went off. I'd been too self-satisfied when I had talked to Vida. Frantically, I back-tracked through my mind to pick up the exact words Vida had used. "He just left here, Roy, and he was half drunk and crazy mad"—I thought that was what she had said, but I was too shaken now to be sure of anything.

If she had, it meant that Sid had left his office, where he had been when Keating had talked to him from the hotel room. It meant that somebody had talked to him after that, but I couldn't believe that it could have been Keating. It was possible that Lola could have got the truth out of her husband, though. His mouth had been split and his face bruised, and Lola would have to have an explanation for that....

I almost ripped the door off getting out of the room and downstairs to the phone, but another roomer was using it. I tore out of the front door and up the sidewalk toward a drugstore two blocks away. The important thing was to get in touch with Vida again and find out for sure.

I was within half a block of the drugstore when the car pulled up to the curb ahead of me. Two men got out, one in his shirt sleeves and one wearing a leather jacket. They cut me off, and the one in the leather jacket said, "What's the hurry, Foley?"

I knew then that all my fine schemes had gone to pot.

"Into the car with him," the one in the shirt sleeves said. They had my arms behind me, jostling me toward the curb, and I knew they must be a couple of Seaward's truck drivers.

"What the hell is this!" I snapped. I tried to break away; then the man in the leather jacket jerked up my arm, jamming my fist against the base of my skull and almost ripping my shoulder out of the socket. The one in the shirt sleeves stepped back, took all the time in the world to get set, and then hit me as hard as he could in the face.

The shock snapped my head back as if I had been hit with a hammer. I could feel my cheek split on the inside and warm, salt-tasting blood began oozing into my mouth. I sagged, half numb, as they went through my pockets rapidly.

"Have a look in his room," the man in the jacket said, and the other went away.

"Get in the car."

He had a leather-covered blackjack in his hand. I got in, trying to choke the sickness down. He got in beside me and closed the door, staring straight ahead at nothing.

After a while the other one came back and got under the steering wheel.

"Did you find it?" the man in the leather jacket said.

"Everything," the one in the shirt sleeves said. "The camera, the pictures, the works." He shook his head. "Geez! How dumb can they get!" He started the car and we headed south, the three of us jammed into the front seat. I was too sick, too hurt, too full of overwhelming disgust at myself to care about anything.

Not until we were well out of town and across the river did I realize that we were headed for Seaward's place. We went through the open gate, around a graveled drive to the back of the house, and I saw four men coming toward us, walking into the bright beam of our headlights. Seaward, Sid, Paul Keating, and Joe Kingkade.

"Get out," Barney Seaward said coldly.

The man in the jacket opened the door and pulled me out after him. Sid stood spread-legged in front of me, red-faced, his little eyes glinting savagely in the headlights. "You lousy punk!" he said thickly. "You goddamn lousy punk!" He took a step toward me, unsteadily, and then lunged drunkenly into the grillework of the car.

"I think we found what you wanted, Barney," the man in the shirt sleeves said, and he handed Barney the pictures. Barney didn't look at them. He handed them to Keating and said "Is this everything?"

Keating looked quickly. "Yes."

Barney took out a lighter, snapped it and set fire to the photographs, the positive and negative prints. They flared up quickly and then died out. Barney ground the ashed paper under his heel, watching me with those cool, business-like eyes, as though he hadn't quite made up his mind what to do with me. Keating stood stone-faced, with a patch of adhesive at the corner of his mouth. How could I have misjudged him? I thought. Kingkade lit a cigarette and studied me dispassionately. If it had been up to him, he would have me killed because it was the neatest way of disposing of the situation.

"Foley," Seaward said finally, "I've thought about killing you, but I've decided you're not worth the trouble and the risk. By tomorrow morning you'll be out of Big Prairie. Out of Oklahoma. I don't care where you go, or how, but you're not ever to come back. Is that clear?"

I looked at them and said, "Go to hell."

Seaward's eyebrows raised slightly. "Max," he said, and the man in the jacket stepped forward. "Joel," he said, and the shirt-sleeved one stepped up. Max hit me solidly in the stomach. As I doubled over, gagging, Joel got my arms and held them behind me.

"All right," Seaward said, "Go ahead."

Max worked as earnestly as a circus roustabout driving a stake. He snapped my head around with a right, drove a left to the gut, low, and then a right to the face again, completely without emotion. He slammed a deliberate low blow and I could feel my insides screaming.

"Wait a minute," Seaward said.

Through waves of nausea I saw a car's headlights cut a long swath in the darkness as it came through the gate and around to where we were. I heard Keating saying, "Lola, you shouldn't have come here!"

"I have a right to be here. God knows what would have happened if it hadn't been for me."

"Your husband's right, Mrs. Keating. This is a necessary job, but not very pretty, I'm afraid." That was Seaward.

"I didn't imagine it would be pretty," Lola said. "Nevertheless, I'm here and I'm staying. You can't deny I have the right." She didn't look at anyone but me.

And all the rage that I thought was dead exploded in. side me. "You bitch!" I twisted hard, breaking Joel's hold for a moment, but Max was in fast slamming a paralyzing fist into my middle. I felt my arms twisted behind me again and a fist smashed at my mouth.

I don't know how long it lasted. My legs gave way but Joel held me up as long as consciousness lasted. It seemed like a long time. My rage kept me fighting long after I should have slipped into darkness. I hadn't really misjudged Keating, but I hadn't accounted for Lola; that had been my fatal mistake.

And now she stood there, laughing without a sound.

I came out of it with the smell of damp earth close to my nostrils, with the feel of dew and grass on my face. I lay for a long time, not even opening my eyes. Finally I tried to move my legs and a warm fluid sickness flowed in and out between the cringing coils in my belly, and I thought: There's no use trying to get up. I'm busted up inside and my legs wouldn't hold me. From somewhere, a great roaring swept in, almost passing over me, and then just as suddenly it was gone. I lay there thinking about it, and after a while it occurred to me that it must have been a car.

I was near a highway. Before long another car passed, and then another, and finally I opened my eyes and I saw that I was lying face-down in a bar ditch, three or four feet away from the edge of the concrete.

Slowly, then, it all came back, the beating, the faces, the glares all mixed up with the queasiness of sickness and hurt. And somewhere in the midst of the sickness saw that smile of Lola's.

I must have gone out of my head for a while. I heard someone screaming obscenities at the night with the monotonous hopelessness of a dog baying at the moon. A long time passed before I realized that the sounds were coming from my own mouth. The grass became spikes to my face, and the dew ice, as I began pushing myself up

I made it somehow, standing upright in the ditch holding myself together with my clutched hands. Sweat poured off my face and ran down my back. I lifted my face and stared up at the darkness, and then I made a savage vow to the great black god. Finally I began walking, walking....

The lights came at me suddenly, a cluster of lights setoff from the highway, and when I got closer I saw that it was a shack of some kind, with three big semi-trucks and trailers parked in front. Somebody was laughing and a jukebox blared. When I opened the door and went in the laughing stopped. But the jukebox blared on and on. Five men were sitting at the counter and there was a man behind the counter with half a pie in one hand and a knife in the other. The five men sat there with their mouths open, not making a sound. The jukebox stopped, changed records, and started again. The man behind the counter set the pie down very carefully and stared. I had to work my mouth several times to get the words out. "Have you got a phone?"

"God, yes!" the counterman said. "There on the wall. Help yourself."

They all watched as I went over to it. I got a coin out and managed to dial. I heard ringing at the other end, and when I heard the click of the receiver coming off the cradle I said, "Vida, I'm at a place called Mac's Truck stop. It's west of town on highway seventy-two, I think. Vida—come get me."

I leaned against the wall, feeling my legs going out from under me. The counterman said, "Catch him, Johnny. He's goin' on his face!"

I pushed myself away from the wall and said, "No. I'm all right."

And I went out.

I was about a hundred yards down the highway when I heard the tires screaming and that red convertible rocked to a stop beside me.

"Roy! *Roy!*"

I let go then. I could still hear the jukebox blaring.

Chapter Eight

It was morning when I awakened. The pain was still with me, but it wasn't as bad. I lay for a long while, my eyes closed, listening to the distant sound of highway traffic. I didn't know where I was at first, and I didn't particularly care. The sheets were clean and the feel of them was good against me.

But Vida wasn't there. The shallow depression in the mattress was there beside me, the place she had lain. Vida was gone.

Instantly I was awake. The night before was vivid now. I remembered waking up in the gutter by the side of the highway. I remembered Sid, Seaward, Max, and all the rest of them, and with near insanity I remembered Lola.

Then panic seized me and I began to shake and couldn't stop. Your nerves are gone to hell, I thought. They've beat the guts out of you, literally. You're scared to death and there's nowhere to go. "Vida!" I shouted.

I pushed myself up in bed, looking around, finally realizing where I was. The room was part of the same tourist court that Vida and I had been in before. I wondered how badly I was hurt. I had to find out sooner or later, so I swung my legs off the side of the bed and sat there in my shorts and undershirt, feeling the sickness race up to my throat. The shock of sudden movement almost numbed me. Sweat was cold on my face as I inspected my body. All I could see were ugly blue bruises turning a dirty green. A rupture on the inside couldn't be seen, I knew, but it made me feel a little better when I tried lifting my legs without making the pain much worse. Those bruises, being where they were, were going to hurt. But they were sure as hell better than a ruptured gut.

Anyway it gave me something to think about until I heard the car outside. It pulled into the car port at the side of the cabin and in a minute the door opened and it was Vida.

She had a large brown bag in her arms. She wore a black wool dress and a little white jacket, and she was as clean as mountain air.

"How do you feel?" she asked, her face grave.

"I'm not sure. I haven't tried to walk yet."

"The doctor said you would be all right in a few days, except for the soreness caused by the bruises."

"What doctor?"

"The one that was here last night. Don't you remember?"

I didn't remember a thing after I had walked out of the roadside eating joint and Vida drove up. She went into the kitchenette and began taking things out of the bag. After a minute she came back in, carrying some things. I was still sitting there, too sick to move again.

"I had to go home this morning," she said, "before Sid got up. You were sleeping and I didn't want to wake you. I would've come back sooner, but I had to wait for the stores to open. I got you a razor and some shaving cream and underwear and things."

I touched her face, letting my fingers slide down the curve of her throat. Her skin was as rich and smooth as waxed ivory. Then I gathered up the new underwear and socks and started pushing myself up from the bed. My insides felt as if they were going to break loose as I stood there, shaking. Vida's face began to break up—a little at a time at first, and then it was all to pieces as she put her arms around me to keep me from going over on my face.

"Why, Roy?" she said tightly. "Why did they do it?"

I held onto her until my legs stopped quivering and I could stand alone. "I made a mistake," I heard myself saying bitterly. "A bad mistake, but I learned something out of it. You can't underestimate anybody in this business, Vida."

She didn't understand and I don't think she cared. "Will you take me away, Roy? I know how Barney works and how brutal he is. You have to get out of Big Prairie, Roy, or he'll kill you."

I thought about that, knowing that she was right but now I didn't know what to do about it. "Maybe. I'd better have something to eat," I said.

Getting to the bathroom was like learning to walk all over again. I was going to be sore for a long time, but even at that, I could consider myself lucky that they hadn't crippled me.

My face was a mess, the cheek split, the mouth puffy and bruised. But I still had all my teeth, and that was something. I turned the hot water on in the shower, got under it, and let it almost scald me. The steaming spray relaxed me, soaked away some of the soreness. Finally I lathered my face and shaved carefully around the cuts in my face.

The smell of frying bacon drifted into the bathroom as I got into clean underwear and socks. I hobbled into the kitchenette where Vida had dime-store plates and cutlery set out on a drop-down table. She looked around and smiled vaguely.

"You look better. Do you want some coffee, Roy?"

"I need something worse than coffee." I took her shoulders and turned her around. "I missed you like hell, Vida, when I woke up awhile ago and you weren't there. I'm not complete without you. I need you, Vida."

I pulled her to me. I pressed my hands to the small of her back and felt the hard-softness of her body flowing against me.

"Roy, no! You're not well!"

I held her closer, pressing her against me until I felt her begin to quiver. "Roy, you can't!" But even as she said it she closed her eyes and that red mouth began searching, and I knew that she had reached the point from which there was no turning back. Somehow we were in the other room and Vida was saying something over and over in a very small voice twisted by some awful ache. I wanted her more than I'd ever thought it was possible to want a woman.

Later, after the electricity of the storm had passed, I lay there sick with pain, too sick to move or make a sound, and still I felt a calmness and peace.

"Roy. Oh, Roy," she murmured, clinging to me, her face pressed to my shoulder. "Roy, you will take me with you, won't you?"

"Where?"

"Anywhere you go. I don't care."

To a skid-row hotel? I thought. Eating in hash houses, smelling of hash houses? How long would a thing like that last before it went sour?

I said, "I think I could use that coffee now."

"Answer me, Roy. Will you take me?"

I looked at her. "Of course. Now, how about that coffee?"

I watched her dress and we didn't say anything else until she went into the kitchenette and came back with the coffee.

"What is it, Roy?"

"I don't know. An idea keeps walking along the edge of my mind, but it's too far away. I can't reach it. Tell me about this load of liquor Barney's bringing in."

She looked away. "They'll kill you, Roy."

"I just want to hear about it," I said. "When is it due?"

"Tomorrow night." And then she told me what she had learned from Sid, her voice as final as an obituary. "Roy, you're not going to try it, are you?"

"I don't know."

It would be tough; twice as tough as it would have been the way I had first planned it. As things were now, I wouldn't have a chance to let it cool off. And even if I got away with the hijacking, where was I going to sell the liquor? I thought vaguely, Maybe Sid would buy it. But I knew that was wishful thinking. He wasn't going to cross Seaward just for one load of liquor. And then that nagging thought came again, How did a dumb guy like Sid get where he is?

I said, "Tell me about Sid, Vida. How did he ever get in the bootlegging business anyway?"

"I'm not sure," she said finally. "Sid was just a runner when I first knew him." She smiled faintly. "That seems like a long time ago, but it was only a little over four years. He was a big ox of a guy, always grinning, making people laugh. He didn't seem to care about anything." Then she shook her head, puzzled. "But he changed."

"What changed him?"

"I'm not sure. He never used to drink much, but he started drinking more and more, and then one day I realized that it had been months since I had seen him sober." She shook her head again, in that strange way.

"What happened then?" I said.

"Nothing. He kept drinking more and more." She sat there looking at her hands. "I think I loved him once," she said finally, "but that was so long ago that I'm not sure any more. I was working in a drive-in joint and Sid used to come out there and kid around with everybody. He didn't have much money then but he was full of life, like a kid who never bothered to grow up, and everybody liked him. And maybe I loved him.

"Well, we were married a little over four years ago, when Sid was still a runner. We moved into a little four-room place over on the east side because that was all we could afford. I guess it was all I ever expected to have, but it was enough. And Sid was good to me. He was big and clumsy and somehow gentle at the same time. Maybe I was mistaking gratitude for love, but I don't know now."

She was quiet for a while, and finally I said, "How did Sid make the big jump from runner to retailer?"

She shrugged. "He just came in one day and said that Seaward was giving him part of Kingkade's territory in Big Prairie. That was all I ever knew about it. He made money fast after that, but things were never the same again, for some reason."

"Was that when he started drinking?"

She nodded. "I think so. About then."

"But why?" The question suddenly seemed important, and I didn't know why. "It doesn't make sense," I said. "He gets promoted from a common runner to retailer, he's making plenty of money, so he starts drinking himself into unconsciousness."

A quiet excitement started deep inside me somewhere and began to rise. It seemed pretty obvious that Sid had found himself a club somewhere and had blackmailed himself into a retailer's position by holding the club over Seaward's head. I wasn't sure just how that was going to help me, but it was. The answer was there, if I could just find it.

Vida was looking at me in that strange way again. "Roy, what is it?"

I grinned. "I think I know how to make the hijacking work." Then, before she could protest, I went on. "The thing that was wrong with it was that I'm fair game for Seaward's thugs and I wouldn't have any way of getting rid of the liquor after I had stolen it. I think I know of a way now. Sid can buy the stuff. And he will. I think he will."

I could see fear jump up behind her eyes. I said, "Look, it's clear that Sid is blackmailing Seaward. When everything fits together, that's the kind of picture it makes. Both of us know that Sid would have been a runner all his life if he hadn't got something on Seaward. And it must be something pretty bad. You say Sid started drinking about the time Seaward installed him as a retailer. That fits with something Sid told me once—he said that he had done Barney a big favor once. It begins to look like this favor was a job of murder."

Vida's eyes were wide. "Roy, no! Sid isn't the kind of man who could ever kill anybody!"

"That's what makes it look like murder. Sid couldn't kill a man and forget it, the way some people could. A man like him would do just what Sid did—try to drown himself in a bottle. The only thing that doesn't fit is why Sid did it in the first place. He wouldn't have the guts to kill anybody unless he had a damn strong reason—a lot stronger than a man's ordinary greed for money." I looked at Vida and her face was as pale as death.

"Do you know of any reason why Sid would do a thing like that?" I asked.

"No." Not looking at me.

"It couldn't be," I said, "that those four rooms on the east side got too small, could it? It couldn't be that you began to want things that Sid couldn't buy on his pay?"

I knew that I'd hit it. She dropped her head, and after a moment she began crying without making a sound. I touched her and she was cold. I put my arms around her and held her close while she got rid of it. I put my face to the softness of her hair and said, "I didn't want to hurt you, but I had to know, Vida." She still didn't make a sound. "Look," I said, "we've been playing make-believe in a flesh and blood world. Now we can stop pretending that we can leave Big Prairie and I can get a hash-house job and maybe you can get a job in a beer joint and everything will be just fine. It wouldn't work, Vida. Living from hand to mouth would kill whatever you feel for me. I love you, Vida. Nothing but grime and poverty can ever change that. Do you understand now why I've got to go through with the hijacking? We'll have money, Vida. Money enough to start again somewhere else."

"Money won't buy peace."

I knew she was thinking of Lola, but I wouldn't let myself think of her now. I said finally, "Tell me again about this shipment of Seaward's."

By the time the next morning came around I knew what I was going to do. Vida didn't come back to the cabin that night because I needed the time to get the thing thought out. It was a little before daylight when I got up and pulled my clothes on. I was still sore and I hurt like hell when I bent over, but I began to get over the feeling that my insides had torn loose. After I was dressed I called a cab.

I got out in front of the house and went up to the front porch and pushed the doorbell. The morning was dead quiet, still dark, and I had to ring two more times before I heard anything moving on the inside. Then Vida opened the door.

She stood there, stunned at seeing me, holding a silk robe together with her hands. "Roy!"

"I've got to talk to Sid," I said.

"This is crazy! Roy, if anyone sees you—"

She left the words hanging as I pushed the door wide and stepped inside. "Is he asleep?"

"He's passed out," she said.

"Then you'd better go to another part of the house. He's going to get a rude awakening, I'm afraid."

I left her standing there and went through the room, down the hall and into the back bedroom where Sid lay sprawled and snoring. I took hold of the front of Sid's pajama jacket and jerked him upright. I slapped him three times across the face, *crack, crack, crack*, like pistol shots in the quiet of the room.

"Wake up!"

He lay across the bed, stunned and drunk.

I went into the bathroom and soaked a heavy bath-towel in cold water. I hit him in the face with it, wielding the towel like a club. The pain finally got through to his whisky-soaked brain, and he threw his arms over his face, cringing back against the headboard. He still didn't have any idea who I was.

"What the hell is this?" he said hoarsely.

I hit him once more, just to make sure. "You'd better be awake," I said, "because this is going to be a big day. This is the day you turn on Seaward and kick him right in the gut."

His arms still over his face, he shook his head as if he couldn't believe it. Finally he lowered his arms. He looked at me for a full thirty seconds before he realized that it was no dream. I could see a kind of sluggish anger burn behind his eyes.

"You cheap bastard," he snarled, "get out of my house!"

I hit him right between the eyes with my fist. His eyes went glassy as he fell back on one elbow. I got him by the throat again and said, "I'm not fooling, Sid."

"You sonofabitch!" Then he lunged at me, but it only got him tangled up in the covers. I hit him with my left fist, then I swung with my right and got him under the eye. I planted my feet and kept swinging, monotonously, like a boxer working out on a heavy bag. Pretty soon I had his face cut up, and one eye turned an ugly blue and began to swell. I landed a punch just to the side of his Adam's apple and he fell back gasping.

I said, "Is that enough to convince you?"

"They'll kill you for this!" he said, his voice almost a whine.

I hit him again, dropped him in the center of the bed and he lay there gasping. "Listen to me," I said. "I've got a lot of hate to work out on somebody, and it's going to be you unless you're willing to listen to a proposition."

"I don't make deals with punk bastards!"

I hit him from behind, just below the ribs, in the kidneys.

"What do you want?" It was almost a sob.

"I want to sell you a load of liquor. The load I'm going to take away from Barney Seaward."

He looked at me, his eyes swimming with hate. "You're crazy!"

"Maybe, but I'm going to do it."

He closed his eyes, trying to pull himself together. "How much?" he said finally, and I grinned because I could see exactly what he was thinking. Agree to buy it, agree to anything, and then call Barney Seaward the minute I left the room.

"Fifteen thousand," I said. "That's five thousand cheaper than you could buy it direct from Barney."

His nose was bleeding. He wiped it. "All right. Now get out of here and leave me alone."

"Don't you want to hear the details?"

He sat woodenly, praying that I would go so he could call Barney. "I want it in cash," I said, "so you'll have to get it out of the bank and have it ready by tonight. And I want a guarantee that you won't have Seaward putting his hoodlums on my tail the minute I walk out of here."

"I give you my word."

"The hell with your word. I want to know how you got to be a bootlegger in the first place."

He looked up then. His face was cut and puffy with bruises on the left side. "What are you talking about?" he said angrily.

"I'm talking about that 'favor' you did for Seaward four years ago. Who did you kill, Sid?"

It was a wild stab in the dark, but the minute I said it I knew that I had hit something. His eyes flew wide, then narrowed quickly to nothing. "Go hang yourself," he grated. "You're a goddamn punk and that's all you'll ever be."

My right fist caught him in the middle of the mouth and knocked him off the bed. Then I went around the bed and kicked him in the kidneys before he could get up.

"Have you got any more words you want to get out of your system?"

He lay doubled on the floor, his mouth working.

"Do you want to tell me who it was that Barney paid you to kill?"

"Go—to—hell."

I kicked again and he groaned and doubled up. He tried to crawl under the bed but I grabbed his feet and jerked him out.

"You're crazy!" It was a very small voice now. "You're crazy! You can't get—

away with this. You won't live an hour—after Barney finds out." He tried to get up; then his face went suddenly white and he dropped as if he had been shot.

I got him up to a sitting position and rolled him onto the bed. Another drink, I decided, was the thing to bring him out of it.

I went back to the kitchen and got a bottle. Vida was sitting like a stone statue at the breakfast table, staring unblinkingly at her folded hands.

When I got back to the bedroom I poured Sid a drink and helped him get it down.

I said, "Sid, I'll sell the load to you for twelve thousand, like you said. You'll be making eight thousand clear on the deal and there's no reason for Barney to ever find out about it. You can get rid of it a little at a time and Barney will never guess a thing."

No sound. Not a word.

"Look," I said, "you can see why I have to have a guarantee, can't you? I want to know what kind of thing you're holding over Barney so I can hold it over you. But just for one day. Until the job is over. Then I'll get out of Oklahoma and you'll never see me again. After you get that liquor in your warehouse, I'm not afraid of you going to Barney then."

It was no good. I could kill him, or I could beat him some more, but neither would get me what I wanted. I was tired and sick now and I wanted to get away and forget all about it.

Then I had an idea. I said, "Sid, listen to me." And he lay there, his eyes glassed with pain. "Sid, I'm going to tell you something that you would have known a long time ago if you'd bothered to stay sober long enough to see what was going on around you. It's about Vida, Sid. Remember a long time ago, Sid, when you were just a runner? Things were good then weren't they? No worries, no problems, no conscience to bother you. That was the way you liked it, but Vida wanted something else, didn't she? She wanted you to be a retailer and make big money like Kingkade, so finally you went to Barney and made a deal with him and got to be a retailer. But was it worth it, Sid? Have you had a good night's sleep since then?"

He said nothing.

"Was it worth it?" I said again. "You did it for Vida, but do you know what she's going to do to you? She's going to leave you, Sid. She's sick and disgusted with you. And do you know who she's leaving with? It's me, Sid. Roy Foley."

Something terrible happened in those little eyes of his. "Get out of here, you sonofabitch."

I got up and opened the door and called, "Vida, come here a minute." She came in from the kitchen looking as pale and cold as marble. I said, "Ask her, Sid."

He didn't have to ask her. He didn't have to say a word and neither did Vida and neither did I.

He lay there looking at her and it seemed to me that he died a little. I took Vida's arm and led her out into the hallway and it was like leading a department-store dummy. I didn't know what to say to her, so I left her there and went back into the bedroom. "So that was what you did it for," I said. "It wasn't worth it, was it, Sid?"

There was no fight left in him. "Get out of here...." That whisper again.

"As soon as I get the story."

He said, "Marty Paycheck."

"Did you kill him?" I asked.

He nodded.

"Tell me about it," I said.

"Paycheck was a wildcatter trying to move in on Kingkade. He had his own wholesale outlet. Seaward couldn't stand for that."

"So you made a deal with Seaward. Did they ever find the body?"

"No."

"Where is it?"

"Copper Lake, about four miles north of town." The words came slowly, indistinctly. He must have understood that he was the same as signing his own death warrant, if Seaward ever found out that he had talked. It didn't seem to bother him.

"Then what?" I said.

"Nothing. It was just a deal. Big Prairie was growing. It was big enough to hold two retailers, but Barney wanted to be sure that they bought from him. That's all there was to it."

Now I could understand why Seaward didn't like this heavy drinking of Sid's. He was afraid that someday Sid would get too drunk and do exactly what he was doing now. Talk. Of course there was no positive proof that Seaward was mixed up in the killing, but if the word ever got out the State Crime Bureau might be interested, and that was the last thing Seaward would want. I could understand why Barney put up with Sid, even when it turned out to be a bad deal. Killing to cover up a killing could be an endless thing, and not even Barney Seaward could hope to get away with it long.

"Now get out," Sid said. He sounded like a very old man.

I went out of the bedroom and into the kitchen where Vida was. "It's all settled," I said, "you start packing. By this time tomorrow we'll be out of Big Prairie for good." I put my arms around her and held her tight.

"Why did you have to do it like that?"

"There wasn't any other way. Christ, I didn't enjoy it." I held her for a minute, letting her cry it out.

"Hold me tighter, Roy," she said. "Hold me as tight as you can."

Chapter Nine

The next few hours, I knew, were going to be dangerous ones. I had to stay out of sight, and still there were a lot of things to be done before attempting to hijack an armed whisky truck. To start with I had to have a car no one would recognize.

So I had Vida rent one at a U-Drive-It place. Next I had to find somebody to help me. Somebody I could depend on. My best bet, I guessed, was a man who needed money and who hated Barney Seaward's guts. A wildcat bootlegger.

As soon as Vida came back with the rented car I got in it and headed south for River Street, a part of town even crummier than Burk. I sweated getting across town and down to River Street. If some of Barney's men spot you, I thought, you'll sure as hell get more than a bruised groin.

But I made it all right. I parked the car behind a second-hand store and went into a beer joint where I knew I'd find a wildcatter if I just waited long enough.

The minute I saw Link Mefford I knew he was the man I wanted. He was a rawboned, sunburned farmer with bitter eyes and a mouth like a steel trap. When we got back to the alley, he said, "I hear you're lookin' for somethin' to drink."

"Not exactly. I've got a deal you might be interested in."

He spat a stream of tobacco juice on a pile of beer cans.

"I know where I can get some merchandise," I said. "Cheap."

"How cheap?"

"It's free, you might say."

"Go on."

"All right, here's the way it is. I happen to know when Barney Seaward plans to bring his next load into Big Prairie. I know the truck, the driver, the guard, and the route they're taking. I've even got the place spotted where we can hit them. Do you want me to go on?"

He nodded, his face bland.

"All right, we'll rent two light trucks at the U-Drive-It place where I got my car. If anything should go wrong and it turns into a race, it's better to have two light trucks than one big one. You'll have to do the renting, though. I can't afford to be seen."

"Why?" he asked flatly, not missing the bruises and cuts on my face. "Seaward?"

I nodded and that seemed to satisfy him.

He thought about it some more, chewing slowly. "It'll take more than two men," he said.

"Have you got a friend?"

"Maybe. If it comes off, what's the split?"

"Three ways," I said, "after I take out for expenses. And we'll need some guns. Two shotguns and a pistol. Can you get them?"

He thought some more and nodded. It was a deal. We didn't shake hands on it; he just nodded. "You better wait inside," he said. "I'll see what I can do about findin' somebody to help us."

Mefford turned and walked off down the alley. I went back inside the beer joint, took a back booth and waited. I thought of Mefford. Like hell I was going to split that load of liquor with him or anybody else, but he wouldn't know about it until it was too late. The stuff would go into Sid's warehouse and Vida and I would be on our way out of Oklahoma.

About thirty minutes passed and Mefford came back with a man he introduced as Burl Cox. Cox was a soft-spoken, squatty little man with tremendous shoulders and arms, and like Mefford he wore faded bib overalls and chewed tobacco. After we'd shaken hands Mefford said, "We can go get the trucks any time you say. While we're doin' that you can wait over at my house."

It sounded all right, so we got into my car and went around to Link Mefford's house, a two-room shack standing almost on the edge of the river, and Link went in with me. From under the bed he got two sixteen-gauge shotguns and from his pocket he took a .38 caliber revolver.

"The pistol is Burl's," he said, "the shotguns are mine. I'll have to buy some cartridges for the .38, though."

"Do it when you pick up the trucks," I said, "because I won't be seeing you any more until I meet you across the river." I looked at my watch and it was almost noon. "We've got plenty of time. I'll give you two hours to get the trucks and drive them across the river on the south highway. That's where I'll meet you."

"Where do you figure on hittin' this truck of Barney's?"

"I'll let you know when we get there," I said.

He shrugged, put the guns on the bed and went out. All I had to do now was wait. And not think. I broke the shotguns open and inspected them. Just keep busy, I thought. Don't think about anything. Mefford and Cox were perfect, all guts and no brains, and greedy. Right now they were probably trying to think up a way to keep me from getting the split they thought I was going to take.

Time dragged. I found a rag and began wiping the guns.

I looked at my watch again and there was still almost an hour to go but I couldn't sit still any longer. I went out to the car and put the guns under the back seat. About an hour later I pulled onto a side road, across the river, and smoked a cigarette until I saw two trucks crossing the bridge. Mefford waved as they roared by. I pulled out and moved up ahead of them and we were on our way.

It was only about a ninety-mile drive to where we were going, so we were in no particular hurry. It was dark by the time we reached the section line road Vida had spotted for me. I blinked my lights two times and turned off, then I looked back and saw that the trucks were following. We were still almost a mile from the highway when I came to a stop and the trucks eased up behind me. Mefford and Cox got out of their cabs. I was in the back seat breaking out the guns when they came up.

"All right," I said. "Here's the way we do it. If Seaward's truck is running on schedule, it will be passing this section line around ten o'clock. We'll leave the trucks here and take my car back down to the highway. I'll go down the road maybe four or five hundred yards to spot the truck when it comes, and as soon as it passes I'll give you a signal with a flashlight. Three quick flashes. Burl, you'll be at the crossroads in my car. When you see the flashes you pull out and block the highway in a hurry. Play like your car's stalled or something."

Burl Cox nodded as I handed him the revolver. "You'd better take the pistol," I said, "because all the attention is going to be focused on you right at first. Keep it where you can get to it, but don't let it show. Maybe it would be a good thing if you get out of the car after you get the highway blocked, because I want the driver and guard to be looking at you."

Then I turned to Mefford. "Link, while this is going on, you'll be crawling out of the bar ditch on the other side of the road. You come up behind the truck—and this has to be fast—and throw your shotgun in the driver's face. By that time I ought to be up to the truck. You keep your shotgun on the driver and force him and the guard out on the other side. Then you get in the truck and drive it down the section line road to where we're parked. Burl and I will take care of the driver and guard and meet you."

Link Mefford rubbed his chin thoughtfully. "What if the guard goes for his own gun?"

"If we have to kill them, then that's the way it'll have to be. You don't get twenty thousand dollars worth of whisky without taking some chances. The thing is, do it fast."

They seemed satisfied. Cox got in my car and backed away from the highway. Mefford went across the road and lay down in the bar ditch, and I struck out across an open field with my shotgun and flashlight. I found a place by a culvert, about four hundred yards up the highway, and sat down to wait.

There wasn't much traffic. It was flat prairie country and you could see the headlights coming for more than a mile in both directions. Two hours must have gone by and I hardly moved. About a half a mile to the south there was a bend in the road, and the cars would come around it, their headlights slicing the night wide open, and I would lie in the gully and hold my breath until they were past. You could see the trucks a long way off because of the lights above the cabs. They would come hurtling up the highway, hellbent for somewhere, but none of them was the right truck.

Ten o'clock came and went and I began to sweat. Then, just as I was about ready to blow up, I saw the truck round the bend.

I lay there watching its headlights take a long cut at the night; then as it roared toward me I raised up just a little. It was in a hell of a hurry, but not in such a hurry that I couldn't read the lettering on the side of the cab. It said "Caney Produce Company."

It was the one.

The minute it got by I stood up and flicked the flashlight three times and then started running across the open field toward the crossroads. I hadn't taken two steps before I saw Cox snap the lights on and begin pulling onto the highway. The truck driver tramped his air brakes and I could hear the squeal of rubber on concrete and the blaring of the horn as he rocked to a stop. I got out of the field then, rolled under a barbed wire fence and began running up the highway. I could hear the driver yelling, "You goddamn farmer sonofabitch! Get that thing off the highway!"

Cox did it just right. He pulled out in front of the truck and stalled the motor, and I could see him standing out in front of the car, in front of the headlights, waving his arms and yelling back at the trucker, just like a damn farmer. But the luckiest part of all was the fact that there was no traffic. I didn't see Link Mefford until I had almost reached the truck myself. He seemed to blend with the darkness, and when I finally saw him he was moving all crouched over like a big cat, holding that shotgun at the ready. Cox had got over on the guard's side of the highway, holding their attention in that direction. I wasn't close enough to hear anything when Mefford sneaked his shotgun into the other window, but I've got a pretty good idea of what was said.

I was blowing hard when I finally got there. Mefford was saying coldly, "Don't sonofabitch me, mister. Just get out of that cab before I blow your face through the back of your head."

They didn't like it, but they got out, all right. Cox had his pistol out now, hustling them toward the car and Mefford was climbing under the wheel of the truck. About that time a car rounded the bend and came toward us.

"Get that thing out of here!" I yelled.

I piled into the back seat of the car, on top of the driver and guard. Cox got under the wheel of the car, and we shot off the highway. In just a few seconds Mefford had the truck rolling. He got off the highway just as the car zipped past us.

It was pretty awkward, three men in the back seat and one of them trying to hold a shotgun on the other two. I got the pistol from Cox and then climbed into the front seat where I could do a better job of watching them.

"What's goin' on back there?" Cox asked.

"Nothing. Mefford's coming along with the truck."

"What do you aim to do with the two in the back seat?"

"I haven't decided yet."

This was the catch in the plan. It was the catch that all of us had thought about, but none of us had brought into the open. The cold fact was, the truck driver and the guard had to die.

For a minute I felt sick. Then I thought of all the thousands of hash houses in the world, of all the three-dollar shoes and hand-me-down suits. I thought of Lola. The revolver cracked five times.

I couldn't stop until I heard the hammer clicking on empty chambers. Then I turned around in the front seat and watched the road. Cox didn't say a thing.

Cox pulled up past our trucks and as we got out Mefford came up with the load. We had to work in the dark and we had to work fast. The first thing we did was break the lock on the back of the truck and open the big swinging doors, then I vaulted up on the tailgate and began throwing the tarps back.

It's no easy job transferring a whole truckful of liquor. It took us well over an hour to get all the stuff shifted from the one big truck to our two lighter ones. After the job was finally completed and we got the tarps tied down, Cox looked at me, then spat wearily in the direction of my car.

"What do you aim to do with them?"

"Well, there's one sure thing. We can't just leave them here; we've got to get rid of them somehow."

"The river?" Mefford asked.

"Maybe. Sure, I guess that would be all right. We can wrap them up in a tarp, throw in a few rocks and tie them up good. They'll stay at the bottom a long time if we find a hole deep enough."

Cox rubbed his chin. "I know a place that might do."

"All right," I said, "that's it, then." We took part of the tarp off the big truck; then Mefford and I went out to get the rocks while Cox dragged the bodies out of the back seat. After we got the bundle made we heaved it back into the car and I said, "Cox, you take my car and get rid of this. I'll drive the truck back to Big Prairie and Mefford and I will meet you at 712 Burk."

Cox nodded, then Mefford said "Why Burk Street?"

That stopped me for a moment because I hadn't meant to take the stuff to Burk Street at all. But I had to take it somewhere, and I didn't think Mefford and Cox would be very enthusiastic about leaving it in Sid's warehouse. The main thing was to postpone making the split.

"That's where we're going to store the liquor for now," I said. "As it is, we've got to work damn fast to get it unloaded before sunup. It wouldn't look good, going from one place to the other splitting up two truckloads of whisky in broad daylight, would it?"

I could see that Mefford didn't like the idea. He wanted his share and he wanted it now—but time was running out.

"What are you going to do with the liquor truck?" Cox asked.

"You can't do away with a thing like that. Leave it here."

I got under the wheel of the lead truck and began pulling for the highway. Then Mefford pulled out. And, finally, Cox, in my car. When we got on the highway, Cox passed us up, hellbent for the river.

It was a little after four o'clock and Burk Street was as quiet as a grave when we rolled the trucks into it. Cox had already finished his job and had the car parked in front of the old man's house.

"Is everything all right?" I asked.

"I got rid of the bundle," Cox said, "if that's what you mean."

"Have you seen anybody?" I said.

Cox laughed shortly. "On Burk Street, at four in the mornin'?"

To me, those trucks sounded like a battalion of tanks, but they don't pay much attention to things on Burk Street. Finally, I pulled the truck into the street, then backed it right up to the front porch. Then Mefford and I got in the back of the truck and started throwing whisky down to Cox. It took us about an hour to get it unloaded and stacked.

"Well," I said, when we finally got finished. "I guess this is the best we can do for now. We can make the split tomorrow night."

"I guess me and Burl'll stay here and just keep an eye on it," Mefford said. "This is a hell of a lot of whisky. I'd hate for anything to happen to it. What're we goin' to do about the trucks?"

"Geez, we've got to get those things out of here! You and Cox take care of that. I'll wait here till you get back."

The minute they left the house I ripped open a case, uncorked a bottle and gulped down a healthy slug. I never needed a drink more than I needed one now. My nerves were screaming. Every muscle ached, and my eyes burned, and more than anything else in the world I wanted to lie down and sleep. But I couldn't do it. The minute I closed my eyes I could see that truck driver and guard.

Forget about it, I thought. That's one thing you've got to forget or you'll go nuts. Besides, you've got other things to think about.

About a million other things, and I didn't know where to begin. The first thing I ought to do, probably, was get in touch with Sid and turn the whole thing over to him.

And there were Mefford and Cox to be taken care of somehow. I'd be damned if I split the liquor with them. I'd take all of it or I'd drown in it. While I was worrying about it, they came in.

They had their shotguns with them and it looked as if they meant to stay—until they could carry off their share of the whisky, anyway. The hell with them, I thought. I didn't have time to worry about a pair of farmers.

"You get the trucks put away?" I said.

Mefford nodded, resting his shotgun against the door.

"All right," I said, "we can take them back to the rental company after a while. Are you two going to stay here?"

"We thought it might be best," Cox said evenly.

I started for the door. "I've got something to look into. I'll be back before long."

"There's just one thing," Cox said as I hit the porch. "The back seat of your car is pretty messed up."

The whisky started to bounce on me. I made it as far as the car, then I leaned on the fender and let it go. I got a hold on myself finally and slid under the wheel. But I didn't look in the back seat.

The sky in the east was growing pale as I pulled out of Burk Street and headed toward the center of town. Big Prairie was quiet. The old day hadn't quite died, the new one hadn't quite started to live.

I found an all-night service station near the edge of town, so I had the boy put in some gas while I went inside to use the phone. I got the number and listened to the ring at the other end—once—twice....

"Hello." It was Vida.

"It's all over," I said. "In another hour or two we'll be out of Big Prairie."

"Roy—!" I could hear the quick intake of breath. Then her voice broke. "Roy! Roy!"

"Take it easy," I said, trying to sound calm. "Everything's all right. It's all over. I've got the stuff at the old man's place on Burk Street. You can stop worrying now. But how about Sid? Did he get the money out of the bank?"

"I—I think so."

I said, "All right, Vida, just sit tight for another hour or so, and you'd better start waking Sid up. I've got two farmers watching the liquor for me, but pretty soon they'll be leaving to return the trucks. I'll let you know when. Then Sid can come down and we'll close the deal."

I could feel myself grinning faintly. There was going to be hell to pay when Mefford and Cox came back and found that their liquor had been bought and paid for by another bootlegger. But that was something they would have to settle themselves. I would be far away by then.

"Roy—" Then she waited a long moment before saying anything else. "Roy, I'm afraid. It's Sid, I think," she said uncertaintly. "He doesn't even seem to care."

"Forget about him," I said. "It isn't that he doesn't care—he just can't do anything about it."

I hung up when the service station attendant came in to collect for the gas. As I got in the car I noticed that it was getting light, and I didn't like that much. A few cars were on the streets now—factory workers, heading for work. I didn't see the pickup truck until it pulled up beside me at a stop light. I sat there behind the wheel, numb with fatigue, and then I heard a voice saying, "I'll be damned!"

I could feel my guts dropping out of sight. It was my old friend, Max. And sitting beside him was his partner, Joel.

Of all the lousy breaks! I thought. For an instant I seemed to be paralyzed. Then I slammed the car into gear, spurting cross the intersection against the red light, but that pickup was right on top of me. There was a teeth-rattling jar as the truck rammed me broadside, shoving my car over against the curb. I made a grab for the door, completely panic-stricken for that moment, and the only idea in my mind was to run—run! The door stuck, it had been jammed somehow in the crash against the curb, and I nearly went crazy as I struggled with it. It came open suddenly. I piled out and ran straight into Joel's arms.

"Geez," Max said flatly, "you never learn, do you, buddy?"

"We can't just stand here," Joel said, "what are we goin' to do with him?"

Max shrugged. "I guess Barney'll decide that." It all happened in a few seconds. They grabbed my arms, hustled me around to the pickup and shoved me in between them.

Max looked at me, puzzled. "Geez, I've seen some dumb ones," he said, "but, friend, you just about take the prize."

Chapter Ten

I didn't really begin to get scared until we got to Barney's place. Until then rage had kept me from thinking about anything else, the helpless rage at myself and at my luck. It was just one of those lousy breaks that Max and Joel had been making a delivery at that time of morning. It was another lousy break that they happened to stop beside me. Happened to see me. God, I thought, how Lola will laugh when she hears about this!

It was still early, not much more than five o'clock when Max pulled the pickup around behind Barney Seaward's house. He went around to the side door and talked to somebody for a minute and then he came back.

"It's dumb punks like you," Joel said, looking at me, "that make things hard for guys like us."

"Well, he asked for it," Max said. "He can't ever say he didn't."

That was when I began to wonder for the first time what they were going to do with me. I thought, I can't stand another beating like that last one. My nerves are gone, I'm ready to crack wide open.

"Get out," Max said.

We went across the back yard and up to the porch. Barney opened the back door and stood there looking at us.

He looked annoyed and that was about all. Anyway, I thought, he hasn't heard about the hijacking yet. "You're causing me a lot of trouble, Foley," he said, coldly. "For a punk, you sure cause a lot of trouble." He lit a cigarette and looked as if it tasted like hell. He said abruptly, "Get him out of here. Take him somewhere, you know what to do. I'm sick of looking at him."

He turned to walk away and I went to pieces for a minute. The fear of pain covered me, almost drowned me. "Barney, for God's sake, I'll tell you something, something you ought to know! But just let me leave and forget about it!"

I don't think he even heard me.

"Marty Paycheck, Barney!" I yelled. "Marty Paycheck! Did you ever hear of a man with a name like that?"

Barney stopped as if he had been shot. He looked at me with the coldest eyes I ever saw and maybe ten seconds went by before he made a sound. He took a deep drag on his cigarette, still looking at me. Then he let the smoke out very slowly and said, "Let him go, Joel. I'd better talk to him."

Joel dropped my arms as though I had suddenly stung him. "Now get out, both of you," Barney said. "I want to think."

Max and Joel looked at each other and Max shrugged the smallest shrug in the world.

Barney didn't say another word or make a move until they were gone. I was too full of relief to feel much of anything.

Then Barney said, "What is this about a man named Paycheck?"

"He's dead," I said. "Sid killed him on a deal he made for you. The body's in Copper Lake, north of town." And I thought, Why are you telling this? It's not going to do you any good. You're getting yourself in deeper all the time; he's going to have to kill you whether he wants to or not because now you know as much as Sid.

It was that sudden sickening fear of pain. The most important thing in the world seemed to be keep talking, keep Barney interested, somehow postpone the time when Max and Joel would come back.

"Did Sid tell you this?" Barney said, and I nodded.

"When?"

It seemed like a long time ago. I had to think back and it startled me when I realized that it had been just a day ago. "Yesterday," I said.

For the first time a kind of emotion came into Barney's face. His mouth seemed to draw tighter, his eyes narrowed down in cold anger. "The drunken bastard!" he said softly. "The goddamn bastard! Go on. What else did he say?"

"That's all." Then I did think of something else, and when I thought of it some of the old excitement rose up again and pushed some of the sickness away. I tried to keep my voice even. "Yes, he did mention that Paul Keating knew about the killing."

I could see him stiffen, but he didn't say a thing. He looked at me for a long time, and finally he said, "I get nothing but punks. All my trouble comes from punks and they're all I ever get." Then, without even calling to Max and Joel, he walked out of the room and left me standing there.

After a minute I heard him talking on the phone. "Sure it's the truth. There's no other way he could have found out about it. He even knows about Copper Lake!"

You've done it now! I thought dumbly. You've talked yourself right into an unmarked grave.

Still, it didn't seem to be me whom he was worried about. It was Sid who had knocked that iciness out of him and put him into a rage. That slow excitement started coming up again as I began to feel carefully along the edges of an idea.

I knew what Barney was going to say. Even before he came back into the room and stood there looking at me, studying me, I knew what he had in his mind.

"All right, Foley," he said quietly, as though he had never been out of the room, "I think we understand each other. You know what will happen if I put Max and Joel onto you again. The last time was nothing, Foley. Less than nothing, compared to what it will be if it happens again."

I knew what was coming, I could see it in his eyes. "You wanted a chance to get out of Big Prairie without being worked again," he went on. "Well, you're going to have to earn your way, Foley. Do you know how you can earn your way, Foley?"

"No."

His smile widened slightly. "Yes, you do. Sid is a luxury I can't afford any longer; you can understand that. If he talks to you, he'll talk to other people, so I've got to get him out of the way. That's going to be your job, Foley, and then you can leave Big Prairie and you'll never see me again."

I stood there, swaying, sick inside and hoping that I looked even sicker than I felt. After a moment, I said, "God, I can't do it! Sid's my friend!"

Barney raised his voice slightly and said, "All right, Max, you and Joel can come in." The door opened and they came in and Barney said, "Take the bastard out of here. I gave him a chance and he wouldn't take it."

I almost yelled, and it wasn't all acting. "Barney, I can't do it! Anything else, but not that!"

"Take it or leave it," he said calmly. "I'll give you a stake to leave town on—we'll say five hundred."

Five hundred lousy dollars! But I kept telling myself to stay calm. He could multiply that by a thousand by the time it was over. I thought of Sid with uneasiness. It wouldn't happen this time the way it had with the truck driver and guard. This time I would have plenty of time to think about it and it wouldn't be easy. I thought of Vida, too. She would hate me if she ever found out—but she would never know. With Seaward's help, a thing like this could be done. But, in the back of my mind, I was thinking of Lola. Every time my bruised guts ached I thought of her. I could hear her laughing.

"What will it be, Foley?" Barney asked impatiently.

"I'll do it," I said.

I looked at Barney and could almost see him thinking the same thing I was thinking, This is too easy—much too easy. He had expected a fight out of me and I hadn't given him any fight, and now he was beginning to wonder what I was thinking about. And on my side, it just didn't make sense to agree to a job of murder for a lousy five hundred dollars. I had the feeling that Barney was trying to make it easy for me, that he was leaving the door open, inviting me to fight and make it convincing.

The sweat on my forehead was cold. I had almost underrated Seaward again.

"All right," I said finally. "I'll do it, but not for five hundred. Five thousand. That's cheap and you know it."

There was no change at all in those eyes of his. No anger. Just that vague smile of self-satisfaction, and I had the uncomfortable feeling that he was reading my mind and thinking ahead of me again.

Finally he nodded. "Five thousand. But you do it exactly the way I say." He looked at Max. "Get him out of here. Take him back to his rooming house and be sure he stays there." Then to me, "Don't think you can run out on this, Foley."

"Run out on five thousand dollars?"

He still smiled that vague half smile. The sonofabitch knows you're planning something for him, I thought, and he doesn't even care! It was still too easy, my willingness to kill for him, his willingness to pay my price. If you fail this time, Foley, I thought, it will be the last mistake you'll ever make.

I said, "I'll have to know how you want it done."

"I haven't decided yet," he said evenly. "I'll get in touch with you after I've done some thinking."

"And another thing," I said, "I want my car your hoodlums smashed up for me."

Barney looked at Max and shrugged. "All right, get it for him. But keep the keys yourself."

We rode back the same way we had come out, with me sandwiched in between Max and Joel. The police hadn't picked up the car yet, probably because nobody had reported the accident. It was still sitting there, jammed up against the curb with the left rear fender crushed in. Joel and I got out of the pickup, and into the rented car and drove on to my rooming house with Max following.

"Just don't forget," Joel said. "Don't try anything. Me and Max will be right out here lookin' for you."

"As long as you're going to keep the keys," I said, "drive my car around to the back and park it."

They stood on the sidewalk, watching me go up the steps into the house. When I reached my room my nerves started screaming again. I lay across the bed, not thinking about anything, too wound-up to sleep, too tired to rest. That back seat in the car, something had to be done about that. The car was rented in Vida's name, and sooner or later somebody would see that blood and would want to have some answers. I went downstairs and out the back door of the rooming house. The car was there where Joel had parked it. I got the back seat out and siphoned some gas out of the tank and soaked it and set it on fire. When it was going good I heard Max and Joel coming around the corner of the house.

"What the hell is this?"

Two roomers came out the back door to see what the excitement was about. The fire shot up higher and higher, and then it began to die down. When it was over there was nothing left but some ashes and blackened springs. Now, I thought, maybe I can rest.

"What do you think you're doin'?" Max demanded angrily.

"Go to hell," I said, and they didn't know just what to do about it with the roomers coming out of the house and wanting to know what had started the fire. "Somebody must have left a cigarette back there," I said. I left Max and Joel and went back into the house.

I went upstairs and lay down again, trying to think calmly, trying to get the most important things first. I looked out the window again and saw Max in the pickup watching the front of the house. Joel would be around at the back. Then I went downstairs and used the rooming house phone.

"Vida," I said, "I want you to listen closely and not ask any questions. Things have gone all to hell, it just blew up in my face, but it still may turn out to be a good thing if we can work it right. The first thing I want is a good recording machine, the finest you can get. Probably a tape recorder would be the best. And I want two microphones, the most sensitive microphones money can buy. And I've got to have some lead wires—get the flat kind that you can lay under carpets so they don't show—and a screwdriver and hammer. Have this stuff delivered to the front door of my rooming house, but not to me. I'm being watched by two of Barney's boys. I don't know how you're going to get this stuff, but you've got to do it and do it fast, or everything's ruined. Everything!"

"Roy—" Her voice jumped at me, as though she had been holding her breath for a long time. "Roy, what went wrong?"

"Everything! But it can still be straightened out if you do exactly as I say."

Then the fatigue and worn nerves caught up with me. I made it back up the stairs, thinking, There's nothing to do now but wait and see. I lay across the bed and felt the tiredness wash over me like a warm ocean, and I closed my eyes. I was going to rest. Everything was going to be all right. I had a sudden, dark vision then and I could see the truck driver and guard, their eyes wide, their mouths open, the way they had looked at me.

Forget it! I thought. You have to forget it!

Finally I went to sleep. About five minutes later I woke up screaming.

Chapter Eleven

"Mr. Foley! Mr. Foley!" Somebody was hammering on the door. I had fallen asleep finally and now the sound came to me as I lay there in a sluggish fog. "Mr. Foley!" It was the landlady—I realized that after a while. My mind jumped headlong into full consciousness.

I opened the door and she was standing there, vaguely puzzled, a tight-mouthed little woman holding an envelope in her hand. "Mr. Foley, some men are downstairs with a parcel," she said. "It's addressed to me, but there's a message with it that says it is to be delivered to you. Do you know anything about it?"

Vida, Vida! I thought. How I love you! "Yes," I said. "Will you please have the men bring it up to my room?"

I looked out the window and saw Max talking to one of the two delivery men. Then he went back to the pickup and looked without interest as the men hefted the crated recorder and started toward the house.

"Is this where it goes?"

I turned and a big blond kid was standing in the doorway holding a package about the size of a small suitcase. The other deliverymen came in carrying two smaller packages.

"This is the place," I said. "Would you mind setting it up for me? I want to be sure it works."

"That's our job," the kid said.

When they got it all set up it seemed like a hell of a lot of machinery, but it wasn't really as complicated as it looked. The kid turned it on and counted up to ten into the microphone, then he played it back and it sounded fine.

"Will that microphone work from four or five feet away?" I said.

The kid was connecting the two mikes. "Sure." He turned it on again and adjusted the input control and stood back and counted. When he played it back it was almost as good as it had been before.

That was all there was to it. They went out and I stood there looking at it, thinking. This is your last chance. And it sure as hell better work! Time was everything now. My watch said twelve o'clock and I knew that Seaward would know about the hijacking by now. And Mefford and Cox were still sitting with that liquor—if I was lucky—wondering what had happened to me, probably.

I disconnected the recorder and began making splices with the flat lead wire. Then, in front of the couch, I cut a small slit in the carpet and slipped the lead wire into it. I pulled the lead wire under the carpet to the far side of the room, and then I fixed the microphone the same way. The recorder itself had to go in the closet. A squat mahogany table that served as a coffee table went over the hole in the carpet. I ran the microphone wires up the legs of the table, on the inside, and then made a bracket of nails on the under side of the table to hold the microphones. There was only one place where the wires showed when I got through and that was on the bare space of floor between the carpet and the closet door. I fixed that by getting a dirty shirt out of the closet and throwing it on the floor. Then I messed the room up even more than usual so the shirt wouldn't look out of place. I piled odds and ends of clothing on the bed and on the other chair in the room, which left only one place to sit—on the couch. Right in front of the microphones.

I heard the telephone ring downstairs and I stood there listening to the hammering in my chest. "Mr. Foley!" It was the landlady.

When I picked up the phone, Barney said, "It's settled, Foley. It happens tomorrow."

He sounded so grim I guessed that he had found out about the hijacking. But not all about it.

Now came the tough part. I had to get him in the room or the plan was no good at all. I said, "I've been doing some thinking. I've decided that five thousand isn't a big enough stake to leave town on."

He didn't like that. "We'll talk about it later," he said coldly. "Max and Joel will bring you out to my place and we'll go over it."

"I've had enough of your place,' I said. "I'm not taking another going-over if I can help it."

"You can't help it, Foley," he said dryly. "Max and Joel can drag you out of that room any time I give the word."

"Not without a hell of a racket."

He thought about that. He could get me out, all right, but that might not be the best way.

"All right," he said evenly. "There's a roadhouse across the river; we can settle it there."

"Like hell. There's a place on the corner of First and Main. If you want to do business, I'll talk to you there."

"Someday," he said softly, "you're going to learn who gives the orders, Foley. But it's going to be too late then."

"I'm ready to do business. I'm just not going to take any more beatings from your hoodlums."

"All right," he said finally, and my arm ached from squeezing the receiver. "I'll come to your place."

He hung up and I stood there with my breath whistling between my teeth. I hadn't suggested that he come here, so there was no reason for him to suspect anything. There were some things that I *could* expect, though. A gun, probably, and Max and Joel. But that didn't bother me. All I wanted was to get him in the room. Then the sonofabitch would soon find out who could give orders.

Less than an hour had passed when I heard the steps on the stairs. I went to the closet and turned on the recorder. Then I opened the door before he had a chance to knock and Barney stood there smiling an iron-hard, humorless smile. I was struck completely dumb for a moment, too stunned to move or make a sound. Barney wasn't alone. And he didn't have Max and Joel with him, as I expected. The man beside him looked grim and uncomfortable—it was Paul Keating.

I must have stood there for a full ten seconds without making a move. Then the impact of the thing hit me like a bullet. Not even in my wildest imaginings had I expected to get Barney Seaward and Paul Keating together. It was perfect.

I stepped to one side and Barney came into the room, watching me closely. Keating hesitated, then followed him in and closed the door. Only then did I remember the tape recorder that was grinding away in the closet, recording nothing.

"I thought we were going to talk alone," I said. "I didn't expect Big Prairie's county attorney to be with you." I had to get names on the tape and establish identities.

"Keating thinks I'm making a mistake," Barney said dryly. "He doesn't think you're to be trusted, Foley."

"Maybe he's right," I said. Then I realized that the recorder wasn't doing a damn bit of good because we were too far away from the microphone. I went over to the bed and motioned to the couch, the only other place in the room to sit down.

They wouldn't sit down. They stood there in the center of the room, each of them nursing his own special kind of hatred. Keating would like to see me dead. Seaward—there was no way of knowing what he was thinking.

Barney looked at me, then he glanced at Keating with that same hard smile. I realized then that he had his own reason for wanting Keating in on this. Barney was an ambitious man—more ambitious than I had realized until now. Maybe one day he would be wholesaling for all the bootleggers in Oklahoma. After he had made Keating governor of the state. Even now he knew too much about the county attorney for Keating to dare refuse him anything. On top of bootlegging, gambling, and prostitution, Seaward had already made him a party to one murder—Marty Paycheck's—and was preparing to make him a party to one murder more. You couldn't refuse a man anything after you had joined with him in crimes like that, and Seaward knew it better than anybody.

I sat there looking at Barney Seaward with a new kind of respect until I realized that all that power could be mine.

But it didn't mean a thing if I didn't get it on the tape. "Did you bring the money, Seaward?" I said.

He lost his smile. "Don't push me, Foley. I've lost a truck of liquor and a driver and a guard this morning, and before long somebody's going to get hurt and hurt bad. It could be you, Foley."

"I told you what my price was. If you want me to kill Sid, you'll have to pay for it."

Keating winced. Suddenly his knees seemed to give away and he dropped to the couch and lit a cigarette, his hands shaking. I looked at him and said, "Keating, you can pay half of it, you're in it as deep as Seaward here." That got their names on the tape. "Now that I think of it," I went on, "I wouldn't have it any other way. If there's an investigation, I want the county attorney on my side. If it ever comes before a grand jury, I want Keating to be in a position to throw up every smoke screen he can think of. And you can think of them, Keating. You thought of them all right when Marty Paycheck was killed."

Barney laughed, in that abrupt, completely humorless way of his.

"The punk's got a head on his shoulders," Barney said.

I said, "Don't call me that again, Barney!"

It startled him. "Maybe," he said softly, "I'd better call Max and Joel in and show you again who gives the orders."

"And maybe I'll raise so much hell," I said, "that it'll be heard all the way to the State Crime Bureau in Oklahoma City!"

I could see kill behind those cool eyes of his, but he kept a strong hand on his emotions. First things first with Barney. "All right," he said, as though he had completely forgotten everything but the business at hand. "Ten thousand dollars. But you'll get it after the job, Foley, not in advance."

If I had said twenty thousand, it would have been the same thing. He would promise it and I would never see it.

"And you'll do it the way I tell you," Barney said. "Tomorrow morning I'll send Sid to Ardmore to make some collections for me. He's going to have an accident on the way. A bad one. Do you know the highway between here and Ardmore, Foley?"

"Not very well."

"About thirty miles west of Big Prairie the highway is straight and the land is flat for the most part. Traffic moves fast out there. There's an arroyo there—a place called Little River—the bed is dry most of the year, but it's deep. It would be a long, hard fall in a car. Especially a convertible like Sid's."

"What kind of a bridge is it?" I said.

"The bridge is concrete, but the approaches are two-by-six railing. It wouldn't take much to shove a speeding car through them. West of the bridge there is a section line road, and beyond that there is a service station. Their business is whisky, but you can buy gas, too, if you want it, or you get a bent fender straightened or a new paint job or even a new license plate. A man by the name of Carter runs the place. He has a couple of trucks that he rents sometimes to friends."

It was clear enough, but not as clear as I wanted it for the tape.

I said, "Let's see if I've got it. First, I go to this service station and rent a truck. You'll have to arrange that end of it. Then I go to the crossroads west of the bridge and I wait until I see that red convertible of Sid's. Then I pull out, force him through the railings and into the arroyo. After that, I take the truck back to the service station where they straighten out any dents that might be in it, paint it, change license plates, and I get in my own car and come back to Big Prairie. What will I do about passing traffic? I can't just drive away as if nothing happened."

"Tell them you're going for a doctor," Seaward said. "Let them see your license plate—it won't make any difference. Thirty minutes after you get the truck back to the service station it will be a different truck. Nobody will ever recognize it."

"What about the highway patrol?"

"By the time they get there, it will be over." He looked at Keating. "Have you got anything to add, Paul?"

Keating looked ten years older than he had when he first walked into the room. "That bridge is within a few hundred feet of the county line. If anything happens in the next county, I won't be able to help you."

"It will happen just the way I said," Barney said, looking at me. "Won't it, Foley?"

I thought of the recorder, all the words going on tape. I thought of Lola—I'd like to see her face when she first heard this recording!

"It's going to be just exactly the way you said, Barney," I said. "You don't have to worry about that."

After they left, I played the tape all the way through, from beginning to end. It was all there, the complete plan for a murder. I could hardly breathe as I sat there listening to Barney's voice, ragged with nerves. The only thing missing was the murder itself. That was up to me.

It didn't worry me at all that I was in it as much as Keating and Seaward, because I wasn't bluffing this time. The power that I held was staggering.

Even as I thought about it I heard the heavy tramp of shoes on the stairs. The knock on my door startled me and for a moment I felt my insides go loose and I thought hopelessly: It's happened! Something's happened and the bottom has fallen out of everything!

"Mr. Foley!" It was the landlady's voice, harsh and indignant.

There was another heavy-fisted knock, a knock that meant business. "Open that door, Foley!" A man's voice this time.

"What is it?" I said.

"It's the police," the landlady said, sounding outraged now.

I couldn't move. I couldn't get my mind to working as the pounding on the door got more insistent. I watched the door give under the weight of heavy shoulders, then the lock snapped and a piece of the door facing splintered and flew across the room as the door came open.

A big plain-clothes cop came into the room with a gun in his hand. "Shake him down," he said, and his partner got behind me and patted me.

"What the hell is this!" I said.

"Get him downstairs," the first cop said flatly, and the two of them got me handcuffed and hustled me out of the room.

"What the hell do you think you're doing!" I was almost yelling by now.

The first cop slammed a sledgehammer fist into the small of my back, and I almost went to my knees. "That's just a sample, Foley," he said. "If you want some more, just try hollering again."

They half dragged me out of the house and all the roomers crowded onto the front porch, staring wide-eyed. I saw Joel come around from the back of the rooming house where he had been standing watch, on me, and Max standing undecided beside the pickup. The two cops were shoving me into their car when Max came forward and said: "What is this?"

"Just stay out of it, buddy. Move away and you won't get hurt."

He got me into the back seat and then got in beside me, the gun still pointed at my middle. The first cop got behind the wheel. We left Max standing there, his mouth open, looking worried.

I said, "I don't know what this is all about, but I know one thing. You're going to get your rump warped when Barney Seaward finds out about this!"

"Jesus," the driving cop said wearily. "Everybody works for Seaward, if you listen to what they say."

I felt like hell. My beard was coming out and I was sweaty and dirty and numb for want of sleep. Then I remembered that recorder in my closet, and that tape. If somebody found that….

They didn't give me time to worry about it. We went straight through the middle of town and then pulled into a parking lot behind the courthouse.

"Get out," the sweating cop said. The two of them got my arms and started walking me across the graveled parking lot, toward the rear of the courthouse.

Big Prairie's courthouse is a three-story, red-brick affair, with the county jail on the top floor and the county and city offices down below. They hustled me through the rear entrance and down a hall, then we stopped in front of a frosted-glass-paneled door and the sweating cop knocked. In black letters beginning to peel on the frosted glass, there were the words: *Thaddeus M. McErulur, Chief of Police.*

McErulur was in his shirt sleeves, sitting behind a battered desk, when we came in. His long, horselike face looked as hard as a granite slab. He leaned slowly across the desk, jutting out his big chin. "You lousy punk bastard," he said harshly. "Foley, you're going to be one sorry punk before this day is over!"

"When this day is over," I said tightly, "Big Prairie is going to be looking for another gutless ape to take over the police department!"

The sweating cop shot that hammer-like fist into the small of my back again and the wind went out of me.

The telephone rang as I was picking myself up. McErulur picked it up, answered it, and the grin suddenly left his face. "I tried to get in touch with you, Barney," he said worriedly. "Hell, how was I to know?" He listened some more, his long face getting redder all the time. "Sure, Barney. There was no fuss, none at all—"

"Like hell," I said. "Everybody on the block knows I was hauled out of the rooming house by your cops!"

The sweating cop was about to let me have the fist again, but McErulur shook his head. "All right, Barney. Whatever you say." He hung up, looking at me with a new kind of hate. "Get him downstairs," he said to the cops. "I'll let you know later what to do with him."

They took me out into the hall again and then we went down a flight of stairs to the basement. "In here," one of the cops said, opening a door to a naked, windowless room. That was when I saw Mefford and Cox.

They came down the stairs at the other end of the hall, handcuffed, two uniformed cops behind them.

"Get going," the sweating cop said. His partner gave me a shove and I stumbled into the room. The only furniture in the room was a long plank table and four straight chairs. I dropped into one of the chairs and sat there raging. I had risked my neck for nothing! I'd hijacked a liquor truck, killed two men, and two goddamn farmers had ruined everything!

The sweating cop sat on the edge of the table and shook out a cigarette. "What's the matter, Foley?" he said sourly. "Did you see somethin' that upset you?"

"Lay off," the other cop said. "Let McErulur take care of this."

"Don't worry about your partners," the sweating cop went on, "they'll be taken care of, all right." He laughed.

I looked at him. "What partners?"

"You goin' to tell us you never saw the two farmers before? That ain't the story they're tellin'. They say a whisky truck was hijacked and you ramrodded the job. They say you killed a couple of men. Now ain't that a hell of a thing for a man's partners to do, turn on him like that? You want to know how we caught up with you? Your partners were stealin' you blind, Foley," he said grinning. "All that liquor you went to so much trouble to get, they were haulin' it away in broad daylight!"

Then the door opened and McErulur and Barney Seaward came into the room. McErulur jerked his head and the two cops went out. Seaward came over to the table, his face white with rage. He put his hands on the table and stood there glaring at me.

"Take it easy, Barney," McErulur said softly. "We can take care of it."

Barney wheeled as if he had been stabbed. "You took care of it all right! You and your dumb cops. The whole thing would be in the headlines right now if I didn't own the newspaper." He turned back to me. "You punk, I should have killed you in the beginning!"

"That would have been smart,' I said. "Kill me, then kill Sid, then kill the man who pulled the trigger for you! Where's the end to it? How long do you think you can get away with a thing like that?"

His hand darted out like a snake, but I hardly felt the sting as it whipped across my face. "You're the big man in Big Prairie!" I said. His rage seemed to have spilled over on me. "All right, keep on killing and it won't make any difference how big you are. The Crime Bureau will get you, Barney. They'll take you to McAlister and strap you in the two thousand volt chair and you'll squirm just like anybody else."

He would have killed me right then if he had had something to do it with. Then the door opened and Paul Keating came into the room.

Barney turned on Keating. "Where the hell have you been?"

"I was out of the office when McErulur tried to get me," he said, not quite able to hold Barney's gaze. He took off his hat and put it on the table and I saw that his hands were shaking.

"Do you know what it's all about?" McErulur said.

Keating reached for a cigarette, not looking at me. "Not all of it."

"I'll tell you what it's all about!" Barney bit out. "This sonofabitch is the one that knocked my liquor truck off last night."

"Him and a couple of farmers," McErulur put in. "The other two are down the hall spilling their guts. They say Foley killed Barney's driver and guard. We've got it all down in writing."

"Bring it to court," I said. "I'll wreck your organization and let it fall around your shoulders!"

"It'll never come to court," Barney said savagely, "because you're not going to live that long, Foley!"

But then Keating said, "Wait a minute, Barney."

"I've waited long enough," Barney grated.

I had an idea then, and I knew that it might be the break that I wanted. "What about Sid?" I said. "You've already waited too long on him. How do you think I was able to hijack your truck in the first place? Who do you think gave me all the information I needed?"

Barney's face wasn't a pretty thing to see.

"You've got Sid to take care of," I said. "Who's going to do it for you, Barney?"

"You," Paul Keating said.

It was strange, but at that moment the county attorney seemed to me the strongest man in the room. In spite of anger, in spite of fear, his mind kept working, and he turned to the chief of police and said, "McErulur, send in a stenographer. I think Mr. Foley wants to make a statement."

Seaward's head snapped around in surprise. He wasn't used to having the play taken away from him. But almost immediately he began to see what the county attorney was thinking. He thought about it and, slowly, he began to relax. "By God!" he said, and it was almost, a whisper. Then he sat in a chair and I could almost see the senseless rage going out of him.

"You'd better do it, Thad," he said finally, not looking at the chief of police. "Send in a stenographer."

McErulur looked at me, at Barney, then, with a bare hint of a shrug, he went out.

A few minutes dragged by in uncomfortable silence, then there was a knock on the door and a uniformed cop came in with a portable typewriter.

"Take this down," Barney said. "I, Roy Foley, of my own free will, do confess to shooting and killing two men on the night of June First, Nineteen Hundred...."

Barney read the full confession after he had finished dictating it, then nodded for the cop to leave the room. He shoved the original and two carbon copies across the table.

"Sign it."

"And if I don't?"

"You won't live to see the outside of this room. And we both know I'm not bluffing, Foley."

"And if I do sign it?"

"Everything will be as it was before. You take care of Sid just the way we planned it, then you get out of Big Prairie. The confession is my insurance."

"What about Mefford and Cox?"

"They're my worry."

I put my name to the original, and then to the three carbons. God! I thought. I hope nobody has found that recorder!

"What now?" I said.

Barney leaned on the table, his face sober, his voice deadly serious. "Foley,

I've got all of you I can stomach. I expect trouble in this business, but not from punks. I want you to get out of my sight while you're still lucky enough to be alive."

I stood up and Barney sat there, his face hard, looking at nothing. "I'll read about Sid in tomorrow's papers," he said. "And if I don't see it in tomorrow's papers, I'll know what to do with this confession. I'm not bluffing, Foley."

I could hardly believe it. I stood up, walked toward the door, and neither of them said a thing. I looked back once before I left the room and Barney was sitting there staring at his fist. Keating was watching me with a quiet viciousness, pleased with the way he had taken care of me. I prayed the recorder would be just where I had left it!

All that liquor. I couldn't allow myself to think of anything except picking up the pieces and hoping that the pieces would be enough. I walked out of the courthouse and down the steps and stood for a moment on the sidewalk experiencing the overwhelming relief that a condemned prisoner must feel at a last-minute reprieve. My knees were weak, there didn't seem to be enough air to fill my lungs.

I turned, looked back at the courthouse and almost laughed. We'll see who's a punk! I thought. We'll see, Barney!

I took the rooming-house stairs two at a time, and the hammering in my chest became almost unbearable as I reached my room, grasped the knob and shoved the splintered door open. Relief almost knocked me down. The room hadn't been touched. I went to the closet and the recorder was still there. The microphones were still under the table, the lead wires hadn't been tampered with.

For the first time in almost a day I thought of Lola. I thought of her with anger and hate—but not with fear. We'll see, I thought! Now we'll see!

I looked out the window and saw that Max and Joel had either been called off the job or they had lost me in the confusion with the cops. It took less than an hour to get everything set. I had to have two recording machines to make copies of the tape. A music store would be the best bet. Rent the machines, make the copies myself, and then I could be sure that there were no leaks.

I made four copies. One I put in a safe-deposit box, addressed to the State Crime Bureau. I dropped the other three in mail boxes, one addressed to Lola and marked "personal." Laugh, Lola! Play this and realize how completely I can wreck you. Then laugh if you can!

There was only one thing left to do. I had to kill Sid, and I had to do it exactly the way Barney and Keating had planned it on the tape. By the time they got copies of the recording, by the time they got machines to play them on, the murder would be a fact.

Chapter Twelve

The bridge, the arroyo, the approaches were all exactly as Barney had described them. It was nearly morning and still cool. The highway traffic was sparse and scattered, so I stopped on the bridge for a few minutes and inspected the wooden approaches. From the middle of the bridge the rocky bed of the arroyo was about forty feet straight down, but it would be practically impossible to blast a car through the reinforced concrete at that point. Back under the wooden approaches there was a narrow shelf about ten feet down, but beyond the shelf there was a sheer drop all the way to the bottom of the dry wash.

The thing would have to be judged carefully. There were less than a hundred feet to the western approach, and both it and the bridge were narrow, with just enough room for a car on either side of the center line.

It was perfect except for one thing—in case of an accident there was a damn good chance of both cars going through the railings!

A thought hit me then and left me cold. Maybe that was what Barney had figured on! And the more I thought about it the more I knew I was right. The bastard! I thought. Sure, that was the reason he hadn't bothered to be so careful. It explained a lot of things that had been only vague half-questions until now.

Had Barney ever really believed that I could be bluffed out of Big Prairie after doing a job like this for him? I doubted it. Had he ever really believed that I would be satisfied with five hundred dollars—or even five thousand? Like hell he had. He had agreed to the thing because it was an easy way of getting rid of me and Sid in one sweep. And at the same time he could tighten his hold on Keating by bringing him in on the murder.

I thought, If you did come out of the accident alive, Foley, do you think he would let you go and forget about it? Not in a hundred years! Killing you is an inconvenience and risk that he hoped to avoid—but he wouldn't side-step the job if it became necessary. He didn't side-step it with Sid.

But you overlooked something this time, Barney, I thought. The recorder!

That thought made me feel big, and the knowledge that I might end up at the bottom of the arroyo with Sid couldn't dampen the feeling. It was a chance I had to take.

About a half mile up the highway I pulled up in front of a service station, a sagging, green-painted frame building with two gas pumps in front and a scattering of wrecked cars at the back. A beefy, red-faced man wearing big overalls came out of the building and I said:

"You Carter?"

"Why?"

"I'm supposed to pick up a truck here."

"Ah—" He made a small, meaningless sound. "You better drive around to the back," he said. "You can leave your car in the garage for a while."

I drove around to the rear and waited until Carter backed an ancient Dodge three-quarter ton out of the garage, then I pulled in. I looked at my watch and it was almost nine-thirty.

I took the Dodge back to the section line road, just beyond the bridge, and waited.

Traffic picked up a little, but it was still scattered and nothing to worry about. I could look out across the prairie and see the cars coming from a long way off. A hammering would start in my chest every time I saw one, and I'd think: This could be Sid! And, in my mind, I'd slam that Dodge into gear and start barreling for the bridge. And every time I'd think: Christ, it can't be done! We'll both be killed. The bridge is too goddamn narrow!

Every time, after the car had passed, I'd have to choke the panic down and get set again, watching for that red convertible.

It was strange, but I hardly thought of Sid as a person at all. He was a way out. He had to be killed—Barney had decided that—so what difference did it make who did it? The only thing that mattered now was whether or not I managed to come out of it alive. Up to that point, everything was perfect, clean, all loose ends tied together. The thing staggered me, every time I thought of it. A murder plan, complete in every detail, designed by Seaward and Keating in their own voices. God, how the crime bureau would love to get their hands on that recording—and how Seaward and Keating would know it! Until the murder was a fact, I was holding an empty gun and that would scare nobody.

Traffic began to pick up on the highway, and as the minutes dragged by I began thinking, What if Barney got suspicious? What if he decided not to send Sid to Ardmore after all? And, even as I was thinking it, I saw that convertible of Sid's, top down, roaring across the prairie like a red comet.

I was wound up, I guess. I had slammed the Dodge off the section line road and onto the highway before realized that I even had it in gear. I had the Dodge up to forty in second gear, then slammed it into high and was reaching for fifty by the time I hit the approaches on my side. That red convertible was coming at me like something out of a nightmare, and crazy panic seized me as I thought: It can't be done! The second you sideswipe him you'll go through the railings! I heard myself cursing savagely.

Then I seemed to grow cold as I heard the tires leave the rattling boards of the approaches and slam growling onto the concrete of the bridge itself. Fleetingly, in those lightning-like seconds, I realized that Barney had understood me even better than I had understood myself. He was a man who understood hate, and greed, and maybe he even knew about Lola. Maybe Barney himself had run from something once. Maybe even the great Barney Seaward had been laughed at, had felt his insides crawl. It was a new thought, but not startling, because how else could he understand that there are times when a man would rather die than fail again.

Roy, you're the funniest thing!

In that last split second it was Lola that I thought of. Not Vida. Not Seaward, and not Sid. It was Lola and I could hear her laughing. It was the last thing I thought and the last thing I had time to think.

It happened too fast to understand. I had the Dodge wide open, roaring straight down the middle of the bridge. Sid must have been making seventy when he first hit the approaches. He didn't even seem to see me. He didn't let up on the accelerator, he didn't tramp his brakes, and I knew in the back of my mind that he was too drunk to know or care what was happening. Sideswipe him! That's enough!

I seemed frozen to the steering wheel. I couldn't move, and that red convertible came at me like a trick shot of a car hurtling out of a movie screen. I must have closed my eyes for a moment, instinctively trying to brace myself for the shock.

The shock didn't come. I heard the ear-splitting crack, like a high muzzle velocity gun exploding. I opened my eyes in time to see the convertible blasting through the gaping hole in the railings. It hit the shelf below and bounced, then it fell end over end down to the bottom of the arroyo. I braked to a stop about fifty yards beyond the western approach, my stomach trying to push its way into my throat. There wasn't a scratch on the Dodge.

I heard another car braking to a stop behind me, and then the sound of running on the highway. I shoved myself out of the Dodge and a man was leaning over the railing, his face pale, looking down at the wreckage.

"Geez," he said softly. "I saw it from almost a half mile up the highway." He turned to me, looking as if he was going to be sick. "This sure is your lucky day, buddy. If he'd sideswiped you, you'd have gone right through the railing with him."

That was the thing that kept gnawing at me. Another car was squealing to a stop on the other side of the bridge, and I finally found my voice. "How about you going down and seeing if there's anything you can do," I said. "I'll find a telephone and call an ambulance and the highway patrol."

There was nothing he or anybody else could do and we both knew it. That convertible was a twisted, smoking mass of scrap, and Sid was under it somewhere. What was left of him.

I got the Dodge into gear, turned it around and headed back across the bridge.

As soon as I got back to Big Prairie I called Vida. It wasn't the smart thing to do, but the only thing I wanted or could think of was Vida. To hold her, to rest against her. Somewhere in Big Prairie all hell was breaking loose, and I knew it, but that didn't seem to matter right now. The mail would have been delivered, and probably Seaward and Keating and Lola had already heard their copies of the recordings. The highway patrol would have already started their investigations at the bridge. I was too tired to worry about it. The only thing I could think of was that red convertible going through the railings. I hadn't even seen Sid's face. What had he been thinking of? I wondered. Why hadn't he done something to save himself? I hadn't even touched him; it was almost as though he had *wanted* to kill himself. I tried not to think about it.

I left the car on a side street at the edge of town and caught a cab to Vida's place. She was waiting at the front door when I got there and the look of her shocked me. She looked as if she had aged ten years since I had seen her last; she seemed thinner, tireder as she clung to me.

"Roy—"

"It's all over," I said. "I fought it out with Seaward, and I won. We're going to be all right, Vida. But I feel a hundred years old. I've got to rest."

My legs almost gave way under me. Vida put her arms around me, half holding me up as we went through the front room and into the hallway leading to the bedroom. "You can stay here," she said. "Barney sent Sid to Ardmore and he won't be back until tonight."

I had almost forgotten about him. Sid won't be back tonight, I thought. Or ever.

"I'll make you some hot chocolate," I heard Vida saying. "It will help you sleep."

I didn't want it, but it didn't seem to be worth the trouble of saying so. I dropped on the edge of the bed and sat there woodenly and Vida went out to the kitchen. I lay back, without even bothering to loosen my tie, but the minute I closed my eyes I saw that convertible going through the railings again, hitting, bouncing, like a nightmare in slow motion, then plunging down to the bottom of the arroyo....

Something was wrong; the thing just wasn't right. It didn't make sense that a guy should go to his death like that, doing nothing to save himself. I thought back, trying to put myself in Sid's position. Would I have done it the way he had? Hell no; I would have tramped on the brakes, even if I hadn't had time to think about it, and I would have jerked the car away from the railing, even if it had meant sideswiping somebody. It was the natural thing. It was the thing that Barney Seaward had planned on all the time.

The only explanation that I could think of was that Sid had been drunk, so drunk that he hadn't realized what was happening until it was too late.

I half turned on the bed and knocked the pillow onto the floor. When I picked it up there was a folded piece of stationery under it—and I think I knew, even before I opened it and looked at it, what would be written there.

There were just a few words. It said: "I'm sorry, Vida. I can't take it any more."

I sat there holding it, looking at it, and then suddenly it hit me. The first thing I thought was, Christ, what a piece of luck! It was a suicide note and I was in the clear, completely in the clear.

But the thing was too impossible to believe. Things just don't happen like that. You don't go to all that trouble to plan a murder that looks perfect and then have the guy commit suicide just exactly to fit the plan, and a note clearing you of all the blame. That was too much luck. Think back—there had to be an answer.

I tried to piece it together—and finally I got an answer, but it wasn't satisfactory. To start with, Sid had written the note last night or early this morning, sometime before he was to go to Ardmore for Barney. He had meant to kill himself—either because of the murder on his conscience, or because of what I'd told him about Vida. Anyway—and the thing was coming fast now—he had planned to kill himself, that much was sure.

But maybe he'd run out of guts. Or maybe he just couldn't think of the right way to do it. If that was the case, the natural thing would be to wait for his chance. So maybe that bridge had seemed like the right place to Sid. When death had come at him, he simply hadn't cared enough to step out of the way.

The thing stunned me for a moment. I sat there clutching the note, feeling as if I had the world by the tail. Then the bottom fell out.

The note wasn't going to do me a bit of good.

In the first place, if I ever proved that it was suicide instead of murder, I'd lose what hold I had on Seaward and Keating. In the second place, it was probable that Sid had insured himself, and I sure wasn't going to stop a double-indemnity insurance claim by producing a note that proved that he had taken his own life.

I tore the note in half and thought: This note could save you from the chair.

But it wasn't the chair I was afraid of.

I tore the pieces, again and again. You've gone to too much trouble and taken too many chances to start playing it safe now, I thought. A stranglehold on Seaward, that's the important thing, and you can't get a thing like that by playing it safe. You'll never hear Lola beg, by playing it safe....

I looked up and Vida startled me.

"Roy, what is it?"

"Nothing. I'm all right." I still had the pieces of the note in my hand. I shoved them into my pocket and lay across the bed again.

"Drink this," she said.

"I don't want anything to drink. I want you."

I felt the bed give as she sank down beside me. Her fingers were cool as she stroked my forehead, her breasts were soft as she held me close. I let my mind wander in darkness as I began to relax. How long would it be before they called on Vida to identify the body? It didn't seem to matter. It would be long enough and I could sleep.

It was almost dark when I woke up. Vida wasn't there. I called out but she didn't answer, and I lay there for several minutes, my mind still in fog, wondering where she had gone. Then I remembered Seaward, and the thought seemed to jerk me half out of bed, bathing my face in sweat. Then I thought: Seaward can't do a thing any more. You're holding the club now, and he damn well knows it!

That made me feel good. By now I realized that the highway patrol must have called Vida and she had gone to the morgue without waking me. I went into the bathroom and stared at myself in the mirror. I looked like hell, but I felt big inside.

I ran some hot water and shaved and Vida still wasn't back. I went into the kitchen and found some gin and limes; I drank the gin straight and sucked a lime for a chaser, and all the time I could feel that bigness growing inside me. If I could only have seen Barney's face when he played that recording for the first time! And Keating's. And Lola's....

Someone came into the front room and I knew it was Vida, and for the first time, I wondered what I was going to say to her.

I went in and she was standing there, pale with shock. She looked at me almost as if I were a stranger and said, "He's dead."

"Who?"

"He went off a bridge. It was a forty-foot drop, they said," she went on flatly. "There wasn't anything left of the car."

"For God's sake, will you tell me what you're talking about?"

"Sid. He just drove off the bridge." Her face began breaking up and I could hear hysteria rising in her voice.

"How do you know all this?"

"The highway patrol came after me and took me down to the morgue. It was Sid. He was...." She began crying then and I felt rotten, not because of Sid but because of Vida.

"You need a drink," I said. "Why don't you sit down and I'll get you something. Sit still and try to relax, Vida."

I went into the kitchen and poured double shots of straight gin for both of us. I put one of the glasses in Vida's hand and she drank it automatically. Suddenly she began to shudder. "God, I keep seeing him, Roy! They said it was an accident, but it wasn't. He meant for it to happen. He planned it."

I could feel my heart hammering. "How do you know that?"

She shook her head. "I just know it. I think I've known it ever since the morning you told him about us." She looked at me now and it was almost as if she was seeing me for the first time. "He loved me, Roy," she said softly, almost whispered. "I guess I loved him, too—once. A long time ago. He wasn't bad, Roy. He was like a kid who never grew up."

"He was a drunken bum," I said suddenly, harshly. It shocked her. "He was no good," I went on. "You're better off without him." Then I remembered something. "Did Sid carry insurance?"

She looked blank for a moment before she answered. "Twenty thousand dollars."

"Double for accidental death?"

"I think so."

I almost smiled then. Geez, forty thousand dollars! "Look," I said, "maybe it was an accident and maybe it wasn't, but it doesn't make any difference now. Sid's dead, and that's all there is to it. You've got to stop thinking about suicide or we won't get a penny out of that insurance."

I was already thinking "we." God, with forty thousand dollars to work with, I could afford to forget about the flop I had made on the hijacking.

Vida was looking at me strangely, her face wet with tears. "Roy... what about us? What are we going to do? Are—are we going to get married?"

"Hell, yes. You know I want to marry you more than anything."

"Hold me, Roy. Hold me close."

I held her and she began crying again. There was only one way I could think of to stop that, so I began unbuttoning the bodice of her dress.

"Roy, no! Not tonight!"

I forced her head back and mashed my mouth onto hers, and as my hand worked she began that shuddering that I knew so well.

Chapter Thirteen

"Goddamn you, this is the last mistake you'll ever make, Foley!" Barney Seward said.

I laughed at him. "I've got you, Barney, and you know it."

He was past rage. He stood there stone-cold, iron-hard, with nothing at all showing in those eyes of his. We were back at Barney's house, right back where it had all started, and that seemed fitting somehow. Paul Keating wasn't on hand this time, and neither were Joel and Max. It was just me and Barney, and I was on top this time.

He said softly, "You goddamn, lousy punk!"

I almost hit him then. I said, "That's the last time you're going to say that, Barney. Do you understand?"

He understood, all right, but still he wasn't ready to give up "All right, Foley," he said evenly, "I made a mistake by letting you live, and a man can't make mistakes in this business without paying for them. How much do you want for all the copies of that recording?"

"They're not for sale."

He smiled faintly. "What do you plan to do with them, Foley? Turn them over to the police? The Crime Bureau? You can't be that dumb."

"Maybe I am," I said.

Barney shook his head, still smiling. "I admit that those recordings are worth something to me, just on the chance that you might let them get away from you. But you're not going to blackmail me with them, if that's what you're thinking, because you don't dare turn them over to the cops. Sooner or later, I'll get those copies. I'll find a way. But if you want to save me the trouble, I'll pay a reasonable price for them."

And I wouldn't live five minutes after you got them in your hands, I thought. Abruptly, anger flared up inside me. My hand grabbed the front of his shirt before he knew what was happening. "You sonofabitch!" I heard myself hissing. I gave him a shove and he reeled against the wall, his smile gone.

"Look at me!" I almost yelled. "Do I look like I'm bluffing? I've failed for the last time, Barney. I've taken my last beating. I'll get what I want out of you and Keating or we'll all go down together. I haven't got anything to lose, Barney. If I fail again, do you know what I have to look forward to? A job in a hash house. And I'm not going to go back to a hash house, Barney. I'll die first."

Barney was beaten. I looked at him, grinning, feeling as tall as a mountain. Still, something in the back of my mind cautioned me not to push him too far. He was still dangerous. Barney knew about hate, and a man like that is always dangerous. I knew.

When I spoke again, my voice was even. I said, "There's no reason why we can't do business together, Barney. You once gave Sid a retailing position in payment for murder—well, I'll settle for the same thing. Nothing will change. You'll go on being the wholesaler; all I want is a shot at the retailing business."

He wasn't sure that he had heard me right. He looked at me very carefully, as though he were having trouble setting his mind on what I had said. Then a coldness touched me—I could almost see behind those eyes of his, see what he had been thinking.

I had stopped just in time. Barney had been slowly drowning in his hate. I knew how he felt, and I realized for the first time that Barney and I were much alike in a lot of ways. Barney, if pushed hard enough and far enough, could be capable of destroying himself just for the fierce satisfaction of satisfying his hate. We stood there looking at each other, and it was almost like looking in a mirror.

A long moment dragged by and Barney didn't make a sound. He knew that I could ruin him. He knew that if I didn't get my way I *would* ruin him, but it didn't seem to matter at that moment. He carefully weighed it in his mind, the satisfaction of his hate against what it would cost. And finally he said, almost dreamily, "All right. Now get out of here."

It was almost two weeks after the funeral that Vida collected on Sid's insurance. The next day we were married. I had Vida sell the house and we moved into one of the new apartment buildings north of town.

As long as I kept a heavy hand on Seaward he kept the chief of police and the sheriff in line for me. With that recording, I had Paul Keating in my pocket, so I didn't have the grand jury to worry about. And the money was just beginning to roll in,

I should have been satisfied, but I wasn't.

There was always Lola.

I couldn't forget about her. She wouldn't let me rest. I would lie awake at nights imagining the things that must be going through Lola's mind. For years I had dreamed of having the power to ruin her, and now that I had it I didn't know what to do with it. At nights I'd lie there with Vida beside me, and I'd think: Christ, are you still afraid of her, even now?

I knew that it would happen sometime. I'd make her come crawling—when I found the best way to do it. The very best way. And in the meantime I could afford to wait.

I invested in some Big Prairie real estate. On the south edge of town, down by the river, there was a rundown tourist court—nine frame shacks and a two-by-four wooden box that served as an office—where some of the factory workers lived. I bought it and moved the factory workers out.

The next thing I did was make another visit to the Travelers Hotel and call for Rose.

"Well," she said dryly, as she came in, "if it isn't the photographer." She came over to the bed, sat down and looked at me. "Do you know that business almost got me in a jam?" she said. "You didn't take care of the bellhop like you promised. I had to give the pimp twenty dollars of my own money."

"That's what you get for working in a hotel." I said.

"What is that supposed to mean?"

"What you need is another kind of setup. Say a crib, where you could operate in the open and be your own boss. Maybe you wouldn't make as much a trick, but the turnover would be a lot bigger in a crib."

She laughed harshly. "Now that's a brilliant idea. Sure, a girl can make money on a crib street, but that's one thing you can't get away with in this town."

"I'll get away with it," I said. "I'm letting you in on a good thing, if you're smart enough to take it. I need seven or eight good girls to pay the rent on the cribs, and I'll give them all the protection they need."

She wasn't quite sure if I was crazy or if I could really do it.

"Where is this place?" she asked finally.

"Down on River Street. The Red Ball Tourist Courts, the place is called. It's near the factories, and you know how factory workers are. I'll have some gambling in one of the cribs, and that'll help draw them in. If the girls want to sell whisky on the side, it's all right. As long as they buy their supply from me."

"Who will the other girls be?"

I grinned, because I could see that she had already made up her mind.

"I thought maybe you could help me there."

I visited Seaward next. Barney was out in front when I drove up, spraying some rose bushes at the side of the house. He came over to the car wearing a battered felt hat and loose-fitting overalls.

"Barney," I said, "I'm going to have to ask a favor of you. I'm taking up a sideline, Barney. I'm opening a few cribs on River Street. I want you to pass the word along to the sheriff and the chief of police that the place is off limits for cops."

An ugliness began to appear in those quick eyes of his. He said, "I told you once, Foley, that I could be pushed too far. I don't furnish protection for pimps."

Pimp. It wasn't a nice word, it tastes rotten in your mouth when you say it. I felt that blind anger start working inside me, and I reached over to push the door open. I got out and stood in front of him, my face only a few inches from his. I grabbed the front of his overalls and wadded them in my fist. I think I would have clubbed him to death if he had made a move.

But he didn't move. At some time—maybe during the long hours of thinking about it—he had lost some of his hardness. When I felt that, I could hold my voice down. I said, "You sonofabitch, I'm tired of handling you with velvet gloves. I can send you to the chair, and you know it. And because you know it, you're going to do exactly as I tell you." I began shaking him. I shook him until his teeth rattled. "Do you understand that? You'll do exactly as I tell you!"

He still didn't say a thing. Those eyes weren't so ugly now. They were frightened eyes.

"All right, Foley! For God's sake, all right!"

I breathed deeply. The sudden fury began to burn out.

Barney wasn't boss any more. I was.

I said, "I'm glad we finally understand each other. Now about these cribs. Do I get protection for them?"

I loosened my hold on him then let him go. He tried to pull himself together, but it was a tough job. He knew that somehow, there in that fit of anger, he had lost the upper hand.

"Foley, you don't know how it is." He was almost pleading. "The chief of police would be run out of town if we allowed cribs to operate. The sheriff would be tarred and feathered. The churches run this state, and prostitution is one thing the churches can't stand. Forget it, Foley—try anything else, but forget that."

"I've decided," I said, "so there's no use talking about it."

I got back in the car. He was still talking as I drove out of the yard.

Chapter Fourteen

"Roy, is something bothering you?"

"Nothing's bothering me. I'm fine."

Sure I was fine. I had the cribs going, collecting two hundred dollars a day from the girls. I had two dice tables in another cabin and they were averaging a hundred a day. On top of that, there was the whisky, and I was gradually squeezing Kingkade out of Big Prairie.

At this rate I'd have the county in my hip pocket within a year.

Still, for two days I'd done nothing but pace the floor and drink.

"Do you want a drink?" I said.

"All right." Vida, curled up on the apartment couch, watched me with those slanted eyes as I got ice out of the refrigerator and brought it in to the portable bar in the sitting room.

It was just getting dark outside. I pulled the blinds and snapped on a table lamp, then I downed my drink in one gulp and went back for a refill. I could feel Vida watching me.

"For God's sake," I said, "can't you look at something else for a minute? You give me the creeps."

"I'm sorry, Roy," she said softly. "I didn't mean to disturb you."

I was sorry the minute I had said it. I went over to the couch, sat down beside her and put my arm around her. "Maybe I have got a case of nerves at that," I said. "I didn't mean to blow off that way."

"It's all right—"

I pulled her close to me and held her. I loved her—I knew that as well as I knew anything. But something else kept gnawing at me, and not even the warmth of Vida's body could stop it.

"Roy—" She was looking up at me expectantly, her damp red mouth parted slightly.

I said, "I guess I don't feel so good tonight," and got up. I could see disappointment in her eyes as I went over to get another drink. If the gnawing would only stop. What's wrong with me, anyway? I kept thinking. What is it that makes people step to one side when they see me coming, like I had some kind of rotten disease. Hell, I already had more money, more power than Sid had ever dreamed of. But they didn't take me in, the way they had Sid. Seaward didn't even invite me to his parties.

"I think I'll go out for a while," I said. "Maybe some fresh air will do me good."

Vida nodded, her eyes still faintly puzzled.

I took her face in my hands and kissed her hard. "I love you, Vida." Then I went out.

I drove around for maybe a half hour, and an idea began to jell. I figured it out in my mind, deciding just exactly what I would do and what I would say. Then I went to a drugstore and used the phone.

"Hello?" she said, her voice slightly impatient.

"Hello, Lola, this is Roy Foley."

It wasn't exactly the way I had planned it, but it was effective. I could hear the whistle of her breath as she dragged it in sharply.

I said, "Don't hang up, Lola. If you do, I'll just come out to your house."

There was a slight jar in my ear and I guessed that she had put her hand over the mouthpiece. Then she hissed, "Speak quickly. What do you want?"

"I want to talk to you. Meet me in a half hour at 1114 River Street—that's the Red Ball Tourist Courts."

"It's impossible!" she hissed.

"It's about a tape recording. You know the one I mean."

"Wait!" The word came like a pistol shot. "All right, 1114 River Street. I warn you, though, I don't have much money, and I can't get any until the banks open tomorrow."

"Never mind the money."

I hung up and sat there in the phone booth for almost five minutes, thinking, Crawl, Lola! Goddamn you, crawl!

Finally I went back to the car and headed south toward the river. I felt head and shoulders above the tallest man in the world. I was drunk. But not from liquor.

The cribs were doing a good business when I got there. Four or five cars were parked inside the horseshoe formed by the cabins. I walked straight down toward an end cabin where an overalled factory worker was just coming out.

Without bothering to knock, I pushed the door open and went in. Rose was in her work clothes, black lace pants and brassiere. She was straightening the bed, and she looked up briefly, without surprise.

I grinned at her. "I want to borrow your cabin for a while."

"When I pay twenty-five a day for it?" she said indignantly.

"All right, I'll knock off the rent for today. Get your clothes on and go to a movie or something." She got her dress on, managing somehow to look more undressed than she had in just the pants and brassiere.

"Remember, no rent for today."

"I'll remember."

Rose went out and I stayed there in the cabin for a minute. It would be hard to find a crummier place. A nine-by-twelve room with worn linoleum on the floor, gaudy paper on the walls, dirty and peeling. A Lysol-smelling bathroom in one corner. A naked electric light bulb hanging from the ceiling, with a piece of string tied to the end of the chain pull switch. The thin mattressed double bed sagged in the center, and, even before I tried it with my hand, I knew it would be noisy. A cheap dresser and a straight chair took care of the furniture. It was a shock when I looked in the dresser mirror. I had somehow imagined that I would look different simply because it was Rose's mirror—but the face that looked back at me was the same. Clean shaven, hair neatly trimmed, tie straight, collar immaculately white. Instinctively, I touched the lapel of my suit and felt the softness of Oxford flannel. A hundred and eighty dollars worth of suit, cut by an artist, and it gave me a good feeling to know that I had nine more of them in my closet at the apartment.

The half-hour time limit had about five minutes to go when the black Cadillac pulled up in front of the office shack where I was waiting. I walked over and said, "You're on time, Lola. I'm glad of that."

She grasped the steering wheel as though she were trying to break it, then, she pressed her hands to her face. Suddenly she reached forward to turn the ignition.

I said, "Just a minute, Lola," and her hand stopped in mid-air. "Give me time to say something, then if you still feel like running, you can run." I waited while she took a long, shuddering breath. But she didn't make another move toward the switch. "All right, that's better. You know about Sid's murder, and you know the part your husband played in it. Now the thing to do is talk sensibly."

"What do you want?" she asked tightly. "How much?"

"I don't think we're thinking along the same line. I've got a cabin—maybe we can get it straightened out over there."

I opened the car door and she got out woodenly. I started to take her arm but she shrank away. "This way," I said, and started walking toward Rose's crib, Lola following behind me.

Until then, I guess, she had been too angry to realize where she was. But she caught on quick enough when she saw the near-naked girls watching us from the open doorways.

"In here," I said.

She went in, half stumbling. She grasped the edge of the dresser as I closed the door, fighting her shame. The soundless struggle went on for a full minute or more—then, at last, she got hold of herself. Finally she looked at me.

Her face was distorted with hate, but she was still beautiful. Dark hair, dark eyes—a ridiculous arrangement of ribbon and straw sitting almost on her forehead. Her suit was a soft gray shantung, straight-hanging and severely tailored, looking as if its principal function was to conceal the fact that its wearer was a woman. If that was the case, it failed on Lola. She was a woman all right. And, God, how I hated her.

"How much?" she asked, and her voice was cold and steady now. "How much do you want?"

I tried to smile, but my face was like stone. "...I'm not sure yet. Your reputation, maybe. Your husband's career."

I watched the blood drain from her beautiful, perfectly made-up, face.

"You wouldn't dare!"

I knew who was holding the whip now. "I wouldn't dare ruin your husband's career? Lola, you don't know how much I hate you. You can't even guess to what length I would go to hurt you. And that *would* hurt you, wouldn't it, Lola? Ruining your husband? You would never get to live in the governor's mansion. That would be bad, wouldn't it?"

She was beginning to lose some of her poise. "You'd really do it, wouldn't you?" she said wearily. "Even if you died for it." Then, for a moment, she almost went to pieces. "But why! What have I ever done to you!"

"You laughed," I said. "One night, long ago. You laughed again." And I was very calm now. "Remember the election night party at Barney Seaward's? And you buried my old man. You knew I didn't have the money for it, and you did it just to make me look cheap. How does it feel to be God?" I said.

And she stared at me with a touch of hysteria in her eyes. "You *are* crazy!" she whispered. "Your brain is sick. How am I going to make you believe that I've never hated you?"

"You could beg," I said. "You could get down on the floor and crawl. But I still wouldn't believe you. I'd never believe you."

A long moment went by and we said nothing. I looked into her eyes and saw the fight go out, the way it had gone out of Sid's eyes, out of Barney's. I got out a cigarette, sat on the edge of the bed and lit it.

"Roy Foley!" she said abruptly. She threw her head back and laughed, and the sound of it shot coldness through me. "The great Roy Foley! Do you know what you are?" She turned suddenly, facing me. "You're dirt! You're filth and crudeness and ignorance and everything else that is unspeakable and comes from places like Burk Street. I never hated you because you were never worth hating, but I despised you the way I despise all things that are never quite clean." She looked wildly about her. "Look at this place. What do they call them? Cribs? A place for whores!" And she laughed again. "A whore-master! That's what you were always meant to be, from the first!"

"Now we understand each other, Lola."

"What do you want? What will it take to satisfy you?"

"Don't you know, Lola?"

Understanding came slowly. She raised her head and looked at me for perhaps for a full minute before anything happened. Then, slowly, the color began rising to her cheeks.

"No."

"All right, Lola. The choice is yours." I got my hat and started for the door.

She stood there frozen. "What are—you going to do?"

"About the recording? A copy will go to the Crime Bureau in Oklahoma City. Tomorrow some Bureau agents will pick me up and charge me with murder—and along with me, they'll take Seaward and your husband. There'll be a big story about it in the paper. Later, they'll take the three of us to McAllister and strap us into the two-thousand volt chair and that will be the end of it for us. But not for you, Lola. It will never be over for you as long as you live."

"Damn you!" she said hoarsely. "Oh, goddamn you!"

I had the doorknob in my hand. I turned it and started to go out when she said:

"Wait...."

When I turned she had taken off her hat, her face like stone. She began unbuttoning her suit jacket. I closed the door, then I went over to the bed and sat down.

She didn't ask me to turn out the light. Standing in the center of the room, in the whitish glare of the light, she took off the jacket and hung it over the back of the cabin's lone chair. She unbuttoned her blouse, shrugged it away from her pale shoulders, then carefully placed it over the jacket. The skirt was next. There wasn't the slightest hesitation as she took the bottom of her slip and pulled it over her head.

The only sound in the room was the whisper of her clothes as she took them off. She didn't look at me. Her eyes seemed to be turned in, and I had the feeling that she had somehow convinced herself that this thing wasn't really happening at all.

The whole thing was so cold and matter-of-fact that it was hard to believe that she was actually standing in front of me, naked.

"Is this what you want?" she asked flatly.

I looked up at her, then took off my hat and sailed it toward the dresser. "Yes."

I touched the flatness of her belly, feeling her cringe. I moved my fingers down her thighs. Where I touched her, the skin crawled.

"Lie down," I said.

Without a word, she sat on the edge of the bed, and then lay back on the soiled spread, her body rigid. She made a small, tortured sound as I put my hands on her again, and not until that moment did I realize that she wanted it. In spite of herself, in spite of her hate. She had it settled in her mind that it was going to happen, and now—God knew why, unless it was simply because her husband wasn't man enough for her—but at that moment I knew it as well as I had ever known anything. She wanted me; the animal part of her craved it while the rest of her hated it.

I kept my hands on her. She made that sound again and raised her arms and they crawled like twin white snakes around my neck.

Suddenly I laughed. I beat her arms away and stood up and let it roll out of me, all the hatred and frustration and anger coming out with the laughter. As I walked out of the crib I heard her whispering, "God, how I hate you! Oh, God, how I hate you!" I was still laughing.

It was past midnight when I finally got back to the apartment.

Vida was in bed but still awake when I came in. "Do you feel better?" she asked.

"I feel fine." I sat on the edge of the bed and took her in my arms and pressed my face to the softness of her hair. "Vida, I know I haven't been any good to live with lately, but all that's over now."

She took my face in her hands and looked at me. I think she knew that Lola had something to do with it, but she didn't ask questions. "I'm glad you're back," she said. "That's enough for me."

It wasn't until then that I saw a difference in the way she looked at me—a shaded worry deep behind the blueness of her eyes.

"Is anything wrong, Vida? Are you mad because I walked off tonight, the way I did?"

She shook her head. "You know it isn't that. It's just something I feel. And a little of what I hear and see. It scares me. They're out to get you, Roy—Seaward, Kingkade, McErulur."

I laughed, but it didn't sound quite right. "Is that all that's bothering you? Sure they hate me, all of them, but they're not going to get out of line unless Seaward tells them to. And Seaward's not going to do that—not unless he's got a craving to try out the two-thousand-volt chair up at McAllister."

She had never asked me about the hold I had on Seaward—maybe she was afraid to. "Forget about it," I said. "There's nothing to worry about."

But was there? Separately I had beaten them—Seaward, Paul Keating, even Lola. But if they banded together, if they really were out to get me.... I thought, maybe I've gone too far. Barney is beaten now, but he can still be dangerous. As long as he can hate, he's capable of ruining me. Maybe I should close the cribs and give in a little to Kingkade and try to keep things smoothed over. But I knew I wouldn't. If I showed a weakness now they would be on me like wolves. When you climb ambition's ladder there's no backing down. As you go up, they take the rungs out behind you. You keep climbing, or you fall. If I took my foot off Seaward's neck, he would tear my throat open. And there was Lola, too. Even now—and I was just beginning to understand this—I wasn't free of her.

The next conclusion in that chain of reasoning was even more bitter to swallow—I would never be free of her for the rest of my life.

Even now, only a short time after I had pulled her down with me, I found myself wondering if it had really happened. By morning the vague doubt would be in full bloom. By the next evening it would no longer be doubt at all. It would be stark disbelief. I had to see her. I had to stand above her and look down on her and laugh at her, night after night.

So it was time for a new decision—and the decision was already made. Reach, reach high, grasp for the next rung on the ladder.

It was almost daylight when I finally got to sleep. When I awoke it was late in the morning and Vida had been up for a long time. I could hear her in the kitchen as I came out of the shower and got the things out to shave. As I lathered my face I saw myself grinning faintly in the mirror. I felt a lot better, now that I had things settled in my mind. To reach the next rung of the ladder I was going to have to knock somebody down, and I had already decided who it was going to be. It was going to be Joe Kingkade.

I went into the kitchen where Vida had the coffee poured and the cream and sugar set out. I kissed her and she knew I meant it.

"How do you feel?"

"Fine," I said. "Sleep is what I needed."

Her face was sober as she sat across from me and poured more coffee. "Roy," she said suddenly, "do you remember what I said last night?"

"About Seaward and the others? Sure. I've decided to do something about it."

She didn't speak until she got cream and sugar in her coffee. It seemed to take her a long time. "What did you decide, Roy?"

"The first thing I'm going to do is move Joe Kingkade out of Big Prairie. The town's not big enough for two retailers. I should have done it a long time ago. After that—" I played with the idea. "After that maybe I'll move Barney Seaward out, too. Who knows?"

She didn't look up. She stirred her coffee slowly. "Oh."

"What's the matter, Vida?"

"Nothing." Then she looked at me and smiled brightly. Too brightly, I thought.

Chapter Fifteen

Chuck Thompson was one of the runners I had inherited from Sid when I began taking over the residential territory north of town. He was a big blond kid, not too smart, but a good runner for just that reason. I was in the telephone office that afternoon when he called in after making a delivery.

"It's Chuck," one of the telephone boys said; "he wants to talk to you, Roy."

I took the phone, and he said, "Look, is this territory west of Twenty-third supposed to belong to us or to Kingkade?"

"It's ours."

"Then, by God, you'd better talk to Barney Seaward and get it straightened out. Kingkade's got his callin' cards and price lists stuffed in every mailbox on this side of town. He's undersellin' us a dollar a fifth and my customers are raisin' hell about it."

For a moment I didn't say anything. My first impulse was to go straight to Seaward and start raising hell with him. But then I said, "Come on down to the office, Chuck. We'll take care of this ourselves."

It was about three in the afternoon when he picked me up in front of the office in a rattletrap '39 Dodge that he used to make deliveries. He told me about it as we headed out toward Twenty-third.

"Well," he said, "I kind of figured that somethin' was crazy about two days ago. Then I began to notice Kingkade's runners cruisin' the neighborhood, but that didn't worry me too much. I thought maybe it was some kind of deal between you and Kingkade. But when I got hold of one of his price lists and saw that he was cuttin' our price, I figured it was time to do some hollerin'."

"It was time all right," I said.

We hit Twenty-third and headed west. The streets in this part of town were lined with young elms; the houses were mostly modest brick or stone. When we reached Twenty-third and Front, one of the through streets leading downtown, I said, "Pull up here," and Chuck pulled the Dodge over to the curb. "We'll wait here," I said, "and when you spot one of Kingkade's runners, let me know. We're going to convince him that this is unhealthy territory for strange bootleggers."

We didn't have to wait long. Less than five minutes had passed when the vintage Chevy pulled up at the stop sign and then turned onto the tree-lined street. Chuck looked at me and I nodded.

We gave him a good block start because there wasn't much sense to losing him in a twenty-mile zone. When we saw him park in front of a corner house I nodded to Chuck and we pulled up. We saw the runner lifting the front seat to get a bottle, then he went up to the front door carrying the fifth in a paper bag. I told Chuck to move up and park behind the Chevy.

While the runner was inside, I looked under his front seat. Sure enough, there was a lug and a half of red stamped bourbon and two bottles of gin. I told Chuck to take the liquor for himself.

The runner was a youngish, wiry little punk who looked as though he might be about half Mexican. He came swinging down the walk from the house, whistling under his breath and not paying attention to anything in particular. He had almost reached the Chevy when he noticed us in the car behind him. He made a quick jump for the car and was already under the wheel before Chuck could get out on his side. The runner wasn't going anywhere, though, because I had his keys.

When he saw Chuck coming, he kicked the door open and made a try for it. He was too late for that, too. Chuck grabbed him and almost tore his head off with a swinging right that sent him slamming back into the front seat.

"What the hell is this?" he yelled.

Chuck had grabbed him by the front of his shirt and was holding him.

"You want to take him somewhere," I said. "Go ahead. If I see anybody coming, I'll let you know."

Chuck had his hands full for a minute or two. When the punk saw what we were up to he started kicking viciously and trying to squirm out the other side of the car. Chuck put a stop to that with a hammer-like blow to the crotch. The punk screamed, bitterly, but it was a thin sound that didn't carry far.

I stood back, watching for anyone that might come along, but it was a quiet residential street and there wasn't much traffic to speak of. Even from where I was standing, about five yards from the car, I had to listen pretty closely to hear the monotonous thudding of hard knuckles smashing against flesh and bone.

Finally, two blocks away a car turned into the street and I said, "All right, Chuck, that ought to be enough."

The big runner brought his head and shoulders through the door and stood up panting. I leaned through the car window to put the key back into the switch. The punk was doubled up in a tight ball on the floorboards, making whimpering sounds.

I made the rounds with Chuck the rest of that afternoon, but we didn't see any more strange runners. It was about seven o'clock when I finally called it a day.

"Vida?"

There was no one in the front room when I came in, but I went back to the bedroom and Vida was sitting at the dressing table, looking at herself in the mirror. She had just come out of the shower, and when I kissed the back of her neck she smelled like spring rain.

"I love you," I said.

She turned around and smiled vaguely. "Did you—have a busy day?"

"The usual." I took off my coat and loosened my tie. "Anything happen here while I was gone?"

She turned back to the mirror. "I read a book. Are you hungry? If you are I'll get you something."

"I'm not hungry now. Maybe I'll have a drink, though, after I shave." Then it occurred to me that we had done the same thing almost every night since we had been married. A drink, something to eat, and then to bed. I had my shirt half off when I went over to her and said, "Why don't we do something tonight? Hell, we've been living like we had to watch our pennies or something." I sat down beside her on the dressing stool and took her face in my hands. "Geez, I'm just beginning to realize what a lousy husband I've been. I keep busy through the day, but you stay here in the apartment. Do you ever go anywhere? Do you ever see anybody besides me?"

"I guess not. Not very often, anyway." Then she smiled—really smiled this time. "Roy, do you really mean it? Can we go somewhere, dancing maybe?"

"Sure I mean it." I kissed her then and her mouth was warm and eager. "I guess I'm not very smart," I said. "I should have seen that you were lonesome here. Get your party clothes on while I shave."

As I got under the shower Vida called to me, and her voice had new life in it.

"Where are we going, Roy?"

"I don't care. Maybe that roadhouse out west of town. The Blue Star."

In a town the size of Big Prairie you don't have much choice. But to Vida, any place with people would probably be an improvement over the apartment. When I got out of the shower, I caught myself whistling, and that was something of a shock because it was something I never remembered doing before. The party mood had me.

By the time I got out to the front room she had some drinks made. She wore a jet crepe dress that clung to her lithe body like the skin on a young panther. In that first instant, when I saw her, a brief, disturbing thought struck me. Christ, couldn't she manage to look a little less like a streetwalker! But the thought only lasted for an instant, the smallest part of a second, and then it was gone completely.

"You're beautiful," I said. And I meant it as much as I had ever meant anything in my life.

Chapter Sixteen

The Blue Star was one of those cement-block and stucco buildings that you see thrown up along highways around towns like Big Prairie. In the daytime they look like misplaced chicken houses, but at night, with their neon trimmings and their tinted floodlights bathing false fronts in soft blues and purples, they take on a kind of cheap glamour. It was still early when we got there but cars were already beginning to crowd the parking space in the rear.

"It doesn't look like much," I said.

"Big Prairie's best," Vida smiled.

"Well, maybe it's better on the inside." I parked the car, then I got the bottle of Scotch we brought and went around and opened the door for Vida.

The place tried hard enough, but it didn't come off somehow. When you went in there was a dimly lighted foyer where you checked your coat and hat and paid the cover. The floor was heavily carpeted and the walls were decorated with large framed photographs of girls who had been in the Blue Star's floor show at one time or another. A big guy in a sports coat, doubling as headwaiter and bouncer, gave us a tight grin and led us into a dark, low-ceilinged room where a five piece bop band shocked the customers with senseless discords. I put the bottle of Scotch on the table, when we got to it.

"How do you like the Blue Star?"

Vida shrugged and smiled faintly. "Maybe a drink will make it look better."

We tried but it didn't work. It was a dirty, small-soured place and no amount of whisky would change it. The noise of the band grated on my nerves. The faintly soured smell of the place and the thick smoke, took the edge off the excitement. We didn't even try to dance.

"Look," I said, "there must be some other place where people go. Something better than the Blue Star. What about people like Paul Keating?"

Vida looked at her drink. "The Keatings?" Then she looked at me. "They have a country club for people like them."

I don't know why I hadn't thought of it. Probably because I had been too interested in other things—in getting my bootlegging business set up. Until now I hadn't had much time for social life. I knew about the country club, of course, because all the Big Prairies in the world have them and they're all exactly alike. It was Cedar Street all over again.... A place where the snotty bastards could withdraw and be free of people like me.

Vida was looking at me strangely. Several minutes must have gone by before I realized that she was holding my clenched hands under the table.

"Roy," she said softly. "Roy, let's go."

I started to get up, but something seemed to push me down again and hold me there. I thought, I won't let them beat me! I'm not going to let them ruin Vida's night for her. All right, I thought—climb higher. Grow bigger.

I got up then, the idea full grown in my mind. I put my hand on Vida's shoulder and squeezed it gently to reassure her. "I'll be back in just a minute," I said. She kept staring at me.

I found a pay phone near the check room. It wasn't necessary to look up the number this time; I had it in my mind.

"Hello." The well-turned, cultivated voice. Paul Keating's.

I said, "Listen to me, Keating. I've decided I want to see how you stiff-front bastards live, so we're going to have a party. I hear that the place to go in Big Prairie is your country club, so that's where we're going. Vida and I are going to be the guests of you and your wife, Keating. I'll give you an hour to get ready and be there. We'll be waiting."

I could hear him swallow. "Of course." It was a weak voice now. "Of course, some other time perhaps, but tonight is impossible. We have company and—"

"Get rid of them," I snapped.

"But I tell you it's impossible!"

I said. "All right. Forget it. But don't be surprised when the crime bureau men come around."

"For God's sake, Foley! I tell you we'd like to, but it's—" I could almost see him wiping the sweat from his forehead. "All right," he said at last, weakly. "We'll be there."

"That's better."

I hung up.

"Roy, are you sure?" Vida said doubtfully.

"Sure, I'm sure. I talked to Keating and he thought it was a fine idea."

"But the country club. You have to be a member to go there."

"We're going as Keating's guests, I told you that. If you like the place, then we'll take out memberships. Keating can swing that, too."

She didn't mention Lola, but I could see that she was thinking of her.

I poured two stiff drinks. "Relax," I said. "We're going to have a look at Big Prairie's society. If we like it, we'll buy it. Besides, if we stay in Big Prairie we've got to have a place to go, a place to entertain our friends." I looked at my watch. "Let's go. We mustn't keep the county attorney waiting."

The country club was a rambling ranch-style building about a mile off the highway, surrounded by low rolling hills and a few trees. There were several cars parked in front of the clubhouse. Muted, danceable music came from somewhere and there were people coming, going, a few of them lounging on the long, hooded veranda. This is the way to live, I thought. Hell, I should have thought of this before. I looked around but I didn't see that black Cadillac of Paul Keating's. But we were early and it didn't worry me. The bastard didn't dare stand us up.

Vida didn't say anything and neither did I. I had a vague picture of me and Vida, the way we would be when we were members. It would do us good to get away from Big Prairie once in a while. You get in a rut when you see nobody but whisky dealers and crooked politicians and whores. What we needed was a place to relax—as soon as I forced Kingkade out of the county and had the business running smoothly.

"Is that Keating?" Vida said.

I looked around and saw the Cadillac pulling in beside me. It was Keating all right. His face was pale, and he looked sick. Lola sat beside him, her eyes as hard as gunsteel.

A white-coated flunkie met us on the veranda, all smiles and teeth when he saw it was the Keatings. The smile vanished when he saw me and Vida.

"A table for two, Mr. Keating?" he asked hopefully.

"There are four of us tonight," Keating said stiffly.

"Yes, sir." He didn't like it, but because Keating was who he was, the flunkie kept his distaste in his eyes instead of his voice. The vision I'd had exploded like a pricked bubble. "Yes, sir. This way, Mr. Keating. Mrs. Keating." The sonofabitch looked at Vida as if she were a two-dollar whore.

I forced myself to grin but inside I was raging.

Vida got it now, as we followed the flunkie through the lounge and into another place where a sign over the door said "The 19th Hole," where people sat at white covered tables, where couples danced, where a band played softly. The women were the most obvious. They stared at us first, then they shrank back as we passed. In our wake I could hear them clucking, outraged, and I knew that they were talking about Vida. "Tart!" I heard one of them say, and I stiffened. Vida held me.

"It's all right, Roy. It's all right."

An immaculate waiter was holding a chair for Lola, beaming at Lola and Paul Keating and ignoring everybody else. I seated Vida. Lola and Paul Keating looked at each other, they looked blankly around the room, at the waiter, at anybody or anything, but not at me or Vida. We were poison. They were making that clear.

"Hello, Keating! Good evening, Mrs. Keating." A hearty, red-faced man stopped at the table, slapped Keating on the back and carried on a moment of pleasant small talk. The only thing wrong with it was that he pretended that the Keatings were absolutely alone. Not a look or a word at me. Not a glance at Vida. He made his point and moved on.

Keating motioned to the waiter. "The usual, Henry." Then, as an afterthought, "Is Scotch all right with you, Foley? Mrs. Foley?"

"Sure."

It was beautiful, the way they brought it off. Freeze you to death, that was the way they worked it. Sure, I could manage a membership, they were telling me. But did I really want it? Did I really think that a membership could make me belong? And Lola sat there beautiful and cold, smiling a smile that couldn't be seen. Laughing laughter that couldn't be heard.

Laugh! I thought savagely. Go ahead and enjoy yourself, because you'll pay for it. It'll be the most expensive pleasure you've ever had!

Slowly, the bitterness left me and strength took its place. Who holds the club? I asked myself. Me or Keating? Me or Lola? Look at them; you can break them in half anytime you feel like it! I took Vida's hand under the table, her cold hand, and held it and warmed it.

"Sure," I said, and I could grin now. "Scotch will be fine. I'm beginning to like this place you've got here. Not bad at all."

The orchestra was playing. A few couples were getting up to dance. I remembered another time and another place. There had been music and there had been couples dancing in the high-school gym. And Roy Foley had been a hero for a little while. I let go of Vida's cold hand and I could feel her watching me as I stood up abruptly.

I said, "It's been a long time since we've danced together, Lola."

She didn't dare refuse.

"What do you want?" Her voice was toneless. She was as cold as ice in my arms as we danced, feeling the eyes of the place on our backs.

"You should know what I want, Lola," I grinned down at her.

She closed her eyes for a moment. "I'll see you dead first! I'll kill you myself!"

"Would you, Lola?" I asked. "Of course not. It takes guts to kill. That kind of guts your kind doesn't have." The music stopped. I said, "The same place, Lola. At eight o'clock tomorrow night. I'll be waiting."

Without waiting for her to answer, I turned on my heel and went back to the table.

Vida and I left the place, and I drove back to the apartment as though the hounds of hell were snapping at my heels. Vida said nothing. When I touched her she shivered. When we got back to the apartment we undressed without speaking and got into bed.

I thought, What can I tell her? How can I explain it to her? There was no way to put it into words, the way I hated Lola and still had to have her. How can you explain a thing like that to a wife who loves you?

And Vida wasn't blind. She had seen.

Almost an hour went by as we lay there in the darkness not touching, not speaking, not sleeping. At last a long, tortured sound seemed to fill the room, and it took several minutes for me to realize that it was coming from my throat. I took Vida in my arms. There were no words in me. Her face was damp, her tears salt-tasting to my lips.

"I love you, Vida. You've got to understand that, you've got to believe me. No matter what happens, I'll go on loving you."

She didn't say a thing. It seemed a long, long time before exhaustion finally slowed the whirling in my brain and sleep began to creep in.

About three o'clock the phone rang. It was one of the runners calling to tell me that my warehouse was burning down.

Chapter Seventeen

I got there as fast as my Buick could take me, but the situation was already beyond hope. The knock-up little neighborhood grocery store that I had taken over from Sid was a roaring furnace, the two-by-four cross beams twisting, snapping like matchsticks, the roof falling in, spewing showers of sparks into the darkness. The firemen were there but they didn't have a chance. From a block away you could hear the cases of whisky exploding. The whole thing went up in a bright flame.

I stood there for several minutes, knowing that there was nothing I could do. Geez, a fortune in liquor! All gone faster than it took to tell about it!

A small crowd was beginning to gather, sticky-eyed men with pajamas stuffed into their trousers, gaping at the fierceness of the blaze. Another fire truck came up and the firemen hooked their hose onto a plug at the end of the block and began spraying the shacks around the burning store. Goddamn it! Goddamn the lousy goddamn luck! Just when I was going good, a thing like this had to happen! I heard myself cursing when the firemen abandoned the store altogether and focused their attention to the surrounding buildings.

A man, his face black with soot, his slicker dripping, came over to me. "This place belong to you?" he said.

"You're goddamned right it does, and what's the idea of quitting? There's still a chance to save something."

"Too far gone," he said hoarsely. "We'll be lucky to save the buildings around it. You know a man named Chuck Thompson?"

"He works for me. Why?"

The fireman looked at me, his eyes narrowed. "He's dead," he said.

After a moment I said evenly, "Where is he?"

"Over by the pumper," the fireman said. "We found him just outside the store when we got here. Looked as if he had been inside when the fire started and had crawled as far as the door and couldn't make it any farther. He was burned pretty bad." He jerked his head toward the big pump truck. "Maybe you better come over and have a look."

I went over to where they had Chuck laid out with a wet, glistening slicker spread over his chest and face. I threw the slicker back.

It was Chuck, but anybody who hadn't known him well would never have recognized him. His face was black, his hair was singed to his skull, his clothing was almost burned off his back. But the fire hadn't killed him. A long, open gash in the back of his head had done that. I put the slicker back in place and stood there for several minutes.

Chuck meant nothing to me. Still, looking at him was almost like looking at myself. The blow that had killed him had been aimed at me. The fire that had cooked him black had been built for me.

I thought, So Kingkade had made his move....

The time for decision had come again. Something had to be done about Kingkade, and what I wanted to do was get my hands around his scrawny throat and choke the life out of him. But something inside me warned me to keep cool, keep a strong hand on my anger. Barney Seaward was still the top man in Big Prairie. Barney would take care of Kingkade for me.

I went back to my car and drove away from the fire, toward town. I found a restaurant and telephoned. Barney wasn't home.

Where could he be at this time of night? I didn't know, but I thought I knew somebody who could tell me, so I dialed again. I listened to the ringing at the other end—five times, six—and then a voice said: "Yes?"

It was Lola.

"I want to talk to Keating."

She recognized my voice. I could almost see her freezing up. I thought she was going to hang up, but after a long moment of silence she said coldly, "My husband isn't here. He went somewhere with Barney Seaward. Barney was waiting at the house when we got back from the club tonight. They talked, but I don't know what about, and then they left in Barney's car."

"Did it have anything to do with Joe Kingkade?"

"I heard them mention Kingkade's name," she said.

I hung up and sat there for several minutes staring fiercely at the phone. What did it mean? Had Barney discovered what Kingkade was up to and set out to stop him himself? That was the only thing I could think of. That was just as well. Let Barney take care of Kingkade for me.

I felt wrung out and tired, and there didn't seem to be anything I could do, even if I had wanted to. The sky was beginning to turn gray in the east as I went out.

It was a quiet ride back to the apartment. I parked the car and got out, standing there for a moment, breathing in the coolness of the early morning air. I didn't see the three men coming out of the shadows until it was too late.

Two of them were my old friends, Joel and Max. The other was a small, thin-faced man, sloppily dressed—Joe Kingkade.

"Just stay where you are, Foley," Kingkade said mildly. "This won't take long."

"What the hell is this?" The words sounded ridiculous.

"A farewell visit, Foley. You're through in Big Prairie."

"Maybe Barney will have something to say about that."

Max laughed. Kingkade smiled faintly. Joel stood stone-faced to one side, watchful.

"I'll explain it to you," Kingkade went on patiently. "Barney isn't boss any more, Foley. I am. I'm the new wholesaler for Big Prairie County and I'll pick my own men. You won't be one of them, Foley."

"You sonofabitch!" The word jumped out angrily. Max started to swing at me but Kingkade stopped him.

"I gather you've seen your warehouse," he said. "That's only half of it, Foley. Your cribs are burned down too. Big Prairie is going to be a respectable town from now on—the tramps will be kept in hotels where they belong. I ought to kill you, Foley, for the way you almost ruined this county. But I won't have to. You'll do it yourself, sooner or later...."

He let the words hang and seemed to be wondering if there was something else he should say. Suddenly he shrugged, turned on his heel.

They were gone.

I stood there with sweat on my forehead and emptiness in my belly. God, had Kingkade actually managed to step into Barney's shoes? I couldn't believe it. As long as Barney was alive, he would fight. And no man like Kingkade would ever outfight or outthink Barney Seaward. Was it bluff? Did the retailer actually think he could bluff me out of town?

I didn't believe that, either. If it was a bluff, he would have backed it up with a beating. But something had happened—that much I was sure of. I had to find out what. The apartment was dark and quiet. I snapped the light on in the front room, went to the telephone and called Barney. He still wasn't home. I sat there sweating, wondering what I should do next. I felt a faint movement behind me, and when I turned, it was Vida standing in the doorway.

"What is it, Roy?"

"I don't know." I rubbed my hands over my face, trying to think of something. "My warehouse has burned down," I said flatly. "The cribs, too."

"Is—it Barney?" she asked, her voice edged with fear.

I laughed abruptly and the sound startled me. "Crossing me would be the last thing in the world Barney would do! It's that goddamned Kingkade."

"I don't understand," Vida said. "Kingkade's too smart to think he can go against Seaward."

"He's trying it," I said bitterly.

I went to the bar, poured a straight shot of Scotch and downed it. I paced the floor, and Vida watched me.

I tried the phone again and again there was no answer. Out of the exhaustion, an almost overpowering feeling of futility began to grow. I had the feeling that my whole world was falling out from under me and there was nothing I could do to stop it.

Abruptly, for no reason, it seemed, Vida said: "Let's leave Big Prairie, Roy. Let's go somewhere and start all over again. Now, before anything else happens."

"What else can happen? Barney will take care of Kingkade."

"Can you be sure?"

I wasn't sure what she was getting at. I stopped my pacing for a minute and looked at her. "I can be sure of Barney," I said finally. "He's the one thing in this world I can depend on."

I could see the questions in her eyes, the questions that she had kept locked up inside her and wouldn't ask. How could I be sure of Barney? What kind of a deal had I made with him? What had I done for him? I remembered Sid for the first time in a long while. I had to look away.

"Everything's going to be all right," I said. "It would be foolish leaving Big Prairie, now, just when things are opening up. As soon as I take care of Kingkade, the town will be mine."

God, I thought in the back of my mind, it would be good if we could go away. If we could go somewhere and rest. Then I heard the spat of the morning paper hitting the front door, and the muffled tramp of the paper boy going down the hall.

"Go to bed, Vida," I said. "Get some sleep and don't worry about anything."

She saw that I wasn't going to answer unasked questions. There was something in her eyes; it could have been relief, or fear, or maybe it was just weariness. Then she looked away and went into the bedroom.

I tried the phone again and still nobody answered. To kill time, I got the morning paper, opened it and looked at the headlines.

PROMINENT BIG PRAIRIE NEWSPAPERMAN, COUNTY
ATTORNEY KILLED IN AUTO CRASH

I must have looked at it for a full minute before I realized that my world had collapsed. The club I held was useless. Seaward and Keating were dead.

Chapter Eighteen

> Two of Big Prairie's most prominent citizens were killed instantly this morning, shortly after midnight, in an auto accident on the Rock Island overpass west of town. One witness to the fatal accident, Robert Manning, truck driver for the Big Prairie Oil Well Cementing Company, explained to the police that he was momentarily blinded by the bright headlights of Seaward's car as it came toward him on the steep western slope of the overpass. Manning stated, under questioning by the police, that Seaward's car had been traveling at a high rate of speed. "He must have hit an oil slick near the top of the overpass," the truck driver continued. "The car seemed to go out of control. It came straight at me, and then the driver tried to miss me by pulling sharply to the left." The car crashed over the cement barrier and fell onto the railroad track below. The bodies of Seaward and Keating were thrown clear of the car and were found some distance away.

I let the paper drop to the floor. The first thing I thought of was Kingkade. The bastard had planned it. But almost instantly I realized that it hadn't been planned at all, unless fate had done it. It was the luck this time; rotten, lousy luck, and in an instant it had torn down everything I had worked to build.

Almost instantly I remembered those recordings. Christ, I had to get them back before Kingkade found out about them. If the crime bureau ever got their hands on those recordings....

Sweat broke out on my face. I remembered Lola.

It was time for decision again, and this one, like the others, was ready for me. Run. It was the only thing to do. Christ—I held my face in my hands, feeling coldness go through me—why did I ever send that recording to Lola! Lola had the club now, and she had nothing to lose by using it, because her husband was dead. Her dreams of the governor's mansion were dead. Like me, all she had left was her hate. And that recording. A one-way ticket to an electrocution.

"Roy, what is it?"

Vida was standing in the doorway again, staring at me. Then she saw the paper on the floor, picked it up and looked at it. She made a small gasping sound in her throat.

"Roy, what are we going to do?"

"We've got to get out of Oklahoma," I said, "and we've got to do it fast. In a matter of hours every agent in the state will be looking for me."

"But why? You didn't have anything to do with this."

And only then did the irony of the thing hit me. That suicide note of Sid's that I had so carefully destroyed, it could save me now, if I had it. But I didn't have it. And, after hearing that recording, who would ever believe that there had been such a note? No one. Not even Vida.

I put my arms around her and held her hard against me. "I love you, Vida. No matter what happens, I'll always love you. Now we've got to pack, Vida. We've got to get out of here."

"Roy, something has happened to us. I can't go on much longer without knowing what it is."

"Nothing's happened. Everything's going to be all right, but we've got to get out of here. We'll head south, maybe to Texas. I know Houston pretty well, we can get lost there. They'll never find us, Vida."

It was a lie and we both knew it. I touched her hair, feeling that strange gentleness inside me. "You don't have to go with me, Vida," I said finally. "After a while, after it's safe, I can let you know where I am and you can come then."

She clung to me as though it were for the last time. "We'll go together," she said evenly. "I'll be packing."

She had to know sometime about Sid. I had to explain it to her before it came out in the papers, but not now. My gaze drifted around the room. So this is the way it ends, I thought dully. One jump ahead of the law, two jumps ahead of the chair. At least I had money this time. Then I noticed the newspaper scattered on the floor where Vida had dropped it, the gaudy colored splashes of comic pages.

Geez! The realization hit me as I looked at those pages of colored comics. It was Sunday. The banks were closed.

All the money, I thought, near insanity, and no way to get it out! I couldn't wait until the banks opened the next day. I couldn't write checks to be traced. There was only one thing to do—leave Big Prairie the way I had come into it. Broke. I went through my pockets and found almost a hundred dollars in bills and change. Maybe Vida would have ten or twenty. I threw my head back and laughed idiotically. I went into the bathroom and looked at myself in the mirror. My face looked back at me, gaunt-cheeked, hollow-eyed, the face of an old man, a broken man. Mirror, mirror on the wall, who's the biggest phony of them all? And the mirror answered—or I imagined that it did—God, you make me sick!

I thought, I'm not beaten! I'll get out of this somehow!

The mirror laughed. Great God, you make me want to puke, Foley! Do you know what you'll be doing a month from now—if you're still alive? A *week* from now? You'll be in a hash house—another grease-stinking sandwich joint, that's where you'll be! Maybe you can get Vida a job waiting on customers. I'll bet she'd love that. Like hell she would! Imagine going to bed with Vida, smelling of onions and mustard, and never quite getting away from the odor of stale grease. There's another thing, too. What about Lola? Oh, Lola's going to love this! God, how she's going to laugh!

"Roy," Vida called, "I'm through packing. Are you ready?"

"Yes." Methodically, I began going through the drawers to see if she had missed anything of mine.

I found an empty wallet in one drawer. A hair brush and two handkerchiefs in another. The last thing I found was a beautifully blued bone-handled .38 revolver that I had bought to carry with me when I made the rounds with the runners. I held the gun in my hand, caressing it gently with my fingers. I checked the cylinder and saw that there were five live rounds in the chambers. For safety's sake, one chamber had been left empty and that was where the hammer rested.

"Roy," Vida called tightly, "are you ready?"

"Yes."

I gripped the cool butt, slipped my finger inside the trigger guard and gingerly tested the double-action. I thought, It's so simple! And fleetingly I remembered the truck driver and guard. Merely by pointing it at a person and then exerting the slightest pressure with your finger, I thought, it is possible to put a complete, irrevocable end to a human life. Any life. A person could put an end to his own life, for that matter....

The thought rose suddenly, unexpectedly out of the darkness of my mind. I heard Joe Kingkade saying, "I won't have to kill you. You'll do it yourself."

Stop it!

My hands were shaking. I told myself that I could pawn the gun or sell it if we got desperate for money and it would be foolish to throw a valuable gun like that away for no reason at all. I wasn't beaten. Somehow I would find a way to beat all of them—Kingkade, Lola. But I was tired. I felt as old as a mountain. I put the gun in the suitcase and locked it.

Chapter Nineteen

We left Big Prairie in the cool quiet of early morning. Sunday morning. In a matter of two hours we had crossed Red River and were heading south toward Dallas.

I kept the radio on, tuning in all the news broadcasts I could find, but there was nothing at all about me. I thought: Maybe Lola didn't turn the recording over to the bureau after all, but I didn't dwell on it long enough for it to become a hope. I had only to remember that hate in her eyes. She would never forget what I had done to her, and she would never stop until she had ruined me.

We stopped in Dallas long enough to trade my Buick in on a '49 Ford. I got only five hundred in cash out of the trade, but I didn't have time to try to do better. We left Dallas and headed south again. There still wasn't anything about us on the radio.

Vida hardly said a thing all day. It was blazing hot and she sat on her side of the front seat, staring flatly at the shimmering highway. I drove until midnight, until I couldn't stay awake any longer, and then I turned the Ford over to Vida and she drove until almost dawn.

Both of us were too tired to go any farther. We pulled into a knock-up little tourist court to rest.

Day broke early. The blazing Texas sun beat down on our clapboard cabin and within an hour it was as hot and stifling as a bake oven. The first thing I did was go out to the car and turn on the radio.

It had happened.

"A statewide search is being conducted throughout Oklahoma," the announcer said, "for one Roy Foley and his wife Vida. Foley is wanted for questioning in connection with the death of Sidney Gardner, Oklahoma bootlegger. The Oklahoma State Crime Bureau has announced that, until recently, the death of Gardner was believed to be accidental. However, new evidence has apparently been brought to light, and the bureau has hinted that other prominent Oklahomans...."

I snapped the set off and sat woodenly, listening to the pounding in my chest. Damn her! Goddamn her! But Lola was out of reach. There wasn't a thing I could do.

But the thing I dreaded now was telling Vida. I went back into the cabin and stood looking down at her, and I think at that moment I loved her more than I had ever loved before. I touched her hair—it was damp with perspiration—and she opened her eyes. Pale, tired eyes.

"Roy!" She put her hands to her breasts. "I didn't know at first where we were," she said at last. "What time is it?"

"Almost one o'clock. We'll have to start driving soon."

Suddenly I took Vida in my arms and crushed her. I felt a dampness as I kissed her. They were my tears, not hers. "Vida—I've got to tell you something. I've got to try to explain, and I don't know where to start."

Finally she spoke. "Is it about Sid?" She worked her fingers into my hair and slowly brought my face down to her breasts and held me close. Then her arms went lax and she lay back, her eyes closed.

"You killed Sid," she said flatly. "I think I've known it all the time. But I wouldn't let myself believe it."

I took her shoulders in my hands. "Vida, you've got to believe me! I didn't kill him, he killed himself. He left a note for you, but I found it and destroyed it."

"Because of Seaward?"

The right words just wouldn't come. I said, "All right, I made a deal with Seaward, and Keating was in on it too. But what the hell, Sid did the same thing, didn't he? But I didn't kill him, it was suicide."

She laughed suddenly, and the unexpected sound shocked me. "We make a nice pair, don't we, Roy? We both killed Sid, just as though we had put knives into him, and whether or not it was legally suicide is not important. We've broken every commandment. What else is left for us?"

She started laughing again, but it sounded like no laughter I had ever heard before. I squeezed her shoulders viciously. "Stop it! I say stop it!"

The laughter broke off, hung uneasily in the silence of the room. "I did it for you, Vida. Anything I may have done was for you and because I loved you."

"And Lola," she said.

I felt myself cringing. She went on, evenly now. Lifelessly. "Remember when you broke your hand, Roy? I told you that she was hurtproof, that the harder you hit her the more you would hurt yourself." She gazed vacantly at the shabby room. "Was it worth it, Roy?"

I had a sudden dazzling vision of Lola as she had looked that night in the crib. I remembered the enormous oath I had taken beside the highway, as I had walked madly through the darkness. I sat there, the white-hot anger bottled up inside me, compressed and hard in my brain. An anger that I knew would be with me always, sealed with hopelessness. Still, there was the savage satisfaction of that night, and— Yes, by God, it was worth it!

Vida could see the answer in my face. She made a small, hopeless sound as she lay back on the bed.

And, at last, I told her. Everything. I heard my voice going on—and on—

and on—I listened abstractedly as the sordidness unrolled. And when it was over I fell across her, there on the bed, and held her hard in my arms.

After a while, she said wearily, "The police must know by now. We'd better go."

We heard on the radio that the police had found the Buick in Dallas, and that scared me. The Texas troopers would be sure to have a pickup on the Ford, and every minute we stayed in it added to the danger.

When we got to the next town I parked it on a side street, then went to a service station and used the telephone to find out when we could catch a bus for Houston. When I got back to the car, Vida was sitting quietly, exactly the way I had left her.

"We'll have to leave the car here," I said. "We can get a bus for Houston, but not for almost three hours. We'll just have to wait."

"Where?"

"I don't know. There's a little hotel about two blocks from here that ought to do. We could use some rest."

Vida looked at herself in the rear-view mirror. "When they find the car," she said, "they're sure to start watching the bus stations. We'll have to do something to change the way we look."

I rubbed the thick stubble on my face. "I can shave and leave my mustache; that may change my appearance some."

Vida thought about it. "Get some hair dye," she said after a moment. "We'll see what we can do after we get to the hotel."

The hotel was a wooden two-story building about two blocks from the center of town. Vida had taken off her lipstick, darkened her eyebrows with an eyebrow pencil, and put a scarf over her head to hide her almost-white hair. We brought two suitcases and there was no trouble checking in—then I went down to a drugstore and bought two packages of dark brown hair tint.

"This ought to do," Vida said. There was no enthusiasm in her voice. She studied herself in the dresser mirror, then said, "See if you can find a razor blade."

I got a package of razor blades out of one of the suitcases, gave her one and she began whacking ruthlessly at her long hair. While she did that, I shaved, leaving the mustache, and by the time I had finished, Vida had hacked away almost half of her hair. "Mine will take longer," she said. "I'll do it first."

She mixed the tint in the wash basin in the corner of the room and began applying it to her hair with a toothbrush. The change was amazing, almost unbelievable. When she finished, she looked like a dark-haired boy who had just been swimming. She went to the mirror, studying herself again, then she began rolling up the ends of her hair, securing the tight curls close to her scalp until her head bristled with hairpins.

"When it dries," she said almost to herself, "it will be all right. Bend over the basin. I'll darken your hair now; later you can go over your mustache with my eyebrow pencil."

It took about an hour. We flushed away that blonde, glistening mass of hair that Vida had chopped off, we cleaned the dye out of the basin, and then we flushed away the paper packages the dye had come in. Vida sat in front of the window, saying nothing, letting the hot breeze dry her hair. I sat on the bed, looking at her, aching to hold her.

Around three o'clock she took the hairpins out and combed her hair and brushed it, and the ends snapped up briskly, boyishly.

I darkened the tips of my mustache and it looked all right to me. It changed the way I looked.

"Hadn't we better go?" Vida said.

I looked at my watch. "Yes, I guess so." We put everything back in the suitcase and went out of the room.

Chapter Twenty

I don't remember the name of the next town. It was a squat, rambling little place, slow-baking in that South-Texas sun, and the bus pulled in there for a fifteen-minute rest stop.

"What are we going to do when we get to Houston?" Vida asked flatly.

"I don't know yet," I said. "But it's a big place and it's easy to get lost in a place like that."

"What if the police have found that Ford?" She was gazing out the window.

"The odds are against it," I said. "We don't have to worry about that." We had the suitcases in the baggage rack over our heads, and I got one of them down and opened it. My mouth tasted sour and dry, so I got out the toothpaste and a toothbrush, and while I was fumbling for them I found the pistol.

Vida made a small sound in her throat when she saw it. "What are you going to do?"

"Clean up a little and brush my teeth and see if it won't make me feel better." But that wasn't what she meant. I was holding the gun between two shirts; the butt was cool, deadly in my palm. Somehow, there was comfort in the feel of that hard, cool steel. I slipped the gun out of the suitcase and pushed it into my pocket.

We went into the bus station where wrinkled, grimy travelers began lining up at a soda fountain. I went into the men's room, a steaming, concrete-floored box. I splashed cool water on my face, and brushed my teeth furiously. Combing my hair, I was startled to see the leathery, haunted face looking at me in the mirror.

A heavy-set bus driver came in and used the next wash basin.

"South-bound bus ready to load," he said.

"All right. I'll be there."

He kept looking at me. *What is it, you sonofabitch?* I thought grimly. *What are you looking at?* After a while he tramped out, frowning.

Had he recognized me? Had they broadcast my description—? Probably, but I looked a lot like a million other guys, and unless he had a reason to be suspicious....

I felt of the gun in my pocket. There was nobody else in the men's room now; I took the gun out, held it, somehow getting a savage strength out of touching it. Suddenly I froze. There was a whiplike sound, *whack!*, of the men's room door slamming shut. I wheeled as though somebody had put a knife into me. Nobody was there.

I snatched the door open, but he was gone now, whoever it had been.

I went back to the front of the bus station, by the soda fountain, but everything looked exactly the way it had been before. Except for that heavy-set driver. He was in a phone booth, his face red, sweating as he talked.

You sonofabitch! I almost yelled.

But that wasn't going to help. I was almost sick with anger at myself. In a few minutes they'll be after you, Foley, every farmer in town who owns a gun!

I looked for Vida then, and she was nowhere. Blind panic seized me then. The bus driver came out of the telephone booth and I started running toward the side exit where the buses were parked. I forgot about Vida, I forgot about everything, I just ran.

"Say, you!" The driver hollered.

I burst through the doors and sprinted headlong up the sidewalk toward the center of town. I could hear them pounding after me, yelling at me. I leaped off a high curb at an intersection and almost ran into the car.

I don't know where it came from. I didn't see it until I heard the sickening squeal of tramped brakes, and then the big chrome front end was crashing down on top of me, looking as big as a tank. I seemed to freeze in the middle of the street. Somehow he missed me, and the car came to a shuddering stop against the curb.

Somehow, that gun came out of my pocket and jumped into my hand. Before the driver knew what was happening, I was in the front seat with him, the muzzle of the .38 almost in his mouth.

"Get out!" I cried.

He was a little bald-headed guy with weak blue eyes and a startled mouth. I whipped the pistol barrel across his face and he fell back against the door, looking as though he wanted to cry. The fat bus driver and three or four others were less than half a block away, and the sound of their shouting almost drove me insane.

I jerked the door open on the driver's side. I shoved him out into the street; then I got under the wheel. The bus driver's posse was only a few steps away when I got the car started, spurted into the street.

It was a Chrysler, with plenty of guts under the hood. I slammed into a corner, and screamed around it.

About a block down I hit a red light, almost crashed into a stream of traffic. I twisted the Chrysler to the right, fell into the stream, then spurted ahead again. Almost immediately the bus station loomed up in front of me. I was right back where I had started!

Then I thought, That's all right. Let them chase their tails for a few minutes. I had been so intent on getting away that I hadn't thought of anything else, not even Vida, until I saw her in the street waving frantically.

I slammed to a stop and people began pouring out of the bus station, yelling, as Vida jerked the car door open and got in.

"Roy!"

"Just keep looking behind us," I said, "and tell me if we're being followed."

She looked back, her eyes big, her face even paler than usual. I spotted a state-highway sign up ahead, turned the Chrysler wide open and headed south. Abruptly, we were on the prairie and the town was behind us.

We blazed over the highway with the speedometer rocking on 90, then 95, and I thought wildly: Catch me! Catch me, if you can! The excitement of speed, the roar, the flash of nameless objects darting by, filled me with a crazy exhilaration.

"Roy!" Vida was shouting in my ear. "Won't they call ahead to the next town and tell them to stop us?"

God, yes! I thought.

"What are you going to do, Roy!"

"I'll think of something."

The answer came as we roared down a gentle slope, past a blue convertible. I began easing my foot off the accelerator and the speedometer dropped down to 90, 80, 70, and finally I saw what I was looking for, a country road winding off into the prairie brush, off into nowhere.

"Just do as I say," I said, looking back at the convertible. We rocked to a stop and I got out and began waving the convertible down. The tires squealed as he slowed down, then he pulled off the highway, onto the shoulder and rolled along in second gear, stopping behind the Chrysler.

"Car trouble, mister?" he called. "There's a garage about five miles down the highway. Jump in, I'll be glad to give you a lift."

I tossed the keys to the Chrysler in Vida's lap and said, "Follow us." Then without waiting for an answer, I went back to the convertible and said, "Move over."

He was a youngish guy with a wide grin and straw colored hair. His hair was cut close to his skull. There was a sticker on the windshield of the convertible that said: Rice Institute. A college kid.

"Move over," I said again, and this time I opened the door on the driver's side and shoved the muzzle of the revolver against his belly.

"What the hell!" He didn't seem particularly scared. He looked at me, then at the gun, grinning faintly, as though he thought it might be some kind of a joke.

"Just keep quiet and you won't get hurt." I got the convertible started and turned onto the country road, motioning for Vida to follow in the Chrysler. The kid didn't say a thing. He kept looking at me, blinking his eyes.

The dirt road wound around in the brush and probably went on to a farmhouse or a ranch somewhere. We were several hundred yards from the highway by now and that was far enough for what I wanted. I stopped the convertible and Vida pulled up beside us in the Chrysler.

"This is where we change cars," I said. Vida got out of the Chrysler and I gave her the keys to the convertible and said, "Look in the back and see if there's something we can tie him with."

She didn't say a thing. I heard her opening the trunk and I sat up front with the kid.

"There's nothing but a suitcase," Vida called.

"Bring it out."

There wasn't anything in it but some shirts, ties and a few changes of underwear and socks. I selected two silk ties and decided that they would do.

"You can't tie me up and leave me out here like this," the kid said nervously.

"Would you rather be shot?"

I got his hands behind his back and lie didn't put up any more argument. Then I made him get out of the convertible and get in the back seat of the Chrysler, and I tied his feet. I gagged him, then rolled all the windows up on the Chrysler and locked the doors and threw the key as far as I could throw it out the window.

We rode back to the highway in silence—Vida, her head dropped, staring down at the floorboards. I thought, Vida, Vida, what has happened to us?

When we hit the highway I turned and began putting the gas to that light convertible. We hadn't gone more than a hundred yards when I heard the sudden blaring of an auto horn in the distance. It was a faint sound, rising and falling in volume as the wind moved it lazily across the prairie. It was a monotonous sound, going on—and on—and on. I slammed on the brakes, and cursed.

Startled, Vida almost went through the windshield. "Roy, what is it?"

"It's that kid! That smart bastard of a kid!"

"What are you going to do?"

"I'm going back. When I get through with him he'll be sorry he was so goddamn smart!" I turned the convertible around in the middle of the highway and we streaked back for the dirt road.

The horn was still blaring, forlorn sounding, seeming to come from nowhere and everywhere. If I don't get him off that horn, I thought, somebody sure as hell will be curious enough to see where the sound is coming from. They'd have roadblocks thrown up for that convertible before we could get out of the county.

We crashed over that dirt road at almost sixty miles an hour. I put on the brakes and was out of the convertible almost before it stopped skidding.

I don't know how he got from the back seat to the front seat with his hands and feet tied, but he had managed somehow. He was lying half across the steering wheel, his chest on the horn button. He seemed frozen there—maybe frozen with fear, now that I was back.

I grabbed for the door but it wouldn't give, and then I remembered that I had locked it and thrown the key away. "Get away from that horn!" I yelled.

He didn't move. He looked as though he wanted to get off that horn more than anything in the world, but his body just wouldn't answer the command of his brain.

"Goddamn you!" I yelled. Raging, I began pounding on the rolled-up window. I didn't even know I had the revolver in my hand until I heard the explosion.

The horn blared on for maybe another five seconds. Then I saw the kid's eyes roll up, as if in amazement, and slowly he began to slump away from the wheel. The abrupt silence seemed enormous when the horn finally stopped. I stood there dumbly as the kid went all the way down to the floorboard in a huddled, lifeless heap.

I found myself thinking, I didn't want to kill him.

When I turned back to the convertible, Vida was sitting there screaming without making a sound.

Chapter Twenty-One

"Roy—I can't go on any longer."

"Have you got any choice?" I said. "You're in this thing just as deep as I am, and don't forget it."

Almost an hour had passed since the convertible blew a tire, slamming into a barditch and ruining the right front wheel. We had been walking ever since, getting as far away from that convertible as possible. We had traveled cross country, through brush, up and down hills.

Vida tripped on some briars and went sprawling in the loose dirt along a creek bank. "Roy!"

"All right," I said, "we can rest awhile."

We sat on the edge of the creek, a sloppy, muddy little stream, coming from nowhere and going nowhere. The sun beat down unmercifully, but Vida sat hunched forward, her legs drawn up, hugging herself with her arms as though she were freezing.

I rubbed my face and it was grimy with sweat and dirt. My shirt stuck to my body in wet patches.

Lola would enjoy this, Foley. If she could only see you now! I thought.

I knew what would happen if I started thinking about Lola. I'd start screaming and I would never stop. I said, "We have to go now."

Vida looked at me blankly, still hugging herself. I started to help her up but she shrank away.

It was late that afternoon when we finally came across the road. Watching from behind a clump of blackjack we saw a truck rattle past, heading for the highway. A farm-to-market road, I thought. And the closest big market was Houston. I looked at Vida, letting an idea have its way in the back of my mind. We had to do something.

"How do you feel?" I asked.

She nodded, woodenly. She looked tired, and her arm was scratched and her hair wasn't clean. But she was all right, if you didn't look too closely at her eyes.

I took her shoulders in my hands and her head snapped back as I shook her. "Vida, Vida!" I said, "You've got to snap out of it. I couldn't help what happened back there. That kid asked for what he got."

Another truck passed and I pulled Vida down behind the scrubby clump of brush. "Vida, don't you understand? We've got to get away from here!"

"Can we ever get away?" she asked flatly.

"Sure we can. This is just the kind of thing we've waited for. We've got to stop one of these farm trucks. You have rather, because we can't risk being seen together now. You can hold the driver's attention while I get in the back end—one of these trucks will take us right into Houston. Vida, do you understand?"

She nodded. Far off to the north I could see a shredded cloud of dust moving lazily across the prairie and I knew that it must be another truck.

"This is our chance, Vida. Now get out there on the road and make the bastard stop."

I got her to her feet, turned her around, and she began walking like a mechanical woman toward the road. Geez, I thought, this is going to look funny as hell, away out here in the middle of God's nowhere. But a woman was a woman, and I could only hope that the truck driver would be all man and not too curious.

I worked myself closer to the road and lay down in a gully about twenty yards away.

She was perfect, standing there in the sand and gravel by the side of the road. She looked as helpless as a child, as lonesome as the moon. The truck stopped.

"Goin' into the city, lady?" the driver called. He was a husky, sweating, red-faced man with small eyes and a loose grin. Vida said something but I couldn't hear what it was. Then he leaned over to open the door on the far side of the cab and I sprinted across the road and vaulted onto the back of the truck.

There was a heavy mud-crusted tarp thrown over stacks of wooden crates, and there was the acrid smell of tomatoes, not quite ripe, and the heavy-sweet smell of cantaloupes. I lifted the tarp and got under it. "By God," I heard the driver saying, "this is a hell of a place for a woman to be all to herself."

Vida must have said something. The driver laughed loudly. "I bet your boy friend made you walk."

You stupid bastard of an ape! I thought. If you touch her I'll kill you.

"Well, from the looks of you, you put up one hell of a fight," he said and laughed again. "Who won?" I sat rigid, smothering as the sun blazed down on the tar smelling tarp. There was no talking for a minute, but I could hear the movement up front, in the cab. "Well, by God," the driver said finally, "is that any way to act? I'm just trying to be friendly."

A great surge of relief flowed through me when I heard the starter grind, and the truck began to move forward. If there was any talking in the cab, I couldn't hear it. I stopped worrying about Vida and began thinking about what we were going to do when we got to Houston. A ship—that would be the best thing, if we could swing it. If not, then I'd have to think of something else. It was a big town and there were plenty of places to hide.

The truck began slowing down, and I thought: We must be nearing the highway. Then the truck rocked to a stop, pulled over to the side of the road, and I listened for the sound of traffic that would tell me where the highway was.

The only thing I heard was a muffled scuffling up front in the cab.

I heard the driver say, "God, you'd think it'd never been done before!"

The sound of scuffling became more frantic, and an enormous anger exploded inside me. The revolver seemed to grow in my hand as I whipped my arm up to throw the tarp back. Touch her, I thought savagely, and I'll kill you!

Then I froze, almost as though a giant hand had been pushed against my chest to hold me back.

Kill him, I thought, and where are you? Another body left behind to help them follow your trail. And how will you get away from here? You can't drive now—the highway will be swarming with cops. And Vida couldn't do it. This is the time for straight thinking.

"All right!" the driver said angrily, out of breath. "Go on, get the hell out of my truck. Walk all the way to Houston and see if you like that."

There was no sound at all from Vida. Was she waiting for me to do something? But what could I do? We had to get away from here and that driver had to take us.

The scuffling began again and the truck driver laughed. "I thought you'd come around!" My insides rolled. I can't vomit, I thought. He'll hear me.

But I could hear them. The rhythmic rustling, the gasping, the banging of heels against the dashboard. It can't be happening! I thought wildly. I had the gun in my hand, squeezing it tight enough to break it, but I couldn't move. I kept thinking: Everything is all right. Vida can take care of herself. It really isn't happening: it's the heat and you're imagining things.

God, a voice inside me said, How you must hate yourself! How Vida must hate you!

Heat swirled under the tarpaulin and I clung to a wooden vegetable crate, telling myself to do something. I didn't move. It seemed a long, long time before the truck began to move again.

It was dark and the night was old when I began to hear the blatant, impersonal rumble of the city. I raised the tarp and looked out in amazement at a million shimmering lights holding back the darkness of the night. Cabs and buses and cars darted through a thousand lighted streets. A cop stood, hands on hips, gazing up at an electric sign. He wasn't looking for Roy Foley. He didn't give a damn about Roy Foley.

The truck stopped.

"All right," the driver said, "this is the end of the line. I go to market from here."

I heard the cab door open and knew that Vida was getting out. As the driver put the truck into gear, I eased off the back of the truck and dropped to the pavement. I thought quickly: if she says anything, I'll say I was asleep.

But when I walked up to her and looked at her, I knew I wouldn't say anything, for she would never mention it.

"We're lucky it's dark," I said. "We won't have to be in too much of a hurry looking for a place to stay."

I started up the street and Vida followed along beside me. Not until we passed a street light did I see that she had been crying.

Chapter Twenty-Two

That was almost six days ago.

We came to another small hotel, Vida and I, in Houston. A dirty little place with peeling wallpaper, dirt-crusted floors and sagging beds. We're almost out of money and I haven't seen a newspaper for four days, or heard a radio, so there's no way of knowing what the police are doing. But I can guess.

Vida hasn't spoken more than a dozen words all day—partly because of the fight we had yesterday.

I know I should be thinking of something, doing something, but I can't seem to make myself move. All I can do is remember, and imagine things as they might have been. Sometimes I hear myself talking to the emptiness of the room.

Vida thinks I am out of my mind—I can see it in her eyes, when she looks at me—and maybe this is the thing that holds her here. I don't know. But I can't help remembering. Some of it is good, but most of it is bitter, and the worst of all is Lola, because sometimes late at night, or almost any time, for that matter, I can hear her laughing.

Vida—I still love her and I wish I could make her understand about things. But I know I can't, so I don't try.

I have been thinking of that revolver and I tell myself that I ought to hock it for whatever I can get for it, but I've been afraid to touch it.

The time has come, though, when something has to be done. I heard Vida crying last night, and when I touched her, tried to comfort her, she was as cold as marble. I held her close, I said all the good things I could think of, but nothing seemed to help. Love, or whatever it was between us, seems to have died.

Yesterday Vida went out to get sandwiches at the joint across the street. When she came back, her face was even paler than usual.

"Roy, we've got to do something! We can't go on like this!"

She hadn't got the sandwiches. She leaned against the ancient dresser, her chest heaving as though she had been running. "Roy, two policemen stopped me in front of the hotel—"

I went cold. "Why?"

Her face colored abruptly. I knew then what had happened, and for some twisted reason it struck me as funny. I sat on the edge of the bed, almost laughed. "By God! They thought you were hustling, didn't they?"

The color in her face deepened. She turned suddenly to the mirror and stared at herself. Her face was strangely hard; her eyes had receded into dark shadows. I looked at her, thinking: Yes, I can see how they could make the mistake!

Then something else hit me, scared me. Those cops would be watching Vida every time she left the hotel. Maybe they would even follow her to the room! Cops were like that, once they got an idea, they hung onto it like a dog with a bone.

"Roy, you've got to do something!"

"What am I going to do?" I said bitterly. Then all the anger inside me directed itself at Vida. I stood up suddenly, shaking with it. "Goddamn you!" I said harshly. "Why did you let them stop you? Do you have to go out on the streets looking like a whore?"

She winced, as though I had slapped her. Then she wheeled on me, her eyes blazing. "Oh, God, why did I ever come with you? Why did I ever marry you?"

"Getting married was your idea."

"It was a mistake and I'm paying for it," she almost shouted.

"You can get out of it any time you feel like it," I said, raging. "You can get out of it right now. All you have to do is walk out the door."

"Don't tempt me!" she yelled.

"I'm not tempting you. It's an invitation. Great God, a woman who can't even walk out on the street without being taken for a tramp!"

"It's better than being taken for a murderer! Than being a murderer!"

I went wild for a moment. I hit her full in the face with the flat of my hand. Her head snapped back, a tiny trickle of blood formed at the corner of her mouth. The sound of the blow remained in the room.

I stood stunned, sickened at what I had done. I heard myself saying stupidly, "Forgive me, Vida. I didn't know what I was doing. I didn't know...."

She looked at me with fear.

I put my arms around her and I could feel her shrinking away from my touch. When I released her, she went to the bed and lay face-down, motionless.

"Is there anything I can do?" I said. "Is there anything I can say?"

She made no move and no sound.

"I must have been out of my mind," I went on senselessly. "You're the last person on earth I would hurt, Vida. You're the only person I love."

"It's all right." It was all over. At that moment both of us knew it. And nothing could be done about it.

That was yesterday. Out of the emptiness, I kept thinking: What are you going to do, Foley? What are you going to do? There had to be an answer—if I could only find it. Lost somewhere in the violence and rage there was an answer, but I would have to go all the way back if I were to find it.

So that's what I have done. I've set it down on paper, all of it, carefully feeling my way back through the red maze of anger. Starting on one Burk Street. Ending on another.

The circle is complete.

Another day is past and Vida is gone. She left during the night.

I think I have the answer—the only one there is. The revolver is in my hand, as cold and deadly as a moccasin—but as yet I haven't had the guts to go through with it.

Maybe I'll never have the guts. I don't know.

THE END

www.ingramcontent.com/pod-product-compliance
Lightning Source LLC
LaVergne TN
LVHW011930070526
838202LV00054B/4571